Originally from Harrogate in North Yorkshire, Robert Gold began his career as an intern at the American broadcaster CNN, based in Washington DC. He returned to Yorkshire to work for the retailer ASDA, becoming the chain's nationwide book buyer. He now works in sales for a UK publishing company. Robert now lives in Putney and his new hometown served as the inspiration for the fictional town of Haddley in *Twelve Secrets*. In 2016, he co-authored three titles in James Patterson's Bookshots series.

TWELVE SECRETS

ROBERT GOLD

SPHERE

SPHERE

First published in Great Britain in 2021 by Sphere

1 3 5 7 9 10 8 6 4 2

Copyright © Robert Gold Ltd 2021

The moral right of the author has been asserted.

*All characters and events in this publication, other than those
clearly in the public domain, are fictitious and any resemblance
to real persons, living or dead, is purely coincidental.*

All rights reserved.
No part of this publication may be reproduced, stored in a
retrieval system, or transmitted, in any form or by any means, without
the prior permission in writing of the publisher, nor be otherwise circulated
in any form of binding or cover other than that in which it is published
and without a similar condition including this condition
being imposed on the subsequent purchaser.

A CIP catalogue record for this book is available from the British Library.

Hardback ISBN 978-0-7515-8276-5
Trade Paperback ISBN 978-0-7515-8275-8

Typeset in Garamond by M Rules
Printed and bound in Great Britain by Clays Ltd, Elcograf S.p.A.

Papers used by Sphere are from well-managed forests
and other responsible sources.

Sphere
An imprint of
Little, Brown Book Group
Carmelite House
50 Victoria Embankment
London EC4Y 0DZ

An Hachette UK Company
www.hachette.co.uk

www.littlebrown.co.uk

For my dad – the real Michael Noel

One

*'I never want to experience
my own past again.'*

CHAPTER 1

The invitation to meet with Madeline landed in my inbox late morning. It came with no subject line but I knew immediately what it was about. Madeline is nothing if not persistent.

I've spent the afternoon killing time. I gave up on the idea of doing any actual work pretty quickly, unable to settle to anything. Drinking three cups of coffee in the past forty-five minutes hasn't helped. Mostly I've been reading the endless stream of celebrity stories on our twenty-four-hour news site.

'The royal family has a new ginger Labradoodle,' I say to Min, who sits opposite me in our open-plan newsroom. 'I'll give you even money they call it Harry.'

Min raises an eyebrow. I've tried repeatedly to engage her in conversation for the last hour, despite knowing she has a deadline to hit.

'Sorry,' I mouth silently, and return to my screen. Another Hollywood couple has announced their engagement, and a Premier League footballer has smashed his team-mate's head into a dressing-room locker. Nice.

A diary reminder that I don't need appears in front of me. I glance across towards Madeline's goldfish-bowl office and see her gesticulating furiously at two marketing executives. Both shrink in her presence. I realised long ago that the only way to successfully work with Madeline is by standing up to her. It's a lesson many of my colleagues have yet to learn.

'You are going to be honest with her?' asks Min, as if she can read my thoughts.

'I always try to be,' I reply. But Madeline instilled in me her own determination to reach the heart of any good story. It's something we now share. And it's why I fear this conversation.

'You're the only person she will ever really listen to.'

'The problem is, on this one I don't think there's any middle ground.'

Min shoots me a sympathetic grimace before putting on her headphones. I glance across again to see the two marketers skulk away, summarily dismissed. Resolved, I close my screen and get to my feet.

Through her open door, I can see Madeline sitting in her white leather chair, her eyes fixed on the screen in front of her. Without looking up, she calls my name. 'Ben, don't linger.'

'There's no reason for us to fall out over this,' I say as I enter her corner office, floor-to-ceiling windows affording a direct view of Tower Bridge. Behind Madeline's curved glass desk hang three striking sunlit photographs, each one taken by Madeline herself, as she has told me countless times. The first is of the Houses of Parliament, the second of the

4

White House, and the third is of her own home overlooking Richmond Park. She calls them 'the three houses of global power' and I think she is only half-joking.

'Twenty-nine point four million,' she says, still not looking up from her monitor. 'Down close to three per cent and those two clowns tell me not to worry. We're less than two million users ahead of *Mail Online*. We will not lose our number one spot on my watch.'

She's not expecting a response and I don't give her one. Instead, avoiding her vast boardroom table, I take the chair opposite her desk.

'And I'm not falling out with anyone,' she continues. 'I know this is a difficult time for you, Ben. With your mum's anniversary approaching, we will all find ourselves reflecting.'

There's a smoothness to her voice. She's rehearsed this, and I refuse to be drawn into it.

'Your mum would be so proud of what you've achieved. Ten years ago all our hearts broke. If only she could see you now. One of the best "true crime" writers in the country. It's been quite a journey, Ben, a real triumph over tragedy. It's your story to tell.'

'However many times we discuss this,' I reply, 'the answer is still no.'

'Ben!' she exclaims. 'You haven't even heard me out.'

'I know what you're after. And that's not me. I write investigative pieces, not tear-jerkers.'

'I'm not after some trashy sob story. This would be your truth – emotional, affecting, raw, and redemptive. The true story, told by the man everybody in this country holds so very close to their hearts.'

'Well, I'm not interested in that.'

'But millions of people are, Ben.' Madeline's voice has taken on the tone she uses when she's determined to get her own way, each word clearly enunciated. 'You underestimate how much people care about you. What happened to Nick, and then your mum's death ... everybody remembers that. People know who you are, and believe they share a genuine connection with you.' She gets up and steps around her desk, perching on the corner next to me. 'I'm not saying a few of them aren't a tiny bit crazy, but, whether you like it or not, they imagine they shared in your grief. They want to support you, while being forever grateful it didn't happen to them. And now they want to read about it in your own words, as our world exclusive.'

Directness is not something Madeline ever shies away from. Her ruthless ability to get straight to the point is what makes her a great journalist. I simply shake my head.

'I've told you I'm not going to write it.'

'Ben, we both know you *are* going to write this. However painful it is, it's too good a story not to.'

'If I write the article you want, I'll spend the next year having people come up to me in the street asking me how I am and telling me I'm always in their prayers.'

'That doesn't sound all bad. Those people mean well, even the slightly peculiar ones.'

'It's a no, Madeline.'

'Ben.' She gets up suddenly, crosses to close the door and

turns back to look at me. 'I'm going to level with you. Our numbers are under pressure. We really are being squeezed. We need a big story.'

'The answer is still no.'

Madeline has schooled me in her own relentless hunt for readers. Now however, I've quickly realised that when the hunt reaches your own door, your perspective changes.

'Nobody is more committed to the success of this site than me,' I reply. 'My stories bring in more new readers than any other articles. Then, for some reason, those readers stay to read the trashy gossip you call news.'

Madeline's eyes flash and for a moment I think we're done. Then her shoulders relax.

'You've said it yourself, I'm the best journalist you've got,' I say.

'One award does not make you my best journalist.'

'It's two, and they're the only awards the site has ever won.'

'We're not here for the awards, we're here for the readers,' she says. 'And we need more of them. Fast.'

I can feel myself losing patience. I take a deep breath. If I didn't know Madeline so well I'd find it hard to believe she was trying to bully me into this. Having grown up near to my home, she knows at first-hand how traumatic my brother Nick's death was, not just for my family but for our whole community. I've gone back and read the articles she wrote at the time. She understood the devastating impact on our whole town.

I turn my chair to face her as she crosses from the door to the window. 'I'm not doing it, Madeline. You need to accept that. You will never have any idea what it was like. Nick's face on every front page – my mum's, mine. I've no desire to publish the last slice of my life I was able to keep private.'

It's not the answer she wants, and I can see her irritation rising. She drums her fingers on the table. Tight-lipped, she goes back to her chair and begins rattling her keyboard. When she doesn't say anything further, I assume I'm dismissed and, relieved, I get up to go. But, just as I reach the door, she speaks.

'Ben, has it occurred to you that, if you don't write this, someone else might?'

I pause, not turning back to look at her.

'And, if they do, I can't control what they might say.'

CHAPTER 2

We leave the office at four in the afternoon with me telling Min I need just one drink. One becomes two and almost immediately has me feeling unsteady on my feet. I stopped drinking ten years ago but I need something to take the edge off my fury with Madeline. While I admire her unique ability to be first with any story, her voracious appetite for readers is at times impossible to stomach.

Word of my conversation with Madeline spreads fast among my team. Our group swells in numbers and when we become too numerous for the cramped City pub we decide to head west, out of the centre of London, towards our favourite restaurant, Mailer's. Standing on the banks of the River Thames in the village of St Marnham, the restaurant, run by high-profile London chef East Mailer, is housed within a converted warehouse. It was me who had introduced the office to it. Most hadn't ventured that far into west London before, but the restaurant's incredible food, combined with breathtaking views across the river, soon won an army of converts.

Even when not in attendance, Madeline has a habit of dominating our team conversations. Over dinner, support for me is almost unanimous, with most of my colleagues suitably outraged at her pushing me to write the article. Only Min remains quiet, and I can see her deliberating as the rest of us rail against Madeline's determination to win readers at any cost. Finally, as she divides the dregs of the last bottle between our glasses, she asks me if Madeline could be right. Or at least partly. Might the tenth anniversary of my mum's death be a moment for me to pause, to take the opportunity to really understand what happened?

In my darkest moments, I've shared with Min my feelings of guilt; my inability to comprehend, even all these years later, why Mum did what she did. Everyone falls silent. I promise I will think about it. In reality, I already know I'm never going to write the article, for all the reasons I've given to Madeline. My job might allow me to explore the lives of others, but I never want to experience my own past again.

As the evening draws to a close and my team head for home, Min and I drift into the exposed-brick bar for one last drink. Despite already knowing that tomorrow morning I'm going to regret drinking so much, I offer little resistance as Min persuades me that one more won't make much difference.

Seated beside the open fire, the restaurant's co-owner, Will Andrews, smiles when he sees us and invites us to join him, signalling to the bartender for three glasses of whisky. More than twenty years ago, Will had been one of my brother's closest schoolfriends. Having grown up to become something incredibly successful in the City, a few years ago Will, along with his partner, East, had invested in the restaurant. I hadn't known him so well myself, but Will had been incredibly generous towards my mum, never forgetting her birthday, and always sending her roses on the anniversary of Nick's death.

We exchange easy pleasantries and Will and I share life's news. He asks about the site and I talk about an article I've recently published, along with the protracted process of turning it into a 'true crime' podcast. Then I tell him about my conversation from earlier in the day.

'While the rest of us have to fall in line, Ben's used to getting his own way,' says Min, laughing. 'He is very much her favourite.'

'No, I'm not,' I protest. 'Well, maybe just a tiny bit.'

'When I asked the question at dinner, I wasn't saying you should definitely write the article,' she continues, 'and of course this absolutely has to be your decision, but you don't like it when you and Madeline fall out.'

'Surely even Madeline has to see this from Ben's point of view?' says Will. 'This is such a personal story.'

'I don't disagree,' says Min, 'but I think Ben should seize the opportunity, not to write Madeline's puff piece but to carry out his own real investigation. Much as it pains me to say it, he is the best in the business.'

'Only Ben can know the right thing to do,' says Will. 'Clare's death had an enormous impact on all of us. And Nick's before that. But, for Ben, they ripped his life apart. Madeline needs to respect that, and appreciate that he's spent a lifetime trying to find a way back to normal. At some point he's got to be able to draw a line.'

'Do I get a say in this?' I say, smiling, before we're briefly interrupted by East Mailer bringing us our drinks. I get to my feet to greet him and he promises to join us after the last diners have left.

'Can I ask you a question?' says Min, as we resume our conversation. I nod. 'How would you approach this if it was any other story?'

'It's not any other story, that's the whole point,' is Will's interjection. 'It's *Ben's* story. And anyway, after all this time, is it realistic to expect to find anything new?'

'Absolutely – it's what we do all the time,' replies Min. 'Ben, I know it's painful – more painful than any of us can ever begin to imagine – but I also know, deep down, there's a part of you that has a million and one questions you're desperate to ask.'

'But it's not just about me,' I say, slowly turning the whisky glass round and round in my hand. 'I don't think it's what Mum would have wanted me to do.'

Throughout my life, my mum taught me that the simplest things can make the biggest difference. For her, that meant letting me behave like any other teenage boy: playing football, talking about girls, sneaking a drink or smoking the odd cigarette. She treated them all in the same way as any other mother would. Not once did she freak out and try to stop me doing something, however overwhelming that desire might have been. Never did she use Nick as an excuse. If I was late back by thirty minutes or an hour, while

I'm sure at times it must have terrified her, she never let it show – no great drama, no overreaction. After her death, it took all of my strength and the support of those closest to me to get my life back on track. I'm sure she wouldn't want me to throw that away to go raking up the past.

'I get that, Ben, I really do,' says Min gently, adding some water to her drink and then turning to me. 'But I think you still have questions about your mum's death, and that's always going to stop you from accepting it. I don't think your mum would have wanted that for you either. So I say, seize the opportunity now to find out the truth.'

'That might not be exactly what Madeline is looking for,' I reply.

'When has that ever stopped you before?'

I smile in spite of myself. 'What I do hate is the way people have always painted their own picture,' I continue. 'They think my mum was so painfully unhappy that she just couldn't cope any more, that she had nothing to live for. But I know it wasn't like that. Even with all we'd been through, she'd found a new positivity. I still can't understand what she did. Somehow there has to be more to it.'

'Like what, Ben?' replies Will gently, as East tops up our drinks.

I pause. 'That's impossible for me to say.'

When the last diners leave, East joins us at our table and our conversation turns to village life. Plans for a Ferris wheel on the green, as part of the village fête, are causing controversy.

'The chair of the organising committee has threatened to resign,' says East. 'And my offer to pay for the bloody thing wasn't quite received in the way I expected. Some members accused me of trying to hijack the whole event. I was mortally offended.'

'Don't listen to him,' says Will, laughing. 'He loves it. And they love him. When he offered to personally host a Mongolian barbecue, you'd have thought he was offering to walk on water.'

'Straight across the village pond!' adds East.

At the offer of just one final drink I hold my hands up, a signal that I am way over my limit, while Min says she has to be back in the office early the following morning. East calls her a cab and I decide to walk back along the riverbank to my home town of Haddley. 'The fresh air will help clear my head,' I say, standing with East as I watch him light a spliff in the restaurant's courtyard.

'Will only lets me smoke outside these days,' he replies, and as he draws on his joint we stand together watching the tail-lights on Min's cab fade away. East pulls off his chef's chequered bandana and, ruffling his shoulder-length greying hair, offers me a smoke.

'I don't think it would help me,' I say, already knowing that tomorrow morning I'm going regret those two large shots of Glenmorangie.

'You're probably right.'

We leave the courtyard and walk slowly towards the river path.

'Ben,' East continues, as the lights of the restaurant fade behind us, 'I couldn't help overhearing earlier and I really wasn't sure if I should say anything . . .'

'Go ahead,' I say, and we come to a halt by the river where the street lamp spills light on to the towpath.

'I know Madeline of old. She was a regular at my first restaurant in Richmond, a lifetime ago. She can be very persuasive. Don't let her talk you into anything you don't want to do. My advice is, carry on just as you've always done and look forward in your life. Nobody ever gains anything from looking back.'

CHAPTER 3

As the morning light creeps through my blinds, I lie awake in bed with no real idea what time it is. I reach across to the table at the side of my bed, fumble for my phone, and a pint glass of water spills on to the floor. I fear if I lift my head the room will spin, so, slowly, I turn and peer over. I can taste the stale alcohol in my mouth.

Ten years earlier, I'd lain in this same bed as my mum shouted up at me for the third and final time to get up. I was in my second year at Manchester University and for the Easter break I was back home in London, working at a sports news website, spending my days fact-checking articles. It had taken me less than a week to realise that sports journalists didn't start work until midday, finished late, and spent most of their spare time in the pub watching football on Sky. It was a routine I'd been happy to adopt and, lying in bed that morning, hungover, I had been in no rush to join my mum's early-morning commute.

Now, with my eyes still tightly closed, my mum's voice plays over and over in my head – her frustration with me, her rising annoyance at my seeming apathy. As she headed out of the door, she called up to me one last time. 'Ben, stop wasting your days lying around in bed. Get up now!' she cried, and I heard her grab her bag before slamming the front door closed behind her.

Those were the last words she ever spoke to me.

That morning, my mum left our house just before eight. She took the path across Haddley Common and continued along the edge of the woods that run alongside the railway line. It would have taken her less than ten minutes to get to St Marnham station, following the same route she took every morning. Usually she made her way to the far end of the platform, where she always stood and waited to board at the rear of the train – the only carriage where she could be certain of a seat for her twenty-minute journey into the centre of London. But as to what she did on that morning, all I know is what the police later came to tell me.

I had made myself breakfast, as well as a sandwich to take into work, and was standing at a downstairs window, drinking a cup of coffee and thinking about heading out for the day. As I absent-mindedly stared out at my elderly neighbour, Mr Cranfield, who was pottering in his garden, a police car pulled up outside.

Two police officers stepped from the car and made their way up the path. Immediately I felt a wrench in my stomach. As a child I'd seen too many officers arrive at our house, and the feeling of dread that accompanied their arrival was all too familiar. After Nick's death, so many times when I'd seen officers approach I'd hidden away, often crouching at the top of the stairs, listening intently as information was relayed to my mum. Suddenly I felt like a child again. Except this time, however much I wanted it, there was no place for me to run and hide.

When the doorbell rang I stood motionless, frozen at the window, watching as Mr Cranfield propped his pitchfork against the wall of his house. Then, he walked around to his front step, sitting to remove his wellington boots. He set them aside carefully before getting to his feet and going indoors.

Only when the doorbell rang a second time did I move. Slowly I made my way out into the hall, hesitating before I placed my hand on the front door latch; desperate to cling on to life as it was. A life which, I already somehow knew, was slipping away.

The bell rang a third time and I opened the door.

A gale was blowing across the common and the two police offers on the doorstep were unconsciously huddled together. I didn't even wait for them to speak but turned and walked back down the hallway towards the kitchen. Behind me, the officers stepped inside and I heard them close the door. The male officer asked if I was Mr Benjamin Harper. With a degree of resignation I called back, 'Yes.' They knew exactly who I was.

In the kitchen, I sat at our old farmhouse table. It was a huge thing that filled most of the room. After Nick it had felt far too big for just Mum and me, but over the years we'd learned to occupy it. Now, as I sat there alone, the vastness of it was suffocating.

As she stood in the kitchen doorway, the female officer asked me to confirm if I was Clare Harper's son. Was anyone else home? she enquired. I shook my head. I saw the male officer move hesitantly across the kitchen, before leaning against the side where my breakfast plates lay unwashed. I'd forgotten to put the butter back in the fridge. You could see it glistening where it had started to melt, and there was a knife sticking out of the top of a jar of Marmite. My mum would have hated it.

The female officer pulled out a chair and turned to face me. I lifted my head and looked at her properly for the first time. The sympathy I saw in her eyes was a look I'd grown to despise.

She asked me again if Clare Harper was my mother and I said she was. Did she work in an office off Welbeck Street? I remember laughing, an involuntary nervous laugh, before I felt the touch of her hand. I turned away, only to catch the male officer's eye before he quickly looked out into our back garden, where the spring sun had helped the grass grow long. My mum had spent the previous week asking me to mow the lawn. I'd told her to stop nagging.

The female officer asked if my mum took the train from St Marnham station. I started to speak, telling her she caught the train from the same spot each morning, how she was a creature of habit, always had the same routine, left the house at the exact same time, walked across the common, rain or shine. The officer tried to interrupt me but I didn't stop talking. She worked as a project manager at an office design company, always took her lunch with her from home, broke

19

for an hour at twelve-thirty, made herself a coffee when she arrived in the morning; she'd be there now and that was where they would be able to find her. The officer squeezed my hand and said my name.

A woman had stepped in front of a train heading to Waterloo station.

I nodded, suddenly silent.

'We believe the woman was your mother, Ben.'

I looked at the other officer, who was looking at me now and nodding slowly, and I found myself imitating him. On the wall behind us, I could hear the tick of our kitchen clock. It suddenly seemed horribly loud.

'I'm sorry, Ben, but she was killed instantly,' said the female officer. We sat in silence until she continued. 'I know this is a lot to take in, so it might be best if you call a family member to be with you.'

I said nothing.

'Or perhaps a close friend,' she added quickly, glancing towards her colleague.

She was waiting for me to respond but I had nothing to say. I wanted them gone. There were formalities to be followed but I didn't hear them. An identification of the body would be needed, but it didn't register with me that I would be the one to make it. I was twenty years old.

'Is there someone we can call for you?' she repeated. 'I really think you should have someone with you.'

For some reason, all I could think of was Mr Cranfield in his garden with his pitchfork.

'Ben?'

I forced my attention back to the officer and lied. I said I would call my father. I didn't even know his number.

The male officer stepped across the room, put his hand on my shoulder and asked if I was going to be okay. I said I would be fine. I wanted them to go. I was sure he felt the same.

I got to my feet and slowly walked into the hall. They followed, the female officer wanting reassurance that I would make my call.

Again I promised I would. I just wanted them gone.

They'd be in touch, they said.

I nodded and thanked them. I didn't know what for.

The wind blew through the hall when they opened the front door to leave. It had begun to rain heavily and the officers made a dash for their car, the woman desperately holding on to her hat. I closed the door and stood alone in the empty hallway.

CHAPTER 4

Dani Cash walked out of her bedroom, flicked on the light and crossed the small upstairs landing to the back bedroom of her Haddley home. How she had loved this house the first time she had stepped inside – its freshly decorated walls, the welcoming smell of soft new carpets and the neatly fitted furniture to keep everything in its place. The house had been perfect: a home she'd always dreamt of. For her it didn't matter that it was a mile away from the Thames and the supposed Victorian charm of Haddley's riverside properties. This would be her home. She had convinced herself that it could become an incredibly happy place.

Four months later, it felt like a prison.

Standing in the bedroom doorway, she pictured the nursery she had planned to create – animal prints on the walls, her favourite penguins on the blinds. Was she fooling herself by hoping that day might still come?

Now was not the time to think about it. She needed to focus her mind back on her work.

She looked across at the uniform she had laid out so

precisely on the on the spare bed the previous night, and for a moment she hesitated. Was she ready?

She had to be ready.

It was her only way out.

She picked up her crisp white blouse, its epaulettes already in place. Her fingers were all thumbs as she fastened the buttons and attached her scarf. As she bent down to tie her shoelaces, she caught a glimpse of her own reflection. Last night she had felt proud as she pressed a sharp crease into her black trousers. She had thought of her dad and the years he had served, and she'd known it was a pride he would share.

Her jacket hung on the outside of the wardrobe. She ripped away the dry-cleaner's plastic, thumbed the top button and slipped it on. She felt it hang loose over her back and hips. It didn't surprise her: her appetite had disappeared over recent weeks. She lifted her hat from the bed and tucked away as many of her blonde curls as possible. Standing in front of the mirror, for a moment she almost didn't recognise herself.

She was a police officer again.

At the top of the stairs, she paused and listened for signs of life. Careful to avoid the second step down that despite a builder's promise still creaked under the slightest pressure, she crept downstairs. When she got to the living-room door, she found it firmly shut, and quietly exhaled.

Outside the front door of her home, Dani briefly closed her eyes, turned her face skywards and let the sun's rays warm her spirits. She stood for a moment before stepping forward, determined to leave the past five months behind her.

Her five years in the force had shown what a good officer

23

she could be. A new recruit at twenty-one, she had immediately impressed. Being Jack Cash's daughter only meant
she was tested more. But from her very first day she had
delivered. Calm and quick-thinking, she'd been a clear
favourite among her supervising officers. Only six months
ago, there had been conversations about her progressing
to sergeant.

Dani brushed the thought aside. She'd been a good officer
then, and she'd be a good officer now.

Halfway down Haddley Hill, she stopped to cross at
the lights. Traffic was already building and children were
heading towards Haddley Grammar School. Smiling at two
teenage girls as they stood next to her at the crossing, Dani
let her eyes drift towards the Thames. She stood and watched
as the riverbus passed under Haddley Bridge, ferrying early-
morning commuters to the City.

The explosion came out of nowhere. The girls screamed
and Dani jumped backwards with such force that the
sudden movement sent her hat tumbling to the ground. She
scrabbled around on the verge but was almost blind with
panic. Where were the girls? She couldn't let them come to
any harm. She quickly got back to her feet but her vision
swam. Then she felt a hand on her arm.

'You okay, miss?' said one of the girls, handing
Dani her hat.

'Stupid boys!' shouted the other, before bursting into
laughter. 'You're like children, you are!'

Dani looked around and saw daily life continuing around
her. On the opposite side of the road, she caught a glimpse

of three boys before they disappeared, racing into Haddley Hill Park.

'They're always messing about with firecrackers,' said the girl who'd passed Dani her hat. 'They think they're such men but they're nothing more than *silly little boys*!' This final comment she yelled across the road at the top of her voice.

'I'm fine, thank you,' said Dani, and, watching the lights change, she paused to fix her hat. The girls crossed the road, and disappeared into the park. Before she knew it, the traffic was moving again, and she once more pressed the button to cross.

As she made her way down the hill towards the high street, the traffic became more congested. A bus heading to Wandsworth blocked the main intersection. Horns blared and Dani turned towards a frustrated driver, quelling his anger with a look. A delivery driver stopped on the red route and, telling him to move on, Dani left with the traffic flowing behind her.

As she approached Haddley police station, her pace slowed. From the opposite side of the road she watched two constables enter the front of the building, and then an elderly woman, leaning on her walking stick. A senior officer leaving the station held the door for the woman before another officer followed her in. Dani didn't recognise either of the constables, and the others seemed strangely unfamiliar to her, like people from another life she'd only vaguely known. Had she been away that long? She had made a deliberate decision to keep away from the station over the past five months. She'd met up with one or two of the younger officers for a drink, but she'd chosen not to reach out to the rest of the team. She was regretting that now. If she'd called in just a handful of times, maybe it would have been easier, broken the ice.

After a moment, she turned away from the station and walked on.

As she reached Haddley Bridge, she glanced at her watch. It was still thirty minutes until the start of her shift. She'd walk across the river, enjoy the views from the bridge and then head back to the police station. By then she'd be ready.

From the bridge, she looked up the river to the Haddley boathouses, already a throng of activity. Beyond them was Haddley Common and then the woods to St Marnham. In the other direction, a glass-fronted tower block loomed on the north side. These were luxury apartments and beneath them was a gourmet supermarket, packed with organic vegetables and fine wines. The perfect location to capture cash-rich commuters on the hunt for an easy dinner as they arrived home.

And the perfect place for an armed raid last Hallowe'en.

They had seemed little more than schoolkids, rushing past her in their monster masks. She had paid them scant attention, her mind already on the bottle of wine she planned to enjoy after a long shift.

They hadn't noticed her when she'd followed them in.

She was still in her uniform.

When they did see her, they'd panicked.

The flash of a knife's blade. And then another.

Shoppers screaming.

Suddenly there were hostages and knife pressed against her back.

Dani could still hear the sirens in her head – just as she had time and again over the past five months. Should she have acted differently?

She pictured her dad's face, the crinkle around his eyes when he smiled. 'Never doubt yourself, Dani,' he would say. 'You can be anything you want.' She turned away sharply and walked back across the bridge, towards the police station. Not breaking her stride, she climbed the three steps at the front of the building. She walked quickly through the doors, determined to prove herself once more.

CHAPTER 5

The light shining into my room feels almost unbearably bright. I push myself up and reach for my phone, flicking on the screen. The clock shows me I'm already late for work. I'll tell Madeline I'm spending the morning researching my next article. Besides, as it's a Thursday, half of our feature-writers will already be thinking about the weekend.

I survey the room. My clothes are strewn across the floor, my empty wallet tossed next to the watch my mum gave me for my eighteenth birthday. My head is still spinning, and as I drop back on to my pillow I stare up at the ceiling. Tears start to surge and I press my fingers into the corners of my eyes. Breathing deeply, I push back my duvet but, as I do, I hear running water coming from the bathroom.

Seconds later, the bathroom door opens and Mrs Cranfield bustles into my bedroom. I would never dare call Mrs Cranfield my part-time housekeeper, especially as I've never paid her a single penny, but she does a great job of helping me keep my house in order. She and her husband are two of the remarkable people who helped me get back on my feet after my mum died. To me they've become more like a surrogate mum and dad than anything else. I'd hate to be without them, although, like all parents, at times they can be just a tiny bit annoying.

'You're awake, then,' says Mrs Cranfield. 'That bathroom's a disgrace.'

'Is it?' I reply, scrambling to drag the duvet back over me.

'Nothing I haven't seen before.' She makes her way across my room, picking up my shorts and throwing them on to my bed. 'You must have been sick again when you came inside. I'll have to come over later to give it a proper going over.'

'Again . . . ?' I ask tentatively.

'After you'd thrown up in our front garden as you made your way home. George is hosing down the clematis now.'

'Jesus, I'm so sorry,' I reply, mortified, trying to reach for my shorts.

'Honestly, Ben, that toilet is filthy. I hate to think when you last gave it a proper clean.'

Under the duvet, I somehow manage to pull my shorts on before sitting up in bed. 'Mrs C, I'm up now, so I think . . .'

She is pulling up the blinds, barely listening to me. 'I'll tidy up in here while you're in the shower. I've got some breakfast on the go downstairs.'

Where Mrs Cranfield is concerned, resistance is futile.

'You look a sight,' she says as I get out of bed, and I realise my shorts are on back to front. 'When you don't drink, it hits you that much harder than when you do. You haven't built up a tolerance the way my George has.'

I hastily head for the bathroom and close the door.

'And what would your mum say?' she calls after me.

The hot steam of the shower does little to clear my head, and when I walk back into my bedroom the pounding continues. Mrs Cranfield has already stripped my bed and cleared my clothes from the floor. The windows have been thrown open, bringing life back into the room. I grab a T-shirt from the wardrobe, pulling it over my head as I go to the window. The early spring sunshine has brought new life to Haddley Common, with daffodils scattered across the grass and cherry blossoms covering the trees. A canopy has formed above the pathway that runs from the roadside, where the buses stop every ten minutes, to the dark, shadowy entrance to the woods.

At the corner of the street I see Mr Cranfield tending the flowers in his garden, just as he had done ten years before. Semi-retired for as long as I can remember, in the past twelve months he's finally stepped away from the opticians he'd run for almost twenty years. Every couple of weeks we try to take in a match at Richmond Rugby Club. I've never had the impression he's a huge fan of the game but we started to go to matches years ago when my best friend, Michael Knowles, made it into the Richmond first team. He only played one season before moving to Bath to play premiership rugby but Mr C and I stuck with our local team. I think the real enjoyment Mr C gets from matches now is quizzing me about the truth behind the stories we run on the news site, always wanting the inside track on the latest political scandal. Even though he rarely stops talking throughout the game, I enjoy the time I spend with him.

I watch him head over to the vegetable patch he keeps at the side of his house. The Cranfields' home is an end-of-terrace, affording them an extra piece of land that Mr Cranfield has carefully tended since the day he moved in. Lifting his pitchfork, its handle bound with string, he looks just as he did on that morning ten years earlier. Perhaps now he carries a few extra pounds and maybe his grey hair is a little thinner, but in every other way I could be looking at the same scene from so many years before.

I hear Mrs Cranfield clattering about in the kitchen. That morning, after the police had left my home and I was standing alone in my hallway, Mrs Cranfield had opened the back door. She'd walked through the kitchen and come to sit beside me at the foot of the stairs. She had held me in her arms as I sobbed. I doubt I would have made it through the day without her.

I make my way downstairs and into the kitchen, and I'm greeted by the smell of freshly brewed coffee and sizzling bacon.

'You're looking more respectable,' Mrs Cranfield says approvingly. 'What made you have such a heavy night?'

'Work,' I reply, picking up the pot of coffee. 'I got into a bit of an argument. Foolishly, I then I said I needed a drink to calm me down.'

'My guess is it made things worse. Alcohol normally does,' says Mrs Cranfield, handing me a bacon sandwich before struggling to balance herself on the bar stools that have replaced my mum's Shaker-style kitchen chairs. 'I'll never understand why you bought these,' she says, grabbing hold of the island to balance herself. Seeing me suppress a smile, she starts to laugh. 'My figure is not made for cutting-edge kitchen design.'

'You look wonderful to me.'

'Charmer,' she scoffs.

It was Mrs Cranfield who had encouraged me to make the house my own over the past few years. After my mum's death, I went back to Manchester, gave up drinking and managed to graduate with a decent degree. The following year I travelled the world. My old schoolfriend, Michael, flew out and joined me for a few weeks when I was in the United States and we spent Mardi Gras in New Orleans. I still hadn't drunk since my mum's death, and seeing him walk through a poolside plate glass window and spend two weeks in the Louisiana University Hospital had confirmed to me the perils of excess alcohol consumption.

When I returned to England I got my first proper job – and it was an easy commute from Haddley. I knew it was time to come home. At first it was difficult, as I'd convinced myself I couldn't walk down Haddley High Street without being recognised, but in time I realised most people were more well-meaning than malicious.

'So why the argument?'

'Guess.'

Mrs C smiles. She has heard the many tales of my roller-coaster relationship with my boss.

'Madeline wants me to write a piece about Mum for the tenth anniversary,' I say. 'I've told her no,' I add hastily as Mrs Cranfield opens her mouth to speak.

'That woman has no morals,' she says, clicking her tongue disapprovingly. 'Asking you to live through that again. As if that would do anybody any good. She really is beyond the pale.'

I take a sip of my coffee and smile. 'So you think I should stick to my guns?'

Mrs C raises her eyebrows. 'Don't tell me you were thinking otherwise?'

'Min thought it might help me put to rest the last lingering questions I have.'

'Min is a lovely girl, but really . . . '

'I still wonder what would have happened if I hadn't been so hungover, Mrs C – if I'd only spoken to her before she left, or gone after her. Maybe everything would have been very different.'

'Ben, we've been through this. It wasn't your fault. You must never blame yourself,' whispers Mrs Cranfield, stepping off her stool and squeezing my arm. She drops her head and crosses to the sink to start vigorously scrubbing at the frying pan.

'You'll scorch your hands,' I say as the steam rises thick from the water, but Mrs C continues to scrub. I walk across to her and turn off the tap. 'You won't get it any cleaner than that; those marks are baked in for life.'

She dries her hands on a tea towel and surveys me for a moment. 'So tell me about your night out,' she says. 'You said Min was with you?'

'Min and some other colleagues.'

'Min is only a colleague?'

33

'Colleague-slash-friend, no more than that.'

'And were the others colleagues-slash-friends? Or does that apply only to Min?'

'Enough!' I say, laughing, going back to the counter and squeezing more ketchup on to my bacon sandwich.

'Very well, I shan't ask any more.' Mrs C holds up her hands in mock surrender. 'Got enough ketchup on that?' I squeeze the bottle again. 'The first time you ever came to lunch with me and George, you refused to eat anything until you had covered it in ketchup.'

'I was ten years old!'

'Some things never change.'

That day, my mum had gone for her first job interview since deciding to return to work. I had been on a half-day from school due to teacher training and Mr and Mrs Cranfield had stepped in with an offer of childcare. Finding herself in a bind, my mum had been delighted to accept the offer from her new neighbours, who had moved to the common only a couple of weeks before. As Mrs Cranfield worked on getting her new home unpacked, Mr Cranfield had taken me down to the river to teach me the basics of freshwater fishing. Once he'd opened the pot of live maggots for bait, it was rapidly to become both my first and last experience of angling.

'She was so happy to be working again,' says Mrs C, and I remember my mum's joy when a letter had arrived two days later, offering her the job. 'All she wanted to do was take care of you.' Mrs C pauses. 'And she was such a very good friend to me . . . ' there's a tremor in her voice ' . . . but it's you I put first now – for your sake and your mum's.' Mrs C rinses her

34

cup in the sink, before adding, 'Come for lunch on Sunday. Bring somebody if you like.'

I laugh, and as she heads out of the back door I pull her into a hug. 'Thank you,' I say.

'For what?' replies Mrs C. 'It's what I'm here for.' And with a quick wave she heads down the alley towards the back of her own home.

I top up my mug before folding open the doors that lead out on to my small back garden. Sitting on the step in the early spring sun, I flick open the screen on my phone and click on our news app. Our celebrity site reports a minor member of the royal family stumbling out of a nightclub with a man who clearly isn't the duke of anywhere, while the main news site leads with the story of three people being killed by a falling crane in Nottingham city centre. Following that is the story of a woman found dead in her one-bedroom flat on the outskirts of Leeds. I click through to the details. Police are refusing to comment further at this stage but are unable to rule out her dying in suspicious circumstances. Any half-decent journalist knows this means in all likelihood the woman has been murdered, but the police aren't ready to confirm it.

I click back and flick further down through the news headlines, stopping suddenly when my mum's eyes stare out at me.

REMEMBERING CLARE HARPER: TEN YEARS ON.

Two weeks ahead of my mum's anniversary, Madeline is promoting a feature that has yet to be written. Her audacity never ceases to amaze me.

I stare at my phone. The image of my mum is one I know well. Taken on a chill summer's evening the year before she died, with the light fading behind her, wrapped in her favourite sweater, she was sitting on the banks of the Thames. That night I'd been out in Haddley and was walking home along the river's edge when I'd spotted her sitting alone as the watery sun dropped behind the woods. Without her realising, I'd captured her image on my phone – an image of a woman at peace with the world. We'd sat together and talked about the trip to Bordeaux she had just taken with two of her closest friends – how they'd visited different wineries each day and sat outside long into the evenings drinking wine on their terrace. The picture captured the new-found freedom the trip had given her. When she died, it was the one I chose to release it to the press.

Below the image are a series of links to related stories. One is for an article from a number of years ago written as part of a *Women of Courage* series. I re-read the story; it celebrated a woman of great dignity and inner strength.

Scrolling through the article, I stop on an image of my brother Nick with his best friend, Simon Woakes. It is an image that became synonymous with Nick and Simon's story, an image that became infamous the world over. Standing on the touchline at Richmond Rugby Club, dressed in their school rugby kit and wearing winners' smiles, were Nick and Simon. Standing with them, their arms around the boys, were two of their classmates.

The two fourteen-year-old girls who weeks later would savagely murder them.

CHAPTER 6

Lingering beside our front gate waiting for Nick to return home, I stood and watched the two girls as they sprawled on Haddley Common's scorched grass. The bus's arrival animated them, and they were quick to scramble to their feet when the number 29 stopped at the kerb. Nick and Simon, rucksacks thrown over their backs, stepped off the bus. I peered over our garden wall and I saw a brief conversation follow.

Then, the first of the girls danced away, her hair twirling in the late-afternoon sun. She reached out her hands, taking hold of her friend and pulling her forward; the pair whirled together across the wide-open space towards the dense woods that separated Haddley from the neighbouring village of St Marnham. From across the common I could hear them shriek as they spun round and round.

For a moment Nick and Simon appeared to hesitate, but then I saw them pick up their pace in pursuit of the girls. Watching, I crossed the road in front of my house and stepped on to the common's parched ground. The grass was dry and crackly. I felt the heat of the sun beat down as the endless days of a schoolboy summer refused to come to an end. Ahead of me, the figures of Nick and Simon blurred in the sun. I was careful to keep my distance, but soon found myself running to keep them in my sights. Like any inquisitive eight-year-old, I was determined to discover where they were heading.

Breathless, I arrived at the overgrown entrance to the woods, gulping in dry air before hunching my shoulders and creeping inside. Instantly I sensed the heat dissipate, the canopy of trees stymieing the sun's rays.

I stole forward, feeling a line of sweat slowly trickle down my spine.

The woods were silent, tree boughs stagnant with no hint of a breeze. The only sound came from the crunch of dead scrub beneath my feet. I strained for a sound to guide me in my pursuit but, as I did, a train rattled past on the railway line running across the top side of the woods.

I waited.

Then, I listened again. My own breath was the only sound – until a distant cry echoed through the trees. Nick would be livid if he caught me, but I moved forward on my toes, keeping low and staying hidden among the overgrown bushes. I headed towards the small open hollow where my brother and his friends often hid deep inside the woods.

The narrow path twisted ahead of me, and I edged through the undergrowth until finally I reached the clearing. Momentarily dazzled as the sunlight poured through the gap in the canopy, I staggered to one side. My bare neck burned under the blaze.

The hollow was deserted.

I skimmed my feet, kicking at cigarette butts, the dust rising. With no sign of my brother and a growing thirst, I decided to head for home.

A distant laugh reverberated through the trees.

Then another.

And then a scream of delight.

Instantly, I knew where they were – a small raised area on the far side of the woods, close to St Marnham – Nick's secret place. To approach unseen, I had to clamber along the overgrown bank at the side of the railway line. As I pushed through the thistles, a thorn embedded itself in the crook of my arm. Pulling it out, I watched a line of blood run down my arm trickling on to my palm. I bit my lip to stifle the pain.

As I stood at the foot of the giant mound, silence returned to the airless woods. I began my ascent, scrambling up the hill, my feet slipping on the dusty ground. Struggling to find a grip, I felt myself sliding backwards until I grabbed hold of a dead root and hauled myself up. Dusting myself down as I reached the summit, I looked down at my favourite football shirt; it was covered in dry soil and blood.

Slowly, I crept forward.

One.

Two.

Three hesitant steps.

Then I stopped.

I held my breath.

On the far side of the mound, Nick and Simon lay naked; their arms outstretched, their feet towards me.

Confused, I crept forward.

My screams broke the silence.

CHAPTER 7

The desk sergeant smiled at her and Dani Cash had to remind herself to breathe as she walked past her and into the women's locker room. It was hard to believe that five months ago this had felt like her home from home. Pushing open the door, she paused to look at the noticeboard – places up for grabs in the Richmond half-marathon, Pilates classes, tai-chi, a trainee officer's twenty-first birthday party. Dani had placed a similar invitation on the noticeboard for her own twenty-first. She'd joined the force just a couple of weeks before it, and she'd celebrated with so many new friends on a night out by the river.

As she went to her locker, Dani wondered how many fellow officers she'd get to come out on a night out with her now. Faced with her padlock, her mind went blank. She tried a combination, then a second and then finally a third – Mat's birthday. Forgetting it only made her feel worse.

When she'd first met Mat she had been bowled over by him. The high-flying sergeant everyone said would be chief one day. With his six-foot frame, his cropped fair hair, five o'clock shadow and soft blue eyes, he was hard to miss. He was eight years older than her but that didn't matter. Much of the station was in awe of him. She'd been in awe of him.

On a wet Monday evening the last thing she had felt like was a gym class but, still sticking to her New Year's resolutions, she'd dragged herself to Haddley Leisure Centre. Members of the Metropolitan Police were given discounted membership, meaning that in most classes you would find yourself sweating alongside senior officers. She'd turned and half-smiled at him when he'd stood directly behind her in a body pump class. At the end of the class, she'd half-smiled again. When she emerged from the changing room, she'd found him sitting on a bench in the hallway, waiting.

Maybe that third gin and tonic at the pub overlooking Haddley Hill Park had been a mistake. Mat had said he only ever drank doubles and he'd bought her the same. Before nine that night they were back in the flat he rented at the top of the hill and, even drunkenly, she'd loved the feeling of him fiercely inside her. Early the next morning he was more tender, and she'd left wanting to see him again. At the station they didn't speak, but late in the day he'd winked at her and that night they were together once more. In the late summer they'd spent a week together on a beach in Croatia and, over chilled glasses of the crisp local white wine, she had begun to imagine them sharing a future together.

The stench hit Dani as soon as she opened her locker door. For five months, her gym shoes and unwashed kit had festered. Gagging, she pulled them out and threw them into the bin by the sinks.

'Didn't think we'd see you back here again.'

Dani straightened and turned to see PC Karen Cooke standing beside her. Somehow Cooke's uniform always seemed half an inch tighter than any other female officer's.

'Word was you couldn't cut it any more,' Cooke went on, giving Dani an unpleasant smile. She had never tried to conceal her dislike of Dani. Dani had always assumed it had stemmed from the days when her dad was the boss, but she was still taken aback by the venom in Cooke's tone.

Dani said nothing and moved back towards her locker. Cooke blocked her path. 'Talk around the station is that you've gone the same way as your dad – lost your nerve.' Dani's face flushed and she felt her jaw tighten, but she held Cooke's gaze. 'Bottler,' said Cooke, a look of hatred in her eyes. Dani edged past her and reached for a cloth beside the sink, but she could sense Cooke standing behind her as she held it under the hot tap.

'At least when it was your dad he did the decent thing and resigned. Nobody wants you here.' Dani felt Cooke's weight press up against her as she forced a whisper into her ear. 'We can't trust you.'

Without warning, she rammed Dani up against the sink – one arm thrown around her neck and the other pressed hard against her breast. Dani could feel the edge of the unit slicing into her, Cooke's weight crushing her against it. Fighting for breath, Dani desperately tried to twist herself free, but Cooke grabbed hold of her belt and smashed her forward against the mirror. 'You need to find another station. And quick.'

In a single, rapid movement Dani jerked herself backwards. With three quick steps, she slammed Cooke back into the lockers and rammed the wet cloth in her face. As she did so, she heard the changing-room door open and she turned to see Detective Sergeant Lesley Barnsdale standing behind them. She dropped the cloth and walked quietly back across the room.

'Good morning, ladies,' said Barnsdale, calmly. Dani was aware of her superior gauging the scene. 'Welcome back, PC Cash. You're with me today. We've got a callout on behalf of the West Yorkshire force. Be ready to leave here in five minutes.'

'Yes, ma'am,' replied Dani, shutting her bag inside her locker.

'Cooke, you look a little damp,' said Barnsdale. 'I suggest you get dried off, and after that I'm still waiting for two reports from you from last week.' Barnsdale crossed the room and handed Cooke the wet cloth before stepping into a cubicle and closing the door.

'Yes, ma'am,' replied Cooke, grabbing a handful of paper towels. 'I'll be looking out for you,' she whispered to Dani. 'And do send my love to Mat; everyone so wants to see him back here soon.'

Dani stepped sideways and snatched hold of Cooke's shirt. 'Fuck you,' she said, before pushing her aside and leaving the room.

CHAPTER 8

Thirteen months after the murders of Nick and Simon, Abigail Langdon and Josie Fairchild were convicted. During their trial, neither of the girls showed any remorse. They had killed the boys, both about to become Year Ten students, in the most inhumane of ways.

It was stated in court that the girls had lured Nick and Simon to the woods. I don't think I really understood a lot of what was said, but I was required to give evidence via a video link. I remember being asked if I'd seen the girls kissing the two boys when they walked across the common. I'd felt an urge to laugh at the question because I was sure Nick wouldn't have wanted to be seen kissing a girl on the common, but, realising the seriousness, I'd simply shaken my head.

I was never asked to recount what I found when I discovered the boys' bodies. Photographs were placed into evidence but the press were required to withhold the most graphic details.

On that horrendous summer's day, I had charged down

the front of the mound, and in my panic become disorientated. Instead of running for home, I'd stumbled on through the woods and found myself in the village of St Marnham. I ran until I reached the duck pond in the middle of the village. Gasping for breath and confused, I fell to the ground. I knelt on the grass and sobbed until I felt a hand rest upon my shoulder. I jumped to my feet. A man was standing beside me and reaching for my hand. I looked at him and screamed – screamed my brother was dead, dead in the woods. He told me to wait as he ran towards the houses that overlooked the pond. Desperate to escape, I had started running again, too, this time along the road that connects St Marnham and Haddley.

I know now that is a distance of close to a mile, and in the intense summer heat on that wretched day I'd begun to wilt. Unable to run any further, I collapsed by the side of the road, curling myself into a ball. As an eight-year-old boy, it had felt as if I was alone on the roadside for hours, but what must have been minutes later a police car approached. Sitting in the back seat being driven back to Haddley, I'd begun to shake. I would have to tell my mum what I had seen.

Three days later the girls were arrested and charged. Their blood-splattered clothes were discovered squashed beneath Abigail Langdon's bed. With the girls' convictions, their identities were finally revealed to the world. Their police mugshots showed them smiling inanely at the camera, seemingly without a care in the world. Sadistic and ritualistic killers, they were turned into figures of hate, representing the depravity of a younger generation.

Immediately following their convictions, they were transported to separate high-security youth detention centres. During the journey, the vehicle transporting one of the girls came under attack, a concrete block dropped on to it from a motorway bridge. Only once roads were closed could their onward transportation be secured. Called to comment upon events, the Prime Minister asked for calm, but his message of strong family values was drowned out in a national desire for revenge.

Two days after Nick's murder, my father had appeared at our door. My mum accepted his right to share in our grief and invited him back into the home he had left when I was just three years old. In the intervening years he'd made random appearances, suddenly arriving with ill-chosen gifts bestowed with exaggerated enthusiasm. Three weeks after my seventh birthday, I'd arrived home from school to find him sitting on a bench by the common. Calling me across, he had presented me with a replica Chelsea kit. When he'd become annoyed at my ingratitude, Nick had taken him one side to explain that we were Brentford fans, not Chelsea.

'Why didn't he know that?' I'd asked Nick, as, later that evening, we had sat together doing our homework at the kitchen table.

'He's been away a long time.'

'But we've always been Bees fans.'

'I know,' Nick had replied, and the following weekend he and Mum had taken me to my first Brentford game. I never wore the Chelsea shirt.

In returning to our home, I think my father did offer my

mum momentary comfort; in the face of a grief so raw, all that had passed between them was briefly forgotten. But I didn't know him. Whenever I was with him, I was still the three-year-old boy waiting at the window for his father to return from his latest work trip. It was from one such work trip that he never did return, and for that I could never forgive him. Four days after Nick's funeral, he was gone.

The first year after Nick's death was intolerable for my mum. A beloved son to mourn, a murder trial to withstand and a media explosion to endure, I often wonder how she survived the year. Her grief must have been all-consuming, and I remember the desolation we shared as we sat together at our kitchen table, Nick's chair empty beside us. Each evening my mum would toy with her food, hardly seeming to eat. Hugging her each night, feeling her bones against mine, I was scared to hold her too tight for fear she would break.

While my mum grieved and, as she told me later, tried to survive by living her life an hour at a time, she was simultaneously trying to coax me back into the world. I needed constant reassurance of my own safety and that she would be there to watch over me. In the weeks following Nick's death, I was terrified to leave our house. I couldn't bear for my mum to be out of my sight for a single minute. Each night she would lie with me until I fell asleep, in many ways finding it as reassuring as me. I missed the following term of school but in the weeks before Christmas I started to catch up on my school work from home. Then, on a frost-covered January morning, Holly and Michael, my best friends for life, arrived at my front door with their mothers beside them. With a tight hold on my mum's hand, I walked down the edge of the common and then along the riverbank towards the primary school I attended on the far side of Haddley Bridge. Halfway along the river path, Michael started to run ahead and I turned to look at my mum. She let go of my hand, and Holly and I chased after him. Seconds later, I turned and waved to my mum as she walked arm in arm with her two friends.

At the end of each school day, she would be waiting at the school gates and we would walk home together. I remained reluctant to go anywhere other than school and home. My love of the common was gone, and even the lure of chasing a football with my friends couldn't draw me away from our kitchen table.

In the months following the conclusion of the trial, the media coverage started to wane and my mum tried to persuade me to start living the life of a ten-year-old boy. Why didn't we go and watch Brentford again? she would ask. The club was far less glamorous than the big London sides, but Nick and I had supported them since we were young, adopting them as our family team. Although Nick was more a rugby fan, the three of us had loved going to matches together. I'd remained a huge football fan but without Nick I steadfastly refused to return to any games. It was only when the Bees were top of their league and heading for promotion that I started to be swept up in the excitement. One Friday evening, my mum surprised me when she came home with two tickets for the match the following day.

The next day I hugged my mum as Brentford scored goal after goal, and for the first time I felt a little of what I'd had before Nick died. Walking away from the ground, I held on to my mum's hand and chatted about the match, endlessly talking about the goals we had scored. I desperately wanted to know when we could go again, and I've always thought that it was on that day that she'd known I was going to be okay.

It took another year, but somehow the two of us together started to find a rhythm in our lives. My mum loved her new job, while I made my way through school and started playing for the Brentford under-fourteens football team, and then the under-sixteens. In the years after Nick's death, my mum sought out ways to slowly rebuild her life. Supported by some close friends and neighbours, she forced herself to socialise and explore new interests. I wept with laughter when she showed me her efforts at pottery. I still have the lopsided mug she painted for me in honour of the Bees. She adored the cookery classes she attended in Hampstead and would walk on the heath with new friends after each lesson. One bright spring evening included a dip in the famous open-air swimming pond, but, with an early season chill, she swore it would be one time only.

However much she did and however much support she had, I knew at times it never stopped her feeling incredibly alone. There were days when it took an enormous effort to simply step outside our front door. Walking across Haddley Common could be an insurmountable task; facing the world exhausting. But, in everything she did, I could see they were challenges she was determined to face, unwavering in her commitment to overcome them.

For my mum, Nick's death had meant the unbearable loss of a beloved son. For me, it meant the passing of a patient superhero. Whether he had sat with me at our kitchen table teaching me to read, coached me on the art of penalty kicks or inspired awe as I watched him dive from the top board, I had seen in Nick all that I wanted to be. After his death, my mum had sought ways to fill that void. So much of her time was devoted to protecting me, while at the same time helping me discover the best opportunities in life. She pushed me through my school exams and came to cheer me on, win or lose, at every football game I played. Cold and damp from standing on the sidelines, she would listen attentively to my post-match analysis as I relived every second while ploughing through a Big Mac and giant portion of fries.

I put in a decent showing in my A-levels and it was ten years after Nick's death when I started at Manchester University. At the beginning of my second year, I moved into a house off campus, sharing with four friends. One evening I was about to head into the city when my mum called me on my mobile. I could hear the despair in her voice. She'd been visited by a police liaison officer. They had informed her that Abigail Langdon and Josie Fairchild were to be released under new identities.

For the murders of Nick and Simon, they had served eleven years.

They were freed six months before my mum's death.

CHAPTER 9

Hanging in my hallway is my mum's favourite picture of Nick. It was taken at the end of his last summer school term; Nick had lost his school tie after a lunchtime cricket match. He had borrowed one from a friend in readiness for the photograph and looped a huge oversized knot. In the image, his dark hair is clipped short and his bright smile lights up his whole face. My mum simply adored the photo. It captures Nick's absolute joy at the end of the school term and the start of the long summer holiday. I stand and gaze at the image. Looking into his bright, laughing eyes, I have to turn away.

I meander out of the front of my house into the bright spring sunshine. I plan to walk across the common in the hope that some more fresh air will help clear my head. As I do, I see a police car turn up from the Lower Haddley Road.

My stomach turns.

I wait by the wall that runs across the front of my garden, and watch as the car stops directly alongside. Two officers climb out, one dressed in plain clothes.

'Mr Harper? Mr Benjamin Harper?' she asks, as she steps out of the passenger side door. Her hair is pulled tight back from her face, giving her what one of the freelancers on the site calls a Croydon facelift. 'I'm Detective Sergeant Lesley Barnsdale,' she says, offering her hand. 'I wonder if we might have a quiet word.' Her accompanying uniformed colleague walks around from the driver's side. 'This is PC Daniella Cash.'

I smile at PC Cash and she offers me a sympathetic look in return. They already know who I am.

'How can I help you?' I say to DS Barnsdale.

'It might be easier if we speak inside,' comes the reply.

I sigh. 'Of course.'

Inside, I show them into the sitting room. It's a room I use rarely as, although I've had it redecorated, it's a part of the house that still feels as if it belongs to my mum.

'Take a seat,' I say, motioning to the armchairs either side of the fireplace. They're the same ones Mum chose more than twenty years ago.

'How can I help you?' I repeat, after an uncomfortable moment of silence. 'I'm a little bit pressed for time.'

'We'll try not to hold you up, sir,' says PC Cash, a few blonde curls escaping from beneath her carefully secured hat. As I glance across at her, she self-consciously tries to tuck them away.

'We wanted to speak to you,' continues DS Barnsdale, attempting to adopt a delicate tone, 'in relation to matters concerning your family history.'

'I see,' I reply, flatly.

'We need to ask you a number of questions,' Barnsdale continues, 'in relation to an incident that has taken place during the last forty-eight hours. The West Yorkshire Police are investigating an unexplained death on the outskirts of Leeds. At this time they are trying to establish the circumstances surrounding a woman's death.'

'You think the woman's been murdered?' I say, remembering the story I had seen online.

'We can't confirm anything at this point, but it is a possibility,' says PC Cash, failing to read a look from her superior. Clearly her contribution would be required only upon request.

'The West Yorkshire Police are still investigating,' continues the detective, 'but they are unable to rule out suspicious circumstances at this point.'

'And how does this relate to me?' I ask.

'Since the body was discovered, a thorough search of the victim's home has been undertaken. During the course of that search, some letters written to the victim were found hidden under the floorboards in the dead woman's living room. We believe these letters, Mr Harper, were sent to the victim by your mother.'

'By my mum?' I say, the surprise showing in my voice. 'You do know she died almost ten years ago?'

'We are aware of that,' says DS Barnsdale, 'and our sympathies remain with you. However, we believe these letters were written in the weeks immediately preceding your mother's death. I wonder if you could tell me of any reason your mother might have been writing to a woman in the town of Farsley, on the outskirts of Leeds, ten and a half years ago?'

I shake my head. 'I'm sorry, no. None whatsoever.'

'She never spoke of … ' DS Barnsdale pauses before continuing with her question. 'Mr Harper, do you know a woman by the name of Demi Porter?'

Both officers give me an expectant look, which I return with a blank one.

'No, sorry,' I reply. 'I've never heard of her. If that's who my mum was writing to, I've no idea who she was. I'm sorry, I can't be of any more help.'

'You're certain you don't know the name?' says PC Cash, lifting her eyes directly to mine.

'Absolutely. As I said, I've never heard it before in my life. But then again lots of people wrote to my mum, and she did write back to quite a few of the people who wrote to her. Particularly around then. You might not be aware, but that was around the time my brother's killers were released from prison.'

The two officers exchange a look I can't read.

'We are aware that a large number of people contacted your mother,' says the DS. 'But these letters, the ones discovered with the dead woman's body, are not of that nature.'

'In what way?' I ask. 'Can you give me some idea what the letters said?'

Cash goes to say something but the detective cuts across her.

'Mr Harper,' she says, completely ignoring my question, 'are you quite sure your mother never spoke of any acquaintances, or of knowing anyone, in Farsley, or indeed in or around Leeds?'

'Not to me,' I say pointedly. 'I don't think there is anything more I can tell you.' I cross the living room and open the door for them to leave. 'You're positive the letters were from my mum?'

'We're as certain as we can be at this time,' says DS Barnsdale, not getting up. 'From reading the letters, it appears your mother was addressing the victim directly. Mr Harper, I have to tell you the woman to whom your mother was writing – her birth name was not Demi Porter. It was Abigail Langdon.'

Two

*'This could be my chance to discover
the truth my mum so desperately wanted.'*

CHAPTER 10

Holly Richardson stood in the doorway of her living room and watched as her four-year-old daughter, Alice, giggled at the sight of Peppa Pig jumping from one muddy puddle to another. Looking down at her daughter, her soft, almost auburn curls touching her shoulders, Holly fought against the desire to rush into the room, scoop her into her arms and run without ever looking back. Instead, she silently closed the living-room door and crept up the three flights of stairs to the attic room of her Haddley home.

When she reached the top of the house she shared with her husband Jake and their young daughter, Holly felt her stomach tighten. She opened the attic door, telling herself she had nothing to fear. The front door to the house was locked – she had checked it twice, but still she found herself feeling for the key in her pocket as she stepped into the room.

Tasting the room's stale and musty air, Holly brought her hand to her mouth. She stood and looked at the chaos of discarded furniture, unused exercise equipment – a legacy of good intentions – alongside boxed Christmas decorations and even a rusting barbecue. Across the room, in the far corner, was the roll-top desk from where Jake had briefly run a successful family business. That was long gone, suffocated by ambition and now shrouded in a thick layer of dust. It was where she would start her search.

A faded red sofa, which Holly had brought to the house seven years ago when she and Jake had married, blocked her path. As she squeezed past it, she felt for the carefully repaired split running down the back. Her mother had stitched it up by hand after they'd dragged the sofa up two narrow flights of stairs and the fabric had torn. Holly hadn't cared that her tiny bedsit was tucked away on the top floor of a pub; for the very first time she had had her own home. Her mum couldn't understand why she'd been so determined to rent what she always described as a 'grotty no-bedroom flat', but to Holly it had meant independence. So many of her friends had moved away, and this had been her chance to stand on her own two feet.

To clear her path, she edged the sofa towards the window, knocking it into Alice's baby cot as she did. The cot fell forward and Holly leapt across the sofa to stop it crashing to the floor. She rested it carefully back against the wall, gently passing her hand along the side. She thought of the first night she had settled Alice into her own bedroom, of how she'd then spent most of the night sleeping on the floor next to her.

Beside the cot stood Alice's high chair, scratches on its tray, its brightly patterned balloons slightly faded. Both high chair and cot kept in readiness for their second child, but, as she tidied the straps on the chair, Holly knew that child would never come.

Moving further into the room, she clambered over a stack of boxes packed with old clothes and the unused bed linen that Jake's mother had gifted them soon after the wedding. Jake had accepted his mother's gift graciously, but then had refused to allow Holly ever to open the boxes. He was adamant they weren't a charity case. They had no need of his parents' hand-me-downs. He had been the same with the antique wooden wardrobe that now stood sadly against the far wall, just in front of the desk. It had taken all their strength to manoeuvre it up the attic stairs and across the room. By the time they'd finished they were drenched in sweat and, catching sight of each other, had been consumed by fits of laughter. They had been married for less than a month and, tearing off their sweat-soaked clothes, had made love on the attic floor. Holly remembered watching Jake's sinewy body in the wardrobe's mirrored door but now, as she looked at herself in the faded mirror, her honey-brown hair tied loosely back, her fringe in desperate need of shaping before she became totally Seventies, she struggled to recall the passion that had briefly ignited her marriage.

Quickly she pushed aside a seatless exercise bike before pulling back the captain's chair that had made Jake's office look more Dickensian than twenty-first-century business hub. The desk lid was locked. Perching on the edge of the chair, she took a small knife from her pocket and attempted to flick open the lock. It moved, but stayed fast. As Holly increased the pressure, the knife slipped, leaving a tiny scratch upon the surface. Licking her thumb, she tasted the dust of the room before vigorously rubbing at the mark.

Did she hear a creak on the stairs? With a start, she turned to look over her shoulder. 'Alice?' she called gently, but there was no reply. How she hated being so fearful in her own home.

She focused her attention back to the room. She had to get inside that desk. She slipped the knife back into the lock.

Click. The lock finally opened and she rolled back the desk lid. Inside were papers piled upon papers: receipts for Jake's business, unpaid invoices and tax demands. Holly pulled out the first stack and started rifling through the pages. A second and a third stack followed before she removed a final stack. Behind it, another two shelves were crammed with documents. Holly felt panic rise in her chest. Alice would surely start calling for her soon. She rummaged furiously through the remaining documents; her husband had clearly never discarded a single record, not since the day of the company's creation. If only he had been able to let it go.

She reached to the back of the last shelf, and felt a crumpled plastic bag pushed to the rear. Pulling it out, she discovered an orange, old-style supermarket carrier bag, already such an alien thing. Scrunched inside was a tiny white baby's sleepsuit. She put the bag to one side and laid the simple outfit with its embroidered rabbit across her lap. Gently, she straightened its arms and legs, smoothing the suit until it lay perfectly flat.

It was obvious the suit had never belonged to Alice.

Almost eleven pounds at birth, her daughter would never have been able to fit into it. This suit was for a tiny newborn.

Holly lifted it up and turned it over in her hands. It had hardly ever been worn. Overcome by an inescapable urge to inhale a newborn's scent, she brought it up to her face. But the scent of whichever baby it had once belonged to was long gone. Instead, Holly spluttered as the dank mustiness the suit had gathered while it lay concealed at the back of Jake's desk caught in her throat.

Neatly smoothing the sleepsuit back across her knees, Holly wondered how long it had been kept hidden. With a mother's care, she fastened the three tiny press-studs up to the collar, before running her fingers across the cotton fabric.

Then her heart jumped.

A *ra-ta-tat-tat* on the front door of her house.

She froze.

And then again.

Ra-ta-tat-tat.

Ra-ta-tat-tat.

CHAPTER 11

Her heart racing, Holly hurriedly put the sleepsuit inside the bag and pushed it to the back of the shelf. Then, she pressed the stack of papers inside the desk before rolling the cover forward, listening for the click of the lock as it closed.

The rapping on the door came again. She scanned her surroundings for any obvious signs of her presence. As she rushed across the room, her sleeve caught on the handle of the wardrobe and she had to stop to free herself. She told herself to calm down. Touching the key in her pocket, she felt a moment's reassurance. The front door couldn't be opened from the outside. She knew he liked the doors locked to keep her and Alice safe. She would tell him she had been in the bathroom.

And then the doorbell rang and her heart raced again.

She scrambled on to the back of her old sofa and peered out of the small attic window. Stretching herself up higher, pulling on the tiny window ledge, she could see directly down on to the footpath below. A uniformed delivery-man was standing at her door with a box in his hand. At the kerb, she noticed a white van with the letters 'PDQ' on the side.

Taking a calming breath, she watched as the deliveryman stepped away from her door, still holding the package in his hand. She cracked open the window. 'I'm sorry,' she called. 'I'm up here. In the attic. I'll be down in a second.'

As she ran down the stairs, her heart slowed. Turning the key and releasing the lock, Holly felt the relief of opening her front door to be met by the sun-blushed face of Phil Doorley, the owner of PDQuick Deliveries.

'Hi, Mrs Richardson,' said Phil, as he handed her the package.

'I'm sorry to keep you waiting. As I said, I was upstairs. I never seem to get around to any tidying. Alice keeps me run off my feet,' she replied, her speech racing. 'If I'd known it was you, I'd have come straight down.'

'Not a problem,' he said, handing her a delivery note for signature.

'Let me just pop this down in the hall,' she said, stepping back and putting the box at the bottom of the stairs before returning to sign the slip. 'I've nothing on order. Can't think what it might be.'

'Hopefully a nice surprise,' replied Phil, taking the slip from her and turning back down the pathway.

'Thanks again for waiting.'

'No worries,' said Phil, with a wave.

Phil Doorley struck Holly as somebody with very few worries in life. He had been in Jake's class at school before attending teacher-training college and then returning to

Haddley Grammar. After three years back in school, he'd decided teaching wasn't for him, and the next thing she'd heard was that he had set up his own local delivery business. Often she'd see him in and around Haddley and St Marnham, always ready with an effortless hello and seemingly at ease with the world.

She stood in the doorway, watching as he climbed back in his van, and as he pulled away she returned his wave. She closed the door and turned the key, and when she heard the double-lock click back into place she breathed a sigh of relief. Blowing out her cheeks, she rubbed her face as she walked back into the living room. She couldn't keep living like this.

She dropped on to the sofa, and as she did she felt her phone buzz.

She clicked on the message.

You know what happens when you go looking.

CHAPTER 12

'I'm glad she's dead,' I say to DS Barnsdale, as I step backwards, steadying myself against the living-room wall. I raise my hand to my face as, for a moment, darkness closes across my eyes. My body begins to shake and I can sense Barnsdale's eyes on me. I force myself to breathe.

PC Cash is quick to her feet and I feel her hand gently rest upon my arm as she guides me back across the room. 'Come and sit down,' she says, as we slowly cross to my mum's favourite armchair. 'Of course, this is a shock.'

I drop my head forward and for a moment we sit in silence as I desperately try to understand what the officers are telling me. As the tenth anniversary of my mum's death approaches, Abigail Langdon has been murdered. In the weeks before my mum's own death, she had been in direct correspondence with her. Neither of these facts makes any sense to me.

'I hope it was brutal,' I say, lifting my eyes to Barnsdale. The rage, the hatred that courses through me, even after all these years, is unconstrained. I try never to think about those two girls. That kind of loathing is too draining.

DS Barnsale doesn't seem surprised.

'Mr Harper, take your time,' she says, mildly. 'A shock like this can be difficult to process.'

'Why would anyone be shocked at her death?' I say, jumping to my feet again, only for my legs to buckle. PC Cash moves forward but I steady myself. 'Abigail Langdon was one of the most hated figures in Britain. She spent much of her life incarcerated as a child-killer. It's not difficult to imagine the company she's kept since her release. The only shock is that this hasn't come sooner.'

'Mr Harper,' replies DS Barnsdale, sitting motionless, 'please be assured that all possible avenues surrounding Abigail Langdon's death will be explored in our investigation. We do, however, need to understand why your mother wrote to the deceased woman, and, more pressingly, how she came by her contact details. Those letters tell us that for over ten years her new identity as Demi Porter was compromised.'

'Compromised by someone who lived in this house,' I say, regaining my thought process and joining the dots for the detective.

'It would appear so, yes.'

'Can I see the letters?'

'I'm afraid not. They're evidence in a murder case.'

'In that case, I don't think there is anything more I can tell you,' I say, somewhat churlishly.

I see PC Cash look in the direction of her superior.

'We appreciate this is very difficult for you,' begins the constable. 'All we're asking for today is your help. We want to try to build a picture of how your mother could have been in contact with Abigail Langdon, and why.'

'Without knowing the content of the letters, it's almost impossible for me to guess, isn't it?'

'It isn't a case of us not wanting to share the content with you personally,' replies Cash carefully, 'but we'd hate for any information to reach the press at this time. And for that in turn to hamper the further progress of the investigation.'

'And you do work for the UK's biggest online news site,' says DS Barnsdale.

'Detective, I've had enough of front-page stories to last me a lifetime. Rest assured, I've got no desire to go looking for more headlines now.'

'Perhaps if you could come and sit down again . . . ' says PC Cash, placing her hand on my mum's chair.

I do as requested before leaning forward towards the constable. 'If you can't show me the letters, can you at least give me a sense of what my mum wanted from Langdon?'

PC Cash glances at her superior as the detective uncomfortably runs her hands down the length of her pencil skirt, straightening its imaginary creases.

'It's our understanding,' begins Cash, 'that two letters have been discovered in the home of the woman now known as Demi Porter. The first has an envelope addressed to Ms Porter but contains a letter directly addressing Abigail Langdon. The author states that she is Clare Harper. We will of course compare handwriting samples but we've no reason to believe the letter is forged. She makes it clear that she knows where Langdon is but has no desire to interfere with her new life.'

I nod in silence.

'Your mum,' continues PC Cash, 'writes of the intense pain she suffered in losing a child in such an inhumane way, and asks directly why Nick, and Simon Woakes, were targeted. She tells Langdon that only when she has a child of her own will she possibly begin to comprehend the pain she has inflicted.'

PC Cash pauses and turns towards her superior. DS Barnsdale takes up the narrative. 'Our assessment of this first letter is that she was seeking to build a level of trust with Langdon. She repeatedly stresses that she will never share Langdon's location or identity. She ends by explaining the emotional impact on herself, and on you, of what the two girls did. She invites Langdon to share with her the impact on her own life.'

DS Barnsdale again looks directly towards me but I say nothing.

'The second letter,' begins Cash, watching me carefully, 'appears to have been sent shortly after your mother received a response to the first. Your mother writes in more detail of your brother – what he lost, how she imagines his life might have been. She goes on to speculate that Langdon must live her life in constant fear but assures her she has nothing to fear from her,' explains PC Cash. 'But she also refers to a request from Langdon which we believe must have been in Langdon's reply to your mum's first letter.' She hesitates. 'We are of course only interpreting one side of the exchange, but it would appear Langdon had made a request for the sum of twenty-five thousand pounds for the secrets she had to share.'

'Twenty-five thousand!' I say, kicking away the footstool in front of me. 'Unbelievable. How dare she demand money after what she did?'

'Your mother makes it clear she has no interest in buying information,' says DS Barnsdale. 'Mr Harper, are you in possession of any letters your mother might have received by way of response from Langdon?'

'No, nothing. Nothing that I've ever come across,' I reply, getting to my feet again. 'The gall of the woman, demanding money! Everything we know about her must be true.'

'In what sense?' asks Barnsdale, calmly.

'In the sense that she was the ringleader, that everything that happened was at her instigation, that she preyed upon Josie Fairchild, lured her into her deranged plans. That she was pure evil,' I say, my voice rising in anger.

'All of that is speculation driven by the press and doesn't help us here today. Langdon and Fairchild received equal sentences.'

'She was trying to extort money from my mum! Perhaps I should ask why the hell she was released in the first place?'

'Mr Harper, for the horrendous events that occurred here in Haddley twenty years ago, you will always have my deepest sympathy, and the sympathy of all the Metropolitan Police . . .'

I stand motionless, looking at the detective as she searches for her words.

'. . . but Abigail Langdon served her sentence, and we have no reason to believe that she broke any of the terms of her release over the past decade. Over recent years, living as Demi Porter in the town of Farsley, on the outskirts of Leeds, Langdon successfully established herself as a member of the local community. She was regarded as a reliable colleague at the local supermarket and rented a small one-bedroom flat in the town. Our focus today has to be on the fact that a woman has been murdered, and, from what the West Yorkshire Police have discovered, we can't rule out a connection between her death and your brother's.'

There is a change in Barnsdale's tone.

'Mr Harper, can you tell me if you have visited the town of Farsley?'

CHAPTER 13

'Never. Next question.'

'As part of our investigation, Mr Harper,' pushes DS Barnsdale, 'I'm required to ask you your whereabouts over the past forty-eight hours.'

'Now I'm a suspect?'

The detective says nothing, just waits patiently for me to answer her.

'I've been in or near London the whole time. Either here in Haddley, or at work. Last night I was with friends the whole evening. There are plenty of people who can verify that if it's really necessary.'

'Thank you,' replies the DS curtly. 'We might ask you for those names in due course.'

PC Cash puts her hand on the arm of my chair and leans forward. I step back across the room and resume my seat.

'Do you have any idea how your mum might have come to discover Langdon's new identity?' she asks.

'None,' I reply. 'If I had known she was in contact with

Langdon, I would have done everything within my power to stop her.'

'Twice over the past ten years,' interjects DS Barnsdale, 'we have enacted injunctions against an increasingly unrestrained media to prevent the revelation of the real identity of Demi Porter.'

'Not against my site,' I retort. For a moment I'm silent. I try to stop my mind wandering to Madeline, and all that she knows about my family's history. 'Anyway, detective, those injunctions came long after my mum's death.'

'That doesn't mean Langdon's true identity wasn't known within media circles prior to your mother's passing.'

'I wouldn't know about that.' I meet Barnsdale's eye. 'Ten years ago, your colleagues concluded my mum had stepped in front of the 8.06 to Waterloo.' I drop my voice and lean forward. 'At that moment, detective, if I'd known where Langdon was, I would have killed her myself.'

In the corner of my eye, I see PC Cash studying her own reflection in her highly polished shoes.

'As it is,' I continue, 'until you told me today, I had no idea where Abigail Langdon was, or that my mum had been in contact with her.' I get up again and cross to the door. 'And I think we're done here. Abigail Langdon was an evil child-killer. Millions of people wanted her dead. Anybody could have found out who she was, and apart from two letters written ten years ago there's nothing to link her death with my family or with Haddley, as far as I can see.'

I open the living-room door. PC Cash starts to rise but Barnsdale remains unmoving.

'If you could wait just one moment, Mr Harper,' she says quietly. 'Because, although you say there is nothing to link this murder directly to you or to Haddley, I'm afraid there is.'

CHAPTER 14

I stand at the side of the common, trying to comprehend what the officers have told me. After I watch their car slowly pull away, I can't stop my gaze turning towards the overgrown entrance to the woods. It feels as though everything that happened to Nick and Simon still exists here in Haddley.

I turn and make my way up the road towards the Cranfields' garden.

'Sore head?' calls Mr Cranfield, as I walk towards him. I feel like a naughty schoolboy returning to the scene of his crime. I reply that I've had better mornings.

'You're not still cleaning up, are you?' I ask, as Mr C greets me with a firm grip on my shoulder. 'Nothing too horrendous, I hope,' I continue, peering into his garden to look at the flowerbed and feeling suitably ashamed. 'One of those work things that got out of hand.'

'Don't give it a second thought. I'd planned to mulch the borders today anyway.'

I smile. 'Sounds painful.'

'It can be,' he replies, 'especially for my back. Everything okay with you?' he asks, with a gentle nod towards the Lower Haddley Road, where Barnsdale and Cash are pulling into a long queue of traffic.

'Courtesy call, I suppose you could call it,' I say, still trying to understand what the officers have told me. I sit on the stone wall that runs across the front of the Cranfields' garden.

'You've had a lifetime of those,' he replies, and takes a seat beside me. 'Mrs C tells me your boss wants you to write an article for your mum's anniversary.'

'I've said no, but more and more it seems there are still so many questions left unasked,' I say, as Mr C kicks his muddy boots against the wall. 'Questions I should have asked right from the start. I just didn't want to face it. Have I failed her?'

'No,' Mr C says firmly, gripping my shoulder.

I think about what I learned from the detectives. 'Should I have tried harder to understand what happened? More than anyone, it was me who could have got the answers she deserved, the answers she was so desperate for.'

'The only thing we know for certain is that Clare would have wanted you to live your life exactly as you have. Don't live with regrets, Ben.'

I survey the street: the orderly façades, the carefully tended gardens. You'd never know this place had seen such tragedy. What have I missed?

'I need to talk to Madeline,' I say. 'If I tell her I'll write something but only on my terms, this could be my chance to discover the truth my mum so desperately wanted.'

Mr C looks at me gravely. 'Whatever you do, it won't bring her back, Ben.'

'I know that,' I reply, 'but Mum's entitled to more than eternal sympathy. She was surrounded by such love and support. There was no reason for her to kill herself. Why would she do it?'

'Ben, I wish I knew.'

'You were there. People wanted to help her, to support her. She'd suffered so much but she always found such strength, such dignity.'

'She was amazing.'

'I wouldn't be where I am without her. It was her strength, her determination that got me through. It makes no sense that she would have killed herself. Not like that, without leaving any note, any sign of what she was going to do.'

'Without saying goodbye . . .'

Tears spring to my eyes and I swallow them back fiercely.

'I was so angry with her for leaving me, so scared it was because I'd failed her in some way, I never stopped to think,' I continue quietly, as much to myself as to Mr C. 'What if it didn't happen the way we think it did?'

Mr C rests his hand on my shoulder. 'None of us can know what somebody else is truly feeling.'

We sit together in silence, our eyes drifting across the common towards Haddley Woods. 'How would you feel about being front-page news again?' he asks after a moment. 'Because that's what it might mean.'

'That's what I said to Madeline,' I reply. 'I said I didn't want it. But if more headlines are the price I have to pay, to really understand what happened, perhaps I have to accept that.'

He shrugs gently. 'Only you can decide.'

'What are you two so deep in thought about?'

We turn to see Mrs C coming down the path from the back door, a mug of tea in one hand.

'Is that for me?' asks Mr C, getting to his feet and taking the drink from his wife.

'Can I get you one, Ben?' she asks.

'I'm good,' I reply. 'Still buzzing from three cups of coffee.'

'It was Min he was out with last night,' says Mrs C, conspiratorially.

'There was a group of us, but let's not get into that again,' I say, glancing up towards Mr C. 'Your wife with her fresh coffee and bacon sandwich was a life-saver.'

'You're sure you don't want a brew?'

'Sure.'

'In that case I'm going to head inside and let you boys talk,' says Mrs Cranfield, already making her way back up the drive. 'Don't forget, lunch on Sunday,' she calls as she heads inside.

I look at Mr Cranfield, who takes a sip of his tea and watches me thoughtfully.

'Madeline taught me to begin with what you know and unpick from there,' I begin. Mr C nods slowly. 'The morning my mum died . . . she shouted at me and stormed out of the house. No note, no sign of what was to come. And then she walked straight across the common without waiting for you, unlike almost every other morning?'

Mr C nods. 'Over time, I guess your mum and I had fallen into an arrangement that never was an arrangement, if that makes sense?'

I smile silently, allowing him to continue.

'My train to Richmond would leave a couple of minutes after hers to Waterloo, so we'd pretty much be heading to the station at the same time. We became synchronised. Clare leaving home was my cue to say goodbye to Mrs C. Then I'd head out and join her on the path just as it turns along the top side of the woods. Took us no more than ten minutes to walk up to the station. Occasionally we'd talk about work, but most days we'd talk about you.'

I blush slightly, but again say nothing.

'When we got to the station, she'd head to her platform and I'd head to mine. Often we'd find ourselves standing opposite each other, across the tracks. Perhaps a wave when she boarded; I'd have another couple of minutes to wait.'

'And that morning?' I ask.

Mr Cranfield sighs. 'I wish it had been different, but you know that, Ben.'

I watch him step away from me and cross the road to the common. I follow him.

'There's not a lot to tell. It wasn't long after a new partner had entered the business, so I'd started cutting down on the number of days I went into the practice.'

Together we walk across the common and join the pathway my mum would have taken that morning.

'I saw her from the upstairs window, waved, but she didn't see me. She'd have been somewhere about here,' says

Mr Cranfield, stopping on the path and turning to face his own house. 'I opened the window and called out that I was planning on spending the day working in the garden; something banal about retirement being harder work than going into the practice.'

'And?'

'And that was it,' Mr Cranfield replies, continuing back down the path towards my home.

Walking alongside, I ask him, 'What did she do?'

'She kept walking,' he replies. 'Maybe she didn't hear me – I don't know. Did I shout loud enough? Perhaps her thoughts were occupied elsewhere.'

'But no acknowledgment?'

'No, nothing. Her head was down and she kept walking.'

'What did you think?'

'I didn't give it much thought at the time. But later, after it happened and the police asked me all the questions you're asking now, I realised there was something not right. I'd say she was a woman distracted, deep in thought. I could have shouted from the rooftop with a megaphone and she still wouldn't have heard me.'

CHAPTER 15

Holly leapt off the sofa, throwing her phone down as she did. How was it possible? Could he have seen her? Was he watching the house somehow?

She felt her face flush as she rubbed her hands down the back of her jeans.

The phone buzzed again.

She looked down and watched the screen flash.

You'll spoil your surprise. Don't open the box! x

She clicked on the second message and saw the sender's name.

Jake.

She exhaled, and collapsed on to the sofa with a nervous laugh.

'Did you get a message, Mummy?' asked Alice, turning away from *Peppa Pig.*

'I did – from Daddy,' she replied. Clutching the phone in her hands, she realised PDQ would have messaged Jake after making the delivery. Typing a reply, she saw her hands were shaking.

No peeking, I promise. See
you tomorrow. Love, H

Jake's reply was instant.

I'll be late. Don't wait up x

She closed her eyes and, slipping the phone back in her pocket, let the relief wash over her. She would search again later.

Leaning forward, she ran her fingers through the curls brushing her daughter's neck.

'Will Daddy be home for your party?' asked Alice.

'Of course, it's our wedding anniversary,' replied Holly.

'Are we getting my party dress from the shop today?'

'We are. And shall we get you some new shoes as well?'

'The ones with the golden toes!' said Alice, jumping to her feet and throwing her arms around her mother. 'Please!'

'I'm not promising. We'll see if they have them in your size. They're very expensive.'

'But I need them for the party,' said Alice.

Holly squeezed her daughter tightly, and her thoughts turned to the tiny sleepsuit hidden in the desk upstairs. What had become of the baby who had once worn it? She recalled her own joy and exhaustion from Alice's first few months at home. How quickly she had realised she would do anything to ensure her daughter's happiness – and her safety.

She knew she had to act.

She knew they must escape.

CHAPTER 16

'Ben!' cries a child's voice, and I look up to see Alice Richardson running down the pavement towards me.

'Alice!' I call back, crouching down before scooping her up in my arms.

'I'm going to leave you to it,' says Mr Cranfield.

'If I could understand what was on her mind that morning, Mr C, I could start to fathom what she was thinking when she arrived at St Marnham station.'

'Be careful, Ben,' is all he says, a hand on my back before he walks back up the side of the common, a wave towards Holly as he goes.

'Ben,' says Alice, her arms wrapped around my neck. 'Mummy and me are going to buy my dress for her wedding party.'

'You mean her wedding anniversary,' I say.

'And I'm going to get the shoes with golden toes.'

'How beautiful,' I reply as my goddaughter grabs hold of my hair.

'Ben, your hair is so curly,' she says. 'Look, if I pull it out at the side, it makes you look like Zog.' She giggles and I can't help joining in.

'I think I need to get a haircut,' I say, as Holly walks towards us.

Holly's friendship has been the one constant throughout my life. I trust her more than I trust anyone in the world. Aged four, we arrived at the same time on our first day at primary school and were placed at a table together. We were soon joined by a boy called Michael. Michael would remain the biggest boy in class throughout school but on that first day he was also the most petrified. When his mum waved goodbye his whole face had quivered, and Holly had reached across to take hold of his hand.

From that first day in school, the three of us had formed a bond of friendship that had bound us together for more than twenty years. Racing home from school together or cycling along the riverbank, we shared in every adventure. And then, on that frostbitten January morning when I'd first returned to school after Nick's death, it was their friendship that gave me hope.

Seven years ago, when Holly married Jake Richardson, we had all celebrated long into the night. Their wedding was an elaborate affair, held in the grounds of Jake's parents' home. As the evening drew to a close, Holly, Michael and I escaped the party to sit on the banks on the village pond and toasted a friendship we believed would live forever.

Three years later, Alice arrived in the world and I could not have been more proud than on the day of her christening when I held her as her new godfather. But pride couldn't eclipse the heartbreak Holly and I both felt at Michael's absence, his death just weeks before, in a mindless hit-and-run, a devastating blow to us both.

CHAPTER 17

'Mr C was waving to you,' I say to Holly, as she joins Alice and me in front of my garden.

'Sorry, I was a million miles away.' She turns to wave back, but Mr Cranfield has already returned his attention to his flowerbed.

'What's on your mind?'

'Nothing, just me getting distracted.'

'I'll make you a coffee if you like?' I say to her. 'I could do with a chat.'

With the doors folded open on to my back garden, Holly and I sit on the steps as Alice digs in the flowerbed at the end of the lawn.

'So?' I say.

'Really, it's nothing,' replies Holly. 'I'm stressing about Saturday night, that's all.'

'Nice of your in-laws to host.'

'Depends on your definition of nice. In the Richardson family, nothing is given without the expectation of something in return.'

'Hol, it's your wedding anniversary.'

'And Francis will use it to remind everyone of his own importance. Military hero, self-made man, the biggest house in St Marnham – and no one must ever forget it. That will make Jake stressed and he'll probably end up drinking too much and saying something he regrets in the morning.'

'Can't wait!' I say, squeezing her arm.

'Ben!'

'Come on, Hol, it's a party!' I say, but she turns away. 'Holly?'

'Everything with Francis is about control and this party is no different. He's throwing a party that Jake and I could never afford, simply to remind us of that very fact.'

'Accept graciously and then move on. It's all you can do.'

'I know,' she replies, resignation in her voice. 'I should stop moaning. What's going on with you?'

'There's something I need to tell you,' I say, pausing, before moving closer to her.

'Ben?' She turns directly to me.

'Abigail Langdon's dead.'

I see the disbelief on Holly's face before she instinctively throws her arms around me. 'I hope she suffered,' she whispers, hugging me tightly. 'How do you know?'

'The police came to see me this morning.'

'And she's definitely dead?'

I nod. 'Yes.'

'Thank God,' she replies. 'I don't care how awful it sounds, but I couldn't be happier.'

'Ben, I found three worms!' calls Alice from the bottom of the garden. 'Come and see.'

'Three!' I exclaim, and Holly and I get to our feet.

'Look, Ben!' cries Alice, triumphantly. 'Another one! And it's all wriggly!'

'That's a monster worm,' I say, crouching down next to Alice.

'I'm going to take it home with me.'

'Why not leave her here with her family?' I say. 'I think she likes living in the soil.'

'I suppose so,' says Alice, and she clambers back into the flowerbed, dropping her prey as she goes. Holly and I turn back towards my house.

'The police think her death might be linked back to Haddley and Nick's murder,' I say.

'What makes them think that?' asks Holly quickly. 'Did they tell you what happened?'

I think of my closing conversation with DS Barnsdale and suddenly I am transported back to that unbearable summer's day more than twenty years ago. The girls' laughter echoes through my mind, and I hear their call to the boys as they race through the trees to the elevated area on the far side of the woods.

I imagine Nick and Simon on their knees, the girls gently pulling back their heads and kissing their open mouths. The glimmering blades are thrust without hesitation. Plunged into the sides of the boy's necks. Ferocious force jamming the knives to the hilt before being ripped forward.

I look at Holly and rub my fingers against my temples.

'You remember how Nick and Simon were killed, with all of the most horrific detail withheld from the public?'

Holly shudders in acknowledgement.

'Well, whoever killed Langdon knew a lot more than the average person about Nick and Simon's deaths. Langdon was killed in the exact same way.'

Three

'We don't really know what happened to those girls after they were taken away.'

CHAPTER 18

Nathan Beavin closed the front door behind him and looked out across Haddley Common. The late-morning sun brought new life, a gentle breeze blew up from the river, and the smell of freshly mown grass filled the air. He filled his lungs with the warm spring air before making his way down the steps at the front of the house to begin his morning run.

His route took him along the footpath that bordered the common. Behind him stood a row of imposing Victorian villas, each housed in its own ample grounds and enjoying uninterrupted views to the Thames. Along one side of the common ran a terraced row of smaller houses, many transformed by new London money. Running down the path, Nathan acknowledged his retired neighbour out tending his garden, but, as he ran, his eyes turned to each of the houses as they gazed down upon the common and the woods beyond. They had seen over a century of family life, from Victorian hardship to the Blitz, now reborn as part of modern-day London. Nathan thought of the unique story each home had to tell as well as the darkest secret they still stubbornly concealed.

Arriving in Haddley the previous month, he'd left behind his home town of Cowbridge, a little outside Cardiff, for the very first time. An easy-going boy, he'd been happy at school, looked out for his little sister, and had parents who cared for him every day of his life. Yet from a young age he'd known there was more to discover: a life to be lived beyond what he'd always known. He didn't know where his journey might eventually take him, only that Haddley had to be his very first stop.

Two days after his arrival, he'd begun working in one of the many bars that populated the high street. Fifteen minutes from the centre of London, Haddley's riverside bars had become increasingly popular nightspots for anyone willing to pay over five pounds for a pint of beer. Serving cocktails on the bar's terrace that overlooked Haddley Bridge, Nathan had soon realised it wasn't only Friday and Saturday nights that were packed with revellers – whether it was City workers stopping in on their way home or the rowers up from the river, every night was busier than the busiest night in Cowbridge. But Friday night was the busiest of all, with the end-of-week celebrations beginning at four in the afternoon and still going strong at two the following morning.

It was on Nathan's third Friday in London when the manager of the Watchman had asked him to cover an extra shift at the start of the evening. He'd been happy to volunteer and already knew the biggest tips came from the City workers heading home for the weekend. The bar had been packed from lunchtime, although Nathan had still found a moment to notice the woman arriving late in the afternoon and joining a group of friends on the terrace bar. Three times that afternoon he'd carried prosecco across to her table, and later in the evening, when she'd edged her way through the crowd to order a fourth bottle, he'd been waiting for her.

Idly chatting with Sarah Wright as he filled a fresh ice bucket, Nathan had soon discovered that she had recently completed work on a million-pound divorce case and was looking forward to spending the weekend with her young son, Max. Leaning across the bar, he'd joked about his own need for a drink, and as he'd looked into Sarah's dark brown eyes she had looked back at her friends and started to giggle. They'd shouted across the bar for her to call him over, and Nathan had felt a rush of desire as he'd seen Sarah flush and curl her fingers nervously through her long, dark hair. Squeezing into the corner booth alongside the four women, he'd played along as they teased him, wanting to know what such a lovely Welsh boy was doing all alone so far away from home. After three weeks, Nathan was ready with practised answers to all those questions.

A fifth bottle of prosecco had followed, and at midnight a sixth, this one just for the two of them. They'd already drunk too much but that didn't stop them. Together they'd swapped life stories – hers consisted of a childhood in Edinburgh, law school in London, then a job at a City firm where she had fallen for one of the senior partners, who was nine years older than her. She was such a cliché, she'd said. Nathan had assured her she was anything but, and she had laughed, saying she wasn't sure what else she'd call it. She'd been qualified for less than a year when she'd married James Wright, and together they had moved into a villa on Haddley Common.

For a while they'd been happy, or Sarah had thought they were. Max was born before their first wedding anniversary; but three months later James had returned home one evening to tell her he was in love with another woman. As part of their firm's commitment to outreach and investing in future generations, James had been teaching a class at King's College. It was there that he had fallen desperately in love with a twenty-two-year-old postgraduate named Kitty.

'I packed his bags and threw him out that night,' said Sarah, as she sipped on her prosecco. 'He's never been back inside the house since. And you know what – he never will. The one thing I do know is how to find a great divorce lawyer.'

Her settlement meant she kept the house, and she would drain James of everything she could until Max turned eighteen. Why should they have to suffer? She had quit her City job and was happier now with her new firm based in Haddley. Max stayed with his father on Friday nights and came home Saturday afternoons. It wasn't perfect, but Sarah was certain she could raise Max better alone.

Nathan had had his story ready to tell. Born in Wales, a happy childhood, a good school and great parents but now it was time for adventure. He was only twenty so was taking some time out to explore. Sarah had laughed.

'Time out? You haven't done anything yet to take time

out from. Come back in ten years. That's when you'll be as old as me.'

Nathan didn't care. That was when he'd leant in to kiss her.

When the bar closed, they'd walked along the riverbank to Sarah's home, arms wrapped around each other. When they reached the foot of the steps that led to Sarah's striking home, Nathan saw what a different world this was from the one he had left behind only three weeks earlier.

He'd kissed her again and they'd climbed the steps to the polished black front door. She'd fumbled for her keys and they'd giggled together as they blindly tried to turn the latch. They had stumbled through the doorway, Nathan quickly grabbing hold of Sarah before she fell to the floor. He'd felt her lean on him for support when he took her by the hand and led her up the elegant staircase. Slowly they had made their way down the hall and into her bedroom. She'd kissed him one more time before precariously stepping into the bathroom. As she closed the door behind her, Nathan had turned full-circle, taking in his new surroundings – the chandelier hanging from the ceiling, the marble fireplace. Running his hand along the back of the fireside chair, he'd felt the soft material beneath his fingertips. He had stood and looked at the painting hanging above the bed – a little boy walking with his mother along a deserted seafront as the sun set upon the ocean. It was the same boy he had watched Sarah chasing across the common the previous week.

Dimming the light on the chandelier, he had taken one last look around before stepping out of the room. Quickly, he'd made his way back along the hall, pausing at the entrance to the boy's bedroom. When he'd edged the door open, light had fallen upon a framed image standing on the bedside table. He'd started at the picture, his grip tightening around the brass door handle. Even with a gap of over twenty years, the man's floppy brown hair and rugby player's nose were unmistakable.

Stepping back, he had gently pulled the door towards him before quickly making his way back downstairs. Leaving the house, he'd stood on the step in the cool night air and let the front door quietly close behind him.

CHAPTER 19

Now, five weeks after that first evening, Nathan picked up his pace, relishing the warm sun on his back. Early-morning rowers were out in force on the river, training crews hitting their strokes as they raced up the Thames towards St Marnham. Once he reached Haddley Woods, he turned and sprinted back across the heart of the common in the direction of Sarah's house. As he did, he saw Sarah and Max walking hand in hand down the front steps of their home. Sarah was looking attentively at her son, tightly gripping his hand as Max made each concentrated step. When they reached the common Max broke free, and Nathan waved as the little boy raced towards him.

'Nathan!' cried Max, running as fast as his uncertain strides would take him. 'I'm running too!'

Nathan jogged towards him, scooped him up and tossed him up towards the clear blue sky, causing Max to scream in delight. Never had Nathan imagined he would so quickly become part of such a close-knit family; never had he intended it.

It had taken only five weeks for Sarah, Max and himself to form such a happy bond, and anyone looking at them playing in the middle of the common would instantly assume they were a family. As Sarah crossed and greeted him with a kiss, Nathan wished that was what they genuinely were.

His feet firmly back on the ground, the four-year-old told Nathan they were heading to Alice's house.

'Holly is going to look after me this afternoon while Mummy is at work and I'm going to have my lunch there but not my tea. Are you coming home for tea, Nathan?'

Nathan crouched down to talk to Max. 'I have to work tonight so I'll have to miss tea today,' he said.

'But you'll be hungry.'

'I'll make sure I get something before I go,' he replied, ruffling Max's hair before standing back up.

'What time do you finish tonight?' asked Sarah.

'I've got a lunchtime shift and then I'm back on again at five. I shouldn't be late, though. Fingers crossed I'll be home by ten.'

'I'll look forward to seeing you then,' replied Sarah, rising up on her toes and kissing Nathan's lips.

Watching mother and son walk hand in hand back across the common, he knew he should feel lucky to have found them. The morning after he'd crept away from Sarah's bedroom, he'd plucked up the courage to return to her house. As he'd stood at the front door, listening to the bell echoing faintly through the house, butterflies had fluttered in his stomach. Moments later Sarah had appeared, perhaps a little tired but just as vibrant as he'd remembered. Crazily, his stomach had flipped.

'Hello,' he'd said as he had stood in front of Sarah, seeing her hesitate for a second. He hoped he hadn't made a mistake in coming back.

'I think I might owe you an apology,' she'd replied, and he'd seen the colour rise again in her cheeks.

'I thought it was me who needed to apologise.'

'Not in the slightest,' said Sarah, her hand reaching to her face. 'I fell asleep on the bathroom floor, I'm so sorry.'

'Really, you don't need to be.'

'I think I made it to bed around five. Thank goodness Max is at his dad's. It was after ten by the time I surfaced.'

Nathan had smiled. 'I'm glad you got some sleep,' he'd said, as Sarah looped her hair through her fingers, 'even if some of it was a little bit uncomfortable.'

'And thank you for getting me home safely,' she'd said.

'The pleasure was all mine,' said Nathan. 'We both probably drank a little too much.'

'A little?' replied Sarah.

'Maybe a couple of bottles too many,' said Nathan, consciously edging back from the top step. 'Anyway, I should go. I only wanted to check you were okay.'

'You don't have time for a quick coffee, do you?' asked Sarah. 'I owe you that at the very least.'

'I'd love to,' Nathan had answered, and then immediately worried he might have appeared too eager. For the next two hours they'd sat together in Sarah's kitchen, and at lunchtime Max had arrived home. Sitting at the kitchen island,

Nathan had been momentarily transfixed, looking down the hall and watching Sarah open the door to an excitable little boy. As she bent down to squeeze hold of Max, James Wright had stared straight past her. His eyes had met Nathan's and Nathan had hastily looked away.

'You've got company?' James had said, stepping forward slightly.

'Yes, and remind me what that has to do with you?' Sarah had replied, moving firmly to block his path.

'Looks like he could be a playmate for Max.'

'I'll see you next weekend,' was Sarah's reply, before she ushered her former husband back through the open door. 'Don't be early.'

That afternoon he, Sarah and Max had walked along the riverbank, stopping for Nathan to push Max on the swings. When Nathan had insisted Sarah get on to the swing next to her son, Max had laughed delightedly, urging Nathan to push Sarah higher and higher till she'd screamed and begged him to stop. Late in the afternoon, they'd walked into Haddley and devoured three bacon cheeseburgers.

After putting Max to bed, Sarah had sat with Nathan and together they'd shared a bottle of red wine. That night Nathan did stay with Sarah. And he'd stayed most nights since. Nathan had never planned to come to London, fall in love and find a family. But, standing on the common watching Sarah and Max walk away, he feared that was just what he had done.

When mother and son reached the edge of the common now, the little boy turned back to look at him and Nathan waved. Then he began his steady run back across the common. As he made his way down the path and into the woods, he looked up at the leafy canopy closing above him. The sun spilt through the covering, casting long shadows across the path. The further he ran, the denser the canopy became, and slowly the sunlight began to fade. The temperature dropped and Nathan felt the woods closing in around him.

Listening to the sound of the trees, he knew these woods harboured a secret.

He had to remember that that was the secret he had come to Haddley to discover.

CHAPTER 20

'Bye, Ben! Love you!' shouts Alice one more time, as she and her mum make their way down the alley that runs behind my house.

'Love you too!' I yell in reply, before I step into my kitchen and close the folding door. As I lock the door, my attention is drawn to the photograph of my mum and me that hangs on my kitchen wall.

A decade ago, at the very start of that year, on a crisp January morning, Mum and I had left home early and driven through Richmond towards our nearest driving test centre in Isleworth. As we crossed the river and then passed the Asda supermarket, my mum had turned to me and smiled. 'I'm impressed,' she'd said, as I pulled up at the traffic lights. 'You haven't driven on the pavement once.'

I had laughed. A few months earlier after a handful of lessons I'd told my mum I was ready for my test. She'd agreed to take me out for extra practice. Leaving the common and turning on to the Lower Haddley Road, I had veered on to the pavement, terrifying Mr and Mrs Cranfield as they walked up from the river. My mum had grabbed hold of the steering wheel and swerved the car back into the road, narrowly avoiding an oncoming black cab. There and then she had promised to pay for another dozen lessons and sworn she would never take me out again.

'The only time I go on the pavement now is when I'm reverse parking.'

'Well, don't!'

'Everybody does. They won't fail me for that, surely?'

'Benjamin, I wouldn't be so sure!'

An hour later, I had presented my mum with my pass certificate.

'No reverse parking!' I'd said with a smile. I drove us back to Haddley and we talked of the road trip she wanted to take to Arran. It was then that I'd made the promise to go with her, as long as we could share the driving. Very reluctantly, she had agreed.

In early March, Mum had met me in Manchester before we travelled up to Scotland. For three nights we rented a cottage overlooking Whiting Bay as we explored the island and enjoyed our anonymous time together. We spent our second morning touring the Isle of Arran whisky distillery, and the picture on my kitchen wall is a captured moment of us sitting outside the distillery on a wooden picnic bench surrounded by rolling green hills. That afternoon, we walked along the coastal path, looking out across the bay towards Holy Island. My mum adored the infinite space and clean air, and as we walked I talked about what I might do after university. My degree in politics offered me no defined career path and I was toying with the idea of becoming a lawyer.

'A solicitor!' my mum exclaimed. 'That's not you, Ben.'

I laughed at my mum's response. 'Why not? I think I'd be pretty good. Can't you imagine me in court?'

'It's not like *LA Law*.'

'What's *LA Law*?'

She shook her head in disbelief. 'It's a wonderful television programme from before you were born that made lawyers look unbelievably exciting and glamorous. The reality of law is that it is incredibly process-driven and hierarchical. You aren't either of those things.'

She had a point.

'I'm sure you could qualify,' she went on, 'but within two years you'd hate it and want to do something else. If it's what you really want to do I'll support you, of course I will, but remember you would have to work alongside other lawyers who love process and respect hierarchy.'

'I don't think I would like those people,' I said, laughing. 'I'm beginning to think I might not enjoy the law.'

Under an endless clear blue sky, we walked on, talking about a few different careers and many different television shows until I asked my mum what it was *she* wanted to do next. It was a question that, up until that day, I'd never thought to ask. For so long the future had been something neither of us felt able to contemplate. My mum had helped me through exams and into university but her own life had seemed like an existence, nothing more. But on that day she talked about herself, about travelling and rediscovering a beauty in our own country which had been lost to her for so many years, about her friends; and we even laughed that one day she might meet somebody new. With my life moving on, I think she had begun to think about companionship, and I encouraged her to sign up to Match.com.

'That's for kids!' was her reply. 'I'd be too embarrassed. What if somebody saw me?'

'That's the whole point,' I'd replied. 'A nice older gent.'

'Not so old, if you don't mind. Most of the older men on there are after some young piece of skirt. They wouldn't be interested in me. It would be so humiliating!'

'Not these days.'

'Absolutely not, Ben, no. I'd be sure to find some pervert who ended up stalking me! No, I just want a friendly companion to join me on a few trips, visit some nice restaurants. I'm even happy to go Dutch with him.'

'Very modern,' I replied, as the light began to fade and a stiffening breeze picked up, and we made our way back to our cottage.

The weather worsened overnight and on our final day on the island we woke to torrential rain lashing against the picture window that fronted our cottage. After a lazy morning reading the newspapers, I built a fire in the hearth while my mum made us a late lunch. Once we'd eaten, Mum curled up on the sofa, sipping a glass of the cream liqueur she had treated herself to at the end of our distillery tour the previous day. Together, we looked out on the wall of rain sweeping across the water.

'Thank you,' she said, suddenly.

'For what?'

'For spending three days with your old mum on a Scottish island. I think it probably does go above and beyond.' I smiled, and she went on, 'I don't want you to spend your life worrying about me or feeling as if you have to be here all the time. It's always nice for me to see you, but I'm going to be fine.' She stopped speaking, and gazed out at the bay, a lone boat ploughing a choppy course.

'I know,' I replied, 'and wherever in the world I might be, I'll always be at the end of the phone.'

'I know that.'

We were silent for a moment. In the bay, the boat continued further and further out, determinedly battling the rising waves.

'You have to live your life, Ben,' she said. 'Not a day goes by when I don't think of Nick, but we can't bring him back.'

'We will always have him in our hearts.'

'He'd be so proud of you.'

'He'd be proud of both of us,' I said, firmly.

'I sometimes feel . . .' She broke off.

I waited for her to continue and when she didn't I pressed her. 'Feel what?'

'I don't know. Those girls – why Nick?'

I stared at her uncomfortably. 'Mum, sometimes there is no reason. Those girls – they were just evil. Pure and simple. If it hadn't been Nick and Simon, it would have been someone else.'

My mum turned to me. 'But do you ever imagine there are more things we don't know? Could there still be people in Haddley who know more? We don't really know what happened to those girls after they were taken away.'

'Don't,' I said, shaking my head. 'Mum, it will only bring you more pain. Remember what you've always taught me. We have to look forward.'

She nodded stiffly. Then she said softly, 'But, if there *was* more, Ben, would you want to know?'

'There isn't,' I said firmly, getting to my feet and closing the conversation, hoping for it never to be reopened. 'Absolutely not, Mum. No.'

CHAPTER 21

My train sits stationary outside Clapham Junction station, held at an interminable red signal. Needing to speak to Madeline face-to-face, I've spent the short journey from Haddley staring out of the window, replaying over and again the conversation I had with Barnsdale and Cash. The exposure of Langdon's real identity and the brutal way in which she was killed connect the murder directly to Haddley.

I think back to what PC Cash said my mum had written in her letter. How had she hoped to find any kind of redemption for such evil? Had she really thought it might be possible? Or had she had some other reason for contacting Langdon? Look forward, not back, that was her mantra. Why, then, in what were to become the final weeks of her life, had she sought out contact with one of Nick's killers? Hadn't she hated Langdon with all her heart? Something, or someone, propelled her to contact Abigail Langdon. I need to understand what, or who, that was.

I flick on my phone and search through my contacts for

Elizabeth Woakes. I feel certain that after Barnsdale and Cash left my home they would have headed to Richmond to meet with Simon's mother. I type her a brief message.

I first met Elizabeth Woakes that long, hot summer a lifetime ago where all our days were spent without a care in the world. Simon and Nick had been inseparable as friends. Running behind them, desperate to keep up, I had loved every second I spent with the two older boys. Days without end we scrambled along the riverbank, sprinting through the water's edge, our faces red in the bright summer sun. The Woakeses' house stood on the embankment and we would often race up from the river, through their garden, before charging into Mrs Woakes's kitchen. She always met us with a welcoming smile and a drink to quench our thirsts before we headed back outside to continue our latest adventure.

My phone buzzes with an invitation from Mrs Woakes to meet for breakfast tomorrow morning. I'm happy to agree.

I stare out of the window at the trains stacking up outside Clapham Junction. My phones buzzes again and I watch as the screen is illuminated with a message from Will Andrews.

A little tired this morning?

I smile and type back a reply.

I've already had my fourth coffee of the day. Thanks again for last night's drinks

Was good to see you. Are you
sticking with your decision?

On the article? Change of heart, I think

There's a pause. Thirty seconds later a response appears.

How come?

A few things don't make sense to me. My
mum was looking for answers. Maybe I
can find them for her. I owe her that

I can see Will is typing a response but no message comes
through. After a minute I message him again.

I'd love to get ten minutes with you to
talk about the summer Nick died

I wait again for Will to respond.
Let's do that some time is his eventual reply.

My train finally crawls into London's Waterloo station and I
click off my phone. I look out at a concourse filled with frustrated travellers milling around, widespread delays leaving
them with nowhere to go. I am halfway out of the carriage
when my phone buzzes again. Thinking it might be Will, I
glance at the message.

Ben, it's East here. I got your contact from Will

I'm surprised to hear from him so soon after Will. Seeing him type more, I wait to reply.

I hope you don't mind me getting in
touch. I've been thinking about our
conversation from last night

Hi, East, I begin, but before I can get any further his next message comes through.

It would be great if we could talk some more.
Nothing urgent but as I said I know Madeline
of old. I'd hate you to do anything rash

I pause before replying.

I'm a bit snowed under right now
but let's catch up soon

Call in any time that works for
you. Fish pie on the house

That's an offer too good to refuse

I'm going to be at the restaurant the next
couple of nights. Would be great to see you

115

As passengers continue to disembark, I stand on the platform for a moment and re-read East's messages. When he opened his first restaurant in Richmond fifteen years ago, East Mailer had quickly become something of a local celebrity. His outstanding food combined with his unconventional character, as well as a picturesque setting overlooking the park, had helped to create a huge word-of-mouth success that had spread way beyond Richmond. And it was there that a City upstart regularly entertained his moneyed clients, only to hit it off with the unorthodox chef. Three years later, East and Will had bought a home together in St Marnham and their lifestyles had begun to converge. When the warehouse which now houses Mailer's came on the market, together they had invested in the building and set about creating London's best seafood restaurant.

As a young reporter starting out in the local press, determined to get somewhere fast, Madeline would have made it her business to get to know East from the very beginning. Looking at East's messages, I can only assume he's spoken to Will. I never knew East had a past connection with my boss but I do know that once Madeline makes a bond she never lets it fray.

With very few trains arriving or departing on time and with further delays on the Underground, I decide to walk along the river towards the glass tower where our office is housed. The sunlight bounces off the water, and, as I head along the Embankment under a clear blue sky, tourists are out in force. After ten minutes of weaving my way through their growing numbers, and still suffering the after-effects of last night, I stop for yet another coffee in the hope that it will breathe fresh life into me. Pausing to sit on a bench across from Shakespeare's Globe, I sip on a flat white and watch the world go by. Three generations of a single family order drinks from the riverside coffee bar. Enthusiastically engaged in conversation, grandmother, mother and daughter all laugh at a throwaway comment from the barista. Smiling and giggling, each enjoys the others' company as they savour their surroundings in the spring sunshine. Together, they share in a family warmth that I miss.

Entering our building, my thoughts turn again to my mum in the immediate days after Langdon and Fairchild were released. Hearing first the anger and then the bitterness in her voice, I had travelled home from Manchester. I'd found her in an enraged and inconsolable state. It was impossible for her to comprehend how the girls had served such a seemingly short sentence. Why should they be given a second chance? Where was the second chance for Nick?

Blanket press coverage had accompanied the release of Langdon and Fairchild, with television crews returning to the common and newspaper journalists badgering my mum for an interview. EVIL was the *Daily Mail* headline, accompanied by the two most famous images of the girls – smiling in their police mugshots. WHAT WILL BECOME OF THEM? asked the paper of the two figures of national hate.

I doubt I really understood how much their release had infuriated and distressed my mum. While I was at first consumed by anger and an adolescent desire for revenge, had she found their freedom impossible to tolerate? Why, only weeks later, make contact with Langdon? The hopeless despair she must have inflicted upon herself while waiting for a response . . . what caused her to make that fatal contact?

Exiting the elevator, I walk directly to Madeline's office.

CHAPTER 22

While Alice and Max clambered around the small climbing frame at the bottom of her garden, Holly Richardson sat on her lawn and picked up her phone to answer her husband's call.

'Hey,' she said, 'how's it going?'

A tale of missed opportunities, buyers who didn't know a great deal when it hit them in the face and harsh words between him and his biggest client was not an unexpected reply. It was nothing Holly hadn't heard before.

'You've got to hang on in there,' she said, trying to muster encouragement in the face of Jake's unrelenting pessimism. 'You never know what's around the corner.'

Lying back on the grass, holding the phone slightly away from her ear, Holly thought of the many times she'd heard the stories of humiliation; the great things they might have achieved with Jake's start-up if only his father had supported them.

'I know, Jake, I know. It was so unfair,' she replied, her tone one of practised validation. Perhaps things *would* have been different, if Francis had backed them for longer, but he'd loaned Jake the money for twenty-four months and on the day after the loan came due he'd called in the debt. Summarily taking control of the business, three months later he'd emailed Jake to tell him he'd sold it. Jake was now employed as regional manager of the company he had founded.

Holly heard Jake's repeated regret at taking his father's money. Even now, five years later, Jake lived with that decision each and every day. Pressurised and goaded, he'd been desperate to prove the great Francis Richardson wrong – the military man who then made millions in the City. Bringing the phone back to her ear, Holly heard Jake's hand slam against his steering wheel.

'Be careful, not too high,' she called as Max Wright made his way up the climbing frame. 'We're out in the garden,' she said to her husband, returning to his call. The cancellation of his afternoon appointments had left him sitting in the car park of a motorway hotel. 'You should come home tonight,' she said, knowing full well Jake's pride would never allow him to return early from a sales trip. It would be late tomorrow night before she saw him. Sitting up, she saw Alice come running towards her.

'Daddy!' called Alice.

'Are you going to say hello?' asked Holly, handing her daughter the phone.

'Hello, Daddy,' said Alice, before launching into an account of their day. They'd been to the swings; another boy had pulled her hair; Max had told him he was a naughty boy; Max had stayed for lunch but wasn't staying for tea.

'Love you, Daddy,' she said, before running back down the garden.

'Love you, Jake,' said Holly, her tone rehearsed. She promised once again not to open the parcel that had arrived that morning. And they both agreed that they would try to enjoy the party on Saturday night. It was so generous of Jake's parents to host it for them and of course, it had nothing to do with their own aggrandisement.

She couldn't help but think of her wedding day, similarly hosted by Jake's parents. Her own mother had been agog at the conspicuous displays of wealth. Before walking her down the aisle, she had made Holly promise she would never become consumed by material possessions in the ways the Richardsons appeared to be. Holly had laughed off such a suggestion but four days later, lying in bed watching the sun rise over Monte Carlo bay, she'd realised she had done exactly that. At the age of twenty-three, swept into a marriage encased by trinkets and charms, she had watched her husband sleeping deeply beside her and known at that moment that she had never really loved him.

Now, marvelling at how seven years had gone by so quickly, she wondered to herself if her husband would marry her again if he had his time over.

She knew exactly what she would do, given that chance.

CHAPTER 23

Corrine Parsons twisted her neck and pressed her hands against the base of her spine. Working a double shift was always gruelling, and each time she seemed to feel the physical effects that little bit more. Earlier this morning, Miss Cunliffe had needed lifting out of bed to relieve herself on the bedside commode and it always took two members of staff to move her. At eighty-eight the woman somehow maintained a weight three times Corrine's. The delivery of fresh cream cakes she received from the local bakery each afternoon no doubt played some small part. Corrine had no idea how she afforded it. The woman had never offered her a single penny.

The Sunny Sea Care Home, housed in the back streets of Deal, paid Corrine only minimum wage, even when she worked fourteen hours straight through the night. At least with last night's double shift she'd have a bit of extra cash at the end of the week.

Leaving the home, she glanced at her watch. It was already gone ten-thirty. The day stretched ahead of her. She'd hung around for an extra half-hour to help Eddie with the kitchen delivery, as he was good for a few supplies whenever she was short at home. Knowing Molly wouldn't pay her for the extra thirty minutes, she'd hidden away a couple of packs of sausages and a nice piece of steak at the back of the fridge. She'd take them home tomorrow morning when Molly was off shift.

Quickly crossing the Promenade, which ran directly along the shoreline, she headed for the Seafront Café. She felt her stomach rumble and realised her last meal had been the cold shepherd's pie left over in the kitchen after yesterday's residents' dinner. A full English and two cups of tea made her feel human again and, stepping back outside, she saw the clouds were beginning to lift. Tourists were emerging for the day and, sensing the sun was about to break through, she headed to the beach path to begin the two-mile walk towards Walmer.

With little else to fill her day until her next shift began, Corrine had recently taken to walking along the seafront every morning. Being outside in the spring air felt far better than sitting cooped up in her tiny flat, and, when she did eventually head home in the early afternoon, she was nearly always so exhausted that she went straight to sleep. At first she'd been hesitant to walk too far along the beach path, and even now she kept her hood pulled up over her head, but she increasingly discovered how much she enjoyed being out in the open space.

Passing the fancy flats that looked down over the water's edge, she imagined herself living a life of luxury inside one of them. She'd employ Eddie as her private cook and each morning she'd instruct him to prepare a full English. After that she'd lie in the sun for an hour before soaking in a long, hot bath. She would keep the windows wide open, day and night, winter and summer, blowing away her darkest memories. And each afternoon she would sit on her balcony and eat three cream cakes until she was just as fat as Miss Cunliffe.

'I'm sorry!' she said suddenly, quickly dropping her head and moving to one side. Without realising, she had walked straight into an older woman heading in the opposite direction.

'You should look where you're going,' reprimanded the woman, 'you could have knocked me over,' but, tugging at her hood, Corrine was already well past her.

Keeping her eyes down and forward, Corrine walked on. As she left Deal, the path became quiet and gradually she was able to turn her gaze towards the sea. On the pebbled shoreline, two ginger-haired boys were laughing as they tried to fly a Chinese dragon kite; Corrine was positive its giant size would prove far too great a challenge for them. She smiled as she passed, briefly wondering why they weren't in school. That was no concern of hers, she told herself; she had long since learnt what other people did was never any concern of hers.

As the shoreline path narrowed, her pace slowed. She paused at the sight of two middle-aged women stripping down to swimming costumes and striding towards the water's edge. In the early spring breeze, she thought them brave, but without hesitation both leapt into the Channel to begin ploughing vigorously through the waves. With the path now almost deserted, Corrine decided to sit for a moment on one of the faded wooden benches, pulling back her hood and letting the sun's rays warm her face. In less than three minutes the first of the women was out of the water and jiggling her way back up the beach to wrap herself in a large pink striped beach towel. The other woman ploughed on, breathing with each energetic stroke. Smiling to herself, Corrine imagined it might be something Miss Cunliffe would have enjoyed when she was young.

Approaching Walmer, she reached a small run of seafront houses, and when an old woman, tending her bright yellow flowers behind her white picket fence, smiled at her, she realised her hood was still down. She yanked it back over her face and hurried on, treading carefully as the pathway became more pebbled. Along one side of the path, a row of pastel-coloured beach huts looked as though they had seen better days. Corrine could never see the pleasure in sitting inside a cramped and decaying shack staring out at the rolling waves for endless hours, and she felt depressed looking at them now. Her spirits lifted, however, when the Zetland Arms came into view.

She had just reached the entrance to the pub when a black Labrador slowly crept away from behind one of the beach huts. Corrine crouched down and extended a hand, waiting as the dog approached her nervously. 'Hello, boy.' The dog sniffed her hand before coming closer to let her pat his side, flinching as she did. Under his patchy coat she could feel the sharp bones of his ribcage and she felt a pang of pity for him. She gave him a final pat, got to her feet and made to go indoors. The dog trotted alongside her.

'You can't come with me. Let's have a look where you live, shall we?' she continued, bending down to look at his collar, only to realise he didn't have one. 'You're going to have to find your own way home. Go on, off you go. There's nothing for you here.' And she gave him a gentle push towards the beach huts before going inside.

At the bar she ordered a pint of cider and a beef and onion pie, turning her back while the barman pulled her drink. She savoured the first sip, quenching her dry mouth, and by the time her pie arrived she had already drunk half. Moving back outside, she was glad to find a wooden table to herself. When she used her fork to break the pie's crust, its generous filling steamed as it spilt out on to her plate. The caramelised onion and soft pastry made her mouth water.

'This isn't for you,' she said, shaking her head as the Labrador appeared again at her side. His sad eyes stared up at her as she relished her first mouthful and then her second. 'Don't you keep looking up at me like that,' she continued, turning her back to the dog as she began to eat the pastry. Feeling his paw reach up on to her leg, she couldn't help but turn back. 'You really are hungry, aren't you?' she said, taking a drink from her pint. 'You can have just one small piece,' she continued, breaking off a chunk of pie crust. Looking down at the dog's sad face, she added a piece of beef. 'After this, no more,' she said and dropped the food on the ground. Instantly the dog snaffled the pie and was back up at her side wanting more. 'What did I say?' she said, smiling and patting the bony body. 'One last bit,' she said, holding up her finger before throwing another piece of pie on the ground.

'Oi!' yelled a voice, approaching from the beach. Corrine looked across to see a bearded man, with his belly hanging beneath his T-shirt, struggling up the shingle path. 'Get your hands off my dog,' he barked.

'You should look after him better,' Corrine shouted back.

'What's it got to do with you?' he replied, but Corrine said nothing. 'Panther, get back here,' shouted the man. 'Panther!' But the dog didn't move. The man walked forward, standing directly across from Corrine's table. The dog inched closer to her.

'Don't think he likes you,' said Corrine. 'In fact I'd say he's scared of you. Perhaps you should try feeding him a decent meal.'

'I said, what's it to do with you?' the man hollered, thumping his fat fingers on to her table as he stuck his face into hers. In a single movement, Corrine picked up her fork and slammed it into the back of the man's hand. Blood spurted skywards, the man shrieking as the dog darted away from the table.

Corrine sprang to her feet, leapt over the pub wall and started to run back down the path towards Deal. 'You fucking bitch,' he screamed, as he attempted to pull the fork out of the back of his hand. 'I'll have you for this,' he shouted, and, looking back, she could see him holding his hand to his chest as blood ran down his arm. 'Run, bitch, run,' he yelled, 'I'll have the police on you.'

'And I'll have the RSPC on you.'

'You mean the RSPCA, you thick minger.'

'Whatever,' yelled Corrine, flicking a finger; but turning away, tears filled her eyes as she realised she probably was.

CHAPTER 24

'I don't want to hear it, Ben,' says Madeline, as I walk into her office and close the door behind me. Without looking away from her screen, she holds up her hand. 'We need more traffic on the site and that means we all do every little thing possible to achieve it. Rest assured, your mum will be remembered in the right way.'

'What if I said I will write it?' I say, walking across the office.

'You will?' says Madeline, only now turning away from her screen.

'I might. If it's on my terms.'

'Your terms? And what might they be?'

'An investigative piece.'

'No,' replies Madeline, bluntly. 'It's not what readers want.'

'There are unanswered questions around my mum's death,' I say, pulling out a chair to sit directly opposite my boss. 'I realise now that I've never believed she would end her life in that way. I want to use this chance to understand what happened.'

'I said no. End of.' Madeline pauses before leaning across her desk. 'Ben, there's nothing new to say. Do me ten thousand words on the bond between you and your mum and your hopes for the future. We'll do a new photoshoot of you at home in Haddley. Readers will love it and we'll syndicate it out. I'll give you a ten-thousand-pound bonus.'

'Is that what my family is worth to you?'

'Okay, fifteen.'

'This is not a negotiation.'

'Fine. I've a meeting in three minutes so if you don't mind ... ' says Madeline, getting to her feet. Dressed in designer athleisure that will have cost more than the average weekly wage, she steps round her desk to stand beside me. 'We're done here.'

'Abigail Langdon is dead,' I say quietly.

Flicking imaginary dirt from her finely manicured nails, for a split second, Madeline is caught off guard. She looks at me for a moment, trying to gauge me. I meet her gaze coolly. Recapturing her composure, she hits a button on her desk phone. 'Cancel my two o'clock.' Still holding the button, she pauses and glances back towards me. 'And my three.'

She walks across the room and takes a can of Coke from her fridge. 'Want one?'

'Diet, please.'

I think I hear her tut as she picks up a can and comes back across the room. She pulls a chair out from the table and sits directly across from me. Opening her can and pouring it into a glass, she says, 'Langdon's dead?'

I nod. 'Murdered.'

130

Madeline rubs her finger across her botoxed lips but says nothing. 'The police believe her new identity was compromised,' I continue. 'Since her release, there have been a series of injunctions taken out against the media to prevent the publication of her new identity.'

'Not against us.' Madeline leans forward against the table and sips on her drink.

'Langdon was killed in the exact same way as Nick and Simon,' I say. I can see the horror in her eyes. 'As the go-to local journalist at the time, I'm sure you don't need me to refresh you on any of those details.'

Madeline's hands tighten around her glass. 'Ben, I was a seventeen-year-old girl, still at school, when your brother and Simon Woakes were murdered.' Living in Richmond, Madeline witnessed the horror and devastation the killings caused to the whole area. Less than a year after the end of the trial, she started working at the local newspaper. She joined straight from school and soon realised there was little future in her grand idea of becoming a photo journalist. She did though have a true talent for discovering great stories.

'You've written more about the case than any other journalist.'

'It's how I started out, yes, but I've never made any secret of that.' As a new recruit, Madeline pitched a story about the impact on Haddley Grammar and its pupils. Her editor liked the idea and the story got a good response from readers. She pitched a follow-up, this time on Simon's father, Peter, who was living rough in Haddley. The story got picked up nationwide.

'Took you all the way to nationals,' I say.

'I only ever wrote stories I believed would help the town. And help your family.'

'And at the same time if they happened to help you . . . '

'I'm a journalist, Ben, just like you are. I didn't want to spend my life writing stories on the Haddley murders . . . '

'But if they happened to propel your career forward and you ended up becoming one of the most influential people in twenty-first century media, then so be it.'

'I don't know what you want from me here, Ben. If you want to write your investigative piece then fine. I'll give you seven days. It needs to be live on the site for your mum's tenth anniversary. Happy?'

I say nothing.

'Ben?'

I look across the boardroom table at Madeline. 'Two letters, written by my mum, have been found at the home of Abigail Langdon, who until she was killed was living under the name of Demi Porter.'

Madeline gets to her feet and steps behind her desk, skimming the keys on her keyboard. I look at her pointedly.

'The police are very keen to understand how my mum could have discovered Langdon's new identity and then found a way to get in touch with her.'

Madeline turns to the window. 'Let's go for a walk,' she says quietly.

The stalls of Borough Market are packed with the usual blend of meandering tourists and harassed office workers.

Silently, we wind our way through the crowds. We walk past a cheese stall and I reach for a sample of a soft blue.

'Are you ever not hungry?' asks Madeline.

'I haven't had any lunch,' I reply. We turn away from the crowds and up towards the *Golden Hinde*, where we find a seat beside its dock overlooking the Thames. 'First thing you taught me on day one,' I say. ' Every good journalist has their sources, and even better journalists have their secrets. And nobody ever discovered more secrets than you. Tell me what happened when the girls were released.'

'You have to remember, it was at a time when I was still looking for my really big break. I'd been at it for ten years and I was ready to edit a national paper.' Madeline's speech becomes hurried. 'I needed one more truly great story and they wouldn't be able to say no.'

'You'd be the youngest editor on any of the nationals.'

'And a woman, Ben. Even ten years ago that was still incredibly difficult.'

'Don't. Just tell me what happened.'

'I learnt pretty quickly that there had been problems surrounding Langdon's release. She'd got mixed up in a drugs bust in Glasgow and her new identity had come under threat. Ironically, it turned out she was an innocent bystander, but she needed to be moved quickly. It meant a couple of local police forces became involved and, once that happens, information has a way of leaking. Pretty soon I knew where she was.'

'Great information to have, but of course nothing you could publish. That must have been galling,' I say. 'Is that when you devised a plan to use the information in a different way?'

'Absolutely not,' is Madeline's instant denial. 'It was never like that. I wrote a few pieces in the paper in the days and weeks after the girls' release, that's all. I said how incredibly strong your mum had been – the dignity she had shown. The articles drew a lot of support for her.'

'And then?'

'That was it.'

'Until?'

Madeline coughs and rubs her throat. 'I happened to be in St Marnham. Your mum was coming out of the doctor's surgery when I was going in.'

'Quite a coincidence,' I say. 'The one thing every journalist wanted was an interview with my mum.'

'I feigned taking a moment to recognise her and then I introduced myself. She thanked me for what I'd written in the paper but said the reality was very different. Ben, you need to know you were everything to her. You have to believe me.'

I ignore her, fixing my eyes across the water. 'What happened next?'

'We sat on a bench by the pond. She asked me about the girls – whether I thought it was possible that others might have been involved with them; could there be people in Haddley who knew more than they were saying?'

'Let me guess: you were ready to feed her whatever conspiracy theory she might be imagining. If you could win her trust, she might give you the interview she'd refused to give to anyone else, and with that you'd be an editor in no time.'

'No, Ben, that's not fair!' But, however earnestly Madeline tries to protest, when I turn to face her she cannot hide the affirmation in her eyes. 'I'm not proud of what I did,' she concedes, and we sit in silence for a moment until she continues. 'We arranged to meet again. Only to talk, nothing on the record.'

'And she asked you more about the girls?'

'Yes.'

'And where you thought they might be?'

'She had a right to know.'

Even though I've had my suspicions since my conversation with DS Barnsdale earlier this morning, hearing Madeline confess it fills me with rage. 'I wonder if the police would see it that way, because I suspect right now I'm the only person stopping you being directly implicated with Langdon's murder.'

'What did you tell them?'

I don't look at her, but I can hear the alarm in Madeline's voice. 'Nothing. Until now I wasn't certain,' I say. I turn again to face her. 'You knew my mum was desperate, and you fed her your little bit of information and reeled her in.'

'No, Ben ... '

'The one thing you could give her was Abigail Langdon. So that's just what you did.'

Madeline drops her head in her hands.

'A few weeks later, my mum was dead.' I can feel myself

shaking with anger. 'Have you ever considered that if it weren't for you, she might be alive today?'

I hear Madeline call after me but I don't turn around. I'm already walking away.

Four

'He became a ghost of his former self and retreated from everyone who loved and respected him.'

CHAPTER 25

I wake early on Friday morning, after a fretful night's sleep. Time and again I woke during the night and imagined my mum sitting at our old kitchen table, poring over the words she would write to Langdon. Then I saw her staring, disillusioned, at the toxic response she had received. Lying awake in the dark, I pictured what would have happened if she had called me, if she had told me that she planned to write to Nick's killer; I imagined spending hours convincing her it was the wrong thing to do. Why do it? It would only cause more pain. I would have been sure of that.

Every child's relationship with their parents changes over time, and in many ways the dynamic between my mum and me was forced to evolve sooner than most. By the time I left for Manchester, I'd grown to appreciate the challenges she confronted every single day of her life. I recognised her need for support and the role I could play in providing it. When I was away at university, I would speak to her two or three times a week, hearing her news and the daily occurrences in her life. Where I could, I might offer advice, often practical, sometimes emotional; but always I tried to listen. However much I might wish she had told me about Abigail Langdon, she never would have. She would have known I'd have talked her out of it.

It's still dark when I wander downstairs and brew my first coffee of the day. Reaching for the legal pad I always leave lying at the side of my kitchen, I start to scribble the notes that will form the outline of my article. I realise now that I'm steadfast in my belief that my mum never took the fateful decision to take her own life.

Wanting to clear my head before breakfast with Mrs Woakes, I step outside for a run. The common is still silent, and the cool early-morning air is refreshing after my rest-less night. I turn along the foggy towpath, Haddley Bridge barely visible in the distance. The faces of Madeline and my mum are just beginning to recede when Nathan Beavin suddenly appears at my shoulder. We've spoken a couple of times over the previous two or three weeks, when I've seen him out on the common chasing a football around with Max Wright. Now, as he runs alongside me, we exchange pleasantries, although I rapidly feel the effects of trying to keep up with his athletic pace.

'You're so lucky to live in a place like Haddley,' he tells me, as I start to regret my choice of route. 'I love running by the river,' he says. 'Have you lived here all your life?'

I manage a sideways glance and raise my eyebrows. If he doesn't already know my story, I'm sure Sarah will have filled him in.

'Sorry,' he replies. 'I wasn't really sure . . . '

'Don't worry, it's fine. I'm more surprised when people genuinely don't know.'

'Does that happen often?' he asks.

'Sadly not.'

'You never thought of moving away?'

'I did for a while, after my mum died. I did some travelling with a mate, but I guess this is still where I'm most at home. And, as you say, it is a nice place to live.'

We are silent for a moment and I catch my breath. I slow down, hoping he might run on ahead, but stays beside me.

'You've clearly settled in?' I say when he doesn't say anything more.

Nathan reddens, and not from exertion. 'Sarah's great. And Max. They're fun to be around.'

We run on some more, our pace increasing and me straining to hold my position at his side. 'You should come down to the bar tonight for a drink,' he soon continues. 'Max is going to his dad's this afternoon, so Sarah will probably be in.'

'I might struggle tonight,' I reply.

'Drinks on the house.'

'I'll see.'

'Do you know him at all?'

'Who?'

'Max's dad.'

'James? Only to say hello to. He tended to keep to himself when he lived on the common.'

'You weren't at school with him? He went to Haddley Grammar, right?'

'Yes, but he must have left a couple of years before I started. He's a fair bit older than me, ten years or so I think.'

'Was he still at school when your brother . . . ?'

I nod again. 'Head boy, no less.'

'You were close to your brother?'

Tired of Nathan's inquisition, I revert to my practised answer. 'Like any kid brother, in many ways I worshipped him. At times, even now, it can still be difficult to talk about him.'

Nathan reddens again. 'Of course, I'm sorry,' he says, but I'm already making my excuses and turning for home.

CHAPTER 26

When you search online for either Nick or Simon Woakes, the photograph of the two boys together with Langdon and Fairchild at Richmond Rugby Club is always the first image displayed. It is the picture everyone remembers, plastered across all of the papers after the murders, and then again after Mum's death. And the heartbreaking image that binds together our two families.

The photograph was taken only weeks before the boys' deaths, at the season-ending school rugby finals day. For the first time in its history, Haddley Grammar's senior team had reached the final, with a team captained by James Wright. Our junior team was captained by Nick. Nick led Haddley to a forty-point win, while the senior team ended the eight-year reign of Twickenham Duke Boys' School as regional champions. As a screaming schoolboy helping to fill the stands, I could not have been more proud. At the end of the match, we all clambered down from the stands and on to the touchline. While the triumphant teams gathered for the prize-giving, photos were snapped with all of the winning players. Scenes of the boys celebrating with family and friends were captured, including one of Nick and Simon standing side by side, arms around each other's shoulders, grinning from ear to ear. And then, in another, joined by Langdon and Fairchild, an image that more than twenty years later still leaves me trembling.

Before that summer, my mum and Mrs Woakes were never especially close, although they would always stop and say hello whenever they stood together on a windswept touchline cheering on their sons. Mrs Woakes's husband, Peter, was known throughout Haddley as the headmaster of Haddley Grammar. Immediately after the death of his son, Mr Woakes was placed on compassionate leave. Losing his own son had devastated him, and his loss was compounded as he became the figurehead of grief for the school and its community, the personification of the town's loss. It was a burden that became impossible for him to bear. Unable ever to return to the job he had cherished, in the two years that followed the deaths of Nick and Simon he spiralled in a very public descent and suffered what I realise now was a complete emotional and nervous breakdown. He became a ghost of his former self and retreated from everyone who loved and respected him. His days were spent walking alone along the riverbank, casting a harrowing figure that all the town helplessly watched slowly disintegrate. Every day he would walk the same route – out along the riverbank, across the bridge, into the village of St Marnham, before heading back through the very woods where Simon and Nick had been killed. Each time he would emerge from the darkness, his eyes bloodshot, before walking across the common and back down to the riverbank. From there he would begin his tortuous journey once again, over and over each day. As time passed, he became more and more dishevelled, and, as new residents arrived in Haddley, with the town trying desperately to move forward, he became an increasingly bizarre and eerie character.

Disengaged from his former life and family, he started living rough. Every morning as I walked to school along the banks of the Thames, I would see him huddled under Haddley Bridge. Occasionally I would see Mrs Woakes making her way along the towpath, simply to take him food or fresh clothing. She told me later that after a while he stopped acknowledging her and she would simply leave a hot meal under the bridge in the hope that he might find it.

Then, one day, three years after Simon and Nick had been killed, Mr Woakes disappeared. Following his same daily walk, he went from Haddley to St Marnham, but, instead of returning through the woods, he simply kept walking.

When her husband walked away from Haddley, Mrs Woakes chose to do the same. She moved to an apartment in Richmond with their daughter, Jane, and, while it was only fifteen minutes away from Haddley, it was far enough to allow her to begin building a new life. It wasn't until I moved back to Haddley, after university, that I bumped into Jane during a night out. Awkward at first, we soon discovered we shared a multitude of experiences and emotions. Like me, she was younger than her brother, idolised him in the way many younger siblings did, and over many years had

had to find a way to manage her own grief while supporting her mother in hers. We began to meet for a drink every couple of months, taking comfort in our shared childhood recollections.

Four years ago, Jane became engaged to a New Zealand builder, Leon, who ran a successful business in Richmond. A year later, as she walked down the aisle of St Catherine's church, I was part of the congregation, all of us hoping she had found a happiness she hadn't known since she was a ten-year-old girl. Once the photographer had done her work, the wedding party headed back along the banks of the river to one of the Victorian boathouses to celebrate the marriage. I'd walked with Mrs Woakes, talking quietly as we'd remembered those in our families not there to celebrate. I'd asked about Mr Woakes. She told me how she had woken to a news story eighteen months after he had disappeared. On a freezing cold January morning, the lifeless body of a homeless man had been found perished outside Windsor Great Park. It was where she and Mr Woakes had walked on their very first date twenty years earlier. She knew, then, that she would never see him again.

CHAPTER 27

On the train to Richmond, I flick through the latest news stories on my phone. No reporting of the death of Abigail Langdon, and only a brief mention in the *Yorkshire Post* that the unexplained death of a woman in Farsley was currently being investigated. The latest strife of the local football team receives more column inches.

From Richmond station, I fight against the flood of commuters making their way towards London-bound trains. I cut through the Victorian side streets and head to the riverside café where I have arranged to meet Elizabeth Woakes. I'm first to arrive, and our waiter shows me to a table near the window.

As I glance over the menu, I feel a hand rest on my shoulder and turn to see Elizabeth Woakes standing beside me. I rise to meet her warm embrace. She takes her seat opposite me, slips off her long red coat and adjusts the clips in her loosely tied, greying hair.

'I'm so sorry I'm late, Ben, I promised I'd drop Finlay at nursery for Jane and Leon. I thought I had more time than I did.'

'How is Fin?' I ask.

'He's wonderful.' Her whole face lights up when she talks about her grandson. 'Almost walking now. It won't be long until I can't keep up with him. Jane sends her love. It's been too long since we were all together. You must come over for supper.'

'I'd love that.'

The waiter returns to our table and I see Mrs Woakes smile as I order a sausage and egg sandwich.

'I'll take the granola,' she says, handing her menu to the waiter. 'And a cappuccino.'

'Make that two,' I say. As the waiter steps away, I lean in to the table. 'I assume they've been in touch?'

Pushing her white-framed glasses back on her head, Elizabeth Woakes inches her chair back from the table and gives me a long look. 'Ben, we're not the criminals here,' she says, quietly. 'I've suffered a lifetime because of those girls. And so have you. So don't you let anyone convince you otherwise.' She pauses. 'They told me how she died.' I nod. 'I want you to know I'm glad; glad she suffered. She'll receive no sympathy from me.'

'Nor me,' I reply, and Mrs Woakes smiles. 'Did they ask about your whereabouts?'

She flicks her hand dismissively. 'I had nothing to tell them. Looking after Finlay, lunch at Jane's, shopping in town. Of course they were trying to pin me with the details, but I don't have to answer to them and I told them so.'

'Did they ask if you'd ever visited Farsley?'

'That was the place she was found? Somewhere near Leeds?'

'Yes.'

'I said I'd never heard of the place. Ben, as I said,' continues Mrs Woakes, deliberately, 'I'm glad she's dead. Delighted. I applaud whoever killed her, and the police will get no help from me in finding them. Whoever it might be.'

The waiter arrives with our food and Mrs Woakes briefly replaces her glasses to examine her breakfast. Slipping them back on her head, she thanks the waiter and waves him away. I cut into my sandwich.

'You look as if you need that.'

'Desperately,' I say, with my mouth already half full. 'I skipped dinner last night.'

'One day we will have to get you settled down. Finlay has a nanny two days a week – Australian, loves children. And she teaches yoga the other three days of the week. I'll invite her to join us for supper.'

I laugh. 'Not you as well! Mrs Cranfield keeps trying to marry me off.'

'Knowing her it'll be to some Irish frump.'

'Don't be mean.'

'I'm only joking. Is she still keeping an eye out for you?'

I nod before continuing. 'The police think there is some kind of connection back to Haddley.'

'Were they asking about the letters your mother wrote?'

'You knew?'

'The police told me,' Mrs Woakes replies hurriedly, 'although they wouldn't share any details.'

'Langdon wanted money,' I say.

'There's a surprise. Did she tell your mother anything?'

'I've no idea. I never found any replies.'

'No, of course not,' says Mrs Woakes, pushing her dish to one side and leaning back in her chair.

'The police are trying to understand how my mum might have contacted Langdon, been able to discover her real identity,' I say, and I watch as Mrs Woakes removes her glasses to brush away a stray eyelash. 'Did Madeline Wilson speak to you?'

Mrs Woakes furrows her brow, feigning confusion.

'I know Madeline better than anyone,' I say. 'She wouldn't have stopped with half a story, not when there was another angle to pursue.'

Mrs Woakes signals to the waiter her desire for another cup of coffee. I wait.

'A number of journalists called me over the years requesting an interview,' she says. 'Always the same questions – how was I coping living without Peter, did I think he might still be alive, did I miss Simon? Bloody stupid questions.'

A crack in Mrs Woakes's voice fleetingly drops her veil. Always so cheerful, always so well put-together – it's easy to forget the fragility she hides. She glances across the restaurant and watches a young couple taking their seats – the past slowly walking by. Her quivering hand touches her face. Turning back to me, she slaps her leg.

'I'm so stupid. It's only when I'm with you. I'd never let anyone else see.' She briefly squeezes my hand and inhales deeply. 'I'd always refused any media request, point blank. Your mother and I were absolutely of one mind.'

I nod in silence.

'Madeline Wilson was different. She didn't have any questions. She only ever wanted to help me. Of course she bloody did. She said she wanted to try to understand what had happened, particularly with Peter. I told her immediately that I had no interest in anything she had to say. Some things are best left in the past. That was the decision I'd made years before. However much you might try to convince yourself that revisiting the past will change the present, it never does. The past is gone. I've learnt that the hard way.'

Listening to Mrs Woakes, I can see that all of the pain I saw in my own mum lives on in her, perhaps more. 'Madeline can be persistent . . . '

'She pressed me on why Peter had left, wanted me to speculate why he had been affected in such a way. I told her grief was impossible to understand but she kept pushing. I knew she had an agenda and I was the only one left to protect Peter's memory, so I agreed to meet her. It was stupid of me. When we met, I lost my temper with her.'

'That's easily done.'

'She told me she knew where Langdon was. I said I didn't believe her, and right there and then she gave me all the details. I said I didn't care. She tried to give me the impression that she was going to speak to Langdon herself, discover a story. I knew she was lying, that she'd never risk contacting her, and I told her so.'

'What did you do?'

Mrs Woakes thanks the waiter as he brings her the second cappuccino. She looks at me for a moment, clearly considering what to say next.

'I went to Farsley. Don't ask me why. I don't know what I expected to find. It wasn't as if I was going to walk down the main street and suddenly there would be Abigail Langdon. I spent a couple of hours in the town and then came home.'

'As you say, grief can make us behave in inexplicable ways.'

'It can,' replies Mrs Woakes. 'A week later and Wilson was back trying to contact me.'

'What do you think she wanted?'

'Whatever story she could conjure. She was muck-raking, looking for some kind of angle on Peter,' she replies. 'Wilson didn't know Peter, didn't know what kind of man he was, and yet here she was, pretending to be my friend, when all the time she was looking to point the finger.'

Sitting across the table from Mrs Woakes, I can see how raw she still feels; how much she needs to protect her husband's memory.

'The day Peter was appointed headmaster of Haddley Grammar was the proudest day of his life – and I'm saying that as the mother of his two children. But that's the thing: Peter saw all of the children at that school as *his* children. Every decision he made was considered, and his overriding concern was always the welfare of every single child.'

I sip on my coffee. 'How long was he headmaster for?'

'For five years before Simon and Nick . . . '

I nod.

'He never expected to get the job, not when he did. When the position was advertised we agreed he had nothing to lose in giving it a shot, but throughout the process he was seen as the outsider,' says Mrs Woakes, rallying. 'The final two candidates were Peter and the deputy head at the time, E.E. Hathaway – Ernest, although I never found out what the second E stood for. He'll be getting on a bit now but I think he still lives in one of the mansion block flats on the far side of St Marnham. He was old-school even twenty-five years ago. He believed in strict discipline and that pupils were to be seen and not heard. He and Peter didn't get on at all. Peter was a moderniser, wanted to put the pupils at the heart of the school, to rip things up and start again. He set out his case and made a passionate plea to the Board of Governors and against all the odds the inexperienced man, who at that time was only head of Year Seven, was appointed as the new headmaster.

'At that point Peter hoped Hathaway might resign, or retire gracefully, but he was determined to continue as a thorn in Peter's side. To try to sideline him, Peter appointed him head of sixth form. He knew the older students would pay little heed to Hathaway, the true culture of the school being set in the early years. Hathaway soon realised Peter had marginalised him, excluding him from any real decision-making. Out on the fringes, he began to look for ways to interfere, to create trouble for Peter. There was still a group of governors who supported Hathaway, and he found easy allies when he called for a reintroduction of far greater discipline.

'Peter believed if he gave Hathaway enough rope he'd be the architect of his own downfall. Agreeing to a review of school conduct and discipline, Peter's only requirement was that the pupils were given a voice. Soon afterwards, concerns began to be raised and then complaints followed, lodged directly against Hathaway. Parents came forward first, then one or two former pupils, and finally some older boys still at the school. Discipline had been taken to extremes – bullying of the boys. At one point there was talk of police involvement, but Peter took his opportunity to act. Asked to resign, Hathaway refused point blank. Peter responded by saying if he didn't receive his resignation within forty-eight hours he would set in train a full investigation, bringing back former pupils from the past twenty years to offer evidence.

'Hathaway resigned the next morning and from that moment forward Peter was adamant he would always do whatever was right for the children of the school. He said his only regret was not preventing Hathaway's appointment as deputy at Twickenham Duke.'

Mrs Woakes pauses and stirs the chocolate on the top of her cappuccino. 'That bloody rugby finals day was one of the few times we saw Hathaway after his resignation. He was so supercilious towards Peter. Slightly childishly, we revelled in the victory, probably a little too much. That night we got so drunk on champagne that Peter had to cancel assembly the following morning.'

Holding her cup tightly in her hands, Mrs Woakes leans towards me. 'What I'm trying to say, Ben, is that Madeline Wilson didn't see that man, a good and genuine man out to do his very best.'

'What did Madeline see?' I ask.

'More like what she heard. Stories around Langdon and Fairchild; misrepresentation and smears. Perhaps discipline could have been stronger; Peter was changing a culture and learning as he went. I wanted nothing more to do with her. I refused to speak to her again.'

Finishing her coffee, Mrs Woakes signals to the waiter for our bill. 'This is on me, Ben,' she says, reaching into her jacket pocket for her credit card. 'Whatever the police might ask, please remember, you and I are the only real victims in this crime.'

I look across the table at Mrs Woakes and hate myself for thinking of Madeline. Madeline Wilson didn't reach the position she has by publishing baseless gossip. She's a hard-nosed journalist with the ability to discover the truth behind any story. It's what makes her unrivalled in our industry.

What was the real story she was trying to pursue?

And, whatever it was, why is Elizabeth Woakes choosing not to tell me now?

CHAPTER 28

Holly Richardson crouched beneath the cushions stacked carefully on her living room floor.

'Mummy, don't stand up or you'll knock the roof off our house,' said Alice, as she and Max pulled two more cushions from the sofa to build another room on to their den.

'I'm not standing up, Alice, I'm just moving my leg before it cramps up,' said Holly, as Sarah Wright edged in beside her.

'Your mummy and I are not as young as we used to be,' said Sarah.

'What's "cramps up"?' asked Max.

'It's when you get a very painful leg from sitting in the same position for too long,' said Sarah, and Holly stretched out her leg.

'I don't get that when I sit crossed-legs,' said Max.

'You will when you're older,' replied Sarah.

'You're old, Mummy!' said Alice, before she and Max charged out of the room in search of more cushions to extend their den.

'I think I'm starting to feel it,' said Holly wistfully to her friend.

Lying on the floor next to Sarah, surrounded by cushions and seeing her daughter busy herself, Holly felt safe. She had met Sarah a few years earlier when Sarah and her ex-husband James had bought a home overlooking the common. They'd instantly connected, and Holly had enjoyed introducing her new friend to life in Haddley. This was her home town, the place she'd lived in her whole life, and where all her friends were.

And the place she now was desperate to escape.

'Please tell me you're coming to the party tomorrow night?' she said, taking a sip from the cup of tea that had mercifully survived the den-building.

'Wouldn't miss it for the world,' replied Sarah. 'A chance to have a snoop around your in-laws' place? Who'd pass up an opportunity like that?'

'I think Katherine has her interior designers on speed dial. Every time I go over there, something's being updated. I dread to think of the cost, but she doesn't seem to care. Nor does Francis for that matter.'

'I wish I had a husband like that.'

'Really?'

'Okay, maybe not, but you could do worse for in-laws?'

'In some ways, yes, I suppose.'

'And they're clearly crazy about Alice.'

'Yes. Well, Francis is. I wonder about Katherine sometimes.'

Sarah raised an eyebrow. 'Oh? In what way?'

'When I first started dating Jake, Katherine couldn't have been more welcoming. She took me into her home, introduced me to so many of her friends, and, when we married, she seemed to love having a daughter-in-law to spend time with.'

'What changed?'

'I don't know really. Once Alice came along she just seemed to lose interest. I didn't have the time to go to her lunches, had no desire to dress up for cocktail parties.' Holly sighed. 'A crying baby didn't fit into her lifestyle, I guess. I'd still meet her for lunch every couple of months, always somewhere very lovely, but all she ever talked about was what was happening in the village or the next trip she might take with one of her girlfriends. I don't think I can remember her once asking about Alice.'

'What about Francis?'

Holly rolled her eyes. 'Same old, really. It's difficult between Jake and his father. The breakdown of the business. Money. The usual things that divide families.'

'I still see him coming to the house, though?'

'That's for Alice. As I said, he adores her,' replied Holly. 'Now, you have to promise me you're going to bring Nathan to the party.'

'I might,' said Sarah, smiling.

'No! You absolutely have to promise. Everyone's dying to meet him.'

'Are they?'

'Sarah, he's gorgeous!' said Holly. 'I watched him running across the common this morning. I had to pull my tongue back in.'

Sarah giggled, almost spilling her tea. 'If he's not working tomorrow evening, then I'm sure he'll come along. I'd hate to disappoint you all.'

At that moment Max and Alice reappeared, each dragging a cushion behind them.

'Alice, pick those up,' said Holly, as her daughter knocked a pile of books off a footstool.

'But Mummy, I need the little seat in my house.'

'I don't care what you need; you don't throw books on the floor.'

Alice stared at her mother and pursed her lips.

'Pick them up,' said Holly, and Alice slowly knelt down and started to pile the books on to the coffee table.

'An impudent streak?' said Sarah, nudging her friend.

'God knows,' replied Holly. 'Every single one of them,' she added, sternly to Alice.

'Is tomorrow your actual anniversary?' asked Sarah.

'Seven long years,' replied Holly, quietly. 'We were married on a Thursday, as Francis was flying to Malaysia the following day for a business meeting that couldn't be moved. I should have realised then: in the Richardson family Francis always comes first.'

'Some happy times, surely?'

'Of course,' replied Holly, 'but just as many when I could have walked out of the front door and never looked back.'

'Really?'

'This is a suffocating family. Everything comes at a price.'

'Hol, I know it must be infuriating, but try not to lose perspective.'

Holly said nothing.

'You're okay, aren't you, Hol?' Sarah touched her arm and Holly could hear the concern in her friend's voice. 'You're not telling me you'd ever really walk away, would you? We all have our ups and downs, although with me and James it was more downs and downs.'

Laughing, Holly twisted on the floor, lying closer to her friend. 'If I wanted to ask your advice,' she said, whispering. 'Professionally . . . '

'Hol, that's not you.'

'I grew up with just me and my mum and I dreamt of being married, of living in a nice house, of being part of a big family. I was twenty-two when I met Jake and got swept along by the parties and the glamour. One minute I was living in a bedsit where you had to press down the ballcock to flush the toilet and the next I was drinking Bellinis at the side of the Richardsons' pool.'

'What's not to love?' replied Sarah, laughing.

Meeting Jake, Holly's life had changed in an instant. Saying goodbye to the bedsit above the pub, she had told herself she had everything she had ever dreamt of. She could see how much Jake needed to be loved and she'd liked that. 'I've always cared for Jake and I still do, but the passion was fleeting and it's long since disappeared.'

'And Jake? How does he feel?'

'His father grinds him down. I don't think I can rescue him. I can't help but wonder if Alice and I would be better off away from Haddley and St Marnham and the whole Richardson family.'

'I'll tell you what I tell all my clients when they first come to see me – take your time and be certain. Don't do anything until you are one hundred per cent,' said Sarah. 'Your whole life has been in Haddley, and that's what you'd be leaving behind.'

'Would that be so bad?'

'Well, there's this house, for a start. We'd fight for your share, of course.'

'Francis pays the mortgage.'

'That makes it a little more complicated,' said Sarah. 'For how long?'

'Four years. We couldn't live here without him. He controls us.'

'You may not love Jake in the way you thought you did, but if you talk to him you might discover he wants a second chance as well.'

'He'd never leave. Francis wouldn't let him.'

'Hol, he's a grown man!'

'And the only son Francis has,' replied Holly. 'Jake tries hard, but he gets trapped into being something he's not. Or something he thinks his father wants him to be.'

'Then you should tell him that.'

'I'm not sure it would make any difference. Losing the business almost destroyed him.'

'You've been married for seven years, have a beautiful daughter. Is there nothing worth saving? Couldn't the three of you take the chance to move away, start again somewhere new?'

'Grandpa!' called Alice, as she ran towards the living-room window.

161

'Alice?' said Holly, getting to her feet.

'Mummy!' her daughter screamed, as Holly clambered over the cushions, destroying the den as she did.

'I'm sorry, sweetheart,' said Holly, picking up her daughter and clutching her in her arms.

'Look, Mummy,' said Alice, pointing out to the common where Francis Richardson, eyes forward, was striding towards the house.

'Speak of the devil,' said Sarah.

CHAPTER 29

Holly looked at her father-in-law as he stood in her hallway and considered what an imposing figure he still cut, even approaching his seventieth birthday. If asked, she imagined he'd describe himself as distinguished – his full head of hair neatly styled, greying but kept longer to soften his face. She imagined his height must have been a useful tool in commanding a room and aweing an opponent. Striking in youth; confident with age.

Always intimidating.

'I hope we'll be seeing you tomorrow evening,' said Francis, focusing his attention on Sarah. 'You would add a certain style to any occasion.'

Sarah laughed as Holly called out to Alice and Max not to leave the front garden. 'I'll do my very best, Mr Richardson,' she replied.

'Francis, please.'

'I'll do my very best, Francis. I can't wait to see your wonderful home. I've heard so much about it from Holly.'

'None of that is my doing. Katherine's in charge of all the

décor. All I do is tell her what a great job she's done. That, and pay the bills.'

'I'm sure you do more than that,' said Sarah, glancing across at her friend. 'You don't strike me as someone who sits idly by.'

'I try to keep busy,' said Francis, taking in a deep breath. 'With my ongoing business interests, it's hard for me to keep up with what Katherine's up to. It's very much a case of she does her thing and I do mine.'

Holly watches him touch Sarah gently on the arm. 'Sarah has promised she'll bring along her new boyfriend tomorrow night,' she said. 'Haven't you, Sarah?'

'I'm certainly going to try.'

'We'd be delighted if he can join us. But, if not, we'd be just as happy to have you on your own,' said Francis.

'Thank you, Mr Richards— Francis,' replied Sarah, taking a small step sideways and turning to Holly. 'Thanks so much for this morning.'

'Stay for another tea, if you like,' replied Holly, as Sarah leant in to hug her. 'I'll be putting the kettle on again for Francis.'

'I would love some time with Alice,' he said, speaking over his daughter-in-law. 'We grandfathers do get possessive.'

Sarah turned to Holly. 'I should get going,' she said, before stepping outside and calling to her son. 'Come on, Max, nearly lunchtime,' she said, as her son raced across the garden and grabbed her by the hand.

Running inside, Alice leapt into her grandfather's arms. 'Grandpa!' she squealed in delight as he lifted her into the air. 'I've got my party dress all ready for tomorrow.'

'You are going to be the prettiest little lady at the party, isn't she, Mummy?'

'I'm sure she will be,' said Holly, closing the front door as Francis sat with his granddaughter at the foot of the stairs.

'Did you get your golden-toed shoes?' he asked.

Alice dropped her lip. 'Mummy wouldn't let me.'

'We've got you some very pretty shoes.'

'But I wanted the ones with the golden toes.'

'We talked about this, Alice, and how expensive they were.'

'But they're shoes for a princess.'

'And you are my princess,' said Francis. 'And a princess can't go to the ball without golden-toed shoes,' he continued, raising his hands in mock horror.

'Can I have them, Grandpa? Really?'

'Nothing is too much for my little girl,' said Francis, as Alice threw her arms around him.

Holly turned and walked into the kitchen. She flicked the switch on the kettle, and stood facing the counter, waiting for it to boil. She sensed him in the doorway behind her.

'Will you push me on my swing now, Grandpa?' came Alice's voice.

'The biggest push ever?'

'Yes!'

'In five minutes,' said Francis, setting his granddaughter down, 'once I've had a cup of tea with Mummy. And only if you give me a kiss first.' Holly turned to see Alice jump up and, as Francis bent down, she planted a huge wet kiss on his cheek. 'You head outside,' she said, 'and I'll come and push you in a few minutes.'

Alice ran through the kitchen and out into the back garden.

'You spoil her too much.'

'If I can't spoil her, who can?'

'She has to learn she can't have everything,' Holly replied, watching her daughter run into the giant Wendy house her grandparents had bought for her third birthday.

'Why? She is our little princess.'

Holly heard Francis close the kitchen door. She held her breath. Suddenly, an arm wrapped around her neck and she was slammed forward on to the black marble counter top. Her face was pressed down on to the cold, hard surface. Feeling her father-in-law reach inside her underwear, she tensed as he quickly pushed up her skirt and forced himself inside her. Instantly, he was pounding hard with a jarring rhythm. She closed her eyes and tried to think of her daughter playing outside.

'Be quick,' she whispered, as Francis stabbed inside her.

'You shouldn't have kept me waiting with your little play date.'

Holly reached around and touched him knowing it would slow his motion. She heard him groan, and as she gently pushed herself back towards him he eased his pace. She clasped the countertop before reaching around and touching him once again.

'No,' said Francis, and as he released himself he emitted a soft moan that turned Holly's stomach. She felt the weight of her father-in-law rest upon her and trap her against the hard surface. 'You really shouldn't do that,' he said, his lips pressed against her ear. She felt him force his tongue into her ear and quickly she turned to free herself.

'Don't, Francis,' she said, pulling up her underwear.

'You just like it to be over as fast as possible, don't you?'

'Alice is right outside.'

'She's fine,' he said. Holly watched him fasten his trousers and belt. 'When's Jake back?'

'Not until late.'

'Time for me to call round again; perhaps you'll be feeling a little more relaxed.'

'No, Francis.'

'I've got my key, so no need for you to wait up. I could pop up and surprise you.'

Holly turned away, determined not to show any weakness. Francis walked across the kitchen and knocked on the window.

'Come outside, Grandpa,' cried Alice.

'Are you ready for the biggest push ever?'

'Yes!' she replied.

'Be careful with her,' said Holly, not looking at Francis.

'I'll see you later,' he said, as he walked out of the back of the house. As he did, Holly watched him drop three fifty-pound notes on to the kitchen floor. 'And get the girl her shoes.'

CHAPTER 30

At the end of her shift Corrine had quickly made her way home, weaving her way through a series of side streets, determined to avoid the seafront. She'd cooked herself sausage and chips but she'd barely done more than pick at it, and as she pushed the half-eaten food across her splintered table she regretted wasting two of the Cumberlands she'd pinched from the care home. At the sink in the corner of her tiny kitchen, she waited for the water to get hot before rinsing her plate and wiping it down with the tea towel one of the residents had bought her on a bus trip to Folkestone Harbour. Corrine had been touched that the old lady had thought of her.

Picking up her glass of water, she headed into her bedroom, setting the glass down on the floor beside her bed. She went to the window and lifted the flattened cardboard boxes into place. Four taped together helped to block out the daytime light. She sat on her bed and pressed yellow foam plugs into her ears, although they never truly blocked the rattle and hum from the amusement arcade below. Lying back, she stared up at the bare light bulb and remembered the paper lampshade she'd seen in Wilko. It was only two pounds, but at that price she wondered if it would really make any difference. Perhaps she could find an old one at Sunny Sea.

Stretching her back, she froze when she heard her door buzzer sound from the street level below. She removed one ear plug and listened carefully, lying motionless, waiting.

The buzzer sounded again.

She climbed off the bed and peered through a crack between two of the flattened boxes. When she stood on her toes and looked down, she could see two policemen standing at her door.

The red-faced fat bastard, she thought. He went to the police after all. Then again, she had stabbed pretty hard through his fat knuckles.

She stepped back and waited.

Silence.

Peering forward again, she could see the two officers start to walk towards the high street. She breathed a sigh of relief and quickly slipped on her shoes before returning to the living room. Opening the window at the back of the room, she clambered outside on to the metal fire escape and made her way down to the rear entrance of the amusement arcade. She stood at the back door and keyed in the security code to let herself in. She walked past the stinking staff toilet, before opening the faulty fire door and entering the clatter and ring of the arcade.

The smell of plastic popcorn turned her stomach and she

blinked at the flashing lights in the airless cavern. Passing a young family as they collected tokens from a Pac-Man game, she stepped up into the raised change booth in the centre of the arcade.

'Police were looking for you,' said Chad, the arcade owner.

'I know,' replied Corrine. 'Did they come in here?'

'I said I hadn't seen you for a couple of days.'

'You're a doll,' replied Corrine. 'I owe you.'

'What you done?' asked Chad, as he took a five-pound note from a pensioner keen to get back to the tenpenny slots.

'Who says I've done anything?'

'Just a social call, was it?'

'Something like that.'

'Next time I'll send them up, then.'

'You've only given me four quid back,' said the woman at the window.

'Sorry, babe,' replied Chad, slipping another little pile of ten-pence pieces under the glass. The woman tossed the final pile into her little plastic pot and shuffled off.

'"Babe"? She's old enough to be your grandmother.'

'You're not the only one who likes a little chat,' said Chad, turning round and running his hand up the inside of Corrine's thigh.

'Get your fucking hand off,' she said, slapping it away.

'You weren't complaining the other night.'

'The other night I was pissed.'

'You seemed perfectly happy to me, especially with your little yelps.'

'Maybe your wife would like to hear them next time.'

'You do that and your friends from the nick will be coming to look for you at the homeless shelter.'

Corrine moved forward and rested against the counter, letting her leg gently lean against Chad's arm. 'If they come round again, will you tell them I've gone away, just for a few days?'

Chad gently tapped his fingers together. 'You're asking me to do you a favour now, is that what you're saying?'

'Don't be like that,' replied Corrine. 'We had a nice time last week but it was a one-off.'

'Last thing I need round here is somebody getting mixed up with the police. There's lots of cash flowing through the arcade and sometimes it's nice if the boys in blue look the other way. I prefer to be a good citizen and help out whenever I can.'

Corrine knew that if she could avoid the police for a few days they would soon get bored of looking for her. The fat bloke from the beach was never going to be their number one priority. She leant across and gently ran her fingers up the seahorse tattoo that decorated Chad's forearm. 'Come on, doll, you and me are the same: neither of us wants any trouble.'

'I've got the afternoon free tomorrow; Dean's covering. I could bring you up some fish and chips, couple of bottles of cider, keep you company.'

'I'd rather Spotty Dean came up with a kebab.'

'Fuck off! I'm only trying to help you,' said Chad, again rubbing his hand up the inside of Corrine's thigh. 'I've a feeling you might be a little old for Dean these days.

Your talents are more appreciated by an experienced man like me.'

'Go on, then, three o'clock,' said Corrine, resigned. 'And if you're bringing fish and chips, make sure there's plenty of vinegar.'

CHAPTER 31

Exiting St Marnham station, I walk through the village before turning along the towpath. When I reach the outdoor terrace of Mailer's restaurant, I find Will sitting alone in the far corner. He is seated at a table he often occupies in the late mornings, while East and his team are setting up for lunch. He's hunched over his keyboard and doesn't see me until I am standing over him.

'Ben,' he says, looking up and closing his laptop. 'I wasn't expecting to see you again so soon.'

'I was passing so I thought I'd stop by and see if you had that ten minutes to talk about Nick and the summer he died?'

'Right now?' replies Will. 'I guess so. I didn't realise it was so urgent. If you are going ahead and writing an article, surely it's about your mum?'

'Absolutely it is, but it's all connected. One way or another, everything starts with that summer. May I?' I reach for one of the deep-cushioned wrought-iron chairs.

'Of course, yes. Can I get you a coffee?' asks Will, glancing towards the restaurant.

'Thanks, no, I'm fully caffeinated.'

'I'm not sure there's a huge amount I can tell you,' he begins. 'Nick and I were friends in school – not so much out of it.'

'You had the rugby team, though?' I say, remembering Will as one of the members of Nick's victorious team.

'Yes and no,' says Will. 'The team was very focused on winning; it didn't leave us much time for more than that. We didn't hang out much outside of school.'

What Will is telling me feels at odds with my own memories: time and again, Nick throwing a rugby ball across the common with his friends. I'm sure Will was among them. But I can see he is uncomfortable and decide not to press him.

'In the time you did spend with him, did Nick ever talk about Langdon and Fairchild, perhaps when you were in class? Or did you see them hanging out together?'

'Not from what I recall. We all knew them in school, but beyond that I couldn't really say.'

'And that summer? Could they have spent time with Nick and Simon?'

'I'm the wrong person to answer that. I don't think I saw Nick more than one day throughout the whole holiday.'

'And on that one day?' I ask.

'Ben, it's more than twenty years ago, I can't remember what we did. I probably bumped into Nick in Haddley and we ended up spending the afternoon in McDonald's. Or perhaps we walked up to Haddley Hill Park. Regular summer holiday stuff, killing time. Nothing more than that.'

'On that day, did Nick talk about Langdon and Fairchild?'

'No, not that I remember,' replies Will, crossing his legs uncomfortably. There's a pause. 'I don't know, maybe a passing reference, nothing more than that.'

'In what way?' I press.

'Schoolboy stuff, laughing and joking. Mucking about. Abigail and Josie were the sort of girls who attracted attention, often from the wrong kinds of people. We might have made a joke about them but honestly, Ben, there is nothing more I can tell you.'

'Can you remember how long it was before the killings?'

'A week, maybe two. I try not to think about it. Is any of this really relevant to what happened to your mum?'

'I'm starting to think it might be. But I can see I'm interrupting you,' I say, nodding towards Will's laptop and getting to my feet, 'so I'm going to let you get on.'

'Firing off a few emails, that's all.'

'Thanks for your time. Say hi to East for me.'

I'm about to step away when I think of East's message, and I pause.

'Ben?' Will asks, looking at me.

'Don't worry, it's nothing.'

It's only when I return to the towpath and head towards Haddley that I flick on my phone. I message East.

> Caught up with Will but I think you were setting up for lunch. Catch you next time

I'm barely a minute down the towpath when I feel my phone vibrate with his answer.

175

How about tomorrow?

I know East wants to persuade me not to write the article. I don't know why, but I do know I'm not going to be talked out of it.

I'll let you know, is my reply.

CHAPTER 32

I walk across Haddley Common and watch PC Cash step out of a police car and make her way towards my home. Seeing she is alone, I quicken my pace and meet her as she approaches my front door.

'Hello again,' I say, smiling. 'I guess you're looking for me?'

'Mr Harper, hello,' she replies. 'I was hoping you might have had a chance to find a sample of your mother's handwriting?'

Her approach is a million miles away from DS Barnsdale's pointed accusations.

'I'm sure I can find something if you'd like to come in,' I say. 'Can I offer you a coffee?' I add.

'Only if you're having one,' Dani replies, evidently relieved at my lack of hostility.

'I'm maintained by caffeine,' I call over my shoulder, as I head down the hallway to the kitchen and click on the coffee machine. 'Dread to think what it must do to my blood pressure.'

Dani has followed me and takes a seat at the kitchen

island. 'Two sugars in mine, please, which I'm certain is far worse.' She smiles, and I see her eyes brighten.

'We all have our vices,' I reply, opening a drawer of kitchen junk that I'm sure exists in every house. Except at the bottom of mine is a brown envelope that isn't really junk at all. Inside are two cards sent to me by my mum which I've kept for the past decade – one for my twentieth birthday, the last for which she was alive, and the second to congratulate me on passing my driving test. I hand them to Cash, and feel a sudden urge to snatch them back as soon as I've parted with them. It's not that I look at them all the time, but knowing they're there is a comfort somehow.

'I'll get these back to you as soon as I can,' says the constable, carefully taking hold of the cards, as if she can sense my reluctance. 'I know this must be really hard for you, having to go over all this again.'

I look at her, and from the sincerity in her eyes I get the impression she really does understand. I shrug. 'It was a long time ago.'

'That's a lovely picture of you both,' she replies, looking across at the photograph of the two of us together outside the Arran distillery.

'It was taken only a few weeks before she died. We asked a passer-by to snap us on my phone as we waited for a taxi.'

'She looks happy.'

'The more I think about it, I really do believe she was.' I hand PC Cash her drink and sit across from her at the kitchen island. 'That trip was important to her.'

'She got to spend time with you,' says Cash, smiling.

'Thanks, and yes,' I say, 'but more than that. She wanted to use the trip to talk to me. I've always told myself that perhaps in some strange way she was reassuring herself I was going to be okay, but I never wanted to believe that.'

'You've never accepted that she killed herself?' asks Cash, and I'm slightly surprised by her directness. I take a moment before answering.

'I don't know if I ever really confronted it. I don't think I wanted to.'

'And now?'

'Now I'm certain there's more to her death than any of us realised.'

'Why so certain?'

'When I think about that trip, I can see she wasn't reassuring herself about me. She was thinking about her own life and her own plans for the future.'

'What's changed your mind?'

I pause. 'Abigail Langdon. Or rather, her death.' I get to my feet and start to pace the kitchen. 'What if, by the time we went on that trip, my mum was already in contact with Langdon? The dates all fit.' I think of the rain lashing across the bay on our last afternoon in Arran. 'She becomes convinced that Langdon knows something. Then she finds a way to get in contact with her but Langdon's only response is to demand money.'

'Twenty-five thousand pounds,' says Cash.

'Exactly,' I reply. I strain to recall our conversation in Arran. 'She asked me if I thought there was more we didn't

179

know and, if there was, wouldn't I want to know? I closed down the conversation, told her didn't want to hear it.'

'What did she think Abigail Langdon could tell her?' asks Cash.

I take the seat next to her. 'I don't know, but, whatever it was, it was a secret somebody else was very keen to protect. Weeks later, my mum was dead.'

'That's a big leap,' says PC Cash, quietly.

'True,' I say, 'but somebody decided to kill Abigail Langdon now. Why?'

'To protect that same secret?'

'That's what I intend to find out. Starting with what happened in Farsley this week.'

'Mr Harper, that investigation sits with West Yorkshire Police,' replies the officer, a mild rebuke in her tone.

'That might be true, PC Cash,' I say, 'but after my own experiences with the police I like to ask my own questions. Perhaps if they hadn't been so quick to assume my mum's death was suicide, I could have asked more questions at the time.'

'I'm sure I don't need to remind you this is an ongoing investigation and that everything we've told you to this point remains confidential,' says Cash, and I see a flash of concern on her face.

'You can trust me,' I reply, smiling. 'I'd never want to get in the way of the police's best efforts. My plan is to drive up to Farsley early tomorrow morning. I simply want to get a feel for the town, maybe find a couple of people who knew Langdon. Nothing more than that. If you think I'm going to misbehave, why don't you come with me?'

'It's Saturday tomorrow, and I'm not on duty,' she replies, hurriedly.

'Well, I'm going to Farsley tomorrow.'

'Mr Harper, I really don't think that is a good idea.'

'Call me Ben. I'm not doing anything illegal. If you come with me, everything is off the record.'

We're interrupted by a rap on my front door. 'Hold that thought,' I say, quickly heading out of the kitchen. Opening the door, I'm greeted by Phil Doorley of PDQ Deliveries.

'Hi, Ben,' he says, handing me a box labelled UNITED STATES POSTAL SERVICE. 'I've another three of these for you out in the van.'

For a moment I am stumped as to what they could be. Then I remember the podcast I'd been working on before my meeting with Madeline. Everything that has happened since has driven it completely from my mind.

'I'll give you a hand,' I reply, and walk with him out to the kerb.

'Are you running an import business from the US?'

'It's a load of old interview tapes. They were never digitised, so this was the only way I could get hold of them. One of the TV networks shipped them over.'

'Everything okay?' he asks, stepping past Cash's parked car.

'Fine,' I reply. 'Just a routine check-in.'

Phil nods as we stack the boxes in my hallway. We return again to the van and, as we do, a Range Rover stops in the middle of the road, next to Phil's van.

'Big man!' shouts James Wright, jumping out of the car

and heading towards Phil. Seeing me follow, he pauses. 'Hi, Ben, how you doing?'

'Good, thanks,' I reply, acknowledging him, before telling Phil I can take the last box.

I walk back down the path and, reaching my front door, turn to see James with his arm around Phil, the two former schoolmates sniggering together as they lurk at the side of the common. Standing on my front doorstep, I take my phone from my pocket and type a quick message.

> Will, something you said has been rattling around in my mind for the past hour. You said Langdon and Fairchild attracted attention from the wrong kinds of people? What did you mean by that?

Two ticks appear next to my message. I wait for him to reply.

> Men. All kinds of men.

When I walk back into the kitchen, PC Cash puts down her phone. 'I'll go with you tomorrow but it's a visit to the town, nothing more,' she says.

'I didn't expect you to agree.'

'To be honest, I could do with a day away from Haddley. Let me know what time.'

'Early,' I reply, as she again picks up the two cards I found for her. 'Somehow I managed to pass first time,' I say, looking down at the congratulations card she is holding in her hand. *'Always warn me when you're going to be on the road,'* I say, remembering what my mum had written inside. 'My mum thought she was hilarious.'

'She sounds wonderful. I can imagine how much you must miss her.'

I resume my seat opposite her. 'It does get easier. I might still think about her, or Nick, almost every day, but now it's often in a good way. I've learnt to remember the happy times. We did have them,' I say, and smile.

'The good times can sustain you through the bad, right?' says Cash, suddenly distant.

'Yes,' I say, and hesitate. 'Is that true for you?'

She shrugs. 'Everybody has their own ups and downs. I'm no exception. It's crazy to expect everything to be exactly as you imagine. Life isn't like that.' I give a short nod and she continues. 'You think life is going to serve you one thing and then all of a sudden you're somewhere else that you never thought possible.' She twists her wedding ring around her finger.

'How long have you been married?'

She drops her hands to her side and eases them under her legs. 'Not long, just a few months. Early days yet.' She finishes her coffee. 'I lost my dad not so long ago. I know how tough it can be.'

'I'm sorry.'

'Never easy with families,' she adds, picking up the second card.

'My twentieth,' I say. 'My birthday is at the end of January but like most students I never threw anything out. I found it when I went back to university after my mum had died.'

'That can't have been easy,' she says.

'I put it up again the following January. I told myself I would put it up every year for my birthday but I never have. I guess I'm not as sentimental as I thought.'

'Was it always just you and your mum? I mean, you know, after Nick . . . ' She colours.

'Pretty much. My dad has never been around much. He left when I was three.'

She nods. 'I'm sorry.'

'Don't be; he's a complete waste of space.' I pick up our mugs and take them to the sink. 'He always travelled a lot for work – something in sales, I don't know what. Suited his flighty personality, I suppose. I can remember standing at the window, waiting for him to come home from each trip. He'd always bring us a present, something and nothing but important to a three-year-old. That last trip, I stood waiting day after day but he never came back.' I look out into the garden. 'That weekend, Nick and I dragged the lawnmower into the back garden and tried to cut the grass.'

'And you've never seen him since?'

'He came back every now and again but never for anything good.' I come back to sit opposite her. 'The day of the rugby finals, he appeared out of nowhere. My mum was working and Nick was excited to see him. He wanted Dad to see him play. He told me to go and say hello but I refused. Nick made me promise not to tell Mum. She'd become fed up with my father dipping in and out and disrupting our lives. He'd make promises to see us but rarely show. She gave him the ultimatum of either committing to see us on a regular basis or staying away. He didn't do either. A few weeks later he appeared again, this time when Nick and I were swimming at Tooting Bec Lido. As we ran for the bus, he promised Nick he'd be there again the following week. Nick wanted to see him and again he made me swear not to tell Mum. He knew she wouldn't like it. A week later, on that blistering hot day, I lied to my mum and told her I didn't feel like swimming. "Suit yourself," she said, but I know she couldn't understand why I didn't want to go and cool off. I kept the secret from my mum. I always wished I hadn't.'

'Your dad didn't show?'

I shook my head. 'Instead of my father, Nick met Simon, and they came home on the bus together. Langdon and Fairchild were waiting on the common.' I rub my hands across my face. 'My father should have been with Nick.'

Five

'You lie with unnerving ease, you impersonate a police officer, and now you remove evidence from a crime scene.'

CHAPTER 33

Street lamps light the way to my car as I walk along the side of the common in the early hours of Saturday morning. As I flick on my phone, the time turns to 03:00. I want to be in Farsley before any of the national press get the scent of a story. With a stiff breeze blowing up from the river, I zip my jacket and button my collar.

As I do, I see a figure start to cross the common from the Lower Haddley Road.

'Is that you, Ben?' says a voice. I peer through the darkness and see Nathan Beavin walking towards me. Great. 'Early start or late finish?' he asks.

'Just leaving,' I reply. 'Late one for you?'

'We close at two and even then there are always a few stragglers. After that we do a quick clear-up before heading home.'

'That must make it a long day.'

'I enjoy it. It's always a fun crowd on a Friday night,' he replies, now standing beside my car. 'I kept an eye out for you this evening but didn't see you.'

'Work got the better of me,' I reply. 'I'm starting on a new story and tried to make some headway on my research.'

'Is that what you're up to now?' he asks.

Our conversation has swiftly assumed the tone of a cross-examination. This seems to be standard with Nathan. 'Something like that.'

'What kind of story takes place in the middle of the night?'

'You'd be surprised,' I say, 'but I've got a bit of a journey ahead, so I thought I'd try and beat the traffic.'

'Get in ahead of the pack?'

'You could say that,' I reply.

'Something interesting?'

I can only admire his persistence. 'It's early days yet. At this stage you never know quite how a story might pan out.' I look around hopefully for PC Cash. I told her I was leaving at three. 'I should let you go,' I continue. 'You must be exhausted.'

'I am pretty much all-in,' says Nathan, 'but you get used to it. With Max away, I'm hoping for a lie-in in the morning. His dad's going to hang on to him for a second night this weekend so Sarah and I can go to the Richardsons' party.'

'Nice,' I reply.

'Decent of him to keep Max for the extra night.'

'He is his son.'

'True. Got himself a nice young girlfriend, from what Sarah says. Don't think she's overly impressed.'

'As I said yesterday morning, I don't really know the man.'

'No,' replies Nathan. 'I've asked around a bit and nobody seems to know much about him. That, or they're just not saying.'

'You seem pretty interested. Sarah's the one you should be speaking to if you've got concerns.'

'Not concerns, no, nothing like that. I'm just interested in what happened before I arrived.'

'I'm sure Sarah would tell you anything she felt you needed to know.'

'Guess so,' he replies, and, as he does, I'm relieved to see PC Cash walking up the road towards us. 'She with you?' he asks, as she approaches dressed in blue jeans and a black sweater.

'Dani,' says PC Cash quickly, introducing herself to Nathan before I have to, and I explain that she is working with me on the story.

'You work with Ben at the site?'

'I'm freelance,' she replies, instantly.

'One of the best,' I add, briefly catching her eye.

'What kind of stuff?' asks Nathan.

'Mostly crime,' she replies, 'but I like to do some human interest pieces as well.'

I click open the car doors as Nathan says, 'Heading out of London?'

'Going north,' I reply, 'but I've promised Holly I'll be back for tonight. I'll look out for you at the party.'

'You wouldn't want to miss that,' he says, stepping away, and in the darkness I watch him walk towards Sarah's house.

CHAPTER 34

Corrine jerked backwards in her chair. A moment later her head dropped forward, her eyes drooping again. Then another thud echoed from down the hall and she sat upright, stretching her neck. They weren't supposed to sleep in the residents' lounge but she hadn't been able to sleep that afternoon and what else were they meant to do all night? Peering at her watch, she saw it wasn't even four. She leant forward and looked down the corridor. None of the doors were open and no lights were lit. She strained to hear any further sounds but, other than Mrs Hinchliffe snoring heavily in room four, all was silent.

She plumped the cushions piled behind her and tried to settle again, twisting her back in an effort to find a comfortable spot. Finally, she rested her head against the padded wing, only to snap it backwards when her nose touched the textured material. She was certain she could still smell stale dinner from the previous evening. She hated the way smells lingered inside the home. Every odour destined to loiter for days, a constant blend of stewed cabbage and urine.

Resting her face against her hand instead, she closed her eyes and began to drift. She'd started work at six the previous evening, clearing dinner plates before ushering the residents to an early bed. 'May I escort you back to your room?' That was what Molly had told her she had say to each of them every night. Corrine couldn't wait to shuffle them off to bed. There were always a few stragglers in the lounge, the ones who wanted to talk. The same stories, repeated night after night. About their families, mostly. They'd tell her how wonderful and successful, how kind and popular their son or daughter or granddaughter was. To Corrine, it felt like showing off. None of them seemed to recognise that those same families left them shut up in Sunny Sea, week after week, with hardly a visit between them. But family was all they seemed to want to talk about, whether it was their own or hers.

In time, she'd started creating her own stories. Sometimes she'd tell them her parents had been killed in a car crash; another time it was a rail crash. She enjoyed the warm feeling she got when people looked at her with eyes full of sympathy. Nearly always she was able to draw a tear from the old biddies but one time one of the old fellas had quizzed her as to the exact location. He'd been something to do with rail safety when he was younger. Paddington, she'd told him, heart in mouth. To her relief he'd seemed to accept it, and had offered her his sympathies. After that she noticed he was always particularly nice to her and at Christmas bought her a box of chocolates. Next time a new resident asked about her family she said her parents had been killed in the Lockerbie plane crash but that she didn't like to talk about it. At the end of the week the old girl slipped a tenner into her hand and she couldn't believe her luck. The time after that it was her sister who died in the London bombings and she was twenty quid up. Then her mother was crushed under a tree in the Great Storm, but the nosy old git started asking questions and soon she realised the dates didn't quite fit. He had a heart attack at the end of the following week and she was glad to see the back of him.

An alarm suddenly blared and, rousing herself, she looked back down the corridor. The light was flashing outside number seven; Mr Talisbrook – at least she thought that was his name. She stretched and was barely on her feet before Molly was down from the front corridor and at her side.

'Mr Talisbrook, room seven, I think it is, Molly. I was just on my way,' she said, hastily. Molly ignored her and walked on ahead. She hated Molly.

Opening the bedroom door, she watched as Molly rushed forward. Mr Talisbrook was lying on the bathroom floor. His pyjama bottoms were down and Corrine thought she was going to gag at the smell. She lingered by the door, breathing towards the corridor, while Molly tried to revive him. When Molly shouted at her to go and call an ambulance, she was grateful for the excuse to head to the front of the house.

The paramedics were fifteen minutes away, the woman at the end of the line told her. Corrine decided she had better wait by the door to let them in. When the ambulance arrived, five minutes early, she was disappointed to see that the paramedics were both women.

Minutes later, they wheeled Mr Talisbrook away, and Molly instructed her to go and clean up his room. She headed to the cupboard at the end of the corridor. Inside it was a mess: old bedding stuffed in alongside cleaning cloths, bottles of disinfectant and hand sanitizer. She pulled out a mop and bucket and then found a new pair of thick rubber gloves still in their packet. Those were hers now.

Back in Mr Talisbrook's bedroom, she opened the window to let a cool breeze blow through. She filled the bucket in the bath and poured in a generous amount of disinfectant. Turning her head away, she began to mop the bathroom floor, relieved as the stench was gradually overtaken by the artificial lemon scent.

She left the floor to dry, and went back into the bedroom to strip the bed. When she threw the sheets out into the hallway, she could see Molly speaking on the phone. For her to call the relatives in the middle of the night, it must be bad news. Corrine meandered back into the bedroom and looked around at the few possessions Mr Talisbrook had left at the end of his life. A stack of paperback books, a pen he used for the crossword each morning, a scratched Victoria biscuit tin filled with a few old letters, and a packet of chocolate digestives on his bedside table. Inside his cupboard there was a tin of unopened Walker's shortbread his niece had sent him at Christmas. She'd come back for those later. Hanging on the wall were two framed pictures. The first was Mr Talisbrook with a woman she assumed to be his wife, taken what must have been at least twenty years earlier. She thought they looked happy, and hoped he hadn't been alone for too many years. The second was of a woman holding a newborn baby. Corrine had seen her visit. She'd guessed it was Mr Talisbrook's granddaughter. The baby was older now, probably nine months. The woman had asked her if she'd like to hold him. She'd desperately wanted to say yes. But in the end she'd shaken her head, and said she had to get back to work.

Walking out of the room, she stopped at the bedside cabinet and opened the top drawer. Three pound coins were loose at the front, and beneath that morning's crossword puzzle lay a ten-pound note. She scooped them into her pocket, and, as she did, she wished Mr Talisbrook all the best.

CHAPTER 35

'*Mostly crime but some human interest stuff?*' I say to Dani, laughing as we make our way around the North Circular.

'Police work is all about people,' she replies. 'I like to think of my main focus as being crime but balanced occasionally with some emotional work that can really pull at the heartstrings.'

'We'll make a writer of you yet,' I reply, as we head towards the motorway.

'So what's tonight's party?' Dani asks.

'My neighbour's wedding anniversary.'

'Good friends of yours?'

'Holly is – we've been friends since school. And I get on pretty well with Jake. I'm godfather to their daughter, Alice.'

'Nice to have them close by.'

'Definitely. Spending time with Alice is great, but it's good to be able to hand her back at the end of the day,' I say. 'I looked after her for a couple of hours the other weekend and we spent the whole time playing hide and seek. On her last hide, I couldn't find her anywhere. After ten minutes of increasingly desperate seeking, I called for her to come out. She didn't, and it was for no more than another two or three minutes, but for those moments, when I had no idea where she was, I was terrified.'

'Where was she?'

'She'd shut herself in a cupboard at the back of the kitchen and couldn't get out,' I reply. 'In the end she did call out, and I charged downstairs to rescue her. She thought it was hilarious, but my stomach was churning for the next half-hour. If I were a parent, my main focus would be keeping the child alive!'

'You'd be a great dad,' says Dani.

'I'm not sure about that. Not for a while, anyway. What about you? Kids on the horizon?'

'Me?' says Dani, her fingers edging towards her wedding band. 'I don't think so, no. We're not even six months married. Children might have to wait for a while yet.'

'Career first?' I ask.

'Something like that.' I wait for her to continue but she doesn't, and I sense she's keen to move the conversation on. 'You do know I can't get you off speeding tickets,' she says, as we start to make our way up the M1 towards Yorkshire.

'They won't do me for eighty.'

'You sound just like my dad, and he was in the police force. And to me that looks closer to eighty-five.'

With an exaggerated sigh, I do as I'm told and ease my foot off the accelerator.

'No point in sulking,' she says. 'You'll only get done by the cameras.'

'I'm not sulking, I'm just resting my lower lip,' I reply,

and, laughing again, we cross over the M25, a lone car early on Saturday morning. 'Surely your dad was exempt from speeding tickets?'

'We're not above the law,' says Dani. I give her a quick look and she rolls her eyes. 'Okay, perhaps a degree of flexibility on parking tickets, but nothing more than that.'

'I'll bet in your dad's day there was a bit more give and take.'

'I'm sure there was, but times have changed.'

We travel on in silence, the deserted road intermittently lit, until Dani turns to me again. 'Talk to me about Elizabeth Woakes,' she says.

I glance across at her. Her face is bright, illuminated by the neon of an approaching service station. 'Is that Dani asking, or Police Constable Cash?'

'Does it make a difference?'

'I want to trust you,' I reply, 'but for today to work it has to all be off the record.'

'I'm okay with that.'

I turn to meet her smile. 'And DS Barnsdale?'

'Ben, we've agreed off the record. Tell me about Mrs Woakes?'

'You met with her, right?' I say after a moment.

'Straight after we'd seen you.'

'And?'

'I asked first.'

'I've always liked her. She's been through a lot.'

'I could see that,' replies Dani. 'She doesn't like the police. I thought you were tough going until I met her.'

'A mother's pain is always far greater, however much she might try to hide it. And then there was her husband.'

'What do you mean?' asks Dani.

'When he disappeared, the police showed no interest. He'd already been homeless for two years, and the fact that he'd drifted away from Haddley was no concern of theirs. Eighteen months later, he was dead. Not your fault, but she blames the police.'

Dani nods in silence. After a moment she continues. 'I never like to say somebody lied outright, but she made a great show of not knowing about Demi Porter or Farsley. My guess is she already knew, either from your mum or whoever told your mum.'

I hesitate and can feel Dani's eyes on me.

'She knew, didn't she? When did she tell you?'

'Yesterday morning,' I admit. 'I had breakfast with her. But she's only been to Farsley once.'

'She's *been* to Farsley?'

'That doesn't mean anything,' I add hastily. 'She only went there for the day. It was more about Simon than anything else – a mother needing a connection. But I can't help wondering if there was something more she wasn't telling me.'

'Go on,' says Dani.

'Before Nick and Simon were killed, there were rumours circulating about Langdon and Fairchild, stories of them hanging out with older men.'

'Mrs Woakes told you this?'

'No, absolutely not, those stories are schoolboy gossip, but I did get the impression the rumours somehow made their way back to the school, perhaps even to her husband. And I got the impression when I spoke to Mrs Woakes yesterday that she was keeping something back. I thought perhaps she wanted to protect Peter's memory.'

'The headmaster and the schoolgirls? It's happened before.'

'That's not what I'm saying. He might have been aware of the stories is all I'm saying, but I've no doubt Peter Woakes was a good man.'

'You knew him?' asks Dani, and I recognise her acute ability to ask a simple question.

'No, but I know he was a good man.'

'That's because Elizabeth Woakes told you he was.'

CHAPTER 36

Holly closed her eyes tightly and controlled her breathing. Turning slowly, she feigned drifting in and out of a deep sleep. She could sense her husband awake beside her, feel his eyes upon her. Then she felt his touch upon her arm and his breath upon her neck. She curled her body to the edge of the bed. Moments later, when her daughter cried out from the neighbouring bedroom, she hated herself for the wave of relief that washed over her.

Jumping from her bed, she grabbed her phone and whispered to Jake as she left the room. 'I'm sure it's just a bad dream,' she said. 'You go back to sleep. I'll see to her. You must be exhausted.'

'Happy anniversary,' replied Jake, stretching his arms above his head. 'Don't be long.'

'Happy anniversary to you,' said Holly, a quick kiss on her husband's cheek.

Holly crossed the landing and entered her daughter's bedroom, where she found Alice sitting on the floor surrounded by her favourite toys. 'What are you up to?' asked Holly.

'Wrinkles was eating all the cakes,' replied Alice.

'Who?' said Holly.

'Wrinkles,' said Alice, holding up her cuddly dog. 'We're having a party. Me, Wrinkles, Woody and Snowflake. Wrinkles was being greedy.'

Holly pulled her daughter's duvet from her bed and nestled next to Wrinkles the dog, Woody the monkey and Snowflake the rabbit.

'Why can't I stay for all of your party tonight, Mummy?' said Alice, as she poured Woody another drink. 'And don't spill this one,' she reprimanded him.

'You'll be there for lots of it,' replied Holly. 'And you've got your new party dress to wear.'

'But I don't want to have to go to bed. I don't want to sleep in Grandma's house. I want to sleep at my house.'

'It's only if you get tired. I'm sure Grandma will have the bed all lovely and cosy for you.'

'Grandma doesn't like me.'

'What a silly thing to say. Of course she does.'

'Not like Grandpa loves me.'

'Grandma loves you as well, I promise. Why don't we walk over to her house this afternoon so you can be the first to see the party?'

'Before anyone else?'

'Yes.'

'Even before Daddy?'

'Yes, even before Daddy. You can help put up the balloons.'

'Can I have one? Or two? Or three, or four, or five, or six.'

'I'm sure you can,' said Holly, untangling the back

of her daughter's hair. 'I think we'll have to wash this before tonight.'

'Can Snowflake come as well? She loves parties. And Max.'

'I think Max might be at his daddy's house this afternoon.'

'Or he might be playing with Nathan. Nathan lives at Max's house now.'

'Sometimes he does.'

'Is Nathan Max's daddy now? He helped me on Max's slide. I wish I had a slide like Max,' said Alice, putting her arm around her mother.

'Max's daddy is still his daddy,' said Holly. 'Perhaps you could get a slide for your next birthday?'

Alice thought for a moment and then said, 'Wrinkles needs another drink. Will you pour it for him, please?' Holly picked up her daughter's teapot and poured an imaginary drink. 'If I can't have a slide until my birthday, can we go and play on the slides in the park?'

'When we're dressed and have had our breakfast.'

'And Daddy as well?'

'Yes, and Daddy as well if he wants to.'

'And Grandpa?'

'No, I don't think Grandpa will be coming round this morning.'

'Daddy can help me on the slide, then. I'm going to fill my teapot,' said Alice, picking up the pot and heading out of the room.

'Not too much water,' called Holly, hearing her daughter enter the bathroom. Quickly picking up her phone, Holly messaged Sarah.

Are you about this morning?

Lying in.

Lucky you!

Happy anniversary.

Thank you. I still need to talk to you.

Have you spoken to Jake?

I'm not going to change my mind.
I have to get away.

I'll help you if that's what you really want.
But what about Alice?

Alice needs to be with me.

Fathers have rights.

I'm not saying Alice won't see Jake.

Doesn't she need to be with her daddy as well?

Holly paused. Just typing the words made her hands shake.

Jake's not Alice's daddy.

CHAPTER 37

We drive up Farsley's main street and out on to the ring road, before turning off into the car park of the local super-market. Stepping out of the car, Dani arches her back and I stretch my arms, relieved to have reached the end of our almost five-hour journey.

'You sure this is the one?' I say to Dani.

She nods. 'It's not that big a town. This is definitely where Abigail worked.'

A shopping trolley hurtles towards us, caught in the wind howling across the exposed car park, and an attendant chases frantically after it. I run to stop it, grabbing hold of it, and the attendant thanks me. We joke that he's in for a busy day and then, as the rain starts again, Dani and I make a dash for the store entrance. Once inside, we take refuge within the McDonald's café, both of us ready for coffee and a breakfast sandwich.

'I'd say she's done a decent job of building the semblance of a new life around whatever it is she's hiding,' says Dani as she flicks her hair dry, scrunching her blonde curls as she does.

'Abigail Langdon?'

'Elizabeth Woakes.'

'You know I'm fond of her and her family. She is a good person.'

'In what way?'

'Dani, her son was brutally murdered and she was left to raise her daughter alone. I think she's done a pretty good job.'

'What you said in the car about her husband . . . '

'Simply that from talking to her I got the impression she was protecting him, or felt she needed to protect his memory.'

'So, hear me out,' says Dani, as we take out seats at a corner table. 'Somehow your mother and Elizabeth Woakes learn where Langdon has been located. Your mother tries to contact Langdon, convinced she has information to share. Who's to say Elizabeth Woakes didn't do the same but for a very different reason?'

'No way, this isn't about Mrs Woakes.'

Dani pauses for a moment. 'Your mother wanted to uncover a secret. Elizabeth Woakes wanted to protect one.'

'You've nothing to substantiate that. We're still speculating that Langdon even had information to sell to my mum. She could have been simply stringing her along.'

'Schoolgirls are groomed every single day of the week. Why not by Peter Woakes?'

Annoyed at my inability to quell Dani's speculation, I'm relieved when a voice comes from behind us to interrupt our conversation.

'Hullo again,' says the attendant from the car park.

'Hello,' I reply, turning. 'Do you want to join us?'

'No, no, very kind of you, but I'm only on a twenty-minute break. Thought I'd have a cup of tea to warm me through.'

'We're not stopping long ourselves, but nice to have a little bit of company,' I insist, getting to my feet.

'That's true enough,' he says smiling, and taking a seat next to us.

'Have you worked here long … Ted?' I ask, nodding towards his name badge.

'Seventeen years,' he replies. 'Started work when I retired,' he says, laughing at a line I'm sure he's used many times. 'Seventy-six, I am now.'

'You'd never believe it,' says Dani. 'You don't look a day over sixty.'

'She's a keeper,' replies Ted, smiling at me, and I think I blush. 'Little cracker. He's a lucky boy,' he says to Dani, looking at her wedding ring.

'We're not married,' I say, hurriedly.

'That doesn't worry me, not these days. Up to you how you live your lives.'

'No, I mean she's married to somebody else.' Now I do blush.

'We're colleagues,' says Dani. 'Journalists.'

'I see – like that, is it?' And I watch the smile vanish from Ted's face. 'That's why you were so keen for me to come and sit with you. Here's me thinking what a nice couple you were. Sometimes even I get the wrong first impression. Isn't it enough the poor lass is dead?'

'No, Ted, it's nothing like that,' I say, trying to row back rapidly. 'We stopped here for coffee and some breakfast,

nothing more. We work on sports radio; Dani's my pro-
ducer. We've come across from Manchester for the United
game this lunchtime.' Dani nods and smiles.

'That so?' replies Ted. 'I like a bit of football myself.
What's your name?'

'Oliver Hughes – you might have heard me. I do the commentary and then a phone-in after the match.'

Ted nods. 'Think I have, although half the time I'm not
sure you really know what you're talking about.'

'You can say that again,' says Dani, and we all laugh.

'Do you fancy Leeds' chances today?' I ask.

'No bloody hope,' replies Ted, emptying two sachets of
sugar into his tea. 'I'm sorry to have got a bit shirty just now.'

'Not at all,' says Dani soothingly, reaching across to Ted.
'Did you say something happened to someone at the store – a
girl died? It must have been a difficult time.'

'Terrible,' says Ted, rubbing his face with his hands. 'The
manager told us yesterday that it was Demi that'd passed.
With her not showing up for work, it didn't take much to
put two and two together when we heard about the discovery of the body in town.'

'That must have put a strain on everyone,' I say, biting
into my breakfast sandwich. 'Are people having to cover
Demi's work?'

'It's not like she ever did much,' replies Ted, dropping his
voice. 'She only ever really stacked shelves. Did a lot of night
shifts. They'd never let her on checkout. "Not customer-
facing", whatever that means.'

We sit quietly for a moment. I can see Ted is warming to

us, and I don't want to scare him off. Sure enough, he soon continues. 'I suppose she was a nice enough lass. Had a bit of a temper sometimes, but nothing too bad. A bit of a past, from what people said.'

'In what way?' I say, avoiding Dani's eye.

'It's not for me to say, but apparently she'd got mixed up in some pretty bad stuff when she was younger.' Ted lowers his voice conspiratorially. 'Drugs.'

Dani and I both try to look suitably shocked. 'Is that right?'

'They say she might have even been dealing.'

'Really?' I say.

'I'm not sure myself,' continues Ted.

'Sometimes you just can't tell,' says Dani.

'Ay, that's true, but these drug dealers, you see them on TV, they've always got plenty of money. Demi only lived in a one-bedroom flat above the curry house on the main street. She never had two pennies to rub together. Every week she was on the borrow to buy cigarettes or booze. I've no idea how she scraped enough money to pay her rent.'

'Did she have many friends here?' asks Dani.

'Now you are questioning me,' says Ted, wagging his finger at Dani. 'Let's just say she kept herself to herself.'

'The quiet type?' I say.

'Not sure about that. She never had a problem finding some fool willing to shout her a drink at the pub.'

I offer to buy Ted another cup of tea before we leave, but he tells us he'll be rushing to the gents' if he drinks any more. We all leave the store together and as we walk back across the car park I ask him, with everything she might have been mixed up in, did Demi ever seem scared?

'Not her. She always thought she'd get away with it one way or another. I guess this time she was wrong.'

CHAPTER 38

The alley behind Farsley's main street's terraced row of shops is deserted. A bottle man is clearing empties as Dani and I walk past the back entrance to the corner pub. Steam billows as we pass the launderette, and standing at the rear entrance of Gracie's hair salon is a stylist lighting an early-morning cigarette. Stairs descend from the first floor of every building along the terrace, each set leading up to two floors of accommodation. The gate at the back of the curry house is open, the yard filled with discarded boxes alongside blue bags ready for recycling.

Dani brushes my arm. She glances up towards a uniformed constable leaning lethargically on the railing at the back of one of the flats. His head is dropping forward, his eyelids drooping.

'That must be her place,' says Dani.

I don't hesitate. Quickly, I take the steps two at a time, signalling for Dani to follow me.

'Ben, no ... ' says Dani, but I am already at the top of the stairs.

'Constable,' I say, in a quick, sharp tone. Turning towards me, he frantically tries to stand upright and straighten his uniform. 'DS Leslie Barnsdale, Metropolitan Police. This is PC Dani Cash. Apologies if we woke you.'

'Sir, no, sorry, sir,' replies the constable. 'I was just . . . '

'Taking the weight off your feet?' I say, with a smile. 'I could see that.'

'Yes, sir,' he replies, gratefully. 'Taking the weight off my feet.'

'You know we're co-operating with the West Yorkshire Police on this. Nasty business.'

'Yes, sir. Up from London, are you, sir?'

'Could I have a word, sir,' Dani says to me, her eyes wide.

'Not right now, constable,' I reply.

'We're just here for the morning,' I say to the local constable. 'Open up, will you?'

He fumbles for a key before opening the door to Langdon's flat.

'We won't be more than ten or fifteen minutes.' I step inside and Dani follows close behind me. 'Close the door, Cash,' I say, as soon as we are inside.

'You know you can be imprisoned for impersonating a police officer? Lesley Barnsdale?'

'Gender-fluid,' I reply. 'Start looking. Anything that might tell us about her life since her release. Or anything to link her with Haddley.'

'Ben, you do know the police crime scene team will have been all over the flat already.'

'The same force that didn't know her identity was

compromised over a decade ago?' I reply, opening drawers and cupboards in the confined kitchen space. 'She was incredibly tidy,' I say, noticing the neatness and precision of Langdon's few possessions.

'Eleven years in custody,' replies Dani. 'You learn very quickly that everything has its place. And if you want to keep it, you put it away at night.'

'Nice that something good came out of it,' I say, as I walk through into a sparse living room. 'Fuck,' I say under my breath, before turning away at the sight of a light grey sofa caked in blood. Dani steps in front of me and looks down at the murder scene.

'A lot of blood,' she says calmly, 'but no major disturbance around the scene. No knife tears in the sofa, nothing to suggest there was a struggle. I'd say a single thrust and she was dead,' she continues, as I rub my fingers around my neck.

'Somebody enters through the kitchen, comes up behind her and before she knows it she's toast,' I suggest, standing at the side of the room.

'There's no sign of a break-in,' says Dani.

'Nice to know you were checking while I distracted the constable's attention. You think Langdon invited her killer in? If so, we can assume that in all likelihood they were already known to her. Could it be a drug deal gone wrong?'

'Not impossible. Somebody finds out how Nick and Simon were killed, then kills her in the same way to create a diversion.'

'Or, far more likely,' I say, 'it was somebody connected to her and the original killings. And connected to Haddley.'

On the far side of the room is a curtain, which I pull back to reveal a neatly made single bed with clothes tidily hanging on an open rail. 'Hardly living the high life,' I say, as I kneel down and pull open a drawer under the divan bed. 'Clean towels and a spare pillow.'

'Feels like she did little more than exist,' says Dani.

I look up at her. 'She had more existence than Nick.'

I crawl across the room and pull at a second drawer under the top end of the bed. It's blocked by a small bedside cabinet. I look inside the cabinet but there is nothing except for a novel by E.L. James. I push the cabinet to one side and open the second divan drawer. I'm hit by a mouldy smell of damp newspapers. Immediately, I recognise them. National editions from ten years ago. As I rifle through them, I see the same picture, over and over, staring up at me. My mum that evening on the banks of the Thames.

These are the reports of her death.

'I've got something,' I say, as I pull the papers out and spread them across the bed. I see Dani taking in my mum's face. I turn the page of a tabloid and again I see the infamous image of Nick and Simon standing side by side, smiling with their arms around the two killers. The day of celebration now only bringing horror.

As I turn away, I feel Dani's hand gently rub my back. 'You okay?' she asks.

'Seeing them here,' I reply, unable to hide a tremor in my voice, 'with her. It's as if she still had a hold on them.'

There is a rap on the kitchen door and, hearing it open, I scoop the newspapers back into the drawer.

'Excuse me, sir,' calls the constable from the kitchen.

'With you in a moment, officer,' I reply, and Dani hastens back through into the living room.

'We're almost ready to leave,' I hear her say.

I bundle the last of the newspapers into the drawer and as I do, from inside a copy of *The Times* falls an envelope. Instantly I recognise my mum's hand. I slip the letter into my inside jacket pocket before silently closing the drawer and edging the bedside cabinet back into place.

'Everything okay, constable?' I ask as I walk quickly across the room, passing him and heading straight for the back door of the flat.

'Yes, sir. I just wanted to let you know,' he replies, as Dani and I begin descending the rear outside stairs, 'that I've spoken to Inspector Kavanagh and he'd like to meet with you here at the crime scene in thirty minutes.'

'Excellent,' I say, as we reach the foot of the stairs. 'We'll grab a coffee and meet him back here.'

'Only thing is, sir, after your call yesterday, he was under the impression you were a woman?'

CHAPTER 39

From the corner of my eye, I see Dani glance back over her shoulder as I lead her through the yard and back out into the alley.

'Happy now?' she says, when we step out on to Farsley's main street.

I retrieve the envelope from my pocket and hold it up to her. I see the recognition in her eyes, before they narrow.

'You lie with unnerving ease, you impersonate a police officer, and now you remove evidence from a crime scene,' she says.

'Three good skills,' I reply, smiling.

'It's not funny, Ben.'

'Let's get into the car,' I reply, taking out my keys before starting to run down the hill towards the pub car park. 'We'll be back on the motorway long before Inspector Kavanagh arrives.'

I click open the locks and Dani pulls open the door to the passenger side. She says nothing until we're almost back on the ring road.

'What happens when he calls Barnsdale?'

'Could have been anybody,' I reply. 'And why would you impersonate yourself? Makes no sense.'

'Somebody impersonated me right down to the blonde curls?'

'That might be tricky, I'll give you that.'

'And who would even know Barnsdale and I are working on the case?'

'Well, what the hell was Barnsdale doing back down in London anyway? F-all, that's what.'

'Slow down,' says Dani, as I hit sixty. 'We don't want to get pulled over. And remember the cameras.'

'Yes, ma'am,' I reply.

'I get the feeling you don't take any of this seriously!'

'I've learnt not to worry about the little things in life. I'm going to find out the truth and I don't care what I have to do to get to it. Barnsdale can arrest me if she likes, but good luck with the press shitstorm that will unleash. I'm going to find out what happened to my mum, and Abigail Langdon's killer is going to help me.'

'I'll let you sell that to Barnsdale. You shouldn't underestimate her.'

We drive to the motorway in silence but, as we pass a convoy of military equipment heading south, I turn to Dani and ask if she can reach my jacket. She twists and pulls it from the back seat.

'It's in the zip pocket,' I say.

'You sure you want to do this now?' she asks, resting the envelope on her lap.

I glance across at the letter. 'I'd recognise my mum's handwriting anywhere,' I say, seeing the envelope addressed to Demi Porter.

'Why don't we read this when we stop? This is evidence.'

'No, let's do it now,' I say, switching lanes to pass a white transit van. 'I want to know what my mum said. If you don't want to do it, I will.'

Dani slowly picks up the envelope and carefully pulls out the letter from inside. I recognise the writing paper – cream, with our address printed on the top. My mum liked to send personal, handwritten notes whenever she could. As Dani unfolds the letter I can see it's just one sheet, single-sided.

'You want me to read it out?'

'Yes, please,' I reply.

'*Dear Abigail*,' Dani begins. '*I want to start by thanking you for writing back to me. That alone took real courage on your part and for that I am grateful. As I promised, I have destroyed your letter.*

'*As I said in my previous note, I don't have the kind of money you are asking for. I understand your current circumstances are difficult, but I believe I can help you in other ways.*

'*I wish I could have helped you when you were a girl. I am beginning to understand how miserable you were, how desperate. I wish I had known you then. I could have helped you find another release for your anger against all who surrounded you. Reading your letter, I have begun to understand the animosity you hold towards Haddley and some of the people who still live here.*

'*Which is why I am writing to you again. I feel certain you keep a deep secret, one you have been told to carry for the rest of your life. As a mother who has lost a child, I know that is an enormous burden to carry alone. I am not in the position to help you in the way that you ask, Abigail. But I believe I can help your child. You just need to tell me what you know.*

'Yours, Clare Harper.'

Six

*'A parent's love can be an irresistible force.
It's something that never fades.'*

CHAPTER 40

I push my half-eaten toasted cheese sandwich to one side. In the motorway café, raised high above the M1, Dani sits across from me slowly eating a quinoa salad. The sound of cars racing by beneath us blends with restaurant clatter and the low hum of self-conscious conversations held quietly in the open-plan space. But Dani and I sit in silence.

I'm aware of the rift that has opened up between us since we read my mum's letter. For Dani, the letter is evidence in a murder case and I have compromised her position. For me, I'm certain if we hadn't gone to Farsley the letter would have gone undiscovered and nobody would ever have known the real reason my mum contacted Abigail Langdon. I know now that my mum's desire to contact Langdon was never about redemption or forgiveness. It was about her belief that Langdon had given birth to a child and her hope that child could be Nick's. There are more questions I need to ask Madeline and Mrs Woakes. I'm not going to stop now.

'Could your mother have kept the letter she received back from Abigail Langdon?' asks Dani, finally breaking our silence.

'No. She was always as good as her word,' I reply.

'You went through all of her things?'

'Yes,' I reply.

'That can't have been easy,' says Dani, after a moment.

'Clearing out my mum's things was just another attempt at a fresh start in life. By the time we'd finished, Mrs Cranfield and I were on first-name terms with the team at the Shooting Star charity shop.' I get to my feet and tidy the plates from our table. 'I'm getting a coffee for the road,' I say. 'You want one?'

'I'm fine, thanks,' replies Dani. 'Going to nip to the loo. I'll meet you back at the car.'

Standing at the counter, I watch Dani walk across the café and head downstairs. I order my drink, clicking open my phone to pay, before hitting the number of Elizabeth Woakes. As the barista foams my milk, Mrs Woakes's voice tells me she can't reach the phone right now but if I leave a message she'll get back to me. I disconnect and type a series of short messages instead, giving a quick nod to the barista who asks if I want chocolate on my cappuccino.

I've been in Farsley this morning

I know why my mum contacted AL

Why didn't you tell me?

Did you know about the child too?

I'm still with the police

Please wait for me to call you

Back in the car and heading south, I see Dani's eyelids slowly droop and I'm glad. I listen to the football commentary of Oliver Hughes. Just north of London we leave the motorway and I'm pleased to be back on familiar roads heading through the capital towards Haddley. By mid-afternoon we're approaching the high street and I quietly call Dani's name. She stirs, and I can see she is surprised to be almost home.

'You should have woken me sooner,' she says.

'I thought you could do with the rest. Can I drop you somewhere?' I ask, realising I don't know where Dani lives.

'No, no, I'm fine,' she says, looking confused. 'Drop me at yours. I'll walk from there.'

We drive along the river road and turn on to Haddley Common.

DS Lesley Barnsdale is standing outside my house.

I glance at Dani but she's looking straight ahead. 'You called Barnsdale?' I say, quickly pulling into a space at the end of the road.

'I had no choice, Ben, I'm sorry.'

'What happened to off the record?'

'That letter is evidence.' And, before I can say anything more, she opens the passenger door and climbs out.

'I trusted you!' I say, slamming my door in frustration as

much with myself as with Dani. Stalking past her, I walk towards Barnsdale.

'Mr Harper,' says the detective, as I approach. I head straight past her.

'Mr Harper,' she repeats.

I get to my front door and slot the key into the lock.

'We need to talk,' she continues.

I open the door and, without invitation, she follows me inside. I walk through into the kitchen and, when I turn, she is standing in the doorway.

'Mr Harper, you are treading on very thin ice.'

I open the fridge door, taking out a bottle of water.

'Removing evidence from a crime scene, impersonating a police officer. I could arrest you now.'

'But you won't,' I say, opening the bottle, 'because the story of Abigail Langdon's murder would be on the front page of every news site and every newspaper in the country exposing your incompetent investigation.'

'Where's the letter?' she asks.

'I have it, ma'am,' replies Dani, now standing behind her superior.

'Give it to me,' says the detective, holding out her hand without looking at Dani. She opens an evidence bag and slips the letter inside. 'Wait for me by the front door, constable.'

Dani glances towards me but I turn my eyes to the window. When I look back, she is gone.

'Mr Harper, I am running this investigation,' says Barnsdale, stepping forward and standing directly across from me. 'Your job as an investigative journalist does not give you latitude to interfere with evidence or police procedure.'

'Detective, I will do whatever it takes to find out the truth about what happened to my mum. If that means stepping on your toes or anybody else's, that is exactly what I will do.'

'I shared information with you in the strictest confidence. You have betrayed that trust.'

'I've broken no confidences.'

'You've accessed a murder scene!' Barnsdale lets her anger show. 'A murder with which both you and Elizabeth Woakes are intrinsically linked.'

'As *victims*,' I reply.

'That remains to be seen,' says Barnsdale, and the threat in her tone is almost palpable. 'What I expect from you now, Mr Harper, is full co-operation with our investigation into the murder of Abigail Langdon.'

It's my turn to let my anger show. 'Detective, I increasingly get the impression I'm being viewed not as a victim but as a suspect. If you want to question me on that basis, go ahead and arrest me and we can make ourselves comfortable in an interview room.'

'Don't think I won't,' replies Barnsdale. 'I'm getting a very uncomfortable feeling that I made a mistake in sharing information with you.'

'Perhaps you did,' I reply.

Barnsdale stares at me across the kitchen. 'We require an additional sample of your mother's handwriting to verify the veracity of the letters.'

'I'm sure I can find something.' I stalk across the kitchen, past the officer and out into the hallway. 'Anything to assist your investigation.'

Dani looks towards me, but I go upstairs without acknowledging her. Standing at the top of the stairs, I hear Barnsdale drop her voice as she walks towards to Dani. 'I've taken a chance on you at a time when others wouldn't. I hope you're not going to let me down.'

'No, ma'am,' replies Dani.

'We have fresh evidence and a potential suspect to pursue. If I accept your explanation that things simply got out of hand, with Mr Harper acting impulsively, I'm sure I can find a way to position this as good police work.'

'Thank you, ma'am,' I hear Dani reply.

'Cash, I need to be one hundred per cent certain where your loyalties lie.'

'Yes, ma'am. Absolutely.'

'Good. Now, go and wait in the car,' she tells her junior, dismissing Dani from my hall.

Never having had the desire to redecorate the room at the top of the house that I still think of as Nick's space, I've let it gradually become more of a store room than a bed-room. I'm surrounded by the junk I've accumulated over the years – boxes of books I brought home from university, the CD collection from my teenage years, my mum's old kitchen table along with the last few possessions of hers I decided to keep. When I push aside the table, the door to the under-eaves storage is revealed. I crouch down to pull it open. Alongside another dusty stack of books are my mum's old Christmas decorations and two tattered old shoeboxes.

Inside the first I find a worn toy lion, his bright orange mane flattened and his tail hanging loose. I go to pick him up but then quickly close the lid and push the box back under the eaves. The second shoebox contains the final papers from my mum's estate. Inside are the handwritten instructions she left for her own funeral, instructions Mrs Cranfield and myself followed down to the last hymn. I glance over them, recognising the same precise penmanship I saw in her letter earlier in the day. I fold the paper and slip it into the back pocket of my jeans.

Having opened the box for the first time in years, I flick through the contents – old insurance documents, birth certificates, and the legal papers transferring ownership of my mum's house to me. I skim through to the bottom of the box and find a faded packet of printed photographs.

For the second time today I'm confronted with the infamous image of Nick and Simon with Langdon and Fairchild. This time it is the colour original. I inhale deeply, taking in the vibrant colours from the day – the bright blue sky, the boys' crisp white rugby shirts, the bright red school crest on their chests, Simon Woakes's freckled face, the rich black of Nick's hair, just the same as Mum's and mine. I flick through the rest of the pictures and realise it's the full set of images taken on the day of Haddley Grammar's rugby triumph.

'Mr Harper,' I hear Barnsdale call from downstairs, and I start to push the photographs back into their packet.

'I'll be down in a second,' I shout, and in my haste I drop the pile into the box. The pictures scatter and I see the photographer's name printed on the back of several of the images.

The name is Madeline Wilson.

CHAPTER 41

I pass the sample of my mum's handwriting to DS Barnsdale. After a quick glance she nods, satisfied. She will return the sample to me as soon as the police experts have had the opportunity to compare its characteristics with the letter.

'I do hope we can rely on your full co-operation from this point forward, Mr Harper,' she says from the open doorway, turning back to look at me. 'We all want to find Abigail Langdon's killer as quickly as possible.'

I don't say anything and she gives me a curt nod before leaving. I close the door behind her, then run back upstairs into Nick's bedroom and spread the photographs across his bed.

I stare at the image of Nick and Simon together. Then, in another, I see Mr Woakes standing with his son, pride radiating from him. I pick up an image where Mr Woakes stands with the whole of Nick's junior team. The boys are assembled under a Haddley Grammar school banner – so many of Nick's closest friends: Simon Woakes, Will Andrews, Gavin

Chance who emigrated to Australia, Neil Milton who runs a ski centre in Scotland. All from a lifetime ago.

I glance over more of the photos. Action shots from the seniors' game show Phil Doorley kicking a successful conversion and Jake Richardson running down the wing, cheered on by his father, Francis. Elizabeth Woakes shaking hands with the members of the winning team before handing the trophy to captain James Wright. And, on the back of each one, the photographer's name is printed. It seems that under every stone I turn, Madeline is revealed.

Surrounded by the images, I dial Elizabeth Woakes's number. Her answer is instant.

'Ben, where are you?'

'I'm back home. The police have just left. I found another letter in Langdon's flat, from my mum. The police have it now.'

'What did it say?'

'I think you can probably guess.' I wait for Mrs Woakes to reply.

'A child?'

'You knew?'

There's a pause.

'We met, your mum and I,' she says eventually. 'A couple of weeks after Langdon and Fairchild had been released. I was so angry. And so was Clare, except she'd already moved on. She'd been reading online; articles about Langdon and Fairchild. I never told you this because I wanted to protect you, protect us both.'

I say nothing.

'There was a huge amount of conversation around their release. I've no need to tell you, Ben, some of the crazy things people say online when anonymity protects them. There are a million and one different conspiracy theories about every famous case. And there are a lot of very cruel people . . . '

'I know,' I reply.

'Clare had started going into chatrooms. She'd begun to believe more and more of what she heard. People would say stupid things – that Simon and Nick were alive, that they'd been abducted, that they'd been taken as part of an alien invasion. She knew all of it was rubbish, of course, but one story was repeated over and over and she became convinced it was true.'

'She became convinced Abigail Langdon had a child,' I reply.

'Yes,' says Mrs Woakes, 'and that either Nick or Simon could be the father. With Madeline Wilson's arrival a few weeks later, your mum couldn't believe her luck. Suddenly she could be in direct contact with Langdon, discover the truth for herself.'

'But Langdon didn't want to tell her anything?'

'Not without a vast payment, and who knows even then what she would have told your mother.'

'And you? What did you think?'

'I never believed it.'

'Why not?'

'They were four children in the same class at school, but all the evidence we heard in court told us there had been no particularly close pre-existing relationship between them.

Simon and Nick were still only boys. On that day, when the boys climbed off the bus, the girls were waiting on the common. Simon and Nick followed them to Haddley Woods. I believe that whichever boys Langdon and Fairchild had found that day, they would have killed them. It just happened to be *our* boys.'

I think of Nick and Simon hesitating as they stepped from the bus on to the parched common. Tentatively following the girls, their rucksacks thrown over their shoulders. Nothing was prearranged; everything was by chance. Horrendous chance.

'Ben, I told Clare what I thought, but she didn't want to hear it. She was determined to press on, to find the child.'

I sit on the edge of Nick's bed and stare at the images spread out in front of me. I pick up the image of Nick and Simon with Langdon and Fairchild.

'I've found some pictures from the day of the rugby finals,' I say.

'From Langdon's flat?'

'No, among some old papers of my mum's. So many familiar faces – you and Mr Woakes, Simon and Nick. Everyone looks so happy,' I say.

'Briefly, we were,' replies Mrs Woakes. 'Langdon and Fairchild?'

'Yes,' I reply.

'Two silly teenage girls, that's all I saw on that day.'

'All anyone saw.'

'Perhaps,' says Mrs Woakes, before letting the line fall silent.

'Mrs Woakes?'

'You're right, I know you are, Ben, but when you spend a lifetime thinking about a single day you can't help wondering what you missed, what fleeting opportunity might have passed you by.'

'What might you have missed?'

'A million and one things, I'm sure.'

'But something in particular?'

Again, she pauses before continuing.

'You remember the senior championship game? It was so close. Some of the tackles during the match had been brutal.'

I gaze at the images spread out in front of me, my eyes drawn towards the blood-covered face of East Mailer.

'Twickenham Duke weren't used to losing, and the animosity between the two schools boiled over. When Jake Richardson scored the winning try in the dying seconds, the whole school spilt on to the pitch. The boys were ecstatic. I was delighted for Jake – he'd spent half the match looking towards the touchline, his father bawling instructions throughout the game. In the mêlée, shirts got ripped. Peter caught a derisive eye from E.E. Hathaway and immediately dispatched a number of boys to change ahead of the prize-giving.'

I pick up a photo of James Wright and Jake Richardson in pristine white Haddley Grammar shirts. 'Go on.'

'Right before the prize-giving, Peter sent Will Andrews back to the locker room. His shirt was torn almost to his waist. Instantly Langdon and Fairchild were in pursuit. Abigail leading Josie by the hand, they followed him straight in. I went in after them, banging the door open as I entered. The two girls instantly ran back out, screaming with laughter. Will claimed not to have seen them. There was nothing I could have said. Just a lifetime reflecting on two silly teenage girls that were anything but.'

CHAPTER 42

Corrine drained a third bottle of cider before stumbling towards the fridge a for a fourth.

'You want another?' she said to Chad, as he stretched himself out across her battered two-seater sofa.

'Better not, don't want to disappoint,' he replied, his inane grin showing the gold tooth at the side of his mouth.

Corrine flipped the top and swigged from the new bottle as Chad again looked at his watch. 'You worrying about getting home to your wife?' she said with a snigger. She sat opposite him on the stained armchair she'd rescued from Sunny Sea, after a resident's bequest of new lounge furniture. She doubted Molly would have spent the money if the will hadn't clearly stipulated it. When the new furniture arrived, she'd asked if she could take one of the old chairs from the yard and Molly had told she could have one for thirty quid. She'd told her to fuck off and two nights later Chad had brought his van to the back door. Molly had never even noticed the chair was missing.

I suppose he has been good to me, she thought, and she

went to sit beside him on the sofa. Curling her legs up, she leant forward and began to kiss his neck, then stopped. 'Chad! Stop looking at your effing watch.'

There was a tap on the window at the back of the living room.

'Four o'clock, bang on time,' said Chad, jumping to his feet.

'What the fuck . . . ?' said Corrine.

'I wanted to give us time to eat our fish and chips.'

Corrine watched as Chad went and opened the rear window, before helping Spotty Dean climb in from the top of the fire escape.

'Your wish is my command,' said Chad. 'Two for the price of one. It's your lucky day, Corrine.'

'You're having a laugh. No way, no fucking way,' she replied, as Dean stood motionless by the window, a tall, skinny streak of nothing in his white T-shirt and skinny jeans.

'Hi, Corrine,' he said.

'Get out,' was her reply, crossing towards them. 'Fucking get out, the pair of you!'

Dean froze, but Chad sprang forward and grabbed Corrine by the arm, pulling her aside into the kitchen. 'You owe me, remember. Those two coppers were back again this morning. I slipped them a few notes and told them you'd gone away for a couple of days, nothing for them to see here, and they were happy with that.'

Corrine pressed herself forward against Chad. 'You are a doll, but it's you I want to say thank you to.'

'Doesn't work like that, babe. I do you a favour and you do one for me. And Dean.'

Corrine closed her eyes. She would do as she always used to. Close her eyes and let her mind take her somewhere far, far away.

'We all good here, Corrine?' She opened her eyes and nodded. 'Come on, then, Deano, let's see what you've got,' said Chad, keeping a tight hold of Corrine's arm and leading her into the bedroom. 'Grab that empty bottle from the table,' he called to Dean, 'we might find a use for it.'

Walking into the bedroom, Corrine saw Dean stare at the windows. 'The skanky cow's only got cardboard up.'

She felt her face redden.

'Don't worry, Deano,' replied Chad. 'You're not fucking the window.'

CHAPTER 43

Holly held her daughter by the hand as Alice danced through the puddles along the edge of the St Marnham village pond. A row of ducks trailed behind, pursuing the chunks of week-old bread Alice was scattering in all directions. She crouched down and held out a large chunk towards the ducks nearest to her, squealing in delight when they pecked at the food in her hand.

'That's enough now,' said Holly, as the birds flapped beside her. 'Throw the bread out on the water.'

'But, Mummy, the ducks like to be near me,' replied Alice.

'I know they do. It's because you're feeding them,' said Holly, jumping backwards as two more birds landed at her feet.

'Don't be scared, Mummy,' said Alice, happily surrounded by the flapping animals. 'They won't hurt you.'

Holly smiled at her daughter. 'Thank you, darling, but I think we've fed the whole bird population of St Marnham. Throw the last of your bread on the water.'

Alice tore apart the paper bag and emptied its remaining contents on to the edge of the pond.

'Come on, let's go,' said Holly, as three geese sped towards them. 'Grandma will be waiting for us.'

Holly moved away from the water and stepped up the sloping bank that surrounded the pond. Seeing her mother leave, Alice splashed along the edge of the pond and hurried after her. 'Mummy?' she said, taking hold of Holly's hand as they crossed towards the Richardsons' home. 'Will I need to take my muddy boots off to go into Grandma's house?'

'You definitely will.'

'But I don't have any other shoes with me, so I might need to keep them on.'

'You can play in your socks inside.'

Alice thought for a moment. 'My feet might get cold,' she said, looking up at her mother.

'Not at Grandma's house, they won't.'

'No,' replied Alice. 'Grandma has hot floors.'

'She does,' said Holly. 'Your feet will be super-cosy.'

'Can we have hot floors at our house?'

'It costs a lot of money, so probably not right now.'

'Grandpa could pay for it. He's got lots of money.'

'Has he?' replied Holly.

'He bought my swing, my house in the garden and Daddy's car.' Holly said nothing. 'He would buy us a hot floor if we asked him.'

'Grandpa can't pay for everything,' Holly said, more sharply than she intended, and Alice looked up at her in surprise. 'It's very kind of Grandpa when he buys something . . .'

241

Holly crouched down to look at her daughter, ' . . . but, Alice, money isn't everything. Us being together and happy is far more important.'

'Grandpa says with money you can buy whoever you want.'

'Well, sometimes Grandpa is just plain wrong.'

Holly took her daughter by the hand and led her up the curved gravel driveway that fronted the home of Francis and Katherine Richardson. Art deco in design, the house commanded an imposing position. With a vista across St Marnham, it cast a shadow on all of the village inhabitants. Arched glass windows dominated the property, with an elongated outdoor terrace on the first floor where that evening's celebration would take place.

As they approached the bright blue front door, Katherine Richardson was waiting outside, immaculately dressed in a cream trouser suit, her hair backcombed with precision.

'Did I see you feeding the ducks?' said Katherine to her granddaughter.

'Three ducks came and ate from my hand,' replied Alice.

'I saw you from my upstairs window.'

'You should have come out and joined us,' said Holly.

'I don't like to go too near the pond.'

'It is very muddy, Grandma,' said Alice. 'You would need to have wellington boots on like mine.'

'And look how much mud there is on yours!'

'I can take them off here,' replied Alice, immediately sitting down on the driveway.

'You are a good girl,' replied Katherine. 'When you're

ready to go home we will wash the mud off under the garden tap.'

'You can't see it, Grandma, but my boots are pink and have yellow flowers on them.'

'How lovely. I wish I had some like that.'

'I'm sure Grandpa would buy you some,' said Alice, before biting her lip and looking up at Holly.

'Shall we go inside?' said Katherine. 'Everything's almost ready for this evening.'

'Have you got lots of balloons?' asked Alice.

'The house is full of them.'

'Can I see?'

'Run upstairs and see if you can find them all,' said Katherine, her tall, slim frame stepping aside as her grand-daughter charged inside. 'Do come in, dear,' she continued, leading Holly inside her home.

Walking across the black and white spiral-tiled hall and up the vast, winding stone staircase, Holly felt constantly overwhelmed. She followed her mother-in-law into the drawing room, where light poured in from the floor-to-ceiling windows with their all-encompassing view of the village. It had taken Katherine years to refine this room, to source each of the exquisite art deco originals, the dramatic lighting, the gold-leaf wallpaper and curved velvet furniture. Above the open fireplace hung an image that struck fear into Holly every time she entered the room. Dominating its surrounds was an original painting of her father-in-law. It portrayed him from only the neck down, dressed in a black suit, white shirt and red tie.

Despite showing no face, it unmistakably depicted Francis Richardson – and the control he exercised.

'No Francis this afternoon?' asked Holly, as Alice, clutching three balloons, skipped past.

Under brightening skies, Katherine and Holly stepped out on to the terrace, where designers were putting final touches to floral decorations. 'He's out entertaining himself,' replied Katherine, before inviting Holly to take a seat beside her at the mosaic dining table, an outdoor heater burning behind them. 'I'm happy, providing he keeps himself out of my hair,' she continued, pouring three glasses of fresh lemonade. Holly gently nodded. 'I doubt he'll be back much before seven,' Katherine went on. 'As long as he leaves himself enough time to get cleaned up.'

Still holding her balloons, Alice came to the table and picked up a drink.

'Careful,' said Holly to her daughter. 'Grandma doesn't want any spills.'

'I am careful,' said Alice, before putting the glass down and wiping her hand across her mouth.

'Good girl,' said Katherine. Alice ran back across the terrace to look down at the ducks in the pond. 'Her daddy used to love those ducks. She must have got that from him.'

'Both Jake and I are hugely grateful to you and Francis. The whole house looks incredible,' said Holly, as two waiters, carrying the base of a champagne tower, cautiously stepped outside.

'Under the awning,' said Katherine, instructing the waiters to a covered corner of the terrace.

'It really wasn't necessary to go to so much trouble.'

'I enjoy it.'

'But the cost! It's so generous of you.'

'I let Francis worry about that. For me, the pleasure is in being able to do this for you both. I only wish I could give you more.'

'This is more than enough.'

Katherine smiled, but weakly, and Holly thought of the gifts amassed in their loft room. As if she could see them too, Katherine said, thoughtfully, 'Jake has always valued his independence. He's been like that from a young age. I remember after prep school he was desperate to go to boarding school like all of his friends. Francis refused, said he'd learn the value of hard work by staying at Haddley Grammar. He thought it would keep him grounded. Jake was devastated. For the next two years he barely left his room, as if it were his own personal dormitory.'

Holly smiled. 'He can be very stubborn.'

'He definitely gets that from his father,' replied Katherine.

'That's always been a difficult relationship?'

'Somehow they've always failed to meet each other's expectations. Occasionally their aspirations collide, just as when Jake set up his business, but, as we know, rapidly they diverge again in different directions.'

'Leaving you caught in the middle?'

'Something like that. I've always wanted to give Jake as much as I possibly could; Francis has wanted him to earn every single thing, including his love. Somewhere through it all, I suppose we should have been able to find a middle way.'

'None of us would ever pretend raising children is easy,' replied Holly. 'Where is Francis this afternoon, anyway? Is he golfing?' she asked before immediately regretting her question.

'I don't think he has his clubs with him, dear,' replied Katherine and, under her mother-in-law's gaze, Holly felt her face begin to flush.

CHAPTER 44

Damp hung in the air as Dani Cash slowly trudged back up Haddley Hill towards her home. She could feel her hair frizz in the dank, but, exhausted, she didn't care. She imagined herself soaking in a long, hot bath as Mat brought her a chilled glass of sauvignon blanc while she submerged herself beneath the bubbles. Trying to remember such a time during their brief relationship, she found it was an impossible image to conjure.

Her conversation with Barnsdale at the station had been short. After again reprimanding her for her actions and seeking further assurances of her loyalty, the detective sergeant had focused her attention on both Ben Harper and Elizabeth Woakes.

'I've briefed the DCI and from this point forward both are to be treated as suspects,' Barnsdale had said.

'I just don't see it,' Dani objected.

'Don't see what? He impersonated a police officer and removed evidence from a murder scene. Elizabeth Woakes lied to us directly. One way or another, both are clearly involved.'

'If Ben's mother had told him Langdon's location ten years ago, why go and kill her now? It makes no sense. Ben isn't a killer,' Dani had argued as she sat with her superior officer in one of the station's claustrophobic meeting rooms.

'Ben, is it, now?' Barnsdale had replied. 'I hope your judgment isn't getting clouded. I don't like him. He's too pushy.'

'Because he found out stuff we didn't?'

'I've warned you, Cash. You need to back off. I want you in here tomorrow and I want you to find everything you can on Ben Harper and Elizabeth Woakes. I will be working with West Yorkshire Police to gain access to the original case files.'

'Do you know if there was a child, ma'am?'

'That is something I'm going to have to find out.'

Dani had gone to leave through the front of the station, only to see PC Karen Cooke sitting beside the desk sergeant. 'Please don't tell me they're letting you work on any real crimes,' she had called, as Dani walked towards the exit. 'Hear you've been moonlighting today. Impersonating a senior officer. You should watch yourself.'

'Or what?' Dani had replied, before immediately regretting engaging.

'Just found it odd that you'd head off on your little road trip, leaving Mat at home all day on his own.'

Seeing Cooke, shoes off, feet up, lounging behind the desk, Dani had felt the urge to throttle her. 'I'm sure Mat coped just fine.'

'He did,' she said with a knowing smile. 'I made sure of that.'

Dani took a single step back towards Cooke.

'No trouble please, ladies,' had been the desk sergeant's unhelpful contribution.

'You keep away from Mat,' said Dani.

'I've already told him I'll pop back later in the week. Hate to think of him being left on his own.'

Dani shoved the signing-in book across the desk towards Cooke.

'That's enough,' said the sergeant.

'Got your dad's temper, haven't you?' said Cooke.

'I said, enough.'

Leaving the station, Dani knew she'd been stupid. She kept staring straight ahead, walking up the hill and past Haddley General's Accident and Emergency department. Each time she passed the building she was transported back to last Hallowe'en, the raw panic she had felt travelling behind the ambulance as it sped Mat to the hospital.

Moments after the alarm had been raised, Mat had entered the rear of the gourmet supermarket. Dani had broken free but chaos had erupted. Only minutes later, she was seated in a police car with another officer driving her under lights. Dani had been desperate to keep the ambulance in sight. Jumping from the car in the ambulance bay, her uniform covered in blood, she'd run alongside the stretcher as the A&E doctors had raced Mat into surgery. As she'd waited, fear had taken hold. Relief had poured over her at the news he would live; and then devastation had consumed her when she was told he was unlikely ever to walk again.

Sitting beside his hospital bed, she'd been desperate to give back to Mat the life they might have enjoyed.

Yes, she said, she loved him.

Yes, they should buy a house.

And yes, they should get married.

Four weeks later, on the day Mat was discharged, they were.

In the months since, Mat's early optimism had quickly faded. Instead his anger had amplified. Each day, Dani had understood more deeply the desperate mistake she had made.

And her guilt had become all-consuming.

Now, as she arrived home, she couldn't face another night of arguments. Silently she opened her front door and quietly made her way upstairs to draw herself a long, hot bath.

CHAPTER 45

Her hair curling softly around her face, Alice Richardson danced across the terrace in her sparkly blue party dress. Waving to her grandpa as she went, she delighted guests as she showed them her special golden-toed shoes. Holly and Jake greeted friends, a few of whom were theirs, many more those of his parents'. Flashing bright white smiles, they kept moving forward, both reaching for a glass from a champagne-laden tray as it glided past. The three of them then posed for pictures, a fairy-lit walled garden beneath them.

While the photographer snapped, Holly looked across the terrace to see her father-in-law in relaxed conversation with Sarah and her boyfriend, Nathan. She watched the three of them break into easy laughter and, as they did, Francis imperceptibly moved forward, touching Sarah on the arm before letting his hand curve down her body and fleetingly rest upon her waist. Holly wanted to open her mouth to scream a warning to her friend.

Feeling a touch upon her arm, she turned.

'He's just testing the water,' said Katherine, suddenly at

Holly's side as the photographer dissolved into the party and Alice twirled across the dance floor with her daddy. 'Walk with me,' she continued, smiling politely at a pair of new arrivals. Holly drained her champagne but as she reached for another glass she felt Katherine's hand firmly upon hers. Her mother-in-law held her arm before leading her back across the terrace and into the quieter drawing room.

'I've been watching you,' said Katherine.

'It's a wonderful party,' replied Holly, anxious to hide her unease.

'I don't mean this evening. I mean over recent weeks, months. I have no wish to cause you discomfort,' continued Katherine, as Holly felt herself colour, 'but sometimes within a marriage an understanding exists; something that allows a marriage to survive.'

From the drawing room, Katherine took Holly through into the music room, where a polished black grand piano stood beside the richly draped window.

'Francis and I have such an understanding. With you I was never certain, not until this afternoon.' Holly felt her face burn red. 'Tell me why,' said Katherine. 'Is it what you need to make your marriage work?'

'No, nothing like that.' There was a shudder in Holly's voice.

'I feared not. Please, then, tell me why.'

'I can't.'

'I don't believe Francis ever forces himself upon a woman, but he's not afraid to use whatever influence he has. Is it money? I know he pays most of your bills.'

Holly shook her head. 'Please,' she said, 'it won't happen again. I promise.'

Katherine took her daughter-in-law by the hand and led her to the piano stool. 'Sit down,' she said. 'I don't care about Francis. It's you I want to help.'

Holly gulped for air and Katherine looked at her steadily. 'Does Jake know?'

'He has no idea,' replied Holly.

'Good, he must never. It would destroy him. And ... Alice?' asked Katherine, hesitantly.

'No, God, absolutely not!'

'No, I mean, is she Jake's daughter?'

Holly dropped her head, and Katherine ran her fingers along the side of the polished piano.

'I've always wished I could play,' she said. 'I was meant to take lessons when I was younger. My mother had an old Steinway that had belonged to her grandmother. The tone had gone, but she still insisted on reciting a piece each morning. She was technically adequate, no more than that. I grew to hate her heavy-handed sunrise performances as they reverberated around the house. You may find it hard to believe, but I rebelled, refused to take any lessons. I regret that now, of course, but I never felt any desire to please her. Throughout my life, when I needed her most, she was oddly absent.' Katherine paused. 'Perhaps Alice would like to learn? It seems such a waste having it here and nobody playing it. I'd love for her to take lessons.'

'That would be nice,' replied Holly, looking up towards Katherine.

'Your eyes tell me something else.'

'No, it would be lovely, really.'

'I wonder if you'd rather just escape the whole Richardson clan. We can't be easy to live with.'

'I don't want to hurt Jake.'

'Especially while he might have a hold over your daughter?'

Katherine walked back down the side of the piano and sat with Holly on the piano stool. Gently touching the higher keys, she faced her daughter-in-law. 'The bond between a mother and a daughter should be impenetrable. That's what I wanted, and that's why I want to help you.' She lifted her hand from the keys and rested it upon Holly's. 'You have to believe me. I made the commitment on the very first day that everything would be different with my own daughter. And it was. But all it did was increase the agony when I lost her. I don't want you to ever feel that pain.'

CHAPTER 46

Having spent the day driving five hundred miles before confronting DS Barnsdale, I've no great desire to spend Saturday evening at Holly and Jake's party and am already running late. Nevertheless, aware that Madeline is on the invitation list and is likely to attend, I set out across Haddley Common. Repeatedly during the afternoon, she hasn't picked up any of my calls nor answered any of my messages. When I think of her photographs from Richmond Rugby Club, I know she has still told me only half the truth.

'Lunch at one tomorrow?' calls Mrs Cranfield, as I walk on to the common. I turn and head back across to her garden, where she is tidying away her husband's gardening tools. 'Best part of the day,' she continues, looking up at the reddening sky. 'Where are you striding off to?'

'Holly's party,' I reply, sitting on the wall at the front of her home.

'You look exhausted,' she says. 'Off before dawn and then partying all night.' She pushes my hair back off my forehead. 'If only we could see your face.'

'I'm going to get it cut but I've been busy.'

'My poor Ben,' she replies. 'What you need is someone to take care of you.'

'You never let up!' I laugh, and as she locks the padlock on her husband's shed she invites me in for a quick drink.

'Just ten minutes, Mr C would love to see you. He'll run you over to St Marnham.'

Unable to say no, I follow her into her steam-filled kitchen where pots are bubbling on the stove. 'Something smells good,' I say.

'Nothing special. Coddled pork with cider.'

'Sounds good to me.'

'One of my favourites,' says Mrs C. 'I remember my own mother making it for me the day we moved back to County Clare. I was distraught at the thought of moving back home and she always knew how to cheer me up. But no doubt you'll all be having some lovely food this evening.'

'Just canapés, I should think.'

'It'll all be very fancy. No expense spared at the Richardsons'.'

'I'm hoping for mini burgers!' I reply.

'Beer, Ben?' asks Mr Cranfield, entering the room and opening the fridge.

'No, thanks, I'm good,' is my unheeded reply as he pops open a bottle. 'Just a small glass for me, then, and nothing strong,' I say.

'Where were you headed in the middle of the night?' he asks, as Mrs C starts peeling potatoes in the sink.

'You don't miss a trick,' I reply.

'When you get to my age there are always a few night-time bathroom visits.'

'Like a jack-in-a-box, he is, some nights,' says Mrs C.

'I drove up to Yorkshire,' I reply. 'I found some people I thought I should speak to.'

'About your mum?' asks Mr C.

'Kind of.' I take a seat at the cloth-covered kitchen table. 'I'm starting to get an idea of what might have been on her mind.'

'That morning?' he continues, pulling his well-cushioned chair from the table and sitting across from me.

'I shouldn't be telling you this, but it looks as though during the last few weeks of her life my mum was in contact with Abigail Langdon.'

A sudden strain appears on Mr Cranfield's face and he glances towards his wife.

'Ben, I know you want answers, but promise me you're being careful,' she says, turning from the sink.

'Don't worry, I promise,' I say, with a smile.

'What makes you think she made contact?' asks Mr C.

'They exchanged letters. I've seen one of them; I can't say how. I think it had something to do with a child.'

Mrs Cranfield puts down her knife and rinses her hands under the hot tap before wiping them on her apron. Taking a wine glass from her cupboard, she says, 'I'll just have half a glass, George,' and then joins us at the table. I see them share a look as Mr C pours a generous half-glass of red wine before pushing the cork back in the bottle.

Mrs Cranfield rests her glass between her hands before she takes her first sip.

257

'We were sat together at this table,' begins Mrs C. 'Your mum and me. It never felt right to tell you before, but perhaps we should have. We were protecting a secret she had discovered.'

My mouth feels suddenly dry and I swallow. 'You knew about it?'

'She told me what she'd found out. Or what she suspected, I should say. She wouldn't tell me how she knew and she swore me to secrecy. I told her she shouldn't listen to silly gossip but she was convinced – *convinced* – that Abigail Langdon had had a child.'

'When was this?' I ask, and as Mrs C looks towards her husband I see she still believes she is betraying my mum's trust. 'Please.'

'It would have been two or three weeks before she died,' says Mrs Cranfield, taking another sip from her glass before gently placing it on the table in front of her. 'She despaired at the thought of Nick having a child and it not being with her. I told her it might be impossible for her even to find out if that girl did have a baby, let alone where it might be. She didn't care. In that way that she could be, she was absolutely determined.'

I slowly nod my head; Mrs C is confirming what I already thought to be true.

'I wanted to help her, of course I did, but I didn't know how. Your mum said she would never give up until she knew the truth.' Mrs C brushes away a tear and I put my hand on hers. 'All I could do was ask her to make me the same promise I ask of you.' She looks at me intently. 'To always be very careful.' Standing up to leave, I hug Mrs Cranfield and make her the promise.

When Mr C pulls out of our road and we stop at the temporary traffic lights on the Lower Haddley Road, he turns to me. 'Eight weeks they've been digging up these drains. I bet the Victorians built them quicker.'

I smile. 'Sorry to drag you out,' I say. 'I could just as easily have walked over.'

'Not a problem,' he replies. 'Dinner will be half an hour yet, and we don't want you being late for the big party.'

'I'm only going for Hol's sake really,' I reply. 'Doubt I'll be staying too late.'

We edge forward towards the lights but they turn red again before we reach the junction.

'Did you know?' I ask, looking at Mr Cranfield under the glowing red light.

'Not until after your mum was gone. Mrs C and I talked about it and we decided it was better letting things rest. It wasn't that we wanted to keep it from you, Ben – we simply wanted to give you the space to live your own life.'

Feeling no anger, I ask, 'If my mum was so convinced there was a child, and it gave her hope, then why ... ?'

'Why would she kill herself?' Mr C turns to me. 'I don't know, Ben. I've never understood that.'

'Would she put herself in danger for Abigail Langdon's child?'

'For the chance to discover a bond with Nick, I think she would. A parent's love can be an irresistible force. It's something that never fades.'

'If there was a baby, I find it hard to believe it was Nick's. There's no evidence of a real relationship between him and Langdon. I spoke to Elizabeth Woakes and she feels the same about Simon.'

We pull forward, making our way past Haddley Woods and into St Marnham. Mr C stops the car alongside the village pond and turns to me.

'Ben, none of us can know for certain if that child was Nick's, or even if there was one. But if I had to put money on it, I'd say there was more to it than that.'

'What are you saying?'

'When we moved to Haddley it was almost a year after the end of the trial. Every day I'd see Peter Woakes taking the same relentless walk, along the riverbank and through the woods. He was pitiful. You couldn't help but feel for him. By then he was basically living rough, and whenever I got the chance I'd slip him a couple of quid. Nobody wants to see a man in that state, especially after all he'd been through. A few times I sat with him by the water's edge, took him a pint from the pub. He was a broken human being.'

'I remember.'

'The loss of a child is a desperate thing but it was more than that: he felt guilt. His regret was not acting when he'd had the opportunity, and that ate away at him. Each time I saw him, he went over the same ground. If only he'd have acted when he had the chance, if only he'd acted.'

I think of my breakfast with Mrs Woakes and then her unease on the day of the rugby finals. 'Before the killings, had he heard stories about Langdon and Fairchild?' I ask.

'Not long before he disappeared for good, I found him sat on a bench by the embankment. I bought him a pint. And as always, he talked of his regret for not acting when he might.'

'But what was it that he felt he should have acted on?' I ask, wanting to glimpse inside Mr C's fractured memories.

'During that last summer term, there had been a call to the school. He'd dismissed it as little more than gossip, but in hindsight he was agonised. He said he kept going over and over it in his mind.'

'What did the call say?'

'I don't know. I never saw him again.' Mr C looks across the pond towards the Richardsons' floodlit party. 'If I'm honest with myself, Ben, my biggest regret is not doing more to help him.'

This time it's me who reaches across and clasps Mr C on the shoulder. I step out of the car and make my way around the edge of the pond. As I reach the driveway of the Richardsons' brightly illuminated home, I turn and see Mr Cranfield slowly walking from his car towards the village pub.

Seven

'One of those damp, misty afternoons where you can't get warm and should be safe inside.'

CHAPTER 47

'Ben! Over here!' Jake Richardson cries as I enter his parents' drawing room and he beckons me to join him and a small group of friends. 'A glass of champagne for this man,' he says, sending one of the waiters hurrying in my direction. I take a half-filled glass before Jake returns his own empty glass and picks up another. 'Just bring a bottle over,' he says, despatching the waiter back to the bar. 'You know Martin and Duncan from the village. Their kids go to nursery with Alice.'

We exchange brief introductory nods and I quickly scan the room in search of friends who might rescue me.

'It was like this. Bored out of my mind, I down a second pint, finish my pork pie and drive through this sleepy little village that made St Marnham look like a bloody metropolis.' Martin and Duncan laugh when required and I realise I have arrived in the midst of Jake drunkenly reciting the highlights of his work week. 'I'm absolutely knackered, having spent two days filling the pockets of those shits my own father sold my company to – the company *I started* – so

I decided to give myself the afternoon off, beginning with a doze under a tree. I'm just dropping off and there's this annoying knocking on the window of my Audi. I half-open one eye to see an old military stick peering through the window. At first I think I'm having a bloody nightmare and that it's my old man – that will tell you exactly the sort I was dealing with. I close my eyes and ignore him but he starts again – *ra-ta-tat-tat, ra-ta-tat-tat*. I crack the window. Calls himself Major Edwards – I cannot stand ex-military types who still use their rank – and says would I mind moving on? "Bloody free country," I tell him, and of course he doesn't miss a beat in telling me he fought for that freedom. Then he tells me my presence is causing nervousness among "the ladies of the village". "Chance would be a bloody fine thing," I say. I push myself up in my seat and ask him to explain. He soon takes a step back when I go for the door but still keeps going on about anxiety among "the ladies". I ask the bloody busybody if he's actually spoken to any of them but before he can say anything more I make like I'm about to jump out. Quick as you like he stumbles back and falls flat on his back in the thick mud. I couldn't resist taking a photo.'

Jake reaches for his phone while grabbing hold of a bottle of champagne from the waiter. He refills his own glass and then tops up those of Martin and Duncan. As he does, I feel a touch on my elbow. I turn to see Will Andrews standing beside me.

'In need of rescue?' he asks, quietly.

'You're a godsend,' I reply, excusing myself from Jake's

group. As we cross the drawing room I can still hear Jake planning to pillory Major Edwards's puce face.

'Sorry for not giving you more time yesterday, Ben. You caught me on a bit of a bad day,' Will says.

'No need to apologise. Nothing worse than being interrupted by a nosy journalist when you're trying to get some work done.'

Will laughs and suggests we step out of the crowded room and into Francis's study, which has been set up for whisky-drinkers later in the evening.

'This is all very *Francis*,' I say, as we enter the wood-panelled room. I look up at the bookshelves filled with first editions.

'I'm not sure how many of those have actually been read,' says Will, 'but they do look impressive.'

'And that's very important to Francis.'

'Of course. Shall we be the first to try the whisky?' asks Will, reaching for one of the four single malts placed on display.

'I think I've had my fill for this week,' I say, holding up my hand.

Will pours himself a double shot before sitting beside me in one of the high-backed leather chairs. 'I really did want to take a moment to apologise. There's no joy for any of us in remembering that summer, but if there's any way that I can help you ... ' He trails off.

'You asked me on Wednesday night at the restaurant what it would mean if my mum hadn't taken her own life,' I answer, 'and I said it was impossible for me to say. If you asked me now, I'd say it means somebody else killed her.'

267

Will takes a sip from his glass. In the cool of the study it is his only reaction.

'I believe my mum's death is linked to what happened that summer, to the possible existence of a child, and to someone who was more involved with Langdon and Fairchild than we could ever imagine.' I turn to Will. 'Tell me what you meant when you messaged me about "all kinds of men". Did you see them with someone?'

'No, I never saw them myself.' Will continues to slowly drink from his glass. 'During the previous school year, though, the chat had gone around that Josie had been with some of the older boys. It gave her a reputation, around school. Let's just say that once it became known ... well, kids can be pretty cruel. I'm not making excuses for her, but she came in for some harsh treatment, even from Abigail at first.'

'My heart bleeds,' I say, coldly.

'Josie was ostracised, bullied remorselessly, and not just by our class but by the whole year. The psychological assaults were relentless.' Will pauses and then he starts to whisper. 'Josie's a slag, Josie's a slag. That was the chant, over and over, every time she entered a room. Anywhere in the school, every hour, every day. And then, the beat would follow, quietly at first ... ' Will starts to beat the rapid rhythm on Francis's desk. *Ra-ta-tat-tat. Ra-ta-tat-tat.* 'Josie's a slag. Josie's a slag. Building and building.' *Ra-ta-tat-tat. Ra-ta-tat-tat.* 'Rising to a crescendo, wherever she went. Faster and faster. Louder and louder. Josie's a slag ... '

'Enough!' I cry, and for a moment we are silent.

'Every boy, every girl, every day. When we couldn't chant, we would simply rap out the beat.'

'There are no excuses for what Langdon and Fairchild did,' I say. 'None.'

'I know that,' he says. 'Abigail saw her weakness and became her only friend. Each seduced by the evil in the other. All I'm saying is, it wouldn't have taken much for someone else to witness their alienation – and find a way to prey on it.'

CHAPTER 48

Holly stood in the drawing-room doorway and watched in horror as a silver tray, loaded with champagne glasses, flew across the terrace. As Jake landed on top of a hapless waiter, she brought her hands to her face and found herself desperately wishing for the night to be over.

'He's drunk already,' called Francis Richardson, with a callous laugh. 'Bloody embarrassment,' he continued, shouting across to his wife, who appeared in the doorway alongside Holly. 'Somebody drag him to his feet.'

'Nothing to see here,' said Katherine, a sharp rebuke to her husband. With a swift wave of her hand, two waiters instantly had Jake propped up in the corner of a burgundy-red velvet sofa. 'Strong black coffee and a glass of water,' she continued, firing instructions as the broken glass was swiftly swept away. 'And then something to eat. Nothing too rich – a couple of slices of toast is probably best.' She took the arm of the head waiter, and spoke to him so quietly that only Holly, the closest to them, could hear. 'Let him drink the coffee and then take him down to the kitchen. Hold him there for thirty minutes at least. And keep him away from his father.'

'I'm so sorry,' said Holly. 'I feel just awful. You've put so much effort into the party and this is how we repay you.'

'Don't give it another thought,' replied Katherine. 'We all know the party is really for Francis. This has only heightened his enjoyment.' Holly turned to look at Katherine, shocked. 'Each takes a cruel delight in the other's failings,' she said, linking her arm through Holly's and leading her out of the drawing room. 'They've always been like that. Has Jake ever told you about his twelfth birthday?'

Holly shook her head.

'Around the age of eleven, Jake became obsessed with basketball. Francis had a business trip to Manhattan and so Jake and I joined him for a couple of days,' she continued, walking slowly down the winding staircase before crossing the crowded hallway towards the front door of the house. 'We took Jake to Madison Square Gardens to see the New York Knicks. It was a happy evening, Jake loved it, and when we came home he was desperate for his own net. His birthday was coming up and I had a small court built at the back of the garden. I know – we do nothing by halves here. On his birthday, he had a few friends around and his father set up two teams, one captained by him and one by Jake.

'Jake's team were good, and despite Francis's best efforts they got ahead in the game. Jake was loving that, but of course Francis couldn't stomach it. He got more aggressive and, unintentionally I'm sure, knocked Jake to the ground. It would have been something and nothing but, as Jake fell,

Francis's signet ring clipped the corner of his eye. When Jake got to his feet, blood was streaming down the left-hand side of his face. He refused to let me tend the cut and sat alone at the side of the court as the game continued. He left the blood unstanched. His only desire was for his friends to witness his father's failings.'

Leaving the clamour of the party behind them, Katherine led her daughter-in-law down her driveway before the pair carefully stepped around the dimly lit banks of the village pond.

'We won't be disturbed out here,' Katherine said, as they reach a freshly varnished bench with a small bronze plaque. 'I wanted to show you this. This is Lily's bench.'

Holly looked at the inscription. She'd never even given it a second glance before.

Laughter and joy were the gifts she gave us.

'You've never spoken of her,' said Holly, only now seeing the sorrow Katherine had always concealed.

'No,' replied Katherine, 'we never do. We tell ourselves it's too painful, but I wonder if things would be better if we did. She was everything I'd ever wished for. My own daughter. Just like you and Alice, I'm sure.'

'I couldn't imagine the world without her.'

'I was the same. I adored every moment I spent with her. All the little things – getting her dressed at the start of each day, reading her favourite book, hours together in the bath, wrapping her in a huge towel afterwards. In many ways it was the same for Francis; somehow he found it easier with Lily.'

'Can I ask what happened?' said Holly.

Katherine looked out at the pond. The lights from the Richardson house danced across the water. 'It was late on a November afternoon. One of those damp, misty afternoons where you can't get warm and should be safe inside. Lily loved being outside, running free, splashing in the puddles. She wore purple wellington boots . . . ' She hesitated.

'We can go back inside if you'd prefer,' said Holly, a softness in her voice.

'No,' said Katherine, 'I don't come here enough.' After a moment she continued. 'I got distracted inside – something and nothing. I think I was peeling carrots or something equally pointless. Lily went out through the gate at the back of the garden. It was dark, but she still found her way around to the pond. She loved the ducks. She'd squeal in delight whenever one came near her. We fed them together almost every morning. She had no fear; just like Alice, she'd feed them straight from her hand.

'The leaves around the pond were sodden, the mud so very thick. I'd told her time and again not to go too close to the edge but she was so inquisitive. "Never go near the edge," that's what I'd say. She knew the rule, but somehow she must have slipped.

'A passer-by found her, pulled her out. The doctors came running from the surgery, just across the road. They did everything they could, but it was too late.'

As Katherine sat lost in her desperate memories, Holly fought an urge to run inside, grab hold of Alice and never let her go.

'I had the gate bricked over,' said Katherine, and then the two women sat together in silence, the low buzz coming from the party the only sound.

CHAPTER 49

Hearing a clamour in the drawing room, Will and I step out of Francis's study to witness Katherine Richardson issuing a series of directions. Jake is sprawled on the floor, there's broken glass everywhere, and standing at the back of the room, ashen-faced, is Holly. I move towards her but, as I approach, her mother-in-law links her arm through hers and they step away. I make my excuses to Will and set off in search of Madeline.

Adjacent to the foot of the spiral staircase is a small hallway alcove, where I spot her engaged in conversation with East Mailer. Seeing me approach, he stands.

'Ben, good to see you,' he says, holding out his hand, before we half-hug the way men do.

'And you.'

'Let's grab a drink – it would be good to catch up.'

'I'd hate to interrupt you and Madeline. You two looked quite conspiratorial,' I say, looking towards my boss.

'Nothing of the sort,' she replies, stepping from inside the alcove, draping her floor-length trench coat around her shoulders.

'Madeline and I go back years. She wrote me some fantastic early reviews when she was at the *Richmond Times*,' says East, hurriedly.

'I'm sure any good restaurateur likes to keep the local press on side,' I say.

'She supported us from the very first day we opened, and I'm pleased to say she's kept coming back ever since. Just not often enough!'

'I really do have to fly,' says Madeline, reaching distractedly for her phone. 'Lovely to see you, East. And you too, Ben.'

'Wait – I need to talk to you,' I say, moving to Madeline's side.

'I'm out of here in two minutes – we've breaking news. You remember breaking news?'

'You've been avoiding my calls all day.'

'Ben, it really would be good to have that chat,' says East, closing in at my side.

'You're going to have to give me five minutes,' I reply. 'Work, I'm afraid.'

'I don't have five minutes, Ben,' says Madeline. 'My driver's on the way. This is going to have to wait.'

'It can't wait,' I reply.

'I should probably leave you to it,' says East, awkwardly stepping back. 'I have to go and check in with the restaurant anyway – but, Ben, we must talk later in the evening.'

'Sure.' I nod, and East air-kisses Madeline.

'Maddy, so good to see you. Promise me you'll be in for dinner very soon.'

'I promise,' says Madeline.

'Ben, I'll be back in thirty minutes. I'll come and find you.' And with that he disappears into the packed hallway where much of the party has now congregated.

'I can't do this now,' says Madeline.

'Great coat, by the way,' I say, walking beside her as she edges past guests, saying a few brief hellos as she goes. 'You and East seemed very cosy,' I whisper.

'An old schoolfriend,' replies Madeline tersely. 'Well, for the last two years of school, when Twickenham Duke deigned to let girls join the sixth form.'

'I hadn't realised,' I say, as we step outside on to the gravel driveway.

'Really, Ben, can't this wait until Monday?'

I take hold of Madeline's arm and steer her towards the kerbside. 'No, this cannot wait. You need to start telling me the truth, *all* of the truth.'

'I don't know what you're talking about,' she replies, stepping back past me as her car pulls up. 'But I do know I've had enough of you trying to bully me.'

'I know about Abigail Langdon's child,' I say.

Madeline stops.

'You never thought to tell me about that – didn't you say something about always wanting what was best for me and my family?'

Under the streetlights, Madeline's bright green eyes flare at me. 'Did you stop for one minute to think that maybe that's precisely why I chose not to?'

The passenger side window on Madeline's car descends

and she calls to her driver to give her sixty seconds. She steps back towards me and we walk the crescent pathway that runs in front of the Richardsons' home.

'You had moved on with your life,' she says. 'When exactly would have been the right moment for something like that?'

'How about now?' I say.

'If that's what you want,' she replies. 'It's all pretty simple. Langdon's and Fairchild's trial date kept getting pushed back. They'd been granted anonymity but of course all of us around Haddley and St Marnham knew exactly who they were. Nobody had any idea why the trial date kept moving, but among the press there was a persistent rumour. When I started at the *Richmond Times* my editor was pretty open about it. At the time, he'd tried to speak to the CPS, off the record, but they'd stuck to their story that the delay was simply to allow for the preparation of evidence. A few years later, when I moved to the nationals, it was taken as fact – one of the girls had been pregnant. The trial date was moved until after she'd given birth, so as not to influence the jury one way or another.'

Madeline's phone buzzes and she glances down before immediately slipping it back in her coat pocket. 'Now I do have to go,' she says, turning back towards her car.

'We're not done,' I say.

'I'm sorry, Ben, but there's nothing more to tell. I sniffed around for years looking for the child, but we were all operating under such tight court restrictions that it was impossible to discover anything.'

'So rather than waste your morsel of gossip, when the opportunity arose you used it to lure my mum.'

'You're twisting facts.'

'But you did use it, didn't you?'

'She had an idea already, but yes, I did and I was wrong,' replies Madeline. 'There, are you happy? I was wrong.'

I say nothing.

'It gave her hope, Ben. Is that such a crime?'

'If it killed her, yes,' I reply. 'And let's not pretend you were doing anything other than looking for the best tale to tell.'

'You and I are both journalists, Ben. End of,' says Madeline, as she turns to face me. 'I agreed you could write the story you wanted about Clare, but I didn't agree you could go off on your usual million and one different tangents. The story here isn't about any supposed child, and I don't want you going after that angle.'

'The child is *everything*,' I respond. 'It's what my mum discovered and it's what's killed Langdon now. The child is the heart of this story, along with the father and what he did to those girls.'

'Back off, Ben,' says Madeline. 'I said you could write about your mother but it goes no further.'

'If you don't want my story, somebody else will.'

Madeline reaches for her car door. 'I'll let you go only so far.'

I put my hand on the door to stop her from opening it. 'You didn't tell me you'd met Elizabeth Woakes. What were you after?'

'Take your hand off the car, Ben.'

'*What were you after?*' I repeat, forcefully.

'I'd picked up something about her husband. There was a

call to the school, while he was headmaster,' Madeline tells me, confirming what I'd learnt from Mr C.

'About Langdon and Fairchild?'

'Broader than that, I think, but I could never be sure. Schoolgirls involved with older men, that was the suggestion.'

'And he failed to act?' I ask.

Madeline shrugs. 'It was one call, but some people said it tipped him over the edge.'

'And the photographs?' I ask.

'What photographs?'

'It was you who took the picture of Nick and Simon with Langdon and Fairchild.'

'I never wanted credit for that photo. It's not the kind of image I'm going to hang on my office wall.'

'And passing the full set to my mum was what, just another act of kindness?'

Madeline closes her eyes and pulls back her hair. 'It might have been,' she says. 'Or I might have been using whatever I had to get where I was going. Is that what you want to hear?' She opens the car door and steps inside. 'But you know what, Ben? Maybe I simply thought your mum might like them.'

CHAPTER 50

Holly held her head in her hands, spreading her fingers across her face. Hearing the shrieks of laughter rise from the Richardsons' garden, she fought a growing urge to cover her ears. Across the pond, her eyes were drawn towards Ben, engaged in animated conversation with Madeline Wilson.

'It was Francis who invited her,' said Katherine. 'He's followed her career since she was at the *Richmond Times*; tells himself he has "influential contacts in the media". I'd forgotten she was Ben's boss. Are you still close to him?'

'He's my best friend,' replied Holly, her mother-in-law holding her eye. 'Never anything more,' she added. 'I should tell you about Alice.'

'Only if you want to. I told you about Lily because I wanted you to know. We keep her hidden too deeply.'

'It terrifies me to even imagine the pain you've suffered. All of you. If only I'd known before.'

'It was such a long time ago, before you were born. What difference would it have made?' asked Katherine, and Holly found herself unable to answer. 'Each of us had to find our own way of coping. Increasingly, Francis had his life and I had mine. I turned a blind eye to the things he did and I realise now that was wrong.'

She looked at Holly fearfully and Holly shook her head. 'Francis isn't Alice's father,' she said, and felt Katherine exhale beside her. 'Nothing happened with him until after she was born. I never set out to hurt Jake, but when I married him I was in love with another man. Maybe I didn't know it – he was a man I'd known since we were only Alice's age – and I try to tell myself my feelings were confused.

'His name was Michael. He, Ben and I all started school together on the very same day. For years the three of us were inseparable, and if I'm honest something inside me even then told me I loved him in a way I would never love anybody else. At Haddley Grammar, Michael and I grew closer, and when we left I thought we were destined to spend the rest of our lives together. But at school everyone was certain Michael would play professional rugby some day, and sooner than even he could have imagined he was offered a contract with Bath. At the time we were still little more than kids, and we knew we had to let each other go. I wanted to stay in London to be near my mum and he was either playing or training every single day. Our lives went in different directions.

'Michael and Ben still stayed close, and after Ben's mum died they did some travelling together. When Ben moved back to Haddley, Michael would hang out at his house. I'd recently married Jake but the three of us started to have an occasional drink to talk about old times.' Holly turned to Katherine. 'The moment I saw him again, I knew. All I wanted was to find a reason to spend time with him, to be close to him. He's Alice's father.'

'Does Jake have any idea?'

'None,' replied Holly. 'I never set out to hurt him – you have to believe me.' Katherine nodded. 'Only Ben knows. And now you.'

'He died, didn't he – Michael?' asked Katherine after a pause. 'The hit-and-run in the woods?'

Holly fought to control her tears. She got to her feet and, wrapping her arms around herself, stood at the water's edge. After a moment, she felt Katherine's hand gently upon her back.

'Did he know he had a daughter?'

In the lights from the party reflecting off the pond, Holly nodded.

'He was able to spend some time with her?'

'Yes: we were intending on leaving together. Michael had been offered a contract to play in Australia. I was arranging a passport for Alice. The week before we planned to leave, we went to visit his mother for Michael to say goodbye. She wasn't well. She'd been struck by Alzheimer's while only in her early fifties. It was so sad to see. When Michael spoke to her, there were moments she appeared to understand him. She was sitting in her chair, staring across the room, when he asked her if she'd like to hold Alice. Her reply always stayed with me. She looked up at him and simply asked, "Should I?" "I think you should," he said, and I laid Alice in her arms. I watched as she squeezed Michael's hand. I always wondered if she knew.'

'She knew,' replied Katherine, standing motionless beside her daughter-in-law. 'And I'm going to help you.'

CHAPTER 51

Returning to the Richardsons' house, Holly hurried up to the bedroom where Alice was sleeping. Cracking open the door, she found her daughter fast asleep. Exhausted from the excitement of the day, Alice was curled in the middle of the vast bed while her party dress hung neatly on the wardrobe door.

Holly crept into the room, climbed on to the bed and lay beside her daughter. Gently stroking her soft curls, she made a promise to Alice to watch over her forever. Closing her eyes, she found herself beginning to drift as she dreamt of a life away from Haddley.

Then she felt a breath upon her neck.

'Sleeping like an angel,' whispered a voice in her ear.

Confused and dazed, not quite awake, for a moment she thought of Michael. Then her eyes adjusted and she sat bolt upright.

'Francis!' she exclaimed.

'Shhh,' he said, putting his finger on Holly's lips. 'You'll wake our little princess. Come with me,' he continued, taking Holly by the hand.

As Francis led her down the hallway towards the master suite he shared with Katherine, Holly felt fear race through her. The buzz of the party continued below but, when Francis closed the bedroom door behind them, they stood in silence. He stepped forward, forcing her to take a step backwards toward the giant bed with its Gatsby headboard.

'No, Francis, not here, not now. No,' said Holly, but Francis grasped hold of her arms, guiding her backwards. 'No, I said.' But she found herself stumbling against the ottoman which sat at the end of the bed, and she fell backwards. 'Francis, I said no!' And she clambered across the bed to the far corner of the room.

Francis came calmly towards her, a menacing smile playing at the edge of his mouth. 'You don't say no to me,' he said, softly. 'You never say no to me.'

Holly could hear the steel in his voice. She felt her back press against the corner of the room. She had nowhere left to go.

'Francis, you're going to let me walk past you and out of this room right now or I'm going to scream.'

'I don't negotiate,' he replied, his eyes locked upon her. 'I own you.'

'Not any more. This has to stop.'

'I'll decide when this stops. We made a deal.'

'No. It's not fair on Jake. It's not fair on Katherine.'

'Don't you tell me what's fair.'

'I can't do this any more.'

'I don't think that's your choice to make.' Francis moved forward and, as he did, Holly slid sideways and jumped back

286

across the bed. 'Don't mess me about,' he continued, turning to make his way back around the room.

Holly grabbed a lamp from the bedside table and yanked it hard, ripping the plug from its socket in the wall. Holding it up, she said, 'I've warned you, Francis, this has to stop.'

'Don't be stupid,' he replied. 'The last thing you want to do is bring an end to our arrangement.'

'Let me go,' said Holly, holding the lamp like a baseball bat and stepping towards Francis.

'You'll regret this.'

'Let me go!' shouted Holly, and, as her father-in-law took a step to the side, she charged forward towards the door, hurling the glass lamp on to the wooden floor as she did.

The glass shattered, shards flying across the room, and Francis turned to shield his face. 'You'll pay for this,' he roared, as Holly threw open the door. 'You will fucking pay for this,' was all Holly heard as she ran out of the room and down the corridor towards her daughter's bedroom. Racing into the room, she scooped Alice from the bed and fled towards the stairs.

CHAPTER 52

Late in the evening, I wander into the Richardsons' glass-roofed kitchen, a room that shares a similar grandeur with the rest of their home. Spying a tray of mini strawberry pavlovas, I walk across to the white granite island.

'I love you, Ben,' says a voice from behind me. Jake rises corpse-like from the bright blue cushioned banquet seating. 'You're like a brother to me and Hol.' Before I can reply, he slumps back down and closes his eyes. As he does, Will walks down the art-lined hallway that connects the kitchen to the black-and-white-tiled entrance hall.

'Dessert?' I say, picking up a chocolate fudge cake-pop to follow my pavlova.

'I'll stick with this,' replies Will, taking a cube of ice from the freezer to freshen his whisky glass. 'I took a walk around the garden,' he continues, leaning against the back of the seating. 'I don't think we quite finished our conversation earlier.'

'Interrupted by Jake's antics,' I say, glancing down at him sleeping soundly.

'I don't want you to get the impression that I was making excuses for Josie or Abigail. There can never be any defence of what they did.'

'I didn't think that,' I reply. 'My mum always appreciated the way you looked out for her, right from the very start when you were little more than a kid yourself.'

'We were all kids,' replies Will, pulling out a chair. 'What I was trying to say was, I knew what it felt like to be ostracised, to be the kid who was different from everyone else.'

'But you and Nick always stayed good friends.'

'We did, but I was a fourteen-year-old kid just realising he was gay. I soon learnt kids could be cruel. The pack mentality takes over. Suddenly I was the boy nobody wanted to change next to at the gym. I found myself outside the inner circle. For a while, I was desperate not to be who I was. It made me feel like shit. That summer was tough. I hardly saw any of my schoolfriends, somehow began to lose touch.'

'That can't have been easy.'

'I didn't just bump into Nick that day in the summer holidays. I'd arranged to meet him. It was a Thursday and we did walk up to Haddley Hill Park. I told him I'd seen Josie and Abigail at the start of the week.'

'You were friends with them?'

'No, I'd seen them by the bridge, hanging around. We were all in the same class at school.'

'On the day of the rugby finals, they followed you into the locker room.'

'That was them being stupid, nothing more.'

'And on this day?'

'I'd agreed to meet them in the woods that evening. I wanted Nick to come with me.'

'What did he say?'

'He said he was taking you swimming that afternoon and didn't know what time he'd be back.'

I look out of the French doors on to the Richardsons' floodlit rear garden. As I think of Nick teaching me to dive into Tooting Bec Lido, I watch East light a cigarette as he stands alone at the edge of the swimming pool.

'Did you still go?'

Will sips on his whisky and nods. 'We met in the clearing. Straight out, Abigail said did I want to try?'

I look at Will. 'You had sex with her?'

Will shakes his head. 'You have to remember, Ben, I was a kid. It's not something I'm proud of.'

'What happened?'

'She was offering me Josie. It was as if she'd groomed her. Abigail sat and watched. A week later they killed Nick and Simon.'

Eight

'Over the past twenty-one years she had grown to hate Abigail. How different her life would have been if they had never met.'

CHAPTER 53

I say nothing more and Will falls silent next to me. Our eyes are drawn towards the garden, and we watch steam, swirling upwards from the heated swimming pool, cast a fog around East as he stands alone.

'I should go and see how he's doing,' says Will, finally.

I let him go and he leaves me standing alone at the open window as he goes to join East. They walk around the edge of the pool, deep in conversation, before heading towards the far end of the garden. I turn back inside, and, as I do, Jake rolls on to the kitchen floor before staggering to his feet.

'I'm going to find Hol,' he says, giving a weary wave of his hand as he goes. 'Love you, Ben.'

I stand and drink my water before following him down the corridor to the entrance hall.

In easy late-night spirits, the Richardsons' guests are beginning to drift away, back to their homes in St Marnham and beyond. Jake has already disappeared but I see Nathan Beavin, sipping from a lead crystal brandy glass as he sits

293

on the curved sofa that loops around the base of the main staircase.

'Please don't tell me you'll be out running at six tomorrow morning,' I say, taking the seat next to him.

'I might have a lie-in until seven,' he replies. 'The rule is never to give yourself an excuse not to go.'

I find myself wishing I were ten years younger. 'You wait until you're my age,' I say and, terrifyingly, I remind myself of Mr Cranfield. Nathan looks at me pityingly as if I'm middle-aged and I instantly regret my knee-jerk response. 'Perhaps I'll see you on the common at seven.' I already know it's an appointment I am unlikely to keep.

'Quite some house they've got here,' says Nathan, charging his glass with Francis's Hennessy cognac, the bottle nestled neatly beside him. 'You been here before?'

'Couple of times,' I reply. 'Holly and Jake had their wedding reception in a marquee in the garden.'

'I bet that was quite a party?'

'As you might appreciate, Mr and Mrs Richardson do nothing by halves.'

'He must be worth a bit. Family money, is it?'

'Not sure,' I say. 'He did well in the City but I don't think he came from the poor house.' Nathan laughs. 'His father had some kind of manufacturing business – textiles, I think. Francis was in the military at first, but soon realised he was far more interested in making his own money.'

'And Jake just married a local girl?'

'You mean Hol? Yes, she's lived in Haddley all her life.'

'He wasn't set up with someone who came with more influence?'

'I guess not,' I reply. 'Francis had enough of that already.'

'You've known her all your life?'

'You love asking questions, don't you?'

'I guess I'm a bit inquisitive, nothing more than that.'

'Really? I'm not so sure.'

Nathan takes a large drink from his glass that must burn as he swallows.

'Why don't you tell me about yourself?'

'About me?' he says and I wait. 'I don't really have a story to tell. Born in Wales, regular childhood, one sister, we went to a good school, had great parents.'

'Nice,' I say. 'And?'

'I went to university in Cardiff and then I wanted some time out. I came to London for an adventure. That's about it. Never imagined I'd meet a woman like Sarah.'

'You tell it well.'

'Tell what?'

'Your story. I've heard a million and one. Make that a million and two.'

'I don't know what you mean,' says Nathan, swirling the remnants of his drink around his glass.

'What are you really doing here?'

'Exactly as I said – bit of an adventure in the big city.'

'The truth. You've asked me about my mum, my brother, my friends, James Wright, my job. Why?'

Nathan puts down his glass, alarm flashing across his face.

'Ben!' I hear Holly's voice cry out. Jumping to my feet, I

search for her face among the remaining revellers. 'Up here,' she calls, and I turn to see her precariously descending the winding staircase, Alice asleep in her arms.

'What's going on?' I say. As she approaches, I can see a redness in her eyes. 'Hol?'

'Can you get a car to take us home? And find Jake.'

I hear the urgency in her voice and immediately take out my phone.

'I should go and find Sarah,' says Nathan, getting to his feet and hurrying away.

'There'll be an Uber here in four minutes. Come and sit down,' I say, but Holly refuses.

'I want to wait outside,' she replies, wrapping a blanket tightly around Alice. As she heads to the front door, Sarah and Nathan quickly emerge back down the hallway from the kitchen.

'Holly, are you okay?' asks Sarah.

'We're leaving. I need to find Jake and go.'

'He's not in the kitchen,' replies Sarah.

'I'll check the living room,' says Nathan, bounding up the stairs as I head into the sun room at the back of the hall. Opening the door, I find Jake sleeping on one of the plush sofas, curled up like a baby.

'Jake, you're leaving,' I say, waking him with a start. 'I think Alice is a little unwell, so Holly wants to take her home.'

He rolls off the sofa before staggering after me through the hall. I walk with him out on to the driveway.

'Party over?' he asks, only half-conscious.

'I want to get Alice home,' replies Holly, as Sarah and Nathan join us outside.

'My baby feeling poorly,' he says, peering at Alice.

'I explained she wasn't feeling well,' I say to Holly. 'Too much cake mixed with a bad dream.' Jake nods and stumbles on ahead of us. 'Hol, are you okay?' I ask.

'I just need to go.'

I say nothing more until we reach the end of the driveway, when East Mailer walks across the garden, from the rear of the house. 'Ben, you're not leaving already, are you? I was really hoping we'd get a chance to catch up.'

'Need to get the little one home,' I reply, as our Uber pulls up. 'Let's have a drink soon.'

East slides open the door and Sarah and Nathan climb into the rear seats. Jake slumps into the middle row of the minivan before Holly climbs in beside him. I hold Alice for her before gently passing her back to her mother. Alice curls into Holly, and I see Holly squeeze her tightly. I step forward to sit up front with the driver, looking across at the Richardsons' home where the last few guests continue to drink on the terrace. A lone figure carefully observes us through the arched window that looks out from the top of the house. As we slowly pull away around the village pond, I turn to see Katherine Richardson standing there, motionless.

Stopping at the temporary traffic lights on the Lower Haddley Road, I flick on my phone and open our news app. Reading the splashed headline, I have to fight for breath.

REVENGE AT LAST! ABIGAIL LANGDON BUTCHERED!

297

'I'm in trouble,' I say, as we drive along the lower side of Haddley Woods. 'Can you slow down,' I ask the driver, needing time to think. 'Just pull over here for a second.'

'Ben?' says Holly, and I pass my phone back to her.

I look across the common to the front of my house. Outside are parked two police cars. Pointing towards them, I say, 'I think they've come for me.'

'What are they doing here?' asks Sarah from the back of the cab. Holly hands her my phone.

'And that article has nothing to do with you?' says Holly. Jake and Alice continue to sleep soundly beside her.

'No, nothing,' I reply, as Sarah leans forward and passes my phone back to me.

'Somebody's talked,' says Holly.

I'm already messaging Madeline.

WTF?

Her reply is instant:

We didn't break it. Look at the Sun on Sunday.
I had no choice but to follow

I need a lawyer

On it

'You all go on,' I say, opening the car door. 'You're better off out of this.'

'Do you want me to come with you?' asks Sarah.

'Surely best to not get involved?' says Nathan, his voice quiet.

'Madeline's sending someone over,' I reply, catching his stare in the rear-view mirror.

'That's the least she can do,' says Holly. 'Are you sure you don't want one of us to come with you?'

'I'll be fine. I'll call you tomorrow.'

Crossing the common, I watch the car's red tail-lights fade away. As I approach my house, I see DS Barnsdale sitting alone in one of the waiting police cars. I walk past her. Instantly she is in pursuit.

'Mr Harper,' she calls. 'Please wait. We have a number of questions we would like to ask you.' I look over my shoulder. Dani Cash appears from the second vehicle and follows three steps behind her superior. Ignoring them both, I open the front door to my house. I go to slam it closed but Barnsdale jams it with her foot. 'Mr Harper,' she says, pushing the door back open. 'We do need to talk.'

I begin taking off my jacket. 'It's almost midnight,' I say, my back to the detective. 'I can't imagine what is so urgent it couldn't wait until morning.'

'We have a number of questions we would like you to answer,' she calls, stepping inside without invitation. 'At the station.'

I face her from across the hall. 'I didn't break the story, and neither did anyone from my site.' Madeline had better be telling me the truth.

'Somebody broke it,' replies Barnsdale, moving towards

me, 'otherwise how the hell would it have ended up here?' She hands me a print-out of the front page of the first edition of the *Sun on Sunday*. Splashed across the cover is Langdon's image. 'When you're ready, Mr Harper, I would love to hear your explanation.'

The leak has humiliated her. I moderate my tone. 'As I said, I had nothing to do with it. But I can see this is a very difficult situation, so I'm very happy to come down to the station first thing, of my own volition.' Barnsdale says nothing, and I look at her. 'Does a newspaper report really change anything?'

'Nothing but the legitimacy of the whole investigation.'

'Langdon's dead. It was going to come out at some point. My attending a bogus interview in the middle of the night is not going to change that.'

'I can arrest you now if you'd prefer?' She is implacable.

'On what grounds?'

'We've been here before, Mr Harper. Impersonating a police officer, removing evidence from the scene of a crime. Would you like me to go on?'

Dani Cash is studying her own reflection in her highly polished shoes.

'You don't like the fact that the story has broken, so you're punishing me.'

'You're making it very easy for us, Mr Harper. You said yourself you'd have killed Abigail Langdon if you had the chance. Your mother was one of a handful of people who knew where she was.'

I realise I have no choice.

We exit the front of my house with Dani Cash escorting me towards the back seat of the waiting police car. As she opens the door, I lower my head and a flashbulb explodes in my eyes. Dani's hand guides me into the back seat and, as she closes the door, I hear the rapid fire of a press camera lens pushed against the window.

'Barnsdale's handiwork, I assume?' I say, turning away from the window. Under the light of the street lamps, we slowly pull away from the side of the common. I look across the open space and think of that blisteringly hot, hate-filled day that has shadowed my life ever since.

Saturday night in Haddley is no different from any other town and entering the police station is a depressing sight. Three drunks, one with a gash above his right eye, sprawl out on a bench in front of me. Having made it clear to Barnsdale that I'm waiting for my solicitor, I spend the next two hours sitting alone in an airless interview room. Dani brings me a mug of tea but again we make no eye contact.

Some time after two a.m., the head of our in-house legal team, Morgan Turner, arrives. 'I take it they're on a fishing expedition and nothing more than that?'

I fill him in on my visit to Farsley.

'So we're talking a little slap on the wrists, but what else would they expect you to do in your situation? You were grief-stricken and desperate.'

'And doing what any competent investigating officer would already have done.'

'We might go easy on that line until we have you out of

301

here,' replies Turner. 'I want you to avoid answering any of their questions unless I tell you otherwise.'

'Absolutely,' I reply.

When the door opens and Barnsdale and Cash join us, I feel a surge of anger and apprehension. As Dani sets up the recording device, the detective takes a seat opposite me.

'Let's agree to put aside today's activities and focus on the matter in hand – the murder of Abigail Langdon. Mr Harper, prior to the events of the past forty-eight hours, were you aware that Abigail Langdon, latterly known as Demi Porter, was living in the West Yorkshire town of Farsley?'

'Mr Harper's knowledge of Abigail Langdon's whereabouts is irrelevant,' says Turner.

'I beg to differ,' replies Barnsdale, flipping open her notebook. 'To quote: *If I'd known where Langdon was, I would have killed her myself.* Those are your words, Mr Harper?'

'For the record, sergeant, this is the woman who brutally murdered Mr Harper's brother. I would be more surprised if he hadn't threatened to kill her on many occasions throughout his life. His words were simply an expression of understandable grief and outrage.'

Barnsdale continues with her next question as if he hadn't spoken. 'Prior to this morning, have you ever visited the town of Farsley in West Yorkshire?'

'Again irrelevant, sergeant. Mr Harper is free to visit any town in the United Kingdom and beyond. He is not under any restrictions.'

'Mr Harper, were you aware that your mother was in contact with Abigail Langdon?'

Turner turns to me and I answer. 'No.'

'But you were aware that Elizabeth Woakes was in contact with her?'

'Elizabeth Woakes wasn't in contact with Langdon.'

'My mistake. But you did know she visited Farsley?'

'No,' I reply again.

'Really?'

'I found out yesterday that Mrs Woakes had visited once. That's all.' I glare at Dani.

Morgan Turner holds my arm. I take a deep breath and lean back in my chair.

'Did Elizabeth Woakes explain to you the purpose of her visit to Farsley?' continues Barnsdale.

'No,' I reply.

'And had she had visited Farsley on multiple occasions?'

Morgan Turner turns to me and nods.

'As far as I'm aware, no,' I say.

'Mr Harper, would I be right in saying that it is your belief that Elizabeth Woakes was protecting her husband, protecting his memory in some way?'

'That is pure supposition,' says Morgan Turner.

'Constable, could you read from your notebook.' Dani's hand trembles as she flips the pages open in response to Barnsdale's request. 'Go ahead, constable, we're waiting.'

'*Simply that from talking to her I got the impression she was protecting him, or felt she needed to protect his memory.*' Dani has recorded my words verbatim.

'What made you think Elizabeth Woakes was protecting her husband?'

'It was just a feeling. Nothing specific.'

'Do you know what she might have been protecting him from?'

'No.'

'We're going round in circles here, sergeant,' says Turner.

'Fine, let's move on,' says Barnsdale. 'Do you know who informed both your mother and Elizabeth Woakes of the new identity and location of Abigail Langdon?'

I pause, and Barnsdale waits for my response.

'Mr Harper?'

'No,' I reply. There is no benefit in putting Madeline in front of Barnsdale.

'If you could clarify for me, so I have this straight in my mind. You met with Elizabeth Woakes on Friday morning?'

'Yes.'

'She told you she had been made aware of Demi Porter's true identity, she told you she had visited Farsley, and as an award-winning investigative journalist you never thought to ask her how she knew?'

'DS Barnsdale, where are you going with this?' asks Turner.

'I'm only looking for Mr Harper's help in establishing the facts.'

'In that case, may I suggest that hauling him here in the middle of the night may not be the best way to ensure his full co-operation?'

Barnsdale puts her hands flat on the table in front of her. 'Did Elizabeth Woakes speak to you about why her husband fled Haddley?'

'Fled?' I reply, before Turner can stop me. 'He didn't flee.'

'Didn't he? Didn't he flee out of a fear that his prior relationship with Langdon and Fairchild would be uncovered?'

CHAPTER 54

Dawn had barely broken when Corrine walked across the harshly illuminated garage forecourt, another fourteen-hour shift behind her. A truck heading up the coast towards Dover rolled in front of her and, stepping behind it, she held the hood of her anorak over her head. Black clouds hung heavy and she wrapped her coat tightly against the unrelenting wind that cut through her as it blew up from the seafront.

There were no other customers inside the garage. An adolescent attendant idly lifted his head from his phone as she went in and picked up a shopping basket, but looked down again, uninterested. Corrine was exhausted from three weeks of consecutive night shifts, and this morning she found herself in desperate need of a drink. During the night, two of the residents had become unwell. Neither case appeared to be anything serious and she'd wondered if it was the salmon fricassée they'd been fed the previous evening. Molly had still made her write up both incidents in the health records and hadn't found it funny when she'd written in Mrs Bell's record, 'had the shits at 3.30'. Arguing with Molly about cleaning up the mess had at least stopped her thinking about Chad and Dean. This morning she knew she would need something stronger to keep them from her mind.

She hated her job.

She hated her life.

Opening her purse, she saw she had enough money for four cans of Skol. Add to that a small white loaf and a chunk of cheese and she would eat her toasted sandwich in bed. As she was picking up a large bag of salt and vinegar crisps, a hidden voice called out from the tiny kitchen behind the bakery counter. 'Tyler, if I have to come out and unpack the papers myself ... '

She couldn't help but watch as, rolling his eyes, the adolescent took his feet down from the shelf behind the counter and slouched his way across the shop. Lethargically he cut open the first stack of newspapers left piled by the shop entrance. 'I'm doing them now,' was his sullen reply.

A sudden waft of maple and pecan Danish, fresh from the oven, made her mouth water. Corrine felt in her pocket in the hope of discovering loose change so she could treat herself to a pastry. Nothing. She still had Mr Talisbrook's ten-pound note but she didn't want to waste it. She'd have to put back two of the cans of Skol and she wasn't about to do that.

The attendant was still crouched over the newspapers when she made her way across to the self-checkout machine. Idly passing the items across the till, she glanced towards him. And that was when she saw it.

The headline screamed from the front page of the *Sun on Sunday*, sending a tremor through her. She had to put her hand out to steady herself. She forced herself to breathe, unable to drag her gaze away from the headline.

CHILD-KILLER ABIGAIL SLAUGHTERED.

Trance-like, she reached down for a copy and in one movement scanned the paper through the checkout before hastily folding it over. Opening her purse, she poured out all of her coins, only for the machine to tell her, 'Approval needed.' Turning towards the attendant, she could feel sweat running down the side of her face.

'Give me a second,' he said, with total disregard.

Corrine opened her coat but still kept her hood across her face. Feeling her heart racing, she told herself to breathe. She focused all her attention on the screen in front of her. When the attendant absent-mindedly tapped in a code, only then did she turn away. As he looked down at the items she had scanned, she took two steps back towards the door. When he clicked on approve, he looked directly at her. Her hand instinctively went to her face, where she felt the moisture on her cheek. Her heart aggressively pumped the blood to keep her standing.

'You can put your money in again now,' he said, paying her scant attention

Her hand shaking, Corrine hurriedly pushed Mr Talisbrook's ten-pound note into the slot before shoving her shopping into her oversized bag. Leaving the shop, she couldn't stop herself looking back at the newspapers now lined up across the floor. Transfixed again by the

Sun's headline, she heard the attendant say, 'Got what she deserved,' and she responded by hastily pushing open the door and hurrying outside.

She made her way back across the forecourt and inhaled deeply. The sea air was calming and she stood at the corner of the terraced side street, leaning against the window of the curry house where she liked to treat herself each Friday lunchtime. Only when she was certain the street was deserted did she pull the newspaper from her bag. Quickly, she turned to the second and third pages. She scanned the article, until she came to the final paragraph. There was the detail she was looking for.

The whereabouts of Langdon's child-killer accomplice, Josie Fairchild, are still unknown.

Corrine closed the paper and stuffed it back inside her bag. How she hated that name.

Corrine Parsons.

If only she could be Josie once again.

And live her life over.

CHAPTER 55

Corrine braced herself against the wind as it blew in from the Channel before she crossed the road that ran along the Deal shoreline. The small seaside town, which to her felt like a prison from which she would never be released, was slowly awakening to its monotone daily life. Cyclists were pedalling along the sea path, a street cleaner was collecting Saturday night's detritus, while a lone dog-walker tightened her headscarf as she headed towards the castle.

Desperate to be alone and safe from interruption, Corrine crossed the seafront park, walking up the grassy bank to the isolated bandstand. She sat on the steps that faced the shore, and took a can of lager from her bag. She felt the tingle of the cold, bitter liquid in her throat, and she closed her eyes, listening to the waves breaking upon the pebbled beach. She tried to imagine herself far from here – a warm beach, waves lapping at her feet – but all she could think of was her second can of Skol and how much she craved the comfort it would bring. Only once she'd finished that too did her nerves begin to calm, and she edged back up the steps of the bandstand in search of a more sheltered spot. Opening her bag, she pulled out the crumpled newspaper and began to read.

Convicted child-killer Abigail Langdon was found murdered in her West Yorkshire home late on Wednesday night. In what we can exclusively reveal is a macabre reflection of her own savage killing of the two schoolboys Nick Harper and Simon Woakes, Langdon's throat had been brutally cut.

Corrine stopped and clutched the paper to her chest. Over the past twenty-one years, she had grown to hate Abigail. How different her life would have been if they had never met. If only she had ignored her on that day when she stood alone in the lunch queue clutching her school meal vouchers, the unbearable rhythm of her schoolmates' taunting ringing in her ears. Instead, she had grasped hold of a fleeting friendship; a moment of triumph to replace the burning shame she felt in her own skin. It was a moment of triumph for which she had paid dearly ever since.

The day they had left court as convicted killers was the last time she had seen Abigail. Rumours had persisted as to her location but she had never been interested. Her friend had controlled her, created the storm around her, only to seek vengeance for its very existence.

After her own release, Corrine had deliberately kept her life offline. She avoided social media and she didn't own a smartphone. Even some of the care home residents had smartphones, but Corrine had no desire to be connected to anyone or anything. She never searched for Abigail Langdon or Josie Fairchild. To her they no longer existed.

Now, for a passing moment, she felt that fleeting friendship again. The love Abigail had given her. The two of them together against the world. The promise to be always there for each other. No one had known a love like they had.

Abigail was dead.

Slaughtered.

The only friend she had ever known.

Corrine read on.

The child-killer had been living in the town of Farsley on the outskirts of Leeds. Working in the local supermarket, she rented a tiny one-bedroom flat above the local curry house on the high street. It was here that Langdon whiled away her nights, and it was here that the killer struck.

Corrine shuddered. It was a shock to realise that Abigail's life had been as depressing as hers. Living alone and in fear of discovery, Corrine felt her days were dominated by regret. At least at work she was surrounded by others, however depressing it might be. Sleeping during the afternoons had made her feel more secure, not having to face the darkness alone. A knife beneath her pillow had convinced her she was safe. But was she?

In the town of Haddley, where the teenage killers committed their vile crimes, revulsion for the pair still burns. Of the boys' parents, only Simon's mother, Elizabeth Woakes, remains nearby, but she was unavailable for comment. A neighbour told the *Sun on Sunday*, 'There will never be any forgiveness for what Langdon and Fairchild did. They stole two lives and ruined many others. Everyone will be glad she's dead. I hope Fairchild is next.'

Corrine scrunched the paper into a ball and, with seagulls screeching above, she hurried back across the park towards her flat. When she approached the amusement arcade, she tossed the newspaper into a litter bin. She didn't want it inside her home. Searching in her bag for her keys, she opened her door and quickly made her way upstairs before turning on the television in her living room. She switched on the news and Abigail's face stared out at her.

Then her own.

'The manner of Langdon's death has given rise to speculation that this is a revenge killing for the deaths of schoolboys Nick Harper and Simon Woakes,' the news anchor was saying. 'The question the police must be asking themselves is: why now?'

Corrine wasn't particularly interested in that question. To her, Simon and Nick's deaths could have been yesterday. Another question was tormenting her.

Would Josie be next?

CHAPTER 56

From inside the entrance of Haddley police station early on Sunday morning, I look out to see three photographers and a television camera crew waiting on the pavement outside. My heart sinks. I believed Madeline when she told me our site followed the *Sun on Sunday*, but who gave the story to them? Could it have been Barnsdale? She has few qualms about making my life uncomfortable, but is she that desperate to pressure me into turning on the Woakes family?

Exhausted, I ready myself for the questions about to be hurled. As I reach for the door, though, I look across to see a man sitting on the bare wooden bench where I had sat the previous night. He is older than when I last saw him – slightly dishevelled, unshaven and his unkempt hair now grey. I'm surprised by how little I feel.

'You look older,' I say to my father.

'Ben!' he replies, quickly getting to his feet and crossing towards me. I take a step back. 'Sylvie saw your picture on the news. I drove all night to get here. I got you this,' he says, offering me a cold cup of tea. 'Oh, and this,' he continues, fumbling in his coat pocket and pulling out a toothbrush and tube of toothpaste. 'I didn't know how long they'd keep you in.'

'I only live ten minutes away,' I reply.

'Of course you do. I just didn't know . . . ' He slowly bends down and puts the toothbrush on the bench behind him. 'So, how're you bearing up?' he asks, turning back to me.

'What are you doing here?'

'I wanted to see if you needed anything.'

'I don't.'

'Or if I could help in any way.'

'You can't,' is my exhausted response. I move forward, forcing him to step back against the bench. He puts his hand down to steady himself. 'After ten years you turn up out of the blue asking if you can help. Why do you think I would want anything from you? Did you think I was going to welcome you with open arms?'

'I didn't know what you might need,' he says, defensively.

I can feel the desk sergeant's eyes upon us.

'I don't need anything from you,' I reply, steering my father towards the door. 'Throughout my life, all you've done is turn up when you're not wanted, and always with some piece of utter tat.' I pick up the toothbrush and push it into his chest.

'The last time I saw you, it was you who sent me away. You didn't even let me sit with you,' he says.

'It was Mum's funeral. You were never there when we needed you. Why would I want you then?'

'I'm here now.'

'Well, you've wasted your time. You only ever turn up when it's bad news.'

'Ben, that's not fair.'

'Not fair?' I reply, my voice rising for the first time. 'The one day you should have been there, the one day your worthless existence would have made a difference, where were you then? Where were you?' I'm scarcely aware of clenching my fist. My father flinches, cowering. '*Where were you?*' I shout.

I feel a hand upon my arm. 'You need to come with me,' says Dani Cash, standing behind me with the desk sergeant.

I don't move.

'Ben,' says Dani, 'come with me. I can take you out the back way.'

I look at my father shrinking into the corner of the station reception.

I walk with Dani through the station and out of a fire exit at the back of the building. The morning air fills my lungs and Dani lets me take a few deep breaths, saying nothing.

'I'm sorry,' I say. 'I shouldn't have reacted like that.'

'You feel he's let you down?'

I laugh. 'In so many fucking ways. I might forgive him most things,' I say, pressing my palms in my eyes, 'but I will never forgive him for Nick. If I'd known he wasn't going to show up on that day, I would have been with Nick. And then we would have come straight home.' I turn to Dani and she touches a tear from my cheek. 'I will never forgive him. Never.'

'You have to start by forgiving yourself,' says Dani,

but I simply look away. For a moment we sit together in silence until Dani says, 'Let me drop you home. You look shattered.'

'A night being interrogated at a police station can do that to you.'

Walking towards a police Ford Focus, Dani turns to me. 'I didn't know Barnsdale was going to do that. I never set out to betray your trust.'

'You didn't?' I snap. 'From where I was sitting, it felt like you couldn't speak to Barnsdale quick enough. You called her from the toilets on the M1!'

'We had found evidence in a murder case.'

'Let's not do this now. I've heard it all from Barnsdale,' I reply.

'It was more than that. I'm lucky not to have been suspended,' says Dani, a hint of irritation in her voice as we climb inside the car. 'Barnsdale's backed me when a lot of others wouldn't.'

I turn to Dani to understand what she means.

'Let's just say my career is not in the best shape,' she says. 'I don't have many supporters at the station, or even in my own house. Barnsdale has stood by me when I needed her, given me a chance. I owe her.'

'So as soon as you had a nice bit of juicy information you were straight on the phone.'

'It wasn't like that. I didn't betray you,' she replies, starting the engine and pulling slowly forward before stopping at the exit barrier. 'I fought for you as much as I dared. I told her I didn't believe you were involved in any way but that we

317

both had questions around Elizabeth Woakes, about what she might be hiding.'

'Is that what you call having my back?'

'I went with you to Farsley so you could talk to a few people in the neighbourhood. Not so you could impersonate a police officer and remove evidence from a murder scene.' The barrier rises and Dani pulls the car forward, before stopping at the junction. 'I argued against bringing you in but she was fuming. She was embarrassed by the press leak. She's convinced that was you.'

'It wasn't.'

'Elizabeth Woakes and your mum can be linked directly to Langdon and to the fact that she was living in Farsley as Demi Porter. Barnsdale can draw a straight line between them.'

'She's clutching at straws,' I reply. 'And she's way off the mark with Peter Woakes. He didn't flee. I remember him living under Haddley Bridge. He was beyond distraught.'

'There are still questions that need answering,' says Dani, as we make our way through the residential streets. 'We're bringing Elizabeth Woakes in for an interview this afternoon.'

'If she was going to kill Langdon, why do it now? She knew her identity ten years ago. She's the wrong focus. My mum got too close to uncovering a secret, one Langdon had sworn to protect. The secret of Langdon's child.'

I watch Dani check her mirror before pulling up at the side of Haddley Common. 'We're receiving new information all the time,' she offers. 'The vast majority of documents relating to the original case were sealed by the court at the time but, because of Langdon's murder, Barnsdale is being granted limited access.'

'What are you telling me?'

'There definitely was a child,' says Dani, switching off the engine and twisting to face me. 'DNA tests were done to see if either Nick or Simon were the father.' I look past Dani towards the runners battling the headwinds on the towpath towards St Marnham. 'The tests shouldn't have been done without parental consent but whoever made the decision probably felt it was better to know and then inform relatives afterwards, if necessary.'

'The child wasn't Nick's?' I say, turning back to Dani.

'No. I'm sorry.'

For the first time, I pause and allow myself to think how I would have felt if it had been my brother's child. My connection to Nick would have been renewed. I would have had a family. However difficult it might have been, it would have been my family and I would no longer have been alone.

Suddenly I can understand what my mum was searching for.

CHAPTER 57

Nathan stood at the kitchen island and flicked through the Sunday papers. Unease had gripped him the previous night when he had watched from the window as the police led Ben away under the gaze of the gathering press. Reading the papers now, with the relentless retellings of the crime committed by Langdon and Fairchild, he shivered at the gruesome details. After all that had happened to Ben and his family, could anyone blame him if he had exacted revenge upon Langdon? Nathan knew he certainly wouldn't.

The *Sunday Times* had a detailed map of Haddley Woods, exactly where he had run only the previous day. Beside it were images of Langdon and Fairchild as teenage girls. Nathan studied their pictures. What had driven such extreme brutality? Were they born evil? Or had moments in life conspired against them? Was it their parents who triggered their actions? Or did their evil come from those around them? He felt more certain than ever that there was evil in Haddley, still waiting to be uncovered.

'It's not even seven,' said Sarah, as she wandered into the

kitchen, seemingly half-asleep. Nathan closed the paper as she stood behind him, wrapping her arms around his waist. 'Come back to bed,' she said, resting her head on his back. 'James isn't dropping Max off until eight. We've got a good hour.'

Nathan laughed before twisting to kiss Sarah. 'I promised I'd work an extra lunchtime shift,' he replied. 'And I could do with a run to blow the cobwebs away from last night.'

'Please yourself,' said Sarah, kissing him on the cheek before crossing the room to press the switch on the kettle. 'Still a few media types hanging around the common,' she said, taking two mugs from the cupboard.

'Do you think they'll be here all day?'

'Surely there's nothing left in Haddley to film? I suppose they might be hoping to get a quote from Ben. Tea?'

'Please,' replied Nathan. 'You don't think he's involved in some way?'

'With killing Abigail Langdon? No way. He's Holly's best friend.'

'When you've suffered in the way his family has . . . '

'Absolutely not,' replied Sarah, her eyes searching around the kitchen. Nathan felt under the newspaper before handing Sarah her phone. 'Thanks,' she said, and Nathan saw her type out a message. 'That doesn't make him a killer,' she continued, putting her phone down on the table. 'Not Ben. However much he hated those two girls, those two women, he would never do that.'

'Somebody did,' said Nathan. 'And in the papers there's a clear suggestion it could be linked to the original killings.'

321

Sarah's phone buzzed and he glanced down.

I haven't heard anything. I still need your help.

'How can they know that?' replied Sarah, putting tea bags into their cups. 'Passions have always run high around those girls, right across the country. Any crazy might have stumbled upon Langdon and decided to take revenge.' Sarah paused for a moment. 'And do you know what – if they did, good.'

'Is that your professional opinion?'

'Sometimes the criminal justice system doesn't serve the victims as well as it should.'

Sarah picked up her phone. Nathan watched her type a reply before she dropped her phone on the island and crossed the kitchen to pick up the kettle. The reply to Sarah's message was instant.

As soon as I can. I have to escape.

Nathan glanced at the screen and then began to turn the pages of the *Sun on Sunday*. 'Whoever killed her wanted her to suffer,' he said, scanning the sickening details in the paper. 'They wanted her to suffer in the same way as the boys, and to me that makes it personal.'

'Impossible for us to know,' said Sarah, pouring milk into Nathan's tea.

'Who else spent time with them – the girls – when they were kids?'

'I've no idea,' she replied, handing Nathan his mug before picking up her phone. 'Long before my time in Haddley.'

'You must have talked about it with Holly?' asked Nathan, as Sarah typed another reply.

'Nathe, it's seven o'clock on a Sunday morning and I'm a bit hungover. Do we really have to talk about this now?'

'Holly was quite a bit younger than those two girls?' continued Nathan, not listening.

'Five or six years, I think, but does it matter?'

'Six,' replied Nathan. 'If she's the same age as Ben, she would have been eight at the time.' Sarah looked across at Nathan. 'It's here in the paper,' he said.

Sarah nodded. 'Nick and Simon were fourteen. Langdon and Fairchild the same,' she said, before adding, 'And my dear ex-husband would have been eighteen.'

'He was at the same school?'

'James was head boy. He's Haddley through and through.'

'Do you think he'd ever want to come back?'

'Not while he has his riverside fuckpad with Kitty.'

Nathan laughed. 'Did he ever talk about the killings?'

'Nathe!'

'Humour me.'

'Only to say that it was a horrible time. Even James was sensitive enough to recognise that.'

'Did he know either of them?'

'Not that I'm aware of. I assume back then he actually dated women of his own age.'

Nathan smiled. 'I wonder if the girls had boyfriends.'

'Nathan, I've no idea,' replied Sarah. 'It was all a long

time ago. The only thing that matters now is making sure Ben is okay.'

'I just think it's interesting,' Nathan said. 'I bet the other one is feeling nervous. Josie Fairchild.'

'No reason to think her identity is under threat. This was probably a case of Langdon being careless, talking to the wrong people.'

'All the same, it wouldn't stop me worrying if I were her.'

'The police will probably move her as a precaution.'

'They didn't move Langdon.'

'I doubt they knew she was at that kind of risk. Fairchild could be on the other side of the world for all we know.'

Nathan slowly nodded and watched as Sarah read the front page of the *Sun on Sunday*. Turning away, he couldn't shake the teenage images of Langdon and Fairchild.

Ra-ta-tat-tat.

Ra-ta-tat-tat.

'I'll go,' said Nathan, grabbing his running shirt and pulling it over his head as he headed down the hallway.

'Nathan!' squealed Max, as he opened the front door, leaping into his arms as Nathan knelt to say hello.

'This is Max's overnight bag,' said James Wright, at the threshold.

'I went on the big dragon at Legoland! And I had two ice creams.'

Nathan stared at James Wright.

'I'll put it here, shall I?' continued James, stepping inside and dropping the bag in the hallway. 'You must be the famous Nathan. He talks a lot about you.'

'He's a good kid,' replied Nathan.

'What time do you call this?' said Sarah, walking from the kitchen.

'I'm an hour early – what of it?'

'Mummy, I went on the big dragon and had two ice creams,' said Max, jumping down and running across to his mum.

'You are such a lucky boy,' said Sarah, scooping him into her arms. 'A call would been nice,' she continued, over Max's shoulder.

'Things have come up that I need to deal with today.'

'Yes, like looking after your son,' said Sarah, dropping her voice. 'It's seven o'clock on a Sunday morning.'

'You're up, and your boy here's all set for a run.' Nathan said nothing. 'See you next week, champ,' said James, kissing his son on the top of his head. 'Might see you again some time,' he said to Nathan as he stepped outside.

'Can I have a chocolate muffin for breakfast?' said Max to his mum.

'Didn't you have breakfast at Daddy's flat?'

'No, Kitty was asleep. She's always asleep.'

'Shall we make dippy eggs?' said Sarah.

'No! Chocolate muffin.'

'I'm heading out,' called Nathan, as Sarah carried her son into the kitchen. Running down the steps at the front of the house, he stopped on the pavement and watched as James Wright climbed into his white Range Rover, his girlfriend dozing beside him. As the car pulled forward, it slowed beside Nathan and the driver side window descended.

'Word of advice. Trade your girlfriend in for a younger model,' said James, squeezing Kitty's thigh. 'You'll have a hell of a lot more fun.'

CHAPTER 58

It was late afternoon when Corrine Parsons stepped off her train and on to platform three of Haddley station. Her breath caught in her throat. Never had she imagined returning to this place. She walked up the steps and out on to the high street to discover little had changed since her teenage years. The shops, cafés and bars – everything felt very familiar. It should have felt like home, but it didn't. Nowhere felt like home to Corrine.

For a moment, she was fourteen again. She realised she was half-expecting to see Abigail – under the bridge or in the park, by the boathouse or in the woods. Corrine shook her head. She hadn't come here looking for ghosts.

Standing outside the station, she couldn't help but stop and look up the hill towards Haddley Hill Park. The houses where she had lived; some for just a few days, others for months, none ever more than that. Never one to call a home. Each had brought its own fear; at times simply the unknown, Josie being a stranger in a strange place. More often was the pure hatred of what she discovered within.

She pulled her hood tightly over her head and began a brisk walk down the high street towards the Thames. Stepping on to the towpath, she caught sight of the river and her spirits lifted briefly. The tide was rising on a fast-flowing current. She paused to let a team of oarsmen pass, and they thanked her, carrying their boat into the boathouse. When she took a seat on the embankment, she wanted the moment to last forever.

A look at her watch told her it could not.

She turned away from the river and looked towards Haddley Common. And then the woods beyond.

A place that still haunted her.

A place she had never wanted to see again.

But she was desperate and needed help. Abigail was dead, and there was no reason to think she wouldn't be next.

She walked quickly along the edge of the common. Ahead of her, the number 29 bus slowed and then stopped for a passenger to exit. She watched as the man, gently leaning on his walking cane, moved slowly down the steps and on to the path in front of her. White hair touching his collar, he reminded her of Mr Talisbrook as, stooping, he crossed towards the common. Resting against the flood wall, she watched and waited. Once the man was out of sight, she slowly moved forward. She needed to be certain she was alone. She looked back over her shoulder and saw each of the houses glaring across the common. Among them was the home of Nick Harper, the setting sun reflecting off its windows.

Accompanied only by the sound of her own breath, she

continued towards the woods. She was to keep walking along the Lower Haddley Road before cutting into the trees only when she approached the village of St Marnham. Making that turn, she looked at her watch. She had ten minutes to wait for the one person in the world she knew would help her.

CHAPTER 59

Late in the day, wanting to clear my head, I walk down to the river and buy myself an egg sandwich from the embankment stall popular with all the Sunday rowers. I sit on a bench to eat it, watching the last of the racers head up river towards St Marnham. Not having slept the previous night, I've spent the day lying in front of the TV watching rolling twenty-four-hour news retell my family's story.

Dani told me Simon Woakes didn't father the child. I've not been able to stop myself wondering if the real father would stop at nothing to keep that secret.

The sun is fading and it's getting cool, so I finish my sandwich and wander back along the towpath towards Haddley Bridge. A homeless man is sleeping under the arches as I pass, and I drop my change into his collection tin.

As dusk settles, I climb the steps from the river path to the high street, crossing at the lights and heading for the Watchman. Inside, I'm pointed upstairs to the cocktail bar, where I find Nathan restocking for the evening.

'I need to talk to you,' I say, as I approach.

'Ben!' he replies. 'What are you doing here?'

'They let me go.'

'Of course they did,' he replies. 'I meant, what are you doing here in the bar? Can I get you something? A whisky perhaps?'

'For once I could do with a double, but I think right now I'll pass.' I take a seat at the bar opposite Nathan as he starts to unload glasses from the dishwasher.

'What kind of questions did they ask you at the station? Was there something specific they wanted to know?'

'This isn't about me,' I reply. There's a flicker of defensiveness across his face and for a moment I think he's going to deny it. 'You need to tell me what you know.'

'I didn't know about Abigail Langdon, I promise.'

'Then you'd better tell me what you do know.'

Nathan puts down the bottle in his hand and stands opposite me, his hands resting on the bar between us. 'My adoption record was sealed. Even though I was eighteen, I was denied any information. My mum and dad told me I was adopted from a single mother who died in childbirth. I told them I wouldn't pursue it, but one of the reasons I went to Cardiff University is that they have a great legal department. The students get involved with pro bono schemes and four of them worked with me to have my adoption record unsealed.'

'And you won?'

'Yes,' replies Nathan, sweating more than he does when he sprints across the common. 'The record was opened to me and me alone. I've shared it with no one. I came here wanting to understand where I was from. You have to believe me.'

'How did it make you feel?'

'Desperate,' he replies. 'I love my mum and dad, but suddenly to know who I am . . . I never imagined it.'

'And now your birth mother is dead.'

Nathan frowns. 'Ben, I've no idea what has happened to her.' My eyes narrow, and he says, 'Abigail Langdon isn't my birth mother.'

And suddenly I'm hit by the assumptions I've made. I replay the conversation I had with Will last night in my head.

'Your mother is Josie Fairchild.'

Nine

'I should have said something sooner. I didn't plan on telling you like this but everything is spiralling out of control.'

CHAPTER 60

'Can I play outside now?' asked Alice, as she finished her last mouthful of Cheerios.

'It's still quite early,' replied Holly, glancing up at her kitchen clock to see that it was approaching eight.

'Please – I promise I'll be quiet. I won't wake up Daddy.' Holly smiled. 'Mummy, do you think Daddy has still got a poorly tummy?'

'Hopefully he'll be feeling much better today.'

'I don't like it when I have a poorly tummy,' said Alice, fetching her wellington boots from by the back door. 'I can only eat toast with no honey.'

'That's true,' said Holly, sitting her daughter on her knee. 'Are going to play on your bike?'

'No, I'm going to go in my house and make some toast for Daddy.'

'Make it quietly, then,' said Holly, as Alice jumped down and crossed to the kitchen door.

'And maybe some porridge,' said Alice, as she went

outside, 'with lots of blueberries and strawberry jam,' she shouted as she ran across the garden.

Holly stood and watched her daughter open the front door of her playhouse. When she turned, she found Jake standing behind her across the kitchen.

'Porridge with blueberries sounds good to me,' he said.

'Alice's special recipe,' replied Holly, leaving the back door ajar. 'You feeling more human today?'

'Still a little delicate, but I'm pleased to say it's not quite a two-day hangover.'

'Breakfast?'

'Sounds like Alice has it all in hand.'

Holly smiled and looked out at her daughter digging in the garden. 'I'm not sure she's using the best ingredients.'

Jake flopped down on the small sofa, which sat beneath the kitchen window. As he knocked, Alice turned and waved.

'Are you better, Daddy?' she called.

'Much,' he replied.

'I'm making you porridge. Will you come and eat it in my house?'

'In a minute I will.'

'I can bring you out the real thing if you like,' said Holly.

'That would be great,' said Jake, getting to his feet and taking a smoothie from the fridge. He grabbed a sweater from the back of a kitchen chair and wrestled it on before finding a matching pair of trainers by the door.

'Are you okay dropping her at nursery this morning?' asked Holly. 'I promised to meet your mum in St Marnham.'

'No problem,' replied Jake. 'Catching up with my mother – there's a treat. Special occasion?'

'I wanted to thank her for Saturday night,' said Holly, beginning to warm the milk.

'And excuse the behaviour of her son.'

'I'm sure she's already forgiven you.'

'Good of you to spend the time with her,' said Jake. He stood by the door. 'You spent some time together on Saturday night as well. Didn't I see you two go into the music room together? Be careful, or you'll be in danger of getting close.'

Stirring oats into the milk, Holly looked away from her husband. 'She asked me if Alice would like piano lessons. It's such a beautiful instrument and nobody ever plays it.'

'Let's wait until she's a little older,' replied Jake. 'A bit too soon yet, I would say. Nice of her to offer but she probably felt obliged. She doesn't really like anyone touching the piano. As a kid I was never allowed to go anywhere near it.'

Holly lowered the gas on the hob and crossed the kitchen to sit on the arm of the sofa. 'Is that because it was meant to be Lily's piano one day?'

Holly watched her husband's hand grip the door handle.

'We never speak of her,' he said, before silently walking out into the garden.

CHAPTER 61

Holly set down a steaming bowl of porridge on the wooden patio table that stood outside the back of her home. Looking across the garden, she saw Jake crammed inside Alice's playhouse.

'Alice, it's time for Daddy to come and have his breakfast.'

'We're having our breakfast in my house,' replied her daughter. 'I've made porridge.'

'I'm sure it's yummy but I made Daddy breakfast as well. He'll only be five minutes and then he can come back and play some more.' Through the playhouse window, Holly could see her husband remain steadfastly with his back to her. 'Jake, I'm going to leave it here.'

Moments later, Alice emerged through the front of the house and Jake crawled out behind her.

'Daddy, I'm going to dig in the garden while you eat your next breakfast for Mummy,' said Alice. 'When you've finished you can push me on my swing.'

Jake kissed his daughter on the forehead and walked up the garden. As he sat at the table, Holly came out of the kitchen to sit beside him.

'I'm sorry if I sprang that on you,' she said.

'My mum told you?'

Holly nodded. 'Why did you keep it a secret from me?'

'It wasn't so much a secret; as a family, we simply never spoke of her. I know it sounds harsh but I think that for my parents it was just too painful, for my mum especially. She told you on Saturday night?'

'Yes,' said Holly, watching her husband eat. 'It's obviously still incredibly painful for her. It helped me to understand her better. You know you could have told me.'

'It wasn't my secret to share.'

'Jake, it's a tragedy. Something your family has had to live with for so many years. I could have helped.'

Jake shrugged. 'Sometimes it can be easier to lock these things away.'

'In your family, yes.'

'That's a bit harsh.'

'Is it?' replied Holly, but, not wanting to start an argument, she added nothing more. 'Do you miss her?' she asked, after a moment.

'It was a long time ago. I can only vaguely remember her. I was seven, I think. I can remember my mother being so desperately distraught. For weeks on end, she never left her bedroom. Days and days would go by and I would never see her. I would creep into her room just to look at her. She must have been sedated; I don't really know. All she would ever do is sleep. I learnt to become very quiet.'

'And your father?'

'He was away a lot. Perhaps in his own way he tried – I

don't remember. He must have been suffering. Can you imagine how we would feel if anything happened to Alice?'

'Don't. I can't even begin to imagine.'

'They developed a way of dealing with the pain by simply not speaking of it. I'm amazed my mum told you, even now. I don't think she's ever told anyone. How did it come up?'

'I'm not really sure. I'd been over with Alice earlier in the day, feeding the ducks. Katherine had been watching us from the window and I asked why she hadn't come out to join us. She said the pond terrified her, that she couldn't go near. I asked her why and she told me.'

'Just like that?' replied Jake.

'Pretty much,' said Holly, getting to her feet and standing, arms folded, at the edge of the garden, watching her daughter fill her watering can. 'Your mum doesn't have any pictures of Lily in the house?'

'Too painful for her. I'm sure she has a few keepsakes.'

'I was looking for Alice's birth certificate last week, to register her for school.' Holly watches her husband as he scrapes his porridge bowl.

'And?'

'I couldn't find it, but I did find a baby's sleepsuit at the back of your old desk?'

'I've no idea why that was there,' replied Jake, picking up his bowl and putting it inside the kitchen door. 'Probably got caught up with the old junk my mother sent over.'

'I find it so sad that Lily is kept hidden away.'

'It's the way they want it,' said Jake, crossing the garden and catching hold of Alice as she raced towards him.

CHAPTER 62

I wake to the sound of someone knocking on my front door. It's well after eight but, after spending the previous night at Haddley police station, I'm in no great rush. When the doorbell rings, I get out of bed and peer through the blinds. A police car is parked outside the front of my house. I find a pair of shorts, pull a T-shirt over my head and quickly ruffle my hair.

Dani is looking across the common when I open the door, clearly lost in thought.

'Hey,' I say.

She turns back to me and smiles. 'I woke you, didn't I?'

'Not a problem. I always enjoy an early-morning visit from the local constabulary.'

'I was on my way in, so I thought I'd stop by and see how you're doing.'

'Very kind of you,' I say, stepping aside by way of invitation. 'Coffee?'

'Please.'

'Do you ever get a day off?'

'No leave, right now. Barnsdale's diktat. She wants *traction*. Her word not mine.'

I smile at Dani as I load a coffee pod before taking milk from the fridge. 'You had breakfast?' I ask.

'I had some toast before I left home.'

'That won't last you through the morning. Bowl of Coco Pops?' I say, taking a box from the cupboard.

'You really do have the worst possible diet!'

'I need someone to take me in hand,' I say, smiling. 'Your husband doesn't know how lucky he is.'

'You should tell him that.'

I turn and wait for her to continue.

'He's had a tough year. He was involved in an accident.'

'How bad?'

'He's in a wheelchair.'

'Shit.' I pass Dani her coffee. 'I'm really sorry.'

'Thanks,' she replies, sipping her drink as I top up the water in the machine. 'I told you he's a police officer?' I nod. 'He got caught up in an incident last Hallowe'en.'

A memory stirs. We covered the story on the site. 'At the supermarket, under the flats by the bridge?'

'Yes.'

'I remember it. An officer almost died?' Dani winces and I stare at her. 'That was your husband?'

'He wasn't my husband then. I suppose you would say we were dating. I was in the supermarket at the same time, picking up a few things after work.'

'You were okay, though?'

'Fine,' she replies. 'I didn't realise they had knives. I should have done. I should have acted differently.'

'How were you meant to know?'

She cuts across me. 'I panicked. One of them got me round the throat, held a knife to it.'

'That's a difficult situation for anyone,' I say, sitting opposite Dani.

'Mat was the first responder. He came in through the back of the store. If I'd realised sooner that there were knives, I wouldn't have put myself in such a vulnerable position. I was naïve.'

'How could you have known?'

'I'm a police officer, I should have known.'

'You were doing your shopping. Were you even on duty?'

'No, but that shouldn't make any difference.'

'You're not superhuman.'

I pour my cereal into a bowl and drown it in milk.

'You got enough in there?' asks Dani.

'I like to drink the milk afterwards.'

'What are you, five years old?'

I laugh. 'Can I ask what happened next?'

'A second guy attacked Mat from behind. He was stabbed at the base of his spinal column.'

'Not good.'

'He's paralysed from the waist down.'

'That's got to be incredibly tough.'

Dani swallows. 'It just feels like such a waste. He could have gone a long way in the police force.'

'Can't he still?' I ask.

'He's lost his fight. I hope maybe one day.' Dani pauses. 'It's my job to help him.'

'You can't blame yourself,' I say.

'Ben, you weren't there.'

We are silent. I'm desperate to tell Dani what I'm thinking: that none of this was her fault. I want her to tell her she is beautiful and smart and funny, and that she doesn't need to punish herself for a tragedy that wasn't of her making. But I don't. The words won't come.

Dani watches me eating my breakfast before reaching across the table to the stack of photographs I discovered among my mum's things. 'Can I look?'

'Sure.'

'Is that your dad?' she asks, picking up the top picture.

I nod.

'So your mum knew he was at the game?'

'From the photo, I guess so,' I reply. 'She never mentioned it, though.'

'All I'll say is, he looks like any other proud father.'

I don't respond.

'Me and my dad went through tough times,' says Dani, 'but I try to remember the fun stuff.'

'You were close to him, though?'

'A bit like you and your mum, for a long time it was just me and him. My mum died when I was very young. In many ways it was my dad who was my hero. He's the reason I'm here today. I wouldn't have been a police officer without him.' Dani pauses, before looking back down at the photograph. 'Maybe one day you'll have this picture up on the wall as well.'

344

I pour myself more cereal. 'I'm guessing you didn't stop by to reminisce and watch me eat my kids' breakfast?'

'Possibly not,' replies Dani.

'Or even just to see how I was doing?'

'We've received more documents from the original trial. A number are from interviews conducted while the two girls were in custody. Both were asked questions around their potential involvement with older men.'

Putting a second coffee capsule in my machine, I turn to Dani. 'Please tell me you're not still thinking Peter Woakes was involved with the two girls?'

'His wife was less than co-operative when we asked about him yesterday.'

'Perhaps because of the character assassination Haddley police are attempting?' I grab the steamer and hot milk spills on to my hand. 'Fuck!' I thrust my hand under the cold tap. 'His son was murdered,' I say, letting the water cool me.

Dani isn't about to be distracted. 'Could the girls have targeted Simon Woakes?'

'You're way off, Dani.'

'We're going to speak to his mother again today.'

I dry my hands and walk across to the counter. 'Come with me,' I say, taking Dani by the hand. We walk quickly out of the back of my house, up the alleyway towards the Cranfields'.

'Ben, where are we going?'

'We both agree that in some way Langdon and Fairchild were involved with older men, groomed by them. And I'd go as far as to say Abigail groomed Josie – used her, and lured

345

her in as the price of friendship. But the Woakes family have been through hell because of those two girls. Mrs Woakes is a good person, but not a woman who would protect her husband's memory out of blind loyalty. I want you to talk to somebody who knew Peter Woakes.' As we approach the top of the alleyway, I call for Mr Cranfield, knowing he will be outside tending his vegetable patch. 'Mr C, can we borrow you for two minutes?'

'Morning, Ben, how can I help?'

'This is PC Daniella Cash,' I say, introducing the pair. 'In confidence, I'd like you to tell her what you told me about Mr Woakes on Saturday night.'

Mr C looks at me, uncertain.

'Please,' I say.

Briefly, Mr C recounts to Dani the conversation he had shared with me – the regret that ate away at Peter Woakes, the opportunity he missed when he had the chance to act. 'I'd say he was haunted by it.'

'Haunted by regret?' I say.

'In many ways, yes. At his own failure to act.'

'Did he consider contacting the police at the time?' asks Dani.

'Sometimes it's only when you've lived with a lifetime of regret that you can piece together the things of real importance,' replies Mr C.

'I understand,' I say. 'We should leave you in peace.'

'Thanks for your time,' says Dani, as we walk away and head back along the edge of the common.

'There were rumours of a call being made to the school,' I

tell her. 'I don't know how true they are, but a failure to act on it might have driven his regret.'

'A call from whom?'

'A parent?' I reply. 'But I'm guessing.'

'And he still chose not to do anything.'

'If he'd had clear evidence pupils were in danger, I believe he would have. In fact, I'm one hundred per cent certain.'

'You might be, but I'm not,' replies Dani. 'We still can't rule out the possibility that it was Peter Woakes's own secret that destroyed him.'

'You're wrong,' I say. 'It was what Peter Woakes *didn't* do that shattered him, made the loss of his son all the more unbearable. Dani, I'm telling you, there is a man, an older man, who was involved with the girls – perhaps even the father of the child – who is still very much alive, and willing to stop at nothing to keep his secret.'

CHAPTER 63

'Why didn't you wake me?' called Sarah, tucking in her blouse as she ran down the stairs before slipping on her suit jacket. 'It's almost eight-thirty. I'm meant to be in a hearing at ten.'

'You've got plenty of time,' replied Nathan, looking up from the floor where he sat with Max eating breakfast. 'You looked as if you could do with the extra hour.'

'I wanted to give myself thirty minutes to review the case one more time. Can you drop Max at nursery?'

'Sure, we're good with that aren't we, buddy?' said Nathan, dressed in his running kit.

'Nathan made me dippy egg with soldiers.'

'That was nice of Nathan.'

'I love soldiers!' shouted Max, standing up beside his own child-sized table.

'I know you do,' said Sarah, smiling at Max. 'Drink your juice before we go.'

'There's something I need to talk to you about,' said Nathan. He got to his feet and crossed the kitchen.

'Now?' replied Sarah, throwing a teabag into her favourite mug, one designed by Max. 'Can't it wait until this evening?'

'I don't know if it can.'

'Really?' said Sarah. 'I'll make sure I'm home in good time.'

'Can you sit down for just two minutes?'

'We could have done this earlier if you'd woken me,' replied Sarah, as Nathan pulled a chair out for her.

'As I said, I didn't want to wake you.' There was an unease in his voice as he twisted a towel in his hands. 'I should have said something sooner. I didn't plan on telling you like this, but everything is spiralling out of control.'

'Nathe?' said Sarah.

'Mummy?' said Max.

'Drink your juice, darling.'

'Can I take a chocolate bar in my bag to nursery?'

'Okay,' replied Sarah, still looking at Nathan.

'And one for Alice?'

'If she's there, yes. Now drink your juice,' said Sarah.

'You need to know that I didn't come to Haddley simply to explore London,' continued Nathan, sitting next to Sarah. 'I came here to try to find out about myself, to understand where I came from.'

'You're from Wales?' said Sarah.

'Kind of. I'm adopted. My adoptive family come from Cowbridge,' he replied. 'My birth parents are from Haddley.'

'You're right, I wasn't expecting that,' said Sarah.

'There's more. I know who my mother is.' Nathan braced himself. He knew there'd be no going back. 'Josie Fairchild,' he said quickly.

Sarah's face froze.

'I only found out recently. I came here to understand what had happened and to see if I could find out who my father is. I know it sounds stupid but I want to know who I am, what this place did to my mother, and whether my father even knew I existed. I had no idea I would meet you, fall in love with you, and love caring for Max.'

Sarah got to her feet, lifting Max into her arms.

'I love being here with you both. Please say something.'

'Mummy, where are we going?'

'Mummy's going to drop you at nursery,' replied Sarah.

'I haven't finished my juice.'

Walking into the hall, Sarah picked up her bag along with Max's backpack, grabbed her keys from the side table and opened the front door. Nathan followed her. 'Sarah, talk to me, please.'

'I can't do this now,' she said.

'I just needed you to know. I didn't want to keep secrets.'

Dropping her voice, Sarah faced Nathan at the door. 'I welcomed you into my home, put my trust in you. And you never thought to mention this until now? Until Abigail Langdon is dead?'

'It wasn't like that.'

'I want you gone by the end of the day.'

Nathan stood motionless as Sarah carried Max outside.

'Mummy, you said I could have a chocolate bar!' cried Max.

'We'll buy one at the shop,' said Sarah, carefully making her way down the steps at the front of her house.

'And one for Alice?'

'And one for Alice.'

Nathan watched her kiss her son on the forehead and hug him close to her, as though shielding him from some invisible threat. She walked briskly across the common, and didn't look back.

CHAPTER 64

Village life in St Marnham was awakening to the new week. Holly stepped aside as the greengrocer dragged punnets of bedding plants out in front of his store. Next door, the baker was filling an empty basket with fresh brown rolls. The first rush of the morning was over, and now the high street was bustling with relieved mums returning from the school run. Holly wished she could be one of the women crammed into the coffee shop on the corner, laughing and chattering and worrying only about getting through the routine of the day.

Katherine had called her late on Sunday evening, still promising to help. Was she right to put her faith in her? She wanted to trust her mother-in-law but Holly was aware of the power Francis could exert. She had let him control her life for years. How could she be certain he wasn't using Katherine now?

Approaching the duck pond, Holly saw Katherine sitting alone on Lily's bench. She quickened her pace and took a seat beside her. For a moment they were silent, until Katherine, looking out across the pond towards her own home, said, 'I'm glad you came.'

'I'm sorry about the lamp,' replied Holly.

'I only wish you'd hit him with it.'

'Well, I'm sorry I missed, then.'

Katherine smiled. 'Lamps are replaceable. There are no prizes for staying trapped inside a loveless marriage. God help me, I should know. Things might have been very different if I'd been honest with myself right from the beginning. You tell yourself so many different truths simply to make life tolerable.'

'You and Francis were happy at first?' asked Holly.

Katherine considered. 'That's a good question to ask. Throughout my marriage, I've never wanted for anything. I've been able to go out and buy whatever I want without a single critical enquiry from my husband. I suppose that's lucky by some standards. He had no qualms about me going out and spending hundreds or even thousands of pounds. He's never cared what I spent it on. It was our very ability to spend which gave him pleasure. It gave him control over people, control over me. Katherine paused. 'But at the same time, in all of our years together, Francis has never given me anything.' Katherine stopped and turned to Holly. 'Does that make sense?'

'It does.'

'Like our first wedding anniversary,' she continued, moving to face Holly, taking hold of her hand. 'I'd spent weeks in the run-up buying Francis a whole series of gifts, each one representative of our first year together. I commissioned a hand-painted replica of the sailboat where we'd spent our honeymoon, a model of our house with its bright blue front door, a tiny crib, a rowing boat for our time spent messing about on the river. All personal to us. Francis bought me a top-of-the-range microwave oven and told me it had only just been released on to the market.' The two women laughed. 'It was a revelation in so many ways, but I chose to ignore it, then and for so many years after.'

'And Jake?'

'I so wanted it to be different with him,' said Katherine. 'Everything I gave him came with love but he grew to resent it all. He would have swapped every single thing I ever gave him to receive one tiny gift of love from his father.'

Holly squeezed her mother-in-law's hand. 'He does appreciate—'

'Don't,' replied Katherine. 'Please don't. I was so desperate for Jake to love me—'

'He does.'

'Let me finish, please. I would have given anything to create a connection between the two of us, a bond, but the harder I tried, the more I pushed him away.' Katherine closed her eyes. 'It was never going to be easy. It's never the same when it's another woman's child.'

Holly stared at her mother-in-law. 'What do you mean?'

'Jake isn't my son,' continued Katherine, her voice surprisingly calm. 'He's Francis's child with another woman, from before we were married. For all I know, Francis may have a whole family of other children.'

'I had no idea. Does Jake know?'

'No. I've always tried to treat him as my own, but somehow it's meant he's needed more from his father; something Francis refused to give him and I simply couldn't find a way to.' Holly saw the sadness in Katherine's eyes, a secret buried deep for so many years. 'I doubt Jake will ever be happy.'

'Not without Francis's approval,' replied Holly. 'I've tried to find a way ... '

'It runs too deep,' said Katherine. 'You don't love Jake?'

'I don't,' said Holly. Hearing herself say the words aloud made her wince.

'Then you don't have to say any more.' Katherine stood and Holly followed, her mother-in-law linking her arm through hers. 'I have some money of my own and I want that money to go to you and Alice,' said Katherine, as the two women began a slow walk around the banks of the pond. 'Use it to take yourself far away from here and to begin your life over.'

'What if they come after Alice?' said Holly, voicing her greatest fear. 'I've been searching everywhere for her birth certificate. If I could have Michael named as her father ... '

'I won't let them come after you. You have my word.' Katherine's voice was firm, urgent. 'Neither Francis nor Jake must have any idea what we are planning. We must get you and Alice safely away and then I will deal with Francis. Do you have your own bank account?'

'Everything is in joint names.'

'Then go straight from here and set up your own account. Send me the details and I will transfer in two hundred thousand pounds. Plan to leave on the most ordinary of days.

355

Walk out of the door as if you are taking Alice to the park. And never look back.'

Holly felt an urge to throw her arms around Katherine. 'I'll never be able to thank you enough,' she said, a tremor in her voice.

'I only wish I'd opened my eyes sooner,' replied Katherine. 'You must be strong.'

The women parted, and Holly stood and watched as Katherine walked around the pond towards her home. Then she turned, and quickly made her way back through the village. Her eyes on the ground, she was unaware of Francis watching every step she took.

CHAPTER 65

'Mrs Woakes, it's Ben,' I say into my headset as I leave my house and begin a walk around the edge of the common. 'I wish you were picking up. I'm sorry if I've put you in a difficult position. I know you're only trying to protect Mr Woakes but I'd ask you just to be honest with the police. He was a good man caught in a bad situation. That wasn't his fault. I'm sure he did nothing wrong and I know you haven't. Call me when you get this.'

I click off my phone before scanning through my contacts. I dial again and this time my call is answered almost immediately.

'Will, it's Ben Harper,' I say.

'Hi.' Will is abrupt, tense.

'You okay?' I ask.

'Yes, I'm sorry, I'm fine, except I'm standing in my driveway where some fuckwit has slashed the tyres on my R8. What is wrong with these people?'

'Just unbelievable.'

'But hey, more importantly, how are you doing?' he asks.

'I heard the police took you in for questioning. They must be crazy.'

'I'm fine, but I wanted to ask you a couple more questions. Just background stuff.'

'Fire away,' replies Will, without hesitation.

'If the police were to ask you about the town of Farsley, how would you answer?'

'Ben, that doesn't really sound like background,' says Will. 'I do read the Sunday papers.'

'Maybe it's more me wanting to give you a heads-up,' I say. 'My guess is, the police will soon start looking at men who had contact with Langdon and Fairchild before the murders.'

'I was only a kid then.'

'So were they,' I reply. 'But I know for certain there is a child; not Langdon's but Fairchild's.' My phone goes silent. 'Will, are you still there?'

A moment later the line reconnects.

'Sorry, Ben, I'm here.'

'I think it's quite possible the police will try to find the father of the child.'

'Not a simple process.'

'No,' I agree. 'I know what you told me was in confidence . . . '

'I have nothing to hide.'

'I don't want to put you in a difficult position,' I say.

'Ben, last week I spent three days in Frankfurt. I arrived back at Heathrow Airport on Wednesday lunchtime, where East was waiting to meet me. There will be plenty of witnesses to confirm that I was nowhere near Farsley.'

'I have no intention of volunteering anything about you to the police.'

'You've already spent a night in Haddley police station,' replies Will. 'I don't need you to spend another simply to protect me. If the police want to speak to me at some point, I'm sure they will be able to find me. I have to go, Ben. Let's get a beer when this is all over.'

Relieved at Will's alibi, I still can't help but wonder if he might be Nathan's father. I look up the road and see Mr C opening his garage door. I wander towards him. 'Thanks for earlier,' I say, as I approach. 'Are you all set for a day in the garden? You can come and do mine when you're finished.'

'Just pottering,' he replies, walking over to greet me. 'I was surprised to see you helping the police after spending a night at the station.'

'Dani's different,' I reply, 'at least I think she is. In the interview they were just fishing, nothing more. They see me as a useful source of information, not a real suspect.'

'You doing their job for them, more like.'

'Maybe I'm better at asking the right questions.'

'Mrs C was all set to bring your lunch over yesterday afternoon,' he tells me, leaning in conspiratorially, 'but I persuaded her you might be happy to have a little time on your own.'

'Thanks,' I reply. 'I have to admit I was exhausted. Is she about?'

'It's her book club in Richmond this lunchtime. She's gone off early to meet one of her cronies for coffee. They'll have a lot to talk about.'

'I'm sure this is keeping everyone engaged.'

'It'll be over soon, Ben,' says Mr C, a hand on my shoulder. 'A run will do you good.'

'Let's call it a jog,' I reply, reaching for my phone to launch Spotify. 'Thirty minutes to clear my head.'

'Enjoy,' says Mr C as I turn and begin a slow jog across the centre of the common.

I'm about to click on my running playlist when, hearing footsteps, I turn to see Jake Richardson appearing behind me.

'Mind if I join you?' he says.

'Of course not,' I reply, clicking off my music. 'No work today?' We begin a conversational jog across the common and down to the Lower Haddley Road.

'I've a meeting up in Paddington this afternoon but it feels like one of those leads that's a bit of a wild goose chase. Hol's over seeing my mother and I've just dropped Alice at nursery so I thought I'd make the effort to get outside.'

'Effort is the right word,' I say as we go single file past the passengers stepping off the number 29 bus. 'Sore head yesterday?' I ask, turning round to smile at him.

'Every time I tell myself I'm not going to do it again. This time I mean it!'

'Until next time,' I reply, and we slightly pick up our pace as we run towards Haddley Woods.

We've just reached the river path when a harrowing noise stops us in our tracks. For a moment, as the bus rumbles past us, and life on the Lower Haddley Road continues as normal, I think we've imagined it. But then it comes again:

the unmistakable sound of a child's scream, echoing from inside the woods.

Jake is the first to react. He sprints up the common to the opening where I had entered the woods more than twenty years before. My heart pounding, I run after him and together we push aside the branches, now far more overgrown than they were that summer.

A few steps into the undergrowth, two boys, aged no more than ten or eleven, come running towards us through the trees, terror stamped upon their faces. The elder of the two stumbles through his words.

'In the middle of the woods, there's a woman ... '

Hopping from one foot to another, sweat covering his bright red face, the younger boy can stay silent no longer.

'She's hanging from a tree!'

'Can you find your way back there?' asks Jake urgently, and I can see hesitancy in the face of both boys.

'Don't worry, we'll be with you,' I say. 'We'll all stick together.' As the older boy turns, leading Jake through the woods, the younger boy takes my hand and we run side by side. Dodging through the trees, I'm eight years old again, following the narrow and twisting path towards the open space at the heart of the woods. As the route becomes increasingly overgrown and hoary tree roots protrude, I call ahead.

'Jake, hold up a second.'

I see him slow, and as he does I turn to the young boy running at my side. 'What's your name?' I ask.

'Oscar, and that's my brother Harry. I'm nine and he's

eleven. We cut through the woods every morning to go to school. We were late this morning because I had to go to the dentist for a filling.'

'My name's Ben, and that's Jake. Are we getting near now?' Oscar nods. 'You okay to go on?' I ask, and he nods again.

'Just through here,' says Harry, an urgency in his voice as he takes the lead again, pushing branches from our path. Ahead of us, daylight breaks through, and as we approach the clearing I see cigarette butts still scattered on the ground.

We enter the hollow and stand together in the centre. Turning to look back above the path from where we have come, Harry points towards a sprawling oak, standing proud in the heart of the woods.

I feel Oscar bury his head into my side. I hold him close but I cannot turn away.

The tree is slightly set apart from the others, its branches reaching in all directions.

And from the thickest branch, swaying eerily in the breeze, is the hanging body of Elizabeth Woakes.

Ten

*'The incessant drip of rain on to the
cold concrete floor had kept Corrine awake
most of the night. That, and the sound of
the woman's deafening scream playing
over and over in her head.'*

CHAPTER 66

The whirr of a television news helicopter fills the room as Dani and I stare out from my living-room window. Barnsdale stands outside the front of my home, briefing a senior officer. A full-scale media invasion has returned to Haddley Common. Indistinguishable voices shout questions in the direction of my house and it's impossible to tell if they are aimed at the detectives or at me. Dani and I turn away from the window and cross the room to sit together on the sofa.

'Barnsdale is still refusing to rule out Elizabeth Woakes being involved in Langdon's death in some way,' says Dani.

'Surely she's letting that go,' I reply. 'The woman's been strangled and then hung from a tree.'

Dani raises her eyebrows. 'She told me we have to *remain open to all lines of enquiry.*' I suspect what this means is that Barnsdale doesn't have any.

'She's clinging on to her theory about Mr and Mrs Woakes because she hasn't got anything else,' I say. 'Can you tell me what happened with Mrs Woakes yesterday?'

Dani rises up in her seat and looks out of my front window. Barnsdale is still speaking to the senior officer. 'Mrs Woakes came to the interview alone,' says Dani, dropping her voice. 'Barnsdale interviewed her for about an hour but we didn't discover anything new. Mrs Woakes was adamant that her husband knew no more about Langdon and Fairchild than he did any about other child at the school. The interview ended just before five. I've reviewed CCTV cameras this morning and they show her leaving from the front of the building. Then she walks up Haddley high street in the direction of the railway station.'

'To catch the train back to Richmond,' I say.

'Yes,' replies Dani, again looking out of the front window, 'but here's the thing. She entered the railway station at nine minutes past five. She bought herself what looks like a cup of tea from Caffè Nero and passed through the ticket gate.' I nod.

'Then she stopped to read the information screen,' continues Dani, 'and passengers started to come off a train arriving from Waterloo. When these passengers exit the station, Mrs Woakes turns and follows them back out on to the high street.'

'Why would she enter and then exit?' I ask.

Dani quickly gets to her feet and crosses back to the window. I follow her and we see Barnsdale still standing on the path at the front of my house.

'Immediately after Langdon's death, a decision was made to contact Josie Fairchild and activate a plan to relocate her,' says Dani, standing close to me. 'Kent Police have been to her home on numerous occasions over the past few days but it's been impossible to reach her. However, CCTV cameras did capture her boarding a London-bound train on Sunday, at lunchtime. In the late afternoon she arrived at Charing Cross before taking a connecting train across London to Haddley.'

'Josie Fairchild was on that train?'

'Yes!' replies Dani. 'And Elizabeth Woakes saw her walk out of the front of Haddley station.'

'She recognised her?'

'It would seem so.'

'Do you think they arranged to meet?' I say. It still seems impossible to me that my mum had been in contact with Langdon, but she was, so why not Mrs Woakes with Fairchild?

'There's no sign of any interaction between them,' says Dani. I touch her arm and point towards Barnsdale walking towards my open front door, and she continues faster and more quietly. 'Fairchild left the station and Elizabeth Woakes followed her. Fairchild set off towards the river with Mrs Woakes in pursuit. The last images we can find are of Fairchild walking in front of the Watchman bar, with Elizabeth Woakes passing around a minute later.'

'And since then?' I ask. 'Do you have any idea where Fairchild is?'

My living-room door is pushed open. Barnsdale looks directly at Dani.

'None,' is the detective's answer to my question.

CHAPTER 67

I invite the detective to take a seat. Dani and I return to the sofa.

'Josie Fairchild's son is living here in Haddley,' I say to DS Barnsdale. 'He's called Nathan Beavin and he works as a barman at the Watchman.'

Controlled, the detective smooths the perfect crease in her jet-black trousers before brushing away specks of imaginary dust. Dani's bright eyes prevent her disguising her surprise but, sitting in silence, she waits for her superior to respond.

'I should have learnt by now, Mr Harper, that you are always full of surprises.'

I'm tempted to thank the officer but instead acknowledge her only with a self-conscious smile.

'And you've known this for how long?' she asks.

'For certain, since late yesterday.'

Barnsdale nods. 'Have you spoken to him?'

There is nothing to be gained by withholding anything from Barnsdale. 'Yes, he's living in a house at the top of the common. Number twenty-one, I think.'

'How lovely,' replies Barnsdale.

'He's staying with a woman called Sarah Wright. And her son, Max.'

Dani writes down the names.

'I've no reason to believe he was in contact with Josie Fairchild, nor that he was involved with the killing of Mrs Woakes.'

DS Barnsdale sniffs at my assessment. 'Mr Harper, while we are grateful to you for sharing this information, perhaps you could let *us* decide who is and who isn't a suspect in this case.'

I resist the temptation to bite back.

'How did you find him?' asks Dani.

'He's been asking a lot of questions, wanting to know about Nick and my family. He's also shown an interest in James Wright, Sarah's former husband.'

'I should at least thank you for the information,' says Barnsdale, getting to her feet. 'We will proceed from here.'

'Please don't jump to any conclusions,' I say. 'He had no reason to kill Mrs Woakes.'

'Mother and son together in Haddley,' she continues. 'It's my job to find out why.'

CHAPTER 68

'Stay in the garden,' called Holly to her daughter as Alice tiptoed out of the front gate to peer up the road at the police officers.

'Is Sarah going to jail?' asked Alice, as she watched two policewomen climb the steps to the front door of Sarah Wright's home. 'And Max!'

'No, the police just need to ask her some questions.'

'Why, Mummy?'

'I've no idea,' said Holly, unsure how to answer her young daughter. 'Come on, let's go inside and get you some tea. It's starting to rain again.'

'I want to play here,' said Alice. 'This is my favourite place to play.'

'Alice, inside, now.' Holly stood by the door as Alice reluctantly came away from the gate, dragging her feet deliberately. 'Hurry up.'

But seconds later, spying two figures coming up the road, Alice charged forward again.

'Max!' she called. 'Max, the police are going to lock you up in jail!'

'No, they aren't,' said Holly.

'Hol, can you take him? Just for half an hour,' said Sarah, as Max ran towards Alice.

'Of course,' replied Holly, taking Max by the hand. 'I can give him some tea, if you like?'

'Thanks,' said Sarah. 'Poor woman, this is just horrendous. I need to find out what's going on.'

'I can't believe it's happened again in Haddley.'

'Are you okay?'

'I will be,' replied Holly, hugging her friend before watching her walk quickly across the common towards her home.

Nathan stood at the window and watched as the two police officers climbed the steps to Sarah's home. He opened the door as soon as they rang the bell.

'Mr Nathan Beavin?' asked DS Barnsdale. The officers introduced themselves to him.

'You'd better come in,' he replied. 'You could say I've been expecting you.'

Standing in the kitchen with the two officers, Nathan heard the front door open.

'Miss Wright?' said Barnsdale, as Sarah walked through into the kitchen.

'Mrs,' said Sarah, 'I'm divorced.'

'Of course.'

'How can I help you?'

'We're here to ask Mr Beavin some questions regarding his mother,' said Barnsdale.

'You mean his birth mother?'

'Yes,' said Barnsdale. 'You're aware?' she continued, allowing her voice to reveal her surprise.

'That it's Josie Fairchild? Yes.'

'Mr Beavin, we've a number of questions we would like to ask you with regard to your movements yesterday, and I was hoping you would accompany us to the station.'

Nathan turned to Sarah.

'Are you arresting him?' asked Sarah.

'No,' replied Barnsdale, 'but I would appreciate it if Mr Beavin would co-operate with our investigation.'

'If you've questions, fire away,' said Sarah, 'but he won't be joining you at the station.'

'Are you representing Mr Beavin?'

'If you want me to,' replied Sarah, to the officer.

Nathan exhaled but Barnsdale pressed on. 'Did you arrange to meet your mother in Haddley yesterday evening?'

'I've never met my birth mother,' said Nathan. 'I've no idea where she is.'

'Have you ever tried to make contact with her?'

'Never.'

'But you did have your adoption record opened?'

'Under a court order, yes,' replied Nathan.

'Did you ever meet Elizabeth Woakes?'

'No.'

'Did you arrange to meet Josie Fairchild or Elizabeth Woakes at the Watchman bar yesterday evening?'

'No.'

'That is your place of work?'

'Yes, but my shift finished at eight.'

'And after that we were here together all evening,' said Sarah.

'All evening?'

'All evening.'

'Can you tell me about your interest in James Wright?'

'James?' said Sarah, turning to Nathan. 'What about James?'

Nathan was silent. Pushing his hand through his hair, he saw all eyes in the room upon him. 'Mr Beavin,' said Barnsdale. 'Perhaps you'd care to enlighten us – all of us?'

'Sarah, I didn't plan any of this. I really didn't think it would turn out like this. I haven't done anything wrong. You have to believe me.'

'What about James?' said Sarah.

Nathan reached for his jacket and took his wallet from the inside pocket. He retrieved the thumbnail image he had found hidden in the depths of an online search. The only unfamiliar image he could find of his mother.

And, beside her, James Wright.

He handed the picture to Sarah.

'After the adoption file had been released to me, I discovered this picture online.'

Sarah hands the image to DS Barnsdale. 'This is your ex-husband?'

'Yes.'

'All I was doing was trying to find out who my father was.'

'We will have further questions in the coming days,' said Barnsdale, 'for both of you.'

'I'm sure we'll look forward to that,' said Sarah, stepping

out of the kitchen and through into the hall. Barnsdale and Cash followed in silence and as they left her home, Sarah closed the door behind them.

'You have to believe me,' said Nathan, following Sarah into the hall. 'I never set out to hurt you.'

'I said I wanted you gone before the end of the day,' said Sarah. 'I'm going to collect Max, and I don't want you here when I get back.'

CHAPTER 69

The incessant drip of rain on to the cold concrete floor had kept Corrine awake most of the night. That, and the sound of the woman's deafening scream playing over and over in her head.

When the woman had come upon them in the clearing, Corrine had turned and run. In the gathering gloom, she had staggered through the trees and out into the village of St Marnham. Racked with fear and convinced she would be recognised, she had pulled her hood over her face and quickly made her way down to the river. The Peacock boathouse had been abandoned for years. Even when Corrine was young, nobody had claimed it. The rear door was almost completely rotten at the hinge. It had been easy to prise it open and take shelter.

Inside, little had changed.

Corrine wrapped her coat tightly around her, but still the wet and dank of the night was still impossible to escape. She huddled against the decaying boat racks, trying to block out the memory of her first visit here.

This was where Abigail had brought her.

The surprise she had promised. The secret they would share.

The man pressing inside her.

The hard concrete floor unyielding.

Time and again, Abigail brought her here.

Their tormenter hidden, watching from behind the racking.

Throughout the day, Corrine couldn't help but wonder whether she shouldn't have made her escape the previous night when the opportunity had offered itself. With the rain pouring, it would have been simple for her to walk unnoticed along the riverbank to Richmond. A train from there and she could be back in Deal now, back above the amusement arcade. Tonight she was due on shift at Sunny Sea. Molly would seize on any opportunity to fire her. Her dismal life suddenly seemed so appealing. At least it was safe. Now, Corrine doubted she would ever be safe anywhere again.

Cold and hungry, she peered through the rotten door at the dreary late -afternoon sky and asked herself why she had ever thought it was a good idea to come back to Haddley. She hated Haddley. Life here had only ever been wretched. Now she had broken the terms of her release. If the police found her, her arrest would be immediate. The sound of sirens whirring for much of the day had paralysed her. She dared not think what had happened to the woman from last night, but she knew she wouldn't be alive today.

He had killed Abigail.

He had killed the woman.

And he would kill her next.

She should leave now while she still could.

She wrenched open the door and watched the tide rising up the bank.

This had been her last chance. Her one final opportunity to escape the life of Corrine Parsons. To become somebody else, somebody new.

She had returned to Haddley to take that chance.

With the woman dead in the woods, perhaps her opportunity was even greater. It would be something he'd be desperate to conceal.

Pulling her hood back over her head, she momentarily stepped outside. The rain was beginning again. Cars on the Haddley Bridge were stationary, their lights illuminated.

Feeling for the knife inside her coat, she retreated back into the boathouse and barred the door. She would wait until nightfall, and then make her way back into the village of St Marnham.

CHAPTER 70

My phone buzzes with a message from Madeline announcing that she is seven minutes away. A second message follows almost immediately, telling me not to answer a single question from any journalist. In every tragedy, Madeline sees an exclusive.

Confusion still consumes the common. The road between Haddley and St Marnham remains closed, with police tape stretched from side to side. Two constables stand at the entrance to the woods and half of the common remains cordoned off. Press vehicles mix with those of the police, while media types report live to twenty-four-hour rolling news channels. I see Francis Richardson striding through the chaos, passing comment as he walks towards Jake's and Holly's home. Barnsdale and Cash come down the steps at the front of Sarah's house; the detective then heads across the common towards the entrance to the woods, while Dani is dispatched to collect their car.

When I open the door of my house, cameras turn their lenses towards me but, stepping outside, I ignore the barrage of questions launched in my direction. Journalists ask about my mum and her relationship with Elizabeth Woakes: were she and I close; does this bring back memories of Nick? Obvious questions. I drop my head, indicating that I have nothing to say. They continue to shout my name, and I tell myself they are simply doing their jobs.

I walk directly towards Dani, gently touching her arm and stopping her as she reaches her car.

'Tell my why,' I say. 'Why would Nathan finally discover who his mother was, only to come to Haddley and get mixed up in a murder?'

'Not here, Ben,' she replies, looking towards the group of reporters following me up the road.

Glancing back across the common, I see a team from my own site, and then Min suddenly steps forward from the crowd. 'Ben, come and talk to us,' she calls. I hesitate. 'Ben, just thirty seconds, let everyone know you're okay.'

'Let's go inside,' says Dani, taking hold of my arm.

'Ben!' calls Min, but Dani leads me back across the road and, with cameras still trained upon us, we step back inside my hallway.

'It makes no sense,' I say, returning to my train of thought. 'Barnsdale can check the court records herself to see when he learnt the identity of his mother, but we're talking weeks, not even months. In that time he's supposed to have discovered her location, formed a murderous bond with her, and hatched a plan to kill first Langdon and then Mrs Woakes? It's ridiculous.'

'I don't disagree and I don't think DS Barnsdale does,

either,' says Dani, as we head through into the kitchen. 'Nevertheless, it would be a dereliction of duty if we didn't speak to Fairchild's son the moment he appears in Haddley. He may not be the killer, but he might be protecting her. The bond between a mother and her child can be strong.'

I have to concede the possibility. 'It's impossible for us to know how Nathan feels towards his birth mother,' I say, 'but there's still nothing to link him to Elizabeth Woakes. He came to Haddley to try to make some sense of his family. I'm certain he's the wrong focus. The bigger question is, why did *Josie Fairchild* come back to Haddley?'

'Nathan could be the reason.'

'Having spoken with him, I just don't see it. Do you?' Dani slowly shakes her head. 'He's looking for his father here, not his mother.'

'He had a picture of Josie Fairchild standing with James Wright.'

I reach for the photographs taken on the day of the rugby finals and quickly flick through them. 'This one?' I say to Dani, passing her the original of James Wright standing with Langdon and Fairchild.

'Yes,' says Dani. 'He was the captain of the senior team?' I nod. 'I guess everyone wanted their picture taken with him.'

'True,' I reply, 'but could there be something more? Mrs Woakes felt deeply uncomfortable on that day. Langdon and Fairchild masquerading as two silly teenage girls; James Wright, captain of the rugby team and heading to Oxford ...'

Dani is thoughtful. 'That was all anybody saw.'

'He was four years older than them – an adult about to leave school.'

'But there's no evidence to make him a killer, any more than any other member of the Haddley first team.'

'That might be true, but I do know that right now he has a huge amount to protect.'

'Barnsdale wants me to check out where he was yesterday. Let's see what that throws up.'

'You don't sound convinced?' I say.

'After you took me to speak with Mr Cranfield, I went back through the original case file again. Enquiries were made into an anonymous call. It was made to the school, regarding two unidentified girls and their potential involvement with an older man. By the time the call came to light, Langdon and Fairchild had already been arrested. After a brief conversation with Peter Woakes, the decision was taken to rest the line of enquiry.'

'Do you know exactly what the caller said?'

'That's all we have. Two girls, but very much the suggestion of an "older man". Is that really James Wright – or anybody else in the school rugby team?'

'When was the call made?'

'From what I can make out, a few weeks before Nick and Simon were killed. We still have to be open to the possibility that Peter Woakes was happy to bury it.'

'No,' I reply.

'Then why didn't he take it further at the time?'

'Because it was one call,' I say. 'Or because he was too scared of the person he might uncover?'

Dani shrugs.

'Do you think Elizabeth Woakes arranged to meet Fairchild last night?' I ask.

'Why would Josie arrange to meet her and then kill her?'

'I agree. If you were Fairchild returning to Haddley, how would you feel?'

'Scared.'

'Definitely,' I reply. 'You're terrified. You see the news about Abigail Langdon and you think you're next. You want protection and you need money. By returning to Haddley, you know you're risking your life.'

'So who in Haddley was worth that risk?'

Suddenly there is a rattle on my front door and a clamour erupts out on the common. As we go back into the hall, Dani and I hear raised voices, and we open the door to a barrage of questions, cameras firing and lights flashing in the fading late-afternoon light.

'We have no comment to make, but if you want to read Ben Harper's heartbreaking story in his own words there is only one place you can do that.' The cameras explode again before Madeline turns and walks inside. 'Bloody animals,' she smirks, before looking across at Dani readjusting her hat. 'You've got company.'

'PC Daniella Cash – she's working on the case.'

'Hi,' says Dani, looking across at my boss.

'I'm afraid Ben and I have things to discuss,' says Madeline, dismissing her as if Dani were a junior member of staff on the website. 'Glasses in the kitchen?' she asks, turning to me and pulling a bottle of Hibiki whisky from her oversized trench coat.

Dani stands open-mouthed as Madeline walks up the hallway. 'Nice to meet you,' she says quietly.

'And you,' calls Madeline, with a wave of the bottle.

'That's Madeline Wilson,' says Dani.

'She's a bit of a one-off,' I reply. 'I should let you get back to Barnsdale.'

Dani nods and rolls her eyes.

'I'll let you know if I find anything,' I assure her.

There is another blinding flash of cameras as Dani steps outside. I close the door behind her, then head to the kitchen, where Madeline has already poured two glasses of whisky.

'You know I hardly drink,' I say.

'Please don't disappoint me any more,' replies Madeline, already seated. I hide my smile as I take three cubes of ice from the freezer for myself.

'First off,' she says, 'tell me that you are okay?'

'I'm fine,' I reply, dropping the ice into my glass.

'And you're not about to arrested for murder?'

'No,' I reply. 'I think I'm in the clear.'

'I was sad to hear about Elizabeth Woakes. I know you were close.'

'Thank you.'

'And second off . . . ' Madeline pauses. 'I'm sorry. There I've said it.'

I nod my head in acknowledgment of Madeline's apology. She says nothing more and we sit in silence, both waiting for the other to speak.

'Goddammit!' she says, after what feels like an interminable wait. 'You're better at this than me. And I taught you.'

I smile.

'Look,' she says, 'maybe I went about it the wrong way with your mother, but I didn't come from a wholly bad place. At the very least, I made her feel as if I was trying to help. That makes me not all bad. And what was so very wrong about her wanting to know about the child, particularly if it was her grandchild?'

'It wasn't,' I reply. 'In fact it wasn't Langdon's child at all, it was Fairchild's.'

'Say more.'

'The child is here in Haddley,' I continue, knowing Madeline's green eyes will illuminate at the news. 'And so is Josie Fairchild.'

'My God, Ben, this is dynamite. We need to publish, but ...'

'But what? Not like you to hesitate.'

'I know you find it hard to believe, but even I have the odd momentary pang of loyalty.'

'You see, you *are* not all bad,' I reply. 'I assume we're talking about East?'

Madeline nods.

'He's been putting pressure on you?'

'Something like that. And of course we must publish.'

'Once we have everything.'

'And you are our exclusive?'

'I'm good to my word,' I say. 'I said I would write this story, but only when I can tell it all. So, tell me about East.'

Madeline coils back into her seat, sipping her whisky. 'We've been friends since school, good friends. Being me, you tend not to attract huge numbers of close friends, and the ones you do you have, you end up stabbing in the back.'

'Or the front.'

Madeline smiles. 'True, but since school East has always been there for me. Right from the beginning we just clicked, shared everything with each other.'

I nod. 'Including the fact that there was a child?'

'Yes,' replies Madeline. 'We'd both grown up around the story, known so many of the people involved.'

'East knew pupils at Haddley Grammar?'

'He was the captain of Twickenham Duke rugby team, even though he hated the game.'

I search for the blood-covered image of East from the day of the finals. 'Brutal game,' I say, passing the photo to Madeline.

She smiles. 'He didn't even play.'

'How did he end up in that state, then?'

'The two of us arrived at the rugby club a couple of hours early. I wanted to check out the light and then take a few pictures of the pitch being set up, flags being raised, that kind of stuff. East wanted to smoke a massive spliff.'

I laugh. 'Great game preparation.'

'What the hell was in it, I don't know, but an hour before the match he could barely stand. I was getting him to his feet when E.E. Hathaway stumbled across us. Even then he walked with a cane, and East was in no position to protect himself when he whipped it across the side of his face.'

I flinch at the thought. 'And this was the result?' I ask, picking up the photograph.

'East spent the whole of the match in the stands.'

'He would have seen everyone, even Langdon and Fairchild?'

'On that day, Langdon and Fairchild were just another two girls at a rugby game.'

'Maybe, maybe not,' I say, increasingly haunted by all of the images from that day. 'And Will?' I ask. 'Did East know him back then?'

'No, Will is four years younger, the same age as Nick. East and Will didn't meet until years later.'

'But years later, when they did get together, East already knew there was a child – and then at some point Will told him he'd had sex with Josie Fairchild.'

Madeline tangles her fingers through her hair. 'We agreed it was best not to tell Will about the child. What difference would it make?'

'And East very much wanted the secret to remain one.'

'Who'd want to be exposed as the father of Josie Fairchild's kid? East is terrified it might destroy them.'

'Let alone what it might be like for the child.'

Madeline sips on her drink. 'Have you met the child?'

'I have.'

'And?' says Madeline, raising her eyebrows.

'Who knows? Let's wait until it's all over.'

Madeline reaches across the kitchen island for the match day photographs. Within seconds she has the stack sorted into three sections. 'Championship game, crowd cutaways, and post-match celebrations.'

'Impressive.'

'Not a day I'm ever going to forget.'

Together we begin to look through the images and once more I see the faces from a lifetime ago.

'You're missing two pictures,' she says, 'one from the match action and one from the post-match celebrations.'

'How do you know?' I ask.

'Back in the Dark Ages we took pictures in film reels of twenty-four. You've twenty-three in both of these sets. They could have been failed exposures, but I didn't have many of those.'

'Ever the perfectionist,' I say.

'Got me a long way.'

'That, and stealing a march on the competition.'

Madeline generously tops up her glass and without comment passes me a photograph of Elizabeth Woakes shaking hands with James Wright. Their faces are wreathed in smiles, and I can only give the picture a cursory glance.

'I know this isn't easy, Ben,' Madeline says, 'but when we publish this story it's going to blow the roof off. It's going to send you stratospheric.'

'Along with your reader numbers.'

'We are running a business.'

'But nothing is published until I say so?'

'You have my word,' replies Madeline, with a smile. 'This is your story, Ben, and your life. I won't publish until you tell me. Where do you go next?'

'Josie Fairchild came to Haddley for a reason. I believe that reason was to meet with the man who groomed her and Abigail, quite possibly the father of her child.'

'To blackmail him?'

'Yes. And if she's still here, she's going to try and meet with him again.'

'But who is it?'

'I know the father's not Nick or Simon, but beyond that ... ?' I shrug.

'And if she already has what she came for?'

'Then I keep looking – but something tells me she doesn't. Killing Elizabeth Woakes can't have been in her plan.'

Madeline makes no response. I glance, and see that she's staring hard at one of the photographs.

'What is it?'

Madeline places the photograph in front of me. The image shows the triumphant senior team, grouped around James Wright. She points at the top corner. Turning away from his winning team is Peter Woakes, his attention drawn to the other side of the pitch.

Only now do I see what he saw. Barely visible on the extreme left are Abigail Langdon and Josie Fairchild. And standing between them, his arms wrapped around them both, is Francis Richardson.

CHAPTER 71

As I lie on the battered sofa at the back of my kitchen, Monday night football playing silently in the corner, Holly gazes at the image of Francis Richardson with Langdon and Fairchild. Madeline's phone had soon called her back into London to track the scent of a political scandal buried deep in Westminster. I told her my hope was that she would have my article in the next week, and said again that I took her at her word that she would publish nothing until then. After she left, I had messaged Holly, wanting to ask her more about her father-in-law. She had come to my door as soon as Alice was settled in bed.

'I can't bear to look at him,' says Holly, tossing the photo across the sofa as she sits curled in the corner.

'Hol?' I say, sitting up and leaning towards her. 'It's only a photo. We don't know anything for definite yet.' I watch as Holly rubs the palm of her hand against her forehead. 'The photo links Francis to Langdon and Fairchild. Yes, it's the clearest evidence we have, but it is still a big jump to Nathan being his son.'

Holly is quiet, and I look at her questioningly.

'There's more I should have told you,' she says.

'About Francis?' I ask, pulling my feet beneath me as Holly crosses her legs and faces me across the sofa.

'I never intended to keep secrets from you.'

'Hol?'

'I was scared to tell anyone, even you,' she says, her body tightening as she leans forward. 'It started with Michael's death. It was then that I should have talked to you. I was stupid. I wanted to tell you, but he convinced me nobody should know; that it would be safer that way. Safer for me and for Alice.'

'Francis did?' I reply, hating to hear the desperation in Holly's voice.

'I was terrified of what he would do.'

'I don't understand,' I say, leaning forward to put my arm around Holly, but she shudders and draws back. 'Hol, talk to me.'

She takes hold of my hands and slowly leans forward. 'I was petrified I would lose you, that you would never forgive me.' I shake my head. 'No, really, Ben. I loved Michael in a way I've never loved anybody. But your friendship with him ran so deep, he'd become another brother.' Our heads gently touch together. 'That night, the night he was killed . . . we'd been walking in the woods, finalising our plans to leave.'

I think of the endless conversations we'd had around my kitchen table after Michael had been offered a contract to play rugby league in Australia. It had promised a new life for him, Holly and Alice. It was a chance they couldn't pass up.

390

'We were sitting together under an oak tree in the woods. My phone rang and it was Jake. I'd told him I was seeing the girls from my NCT group. He said he couldn't settle Alice. I ran back to my car. A minute later, I raced around the corner. Jake was calling again. I reached for my mobile. Michael must have come running out of the woods.

'I only saw him the second before I hit him. It was me that killed him.'

I let her words echo round in my head. I can't make sense of them.

'Ben?'

When I look at her, her eyes are huge and filled with tears. And she looks so afraid. 'I'm so, so sorry,' she says.

'You could have told me,' I say, my voice barely audible. 'How did you bear it?'

'I don't know, it was . . . it was horrendous. It still is. Even now there are times when I can hardly breathe just thinking about it. But I was desperate; I had to think of Alice.'

'What happened?'

'I knew I couldn't tell Jake. I thought of calling you, but I needed somebody who could make it all go away.'

'Hol, I would have helped.'

'I couldn't risk being parted from Alice. I wasn't looking at the road, I was reaching for my phone,' says Holly, climbing off the sofa and slowly walking across the kitchen. Wrapping her arms around herself, she continues. 'I knew Francis was the one person who could make it all go away. Three minutes and he was there. Michael was dead, Ben – there was nothing I could do.' I slowly nod. 'Francis sent me home, told me to leave the car outside my house with the keys inside. Like everything else, the car belonged to Francis, and the next morning it was gone. I never saw it again. I don't know what he told Jake, but two days later we had a brand-new car.'

'And Michael?'

'Exactly as it was reported in the press. He was out running on the Lower Haddley Road. It was dark, a quiet road by the woods. A hit-and-run. There were no witnesses. The driver was never caught. Nobody knew – except Francis.'

I cross the room to hold Holly in my arms but she steps away.

'Hol?'

'The thing is, everything with Francis Richardson comes at a price,' she says, turning and looking out towards the moonlit garden. 'He came to me the day of Michael's funeral, told me I had a debt to pay. He raped me, Ben. Raped me as Alice lay sleeping in her cot.'

Eleven

'He has money and that gives him power; power to control. He exudes entitlement.'

CHAPTER 72

An eerie calm has descended over the common when I step outside early on Tuesday morning. In place of the previous day's commotion there's an empty silence. Residents remain hidden while the assembled press corps has departed as the twenty-four-hour news cycle rolls on. At the entrance to the woods, a lone police officer stands sentry, crime tape flapping across the opening as the river breeze stiffens.

My phone buzzes and I read a message from Dani Cash.

> James Wright took a helicopter flight from
> Battersea to Sandbanks Sunday morning.
> He was more than a hundred miles away
> when Elizabeth Woakes was killed.

I don't reply.

I take the pathway that runs across the heart of the muddy and downtrodden common. Holly crosses the road in front of her home and, when we meet, she gently takes my hand.

I see the dark circles devouring her naturally sharp eyes, her sparkle extinguished by exhaustion.

'Are you sure you want to do this?'

'Absolutely,' comes her firm reply as we turn along the Lower Haddley Road.

'How's Alice?' I ask.

'Up at five and ready for breakfast,' she replies, her daughter always conjuring a lightness in her voice.

'I don't know how you do it. I like my sleep too much.'

'I was awake long before Alice, if I slept at all. You?'

'Off and on,' I reply, turning towards St Marnham with the commuter traffic starting to build.

'I couldn't get him out of my head,' says Holly.

We quickly cross in front of the packed number 29 bus before it turns towards Richmond. 'He's a revolting human being,' I say, as we take the path into the heart of the village.

'Does that make him a killer?'

'When I think what he's done to you – his daughter-in-law. He has money and that gives him power; power to control. He exudes entitlement. His arrogance makes him believe he's untouchable and he relishes the position he holds. My bet is he would do anything to protect himself – even kill.'

'But why kill Elizabeth Woakes?'

'Fairchild comes backs to Haddley, having arranged a meeting with him. She wants money. She walks towards St Marnham and the agreed meeting point. Mrs Woakes sees her, follows her, only to discover her meeting Francis in the woods.'

Holly and I walk through the village, around the banks of the pond and stand at the entrance to the Richardsons' driveway.

'Ready?' I ask.

'Yes,' she replies. 'Katherine genuinely wants to help. She knows Francis better than anyone. I think she will tell us the truth.'

'Except she doesn't know what we're going to ask.'

We walk up the gravelled driveway, and, as we approach the Richardsons' home, the front door opens. We are invited through into the sun room at the rear of the house, where we find Katherine Richardson already seated. 'Thank you, Monique,' she says as we enter, offering us a seat on one of the deep white sofas. 'We are not to be disturbed.' Monique departs the room as Katherine pours us each a coffee from a glass pot. 'I should have asked if you'd like anything to eat. I don't take breakfast myself, but let me call Monique back.'

'No, no, I'm fine,' I say, sitting opposite Katherine and taking a cup from her.

'Not for me, either,' adds Holly.

'We must thank you for seeing us so early,' I say.

'I've always been an early riser. I like to make the most of the day. My husband is more of a night owl, perhaps an expedient way of limiting our interaction.'

I say nothing as Holly adds milk to her drink and takes a first sip.

'Mr Harper . . . ' says Katherine.

'Ben, please.'

'Holly asked if I would be willing to meet with you to answer some questions about my husband.'

Holly looks across at her mother-in-law. 'Ben knows about . . . ' Her voice trails away.

'Then, at the very least, let me begin there.'

'Thank you,' I reply.

'It would be wrong of me to describe my marriage as one of convenience,' says Katherine, her arm resting on the corner of the sofa. 'Our relationship has been one which has worked for us mutually. There was a bond between us, and there were times in the past when I might have described myself as happy.' Katherine stops and leans forward, talking directly to Holly. 'I did know what Francis was like, and, wherever opportunity presented itself, he seized it. However, I never believed he had forced himself on any woman – until now. For that, I will never forgive myself. Never.' Holly closes her eyes. 'I totally misjudged him.'

'Is it possible that Francis could have done this to other women?' I ask.

Katherine flinches. 'I suppose it is. It makes me sick to think of it, though.'

'You may have read that Abigail Langdon, the girl, now woman, convicted of murdering my brother, was herself killed last week.'

Katherine slowly pours herself a cup of black coffee before leaning back into the corner of the sofa. 'I did.'

'The police are pursuing a line of enquiry that at the time of the murders Langdon and Fairchild could have been in contact with a man, or group of men, in a grooming scenario.'

I look at Katherine for a reaction, for a flicker of acknowledgment or recognition, but she reveals none.

'May I show you a photograph?' I ask.

'Certainly,' says Katherine, and I take the picture showing Francis Richardson with the two girls from my jacket pocket.

Handing it to her, I say, 'At the edge of the photo you can just see . . . '

'I can see.'

Katherine stares at the image, an intensity in her deep brown eyes. She places the photo on to the black marble coffee table, edging it towards me.

'Mrs Richardson?' I ask.

'You want me to comment on whether I believe my husband could have been involved in a sexual relationship with those two girls? I can't say that. I'm sorry.'

'Are you saying it's impossible?' I ask.

'I have no reason to believe his relationship with those girls went beyond what you see in that photograph. A celebration at a school rugby match. Over-enthusiastic, yes. Inappropriate? Probably. But nothing more.'

Holly lifts her eyes and locks them upon Katherine.

'I know of nothing that would suggest a relationship with those particular girls,' continues Katherine, gripping her hands hard together to stop them trembling, 'but he did father a child with a girl, a sixteen-year-old girl. I imagine she was little more than a child herself.'

Letting her words hang in the room, Katherine reaches forward for the jug of iced water that sits upon a silver tray in the centre of the coffee table. Pouring three glasses, she takes one for herself before propping a scarlet red cushion behind her back.

'I became engaged to Francis on my twenty-first birthday,' says Katherine. 'In many ways, the marriage was arranged long before then. My father had known his for years. From the moment I was born, they had imagined bringing our families together. The lure of combining history and money, perhaps. Or was it simply male arrogance?

'By the time of our engagement, Francis had already served ten years in the military and was working in the Ministry of Defence. After the wedding, he was to resign his position and take up a new role with a City firm. He needed the perfect wife to present to City investors, to play hostess at all the corporate parties.

'I'm not saying we didn't have a romance, but I would describe it as whirlwind, almost frenetic. Within six weeks we were engaged and three weeks later he came to me, telling me he was pulling forward the wedding date. We had planned an engagement of several months and suddenly we were to be married in just five weeks. He refused to explain why, and when I spoke to my father he simply told me to accept the plan as proposed and to be grateful. Like everyone else, he assumed I was pregnant. I was not.

'The night before the wedding, Francis came to my home. In my darkest times, I've wondered why he waited until that night. Maybe to prevent me having any time to back out? Or was it simply the vicious streak that runs through him, using adversity to establish control? We sat together in my father's study, and our conversation was incredibly matter-of-fact.

A sixteen-year-old girl was pregnant. Her father worked on Francis's parents' estate, and the girl's family lived in the gatehouse. Francis's father had stepped in to take care of things – pay the family off, as it were. The child was due in two months' time. Francis and I were to take it as soon as it was born.

'Francis was thirty-one.'

CHAPTER 73

A train rattled by as Corrine stole along the overgrown path that ran along the top side of Haddley Woods. Carefully pushing her way through the dense thistle bushes, she stood at the base of the elevated mound, looking up at the summit that had haunted her for so many years. Young saplings, now grown, covered the bank with a new forest of trees.

Creeping around to the opposite side, she found the hollow where he had concealed himself on that day so many years before, now smothered by a thick hawthorn bush. Everything had been prepared one week earlier, but only one boy had emerged through the trees. He had been insistent it must be two: both she and Abigail compelled to prove their devotion.

Seven days later, once again everything was in place.

Abigail's heightened anticipation had been palpable as they danced away from the bus at the side of the common.

The chase through the airless woods.

The knives concealed beneath the creeping ivy as it grew across the mound.

When the boys knelt, Abigail hadn't wavered. She had let out a scream of delight as she plunged the knife.

For Josie, a moment's hesitation. Nick Harper's eyes upon her; his fear and confusion matched only by her own.

The yell from the hollow. Her plunge of the knife; Abigail grasping her hand to rip it forward.

He had stood over them while they maimed the bodies.

And she had felt the thrill emanating from him. The knowledge that she and Abigail were forever his.

Yesterday evening, under the darkness of the night sky, she had made her way from the Peacock boathouse, through the village of St Marnham and towards his home. In the cold she had waited, shivering in the trees, straining through the mist to see the burning lights of his house. Tensing when she'd seen the front door open, leaving him alone; she'd felt that was her moment.

Keeping her hood pulled down over her face, she'd scampered across the open ground, chasing along the path towards his house. The front blinds were open, and she'd found herself frozen, staring inside. Watching him cross the room, radiating his impregnable arrogance, had sent a tremor through her.

His hard fingers, holding his glass, touching her skin.

His strong hands, running through his hair, rubbing her shoulders.

His legs, neatly crossed, pressing against her back.

His eyes at the window, glaring out, seeing her every move.

Turning, she'd run, racing back into the trees, seeking sanctuary under the darkness their canopy created. Weaving through the woods, she'd realised she must return only when she could force her ultimatum.

Silently, she had crept back into the boathouse. Desperate for warmth, she had tried to wrap herself in the life vests that hung on the wall. All night she had sat awake, trembling with fear.

Until this morning, when at last she had her plan.

She would take the child.

CHAPTER 74

Holly rises and moves across the room to sit next to Katherine.

'He left you with no choice,' she says. 'He told you at the last possible moment.'

'I could have walked away that night, or any night since,' replies Katherine. 'I chose to disengage from the truth. Throughout the marriage, I tried to rationalise what had happened – convince myself it was a one-time lapse.'

'Can I ask what happened after the wedding?' I say.

'For seven weeks we honeymooned, a private yacht taking us around the Maldives. We were safe there, no risk of meeting anybody we knew. If by chance we did, I could be spirited away on board. When we returned, a car met us at Heathrow Airport and drove us directly here: our new family home. Two days later Jake was born, and two days after that he came to live with us. We never even really had to lie. People made their own assumptions – the change in the wedding date, the extended honeymoon. From that day forward, I was Jake's mother and he was our son.' Her mouth tightens. 'But I still believe this was Francis once with a girl – a mistake. I believed him then and I still do now. Grooming schoolgirls – no. That's not Francis. I gave him his freedom, especially after Lily.'

'Lily?' I say, as Holly reaches her hand towards her mother-in-law.

'Our daughter. She was with us for less than three years. I still think of her every day,' says Katherine, before turning to Holly. 'And I know Francis does as well.'

'I can see it in the way he cares for Alice,' says Holly, as I look at her with an unforgiving eye. 'He does, Ben.'

'Lily drowned in the village pond after letting herself out through the gate at the back of our garden,' says Katherine, turning back to me. 'We did all we could to save her. The woman who raised the alarm, the team from the doctor's surgery – it felt as if the whole village tried to help. But we were too late.'

Quietly, I flick open my phone and message Min as Mrs Richardson continues to talk.

'Francis adored her, as did I. He bullies women, treats them like possessions and then discards them, but he adored Lily. She really was his. I think that's probably why he loved her so, in the same way he dotes upon Alice.'

'She loves you both,' says Holly, kindly.

Katherine tilts her head and closes her eyes. I imagine what it must be like for her. To have her vulnerability exposed for the first time in her life, when she has spent decades concealing it.

'Neither Francis nor I wanted any more children after Lily.

Our life's course was set – separate lives. In business we were a team, appearing at events, charming investors. The rest of our time was our own. I gave no heed to what Francis did.

'Until Holly. I should have done something sooner. Questioned him, spoken to him at the very least,' continues Katherine, turning to Holly as she does. 'I should have stopped him; I should have stopped him from that very first day. And I should have spoken to you sooner, been ready to help you. When I looked at you, I saw another of his conquests. I was so wrong. I didn't want to think about it, and that was so selfish of me. I blocked it out, terrified of what Jake would do if he ever found out. He harbours such resentment for his father.'

'You've done everything possible to support Jake and me.'

'His father's support came at such an enormous cost.'

'Jake still had you.'

'That is kind of you,' says Katherine, 'but I always wonder if I could have acted differently; often ask myself if I over-compensated in trying to be his mother.'

'Jake never had any idea?' I ask.

Katherine shakes her head. 'He was our son.'

'His relationship with Francis is complex, but Jake does care for you,' says Holly.

My phone buzzes and, briefly excusing myself, I step to the back of the room and read Min's message. She has sent through the *Richmond Times* report of Lily's death from over thirty years ago. Looking at the bleak images of the barren trees surrounding the wet mud on the banks of the pond, I feel the wretchedness of the day. Police tape borders the water's edge, torn and grimy. The black and white photographs from the newspaper capture the hopelessness of the day.

I read the copy and learn that a woman named Mary Hess, visiting St Marnham for the day, had discovered the tragedy, dragging Lily's body from the water. Despite all of her efforts and those of the health workers from the nearby doctor's surgery, nothing could be done to revive the two-year-old girl, and she was declared dead at the scene.

The article closes with a statement from a council official expressing their sympathy for such a tragic loss. The instigation of a full safety review with the future consideration of all options, including fencing in or even draining the pond, was the council's commitment. Remembering the scene we passed earlier, I struggle to think of any change in the intervening years. That horrendous day has affected countless lives, but I wonder if it's acknowledged by anything more than a small plaque on a wooden bench.

I scroll to the bottom of the article, where more photographs show the outside of the Richardsons' home, the village of St Marnham, and a finally a blurry image of Mary Hess.

I stare at my phone, and my hand begins to shake.

CHAPTER 75

Ra-ta-tat-tat.

Ra-ta-tat-tat.

A rap on the sun-room door fractures my thoughts. I click off my phone, quickly slipping it into my jacket pocket.

Ra-ta-tat-tat for a third time and the door opens.

Francis Richardson steps in from the hallway.

'You're scum,' I shout. My anger boils over and I charge across the room.

'Ben, no!' cries Holly, as I jump across the white sofa, my boots leaving an indelible imprint. I hurl myself towards Richardson, momentum gathering behind my six-foot frame. My fist flies forward, my knuckle cracking his jaw as he crumples to the floor. With him sprawled in the doorway I reach down, drag him to his feet and hit him again. His head recoils and blood spurts from his face across the white stone floor. As he cowers in the doorway, I lift him again, my arm twisting as I hit him for a third time.

Holly grabs hold of my arm and drags me back. Only then do I hear a cry from Katherine.

'No more,' she says. 'No more.'

CHAPTER 76

'Call a cab, go straight to Alice's nursery and make sure she's safe,' I say to Holly, as I step over Francis Richardson and into the hallway.

'Alice?' replies Holly.

'We need to make sure she's safe,' I continue, backing away across the hall as Katherine goes to her daughter-in-law.

'Let me drive you,' she says, taking Holly by the hand. 'We'll be there in no time.'

'Ben, where are you going?' calls Holly, as I turn and run out of the front of the house.

'Make sure Alice is safe,' I shout, before sprinting down the driveway and out into the village. I realise my fastest way back to Haddley is running straight down the Lower Haddley Road. Dodging in front of clogged school-run traffic, I head swiftly along the river side of the woods and back towards the common. Images race through my mind. My eight-year-old self, running from the woods, the blistering heat scorching my neck. Michael being hit by Holly's advancing car. The faces of Nick and Simon. My mum falling in front of the 8.06 to Waterloo.

So many killed to protect a secret.

I sprint across the common.

I open the front door of my house and charge upstairs. Standing at the entrance to the loft room, catching my breath, I look at the remaining fragments of Nick's life. My mum would often spend quiet moments here, alone with her eldest son. Memories trapped in time, connecting him to her.

Little now is left untouched. My life has gradually encroached upon the room but in the corner Nick's desk remains, covered in boxes and old books. I rapidly flick through my mum's old papers but there is nothing there I haven't seen before. I know it will have been searched already. I open a box filled with Nick's schoolbooks, rifle through them but find nothing. I empty a brown envelope filled with our school reports, scattering them across the floor. Inside another box, I find the year prize Nick won for English. His prize was for an essay on Thomas Hardy's *The Return of the Native*. My mum had been so proud when he walked on stage at our school assembly to collect his award. It was Nick who dreamt of becoming a journalist, not me.

I sit on the floor, blowing dust off the jackets of a stack of books piled in the corner. Rifling through them, I find Nick's copy of the book. Grabbing holding of it, I quickly flick through the faded pages.

Tucked inside the back cover are two photographs.

The two missing photographs from the day of the match. The two images that tell me my mum was murdered. And why.

CHAPTER 77

I look down at the two images. They've remained hidden up here all these years. My mum would have been the last person to touch them.

She would have seen what I see now. And she'd have wanted answers.

The evening before her death she went in search of those answers, still hoping she was wrong. She would have wanted to believe the best.

Whatever happened that evening, it wasn't enough to put her worries to rest. The next morning, when she shouted up at me as I lay hungover in bed, she would have been distressed by what she had discovered. Agitated and unsure, she would have left home feeling both confused and betrayed.

Resting on Nick's bed, I pick up the first photograph – a snap taken moments after the championship team had posed with their trophy. As the group breaks up, James Wright still has a tight hold of the cup, but now his back is turned to the camera.

Phil Doorley leaps through the air.

Abigail Langdon and Josie Fairchild stand at the side of the group.

No longer does Francis Richardson hold them.

In his pristine white shirt, it is his son, Jake, who now has his arms wrapped tightly around them.

I have to force myself to pick up the second photograph. It's the one my mum will have found impossible to understand.

Taken after the final victorious points had been scored, it captures a moment of pure joy, but one that now leaves me desolate.

Jake Richardson stands triumphant by the corner flag. His arms outstretched, he smiles towards the woman who stands, arms aloft, celebrating on the touchline. Her face lit with pride, it is the woman named years earlier by the *Richmond Times* as Mary Hess. Only, by the time of this match, she would have been known by her married name.

Mary Cranfield.

Twelve

*'Now we had our very own secret —
one we could never share, but one that
would bind us together for ever.'*

CHAPTER 78

My legs are dead weights as I make my way down from the top floor of my home. Resting my hand on my front door latch, I stop. The Cranfields' home has been my safe haven – a place where I went to feel loved. A place to hide from the world. When I next enter their home, that will end.

I open my front door and begin a slow and heavy walk along the side of the deserted common. Only the noise from a plane passing overhead breaks the morning silence. Taking the steps I've taken a thousand times, the same steps my mum took on the very first day the Cranfields arrived in Haddley, I look up towards the sky. I remember the happiness she found in the arrival of our new neighbours, two years after Nick's death. To her they brought hope of a new beginning.

Standing outside the front of their house, I look again at the photographs and know how they would have set my mum's mind racing. With no connection to the area, why had Mrs Cranfield been celebrating so spiritedly on the touchline of a school rugby match played so many years before? Would my mum have made an immediate connection? I don't know, but I do know she would have given Mrs C every opportunity to explain. She would have sat with her friend on the night before she died, seeking answers and understanding. Whatever the answer given, it didn't satisfy. Consumed by her discovery, she made her walk to St Marnham station the following morning wrestling with the gravest possible betrayal.

Walking down the side of the house, I look through the Cranfields' kitchen window – battered pans hang above the hob, well-thumbed recipe books are stacked one upon another; a conjured a smell of home cooking.

Gently, I push open the back door.

Mr Cranfield sits alone at the table, its faded blue linen tablecloth slightly worn. In his stupor he stares blankly at a train ticket resting against the wooden pepper mill. Sensing me step inside, he picks up the ticket and pushes it across the table towards me. Looking down, I see it is dated last Wednesday. A return ticket from King's Cross to Leeds.

'She told me she was on a coach trip with her book group to Chawton House. I said how lucky she'd been with the weather.'

Slowly I edge the ticket back across the table. Taking a step forward, I notice the door through to the garage standing ajar. A cushioned kitchen chair is placed in the middle of the floor. Above it hangs a home-made noose.

I place my hand upon Mr Cranfield's shoulder and he raises his eyes.

'No,' is the only word I say.

CHAPTER 79

'Mrs Cranfield,' I call softly, 'we need to talk.'

There is no reply, and I walk carefully from the back of the kitchen into the hallway and then down towards the living room at the front of the house. The doorknob scrapes as I turn it to enter the room. Sitting in her favourite high-backed armchair, next to the fireplace, is Mary Cranfield.

'I so hoped it wouldn't be you, Ben,' she says, as I walk quietly in. 'George?' she asks, closing her eyes for a moment. 'He was a good husband,' she says.

'He still is,' I reply, and I hear her slowly exhale.

'Sometimes the deepest secrets are the ones you keep from yourself,' she says. 'I don't think he ever wanted to know.'

My arms tighten and I find myself gripping the two photographs still in my hand.

'Come and sit with me,' says Mrs Cranfield, gesturing to her rug-covered sofa, 'one last time.' I cross the room and take a seat next to her. 'I desperately wanted to be the person who found those,' she says, looking at the images in my hand. 'It wasn't for want of trying, I have to admit. I looked everywhere,' she continues with a smile, 'but it was your family, Ben, so in the end it's only right that you found them. May I see?' Mrs Cranfield undoes the clasp on her handbag before searching inside for her glasses. 'I know they're in here somewhere. You didn't see them in the kitchen, did you?' she asks. 'No, here they are. I can't see anything without them these days.' Her conversation is almost trivial.

I pass her the photographs.

'I look so young,' she says, 'I'm surprised you recognised me. So does Jake. Such joy in his face.' I tell myself I hear regret in her voice.

'You're Jake's mother, aren't you?' I ask.

'I am,' she replies, nodding gently while still looking down at the photographs she holds in her lap. 'And I like to think I'm his guardian angel.' I stay motionless as she reaches out her hand towards me. 'He was taken from me, Ben,' she continues, a sudden harshness in her voice. 'Taken from me after only two days. They left me with nothing except the little suit I had dressed him in. Even that wasn't good enough for them.' She looks over her glasses, anger flaring in her eyes. 'He is my son.'

'Tell me what happened,' I say.

'I did what they asked when they packed me off back to Ireland. I tried to forget about him but it was impossible. I was his mother. I needed to be with him, to care for him. Katherine Richardson was never going to give him the love he needed. And as for his father ... ' Mrs Cranfield stops. 'We all know what his father wants. Jake needed me. He needed his mother.'

'How did you find him?'

'That was the easy part. Francis Richardson was never going to live an inconspicuous life. I started watching them. Occasionally at first, over time more regularly. After a few years, I established a routine of travelling to St Marnham once or twice a week. They were happy days. I would arrive from north London in time to watch Jake in the playground during morning break. Then I'd eat lunch in the village and watch him later in the day running by the pond. His mother was hardly ever with him, always the help. They paid no attention to me. I longed to speak to him, to hold him, but I knew I had to wait for the right moment.'

'And that moment was Lily's death?'

Mrs Cranfield nods. 'Once you discovered about the girl, I knew you would put the pieces together.'

'What happened?'

'Nobody had taught Jake right from wrong. It wasn't his fault. Neither of them really cared for him.'

'Tell me about that day.'

'She was a silly little girl. Always screaming, running to her mummy. Anybody could see she was her mummy's favourite, including Jake. He'd been out by the pond with the girl, feeding the ducks. It was getting dark and Jake told her it was time to go inside. I was so proud of him but she simply started wailing. The problem was, she always got her own way. Somebody needed to teach her a lesson.

'Jake said he was going in and, unless she wanted to stay out in the dark on her own, she should go with him. He walked away from the water's edge and eventually she did follow. I decided to sit by the pond for a few minutes more until it was time to head for my train. I was surprised when, no more than three or four minutes later, they reappeared through the gate at the back of their garden.

'Jake led her by the hand across the road, looking for traffic both ways. The streetlight illuminated the glee in her face as they stepped back on to the muddy bank. Her satisfaction in her getting her own way was plain for all to see.

'Closer and closer she went to the edge and it was then she started to slip. I saw her try to grab hold of Jake but by then she had mud all over her hands. It was natural for him to jump away. She slipped down a little further. I could hear her piercing scream. Her wellington boots filled with water. Jake steadied himself on the bank and then edged forward. He reached out his hand.

'And then he pushed her down.'

After taking a last look at the photographs, Mrs Cranfield unclasps her bag, removes her glasses and puts them away inside their case.

'She splashed at first, kicking in the muddy water. He had to hold her down but for a seven-year-old boy he was strong. And then the kicking stopped. Even if I'd wanted to, I couldn't have got to them in time.

'I watched him hold her face under for another few seconds until he was sure and then I made my way around the bank. It was the first time I'd spoken to him since he was two days old. I took hold of his hands, cleaned him up, and told him to go inside and never speak of this again. I was there to make everything right.'

I stare at her in horror. 'You saw what he did and you told nobody?'

'What would you have done?' asks Mrs Cranfield, a frown of puzzlement creasing her forehead. 'Nobody could possibly blame him. All he needed was a mother.'

'You let him drown her!'

'I had to,' replies Mrs Cranfield. 'Now we had our very own secret – one we could never share, but one that would bind us together forever.'

CHAPTER 80

'You're mad,' I say, jumping up from the sofa. 'Deranged,' I cry, shouting directly at Mrs Cranfield. 'You let him kill a two-year-old girl. And then you let him destroy one life after another.'

'I didn't want that, Ben,' replies Mrs Cranfield, calmly. 'But life was so difficult for Jake, particularly after Lily. His relationship with his father was always so strained. I've often wondered if Francis saw my photograph in the paper. If he did, I hope it's haunted him ever since; eaten away at him like a cancer in his soul. Did it make him suspect there was more to the girl's death? I don't know. We've never spoken. All I knew is that I had to be here to try and guide Jake.'

'You didn't guide him. You let him become a monster! How could you? How could you do that to me?'

'I never set out to hurt you. If those girls hadn't come along, things would have been so different. I know they would.'

Dumbstruck, I pace the room before sitting opposite Mrs

Cranfield on the edge of her husband's reclining armchair. 'Tell me about them.'

'They were poison, Ben, those two girls.'

I wait for Mrs Cranfield to continue.

'I did my best – you have to believe me. I really did try to steer him. He'd made such progress, done well in his exams, been selected for the rugby team. He was a handsome young man with prospects,' she says, glancing towards the photographs lying on the sofa. 'If only he'd met a nice girl his own age . . . but instead those two came along. They were cultish in their veneration of him. Unquestioning. He delighted in their awe. Throughout that summer, I could see it getting worse and worse. They awakened something in him, something of his father. His father controlled him, and now he wanted to exert a control of his own.'

'He was there when they killed Nick and Simon?'

Her eyes close. 'You've no idea what it's like, Ben.'

And though, in this moment, I want to hate Mrs Cranfield more than I've ever hated anyone, I find I can't quite hate her absolutely. I see the pain on her face. I feel the tragedy of her life.

'Once Jake became a teenager, my visits to St Marnham became less frequent and instead we would meet in the centre of London; I'd buy him lunch or even take him to the theatre. But as he got older he wanted to see less of me. That summer he'd started driving and time and again he would cancel our meetings. I came to St Marnham to speak to him and when I saw the three of them together I warned him. I even contacted the school, telling them the girls were

425

involved with older men. I was desperate. If I'd known, Ben, known what the three of them were planning, you have to believe me . . . ' says Mrs Cranfield, and, as she reaches across to me, for the first time I hear a crack in her voice.

I move away.

'I would have done anything to stop them,' she continues. 'At the start of that week, he had refused to see me. I should have acted then. On that dreadful day, he was waiting in the woods. He wanted to test his control, to see how slavish they would be.

'He watched them kill.'

CHAPTER 81

Panic surged through Holly as she ran from Alice's classroom, to the breakfast club and out into the playground. No one at the nursery had seen her daughter that morning. Her body began to shake as Katherine held her by the arm and dialled 999.

Within minutes the police were at the front of the nursery. Holly recognised the blonde policewoman she'd seen with Ben.

'Mrs Richardson?' Dani Cash put a hand on her arm. 'Could you tell us again what has happened?'

Holly repeated what she knew. Alice had not arrived at nursery that morning.

'Her father was meant to drop her off,' said Holly, as Dani led her out of the school gates towards the waiting police car. 'Except he's not her father and I don't know if he knows that. Ben said to get Alice, to make sure she was safe.'

'Where is Ben now?' asked Dani, as Katherine stood with her by the car.

'He came back to Haddley,' Katherine replied, 'but we don't know where he went.'

'He believes your husband may have been involved in the killing of his mother?'

'Not my husband,' she replied. 'My son.'

CHAPTER 82

'Tell me about Mum,' I say.

'I never wanted that,' replies Mrs Cranfield. 'I promise you I never did.'

'Tell me.'

'After your brother and Simon Woakes, I had to find a way to control Jake. He was contrite, full of remorse, genuinely repentant. Moving to Haddley was my way of ensuring that continued. For a while, things did get better. He met Holly, started his own business – things really improved. He deserved a second chance.'

I want to scream at Mrs Cranfield, scream that no one ever gave Nick a second chance, but I simply ask her to go on.

'Clare came to me the night before she died. She had collected so many pieces and simply couldn't make them fit. Why had I been at a school rugby match so many years before? Of course, it had been stupid of me, but all I'd wanted to do was watch my son. I tried to deny it, say it wasn't me, that she must be mistaken, but it was useless. She had the letter.'

I sit and watch as Mrs Cranfield again unclasps her bag, removing a tattered white envelope. Opening the fold, her hand begins to shake. She passes the letter to me.

'You should read it,' she says.

I unfold the single sheet of thin, greying paper. A brief, handwritten note spiders across the page. An increasingly desperate and illegible scrawl tells my mum that her money would be well spent. I scan to the last line.

> I can tell you about all of them. Francis Richardson, Mary Cranfield, all of them. You wouldn't believe the things I could tell you.

'I couldn't explain that away. When we cleared your mum's things from your house, I found the letter. What a relief that was, even though I could never find the photos.

'That night, I tried my best to convince your mum, but there was no way. The following morning I watched her walk across the common, consumed in her own thoughts. I had to protect Jake. He'd made such strides. I wish it could have been anybody but her, I really do.'

'You pushed her,' I say, barely controlling the anger in my voice. 'And then you came to comfort me. How dare you!' I yell. 'I loved you like a mother, and all the time it was *you.*'

Mrs Cranfield sits motionless.

'Tell me the rest,' I say, getting to my feet to tower over Mrs Cranfield.

'Ben, don't, please.'

'Tell me!'

'Your mum's death served as a warning to Langdon. It was another three years before she got in touch directly, but by then she was threatening – there was real menace. While Jake had the business, we managed. But increasingly over time she wanted more and more, and in the end there was no money left. Jake started to spiral downwards. He grew suspicious about Michael Knowles and stupidly decided to handle it himself. He pushed him into the road, but all too clumsily. His paranoia increased. I took the chance of the approaching anniversary of Clare's death to act.'

'Throwing suspicion on me.'

'Not on you, Ben. I knew everyone would be talking about her anniversary. Anyone could have tracked Langdon down and killed her. I was just causing confusion. She was scum, Ben.'

'And Josie Fairchild?'

'She never had Langdon's greed. Following Langdon's death she just wanted to escape, start a new life. She hoped Jake would give her the money to do that. I'd have given her that. I didn't want more blood.'

'But Elizabeth Woakes followed her into the woods?'

'Yes – with everything suddenly so fresh again she recognised her at the station. Fairchild fled and Jake was left with no other choice. He strangled her and returned during the night to hang her from the tree.'

I look at her in disgust and she says, 'I had to look after my baby, Ben.' She reaches out to take my hand and I reel back. I don't want her anywhere near me.

'Where's Jake now?' I say, quietly, looking down on Mrs Cranfield as she wanes before me. *'Where is he?'*

'I don't know,' she says, fear now in her voice. 'What are you going to do?'

'I'm going to kill him.'

CHAPTER 83

I sprint across the common towards the home of Jake and Holly. I pound on the front door of the house, but there is no reply. I go to the window, see no signs of life, but the coffee table in the living room lies upturned. I run to the rear of the house and scramble over the back fence. The door to the garden is open and I run inside.

'Jake,' I call into the silence. I make my way through into the hall and call again as I climb the stairs. 'Jake, it's Ben Harper. I know everything.'

'Ben. Help me!'

The cry sends terror through me. I race forward.

'Alice, where are you?' I shout.

'Ben, we're in Alice's bedroom.' His voice punctured with fear, Jake calls from across the landing. 'Please come in slowly.'

I gently push open the door.

Jake stands paralysed at the side of the room while Alice sits in the middle of the floor, surrounded by her toy's tea party.

A woman crouches behind her, holding a knife to her throat.

I crouch to my knees.

'Alice, I'm here now and everything's going to be okay. You just sit very still and do everything this lady tells you.'

Alice barely nods her head. I look across at the woman.

'Hi, Josie,' I say, looking directly at my brother's killer. My only thought now is for Alice. 'My name's Ben Harper.' I see the recognition in her eyes. 'You didn't come here to hurt Alice.'

She shakes her head and I hear the wail of a police siren. Her hand flinches.

'Put the knife down and let me help you,' I say. 'I know you didn't hurt the woman in the woods.'

'I didn't. He did. He did it all. Right from the very beginning, him and Abigail,' she says, fear in her eyes as she looks towards Jake.

'And now he'll pay. Josie, put the knife down and all this can be over.'

Her eyes widen when I again say that name. 'I'm Corrine now,' she whispers.

'Alice has done nothing wrong, Corrine. Let her go.'

Behind me, I hear the creak of footsteps on the stairs.

'Hurting Alice won't get you what you want,' I say, holding my breath and making a tiny move forward.

'I just want to start all over again,' says Josie. She looks at me pitifully. I sense the wretchedness of her life but feel no forgiveness.

'You can still do that,' I reply, edging further forward. 'You just need to put the knife down.'

434

She stares at me. Then, very slowly, she drops the knife.

Breath rushes out of me as Alice charges into my arms and buries her head into my shoulder. I hold her close as Josie Fairchild crumples, sobbing on the floor. As the front door bursts open, the door to Alice's room is thrown open.

Confused, I turn to see Mary Cranfield standing in the doorway.

'This has to end,' she says grabbing the knife from the floor.

With one hand, I push Josie backwards against Alice's bed. 'Mrs C, no,' I shout.

'Ma!' calls Jake, from behind the door.

Without hesitation she turns, and in a single movement steps forward, plunging the knife upwards into his heart before clasping him to her breast. Holding him close, smothered in his blood, Mary Cranfield cradles her son as he falls to the floor.

'Shhh,' she whispers, as Jake shudders in her arms. 'It's over now. It's all over.'

She turns to me, tears in her eyes.

'I should have ended this years ago. I'm so sorry.'

EPILOGUE

I gently picked up Alice and carried her down from her bedroom. Holly met us at the foot of the stairs. I passed her her daughter, and Alice wrapped her arms so tightly around her mum's neck, I thought she would never let go. Together we walked slowly back to my house.

I followed Holly and Alice inside, knowing that I have to protect them now in the same way my mum protected me. Over time, I will help them build new lives, and I know one day I will again watch Alice charge blissfully across the common. She is my family now.

Every day since, the woman Alice thinks of as her grandma has visited, spending time with her in the garden and getting to know her a little better each visit. Katherine's solicitor has already agreed a divorce settlement with Francis.

Dani Cash arrested Mary Cranfield and charged her with my mum's murder as well as that of Abigail Langdon and Jake Richardson. I spoke to Dani yesterday afternoon and she said the police are expecting a guilty plea. I doubt I will ever see Mrs Cranfield again.

Dani ended our call with a reprimand. 'I know I'm probably wasting my breath,' she said, 'but you do know you should have waited for the police before going into Jake Richardson's house.'

'I think you know by now that I don't always like to wait for the police.'

'She had a knife, Ben,' replied Dani, firmly. 'Anything could have happened, I should know. I've seen what happened to one good man. I couldn't bear for it to happen to another.'

I swore I'd be careful in the future. I said it would be nice to meet for a walk along the river one evening. She promised she'd call.

In the days after Jake's death, Nathan Beavin and Will Andrews visited a private clinic in Richmond for a paternity test. When I suddenly saw them together, the result didn't come as a complete surprise. Nathan has moved to St Marnham and is working in his dad's restaurant. Holly and I babysat Max on Saturday night, while Sarah went on what she called her 'second first date' with Nathan.

This morning I opened a card with a photograph of Hampton Court maze on the front. My mum loved to tell the story of how as a family we spent an hour trying to find our way through the intricate puzzle. Nick ran ahead with my father while my mum, struggling with my buggy, settled on her own route. We were first to the middle by some distance, something she relished. I was too young to remember the day. It was my mum's memory.

Inside the card, my father wrote how he hoped one day

we might see each other again. Holly stopped me ripping up the card. She placed it on the mantelpiece in the living room. I've left it there for now. I went back to the cupboard under the eaves and pulled out the other shoebox. The brightly coloured lion has joined Alice's latest tea party. It was the last gift my dad gave me before he left our family.

Last night, when Max and Alice were at last asleep, I read the final draft of my article to Holly. Then I emailed it to Madeline for her to publish today. I wrote of my mum's strength, of how her bravery had given me hope, and of how proud I was of her building a new life – a new life that was brutally stolen away.

For over twenty years, dark secrets were kept hidden throughout Haddley and St Marnham. Along with many others, my mum now has justice. And the lesson she taught me when I was a boy rings truer than ever – secrets are a dangerous thing.

ACKNOWLEDGEMENTS

It might seem a strange thing to say but writing a book really is a team effort. So many people have helped with the publication of *Twelve Secrets* and a huge thank you goes to each and every one of them.

There are a small number of people to whom I am especially grateful and it would be remiss of me not to thank them now. For many years, both Selina and Susan offered me nothing but encouragement. Every debut author needs someone giving them a shot of self-belief.

James Patterson gave me an opportunity for which I will be forever grateful when I worked with him on his Bookshots series.

My agent, Juliet, is a force of nature. I first approached her on a Sunday evening with the hope she might see my email on the following Monday morning. She responded to me that same Sunday evening and by the Monday morning was already sending me great feedback. She has been nothing but brilliant throughout the publication process.

I want to thank everyone at Little, Brown and Hachette

for taking a chance on me and *Twelve Secrets*, when my day job might have made them think twice. Also, I want to thank my boss at my day job for being nothing but supportive and wanting to see the book succeed.

All of the team at Little, Brown and Sphere have been a joy to work with. Their enthusiasm from my very first meeting with them was infectious. They gave me genuine belief. A huge thank you to all of them.

Gemma is not only a brilliant marketer but has also been a great former colleague and friend. My editorial partnership of Ed and Rosanna has been encouraging, honest and direct at all the right times. Working through structure and plot details, Rosanna was insightful, creative and incredibly patient.

Love to all of my family, especially O, H and W for the loan of the name. And to my mum who lost my dad, her husband of fifty-five years, in the run up to the publication of *Twelve Secrets*. Hopefully he is reading from somewhere.

And finally to you, the reader, for reading *Twelve Secrets*. I hope you have enjoyed meeting Ben, Dani and all the characters from Haddley and St Marnham. I should say they exist only in my mind, and in reality I love living between Putney and Barnes.

Thanks all for reading.